Douglas Lindsay was born in Scotland in 1964.
He is the author of *The Long Midnight of Barney
Thomson* and *The Cutting Edge of Barney Thomson*,
also available from Piatkus.

A Prayer For Barney Thomson

Douglas Lindsay

PIATKUS

Copyright © 2001 by Douglas Lindsay

First published in Great Britain in 2001 by
Judy Piatkus (Publishers) Ltd of
5 Windmill Street, London W1T 2JA
email:info@piatkus.co.uk

The moral right of the author has been asserted

A catalogue record for this book is available from the British Library

ISBN 0 7499 3228 7

Set in Times by
Action Publishing Technology Ltd, Gloucester

Printed and bound in Great Britain by
Mackays of Chatham plc, Chatham, Kent

For Kathryn

Contents

part 1
this land of giants

prologue:	it's beginning to look a lot like christmas	3
1	my name is billy	6
2	larry bellows sings the blues	16
3	my name is barney	25
4	an instance in the life of blue hawaii	31
5	my name is socrates	34
6	a new beginning	42
7	the unexamined life is not worth living	48
8	back at the con	53
9	a name of kings	60
10	eureka!	66
11	and to them were given seven trumpets	73
12	and that's all from caesar's palace	82
13	the clothes-horse of senility	89
14	don't dum-de-de-dum-dum	97
15	and you only live twice	104
16	the reason why some people get murdered	114
17	ride a pale horse	126

18	down among the dead men	136
19	and the beast enters once more the fray	142
20	so lonely steps	155
21	a bigga bigga bigga hunka metal	158
22	love's labours and barbershop floors	164
23	the peter mccloy	169
24	nine o'clock in the evening, and i can't go to bed, no, no	174
25	the stankmonster, the plain jane & the sophie marceau	181
26	giant octopus eats mum of five	189
27	been going down this road so long	203
28	now ye need not fear the grave	211

part 2
i'll be your buzz lightyear

1	on cordoba's sorry fields	219
2	barney sings the greens	229
3	punch drunk	237
4	into the river of night where the waters run cold. hey! hey! hey!	245
5	the sixth bottle	253
6	the african dawn	260
7	my friends, these clowns	268
8	the magnificent hugh rolanoytez extravaganza	276

9	liz taylor? she's a woman. no question	284
10	tidings of comfort and joy	287
11	frontier justice	296
12	be thou my battle-shield, sword for the fight	301
13	the last supper	310
14	lesbians roasting on an open fire	322
15	don't suppose it can get any weirder than it already is	331
16	the sorrow of hertha berlin	343
17	and they walk on in silence, down the road darkly	350
18	will the real morty goldman step forward?	361
19	fall on your knees	367
20	the eternal midnight of barney thomson	382
21	i'll be your jade weapon	393
epilogue:	a warm evening in august	400

part 1
this land of giants

prologue
it's beginning to look a lot like christmas

Silver bells, grey clouds, Christmas-time in the city. Sleigh rides on snow. Santa Claus and bright-eyed children. Mulled wine and mince pies. Tinsel on pine trees, snow falling on oaks. Mistletoe and indiscretions. Peace on Earth, goodwill to men. The baby Jesus, shepherds, the Three Wise Men, Bing Crosby and Perry Como. Ding dong merrily on high, hark! the herald angels sing, good Christian men rejoice. Turkey, sage & onion stuffing and roast tatties. Cold and frosty mornings, sledging on hills of thick snow. School's out, work's closed, cold feet roasting by an open fire. In the air there's the feeling of Christmas.

Of course, it's still only October.

Santa Claus rings a mournful bell outside the St Enoch's centre on Argyll Street. Passers-by give him barely a glance, though none is surprised to see him. The adverts have already been on television for a month, the decorations already adorn the shops. Cliff Richard has just released some gawping syrupy mince about love and understanding and all that jazz. And so they come and go and some of them dip into their pockets to toss a desultory coin into the green-tinsel-rimmed red bucket; but most pass on by. It'll be many weeks before the majority feel the guilt associated with the time of revelry, and begin to hand over wads of dosh to the army of charities.

The mournful bell is this scene incarnate. Weary shoppers trudge the precinct, dodging the *Big Issue*, heads down against the wind. A mild day, but bleak and drab. A hint of rain in the air, the low cloud oppressive. Not a Scottish team left in Europe, the Premier League already decided after the first Old Firm fixture; draws with Latvia, Scotland playing ten men at the back; the parliament going down the toilet, ignoring Glasgow as it goes; prices going up, buildings coming down, the summer gone, and all with nothing to look forward to. Except Christmas.

This particular Santa Claus, as it happens, Wee Magnus McCorkindale from Bishopbriggs – Corky Nae Nuts to his pals – is representing no other charity than himself. But who's to know? The occasional passer-by who tosses a dejected coin into his bucket assumes what anyone would.

'Save the Children!' shouts Corky Nae Nuts every few seconds. On the assumption that no one is listening, he occasionally shouts 'Save the Whale!' or 'Save the Rainforest!' or 'Save the Thistle!'

Bleak but mild goes the day, this late October. Still some in shirtsleeves, despite the threat of rain, still women in summer skirts and men in T-shirts. Corky, the poor bastard, is boiling in his thick red jacket and horsehair beard. Another couple of hours, goes his plan, and he'll have enough for a weekend at the boozer, a good trip to William Hill's, and maybe even sufficient remaining to tempt Sandra Dougan, a lady of available

4

reputation, into a rampant ten-to-fifteen-minute gropefest.

None of these pedestrians knows what goes through this uncomfortable-looking Santa's head; and nor does he know what they are thinking. Which is good. Best not to know the secrets that others keep. Definitely best not to know.

This year's serial killer emerges from the shopping mall empty-handed, and heads off up Argyll Street. A slow day at work, so he's taken the afternoon off to wander the town. Not thinking of Christmas. Hasn't done so in a long, long time. Wearing a jacket and too warm with it.

He looks at the women on this grey day, wonders at the clothes and the shoes that some of them wear, but appreciates the acres of skin and cleavage still bared to the warm, dull day. Hears the bell of Corky Nae Nuts, but it penetrates no further than his subconscious at first, for he does not see the dingy red of his last year's Santa outfit, he does not see the green-tinsel-rimmed red bucket. Thinking of nothing much but vague musings on the disintegration of the ozone layer and of moral standards and of the values of the current generation; the rules that now apply that didn't used to, and the rules that apply no longer; the in-your-face generation; the age of marketing, with limited-edition chocolate bars and bags of crisps.

But Corky's bell is loud, and eventually, as our killer is already ten yards beyond, the sound penetrates and he turns and he looks through the crowd. The bell rings, a pound coin clinks into the bucket and nestles beside a brace of tens. And he does not see Corky Nae Nuts. He sees red.

He sees Santa Claus.

5

1
my name is billy

'My name is Billy, and I'm a murderer.'

A ripple of applause circles the room. Ten people clapping slowly, but appreciatively. 'Good lad, Billy,' says a voice, and he's not sure who says it, but it's good to hear. Might be the blond guy, might be one of his mates, might be the Fernhill Flutist, might even be one of the women, for the voice is lost in his relief.

The applause dies away. Billy Hamilton looks around the room, engaging the eyes of a few. A good turnout on this mild evening in mid-December. No football on the TV.

The small moustache that has plagued his top lip since he was fourteen gets sucked briefly under the confines of his thin bottom lip. His right thumb vigorously rubs the palm of his left hand. He lets go of the moustache then bites his lips. Eventually his eyes settle upon a woman at the back of the small group. Blue jeans, blue jumper, blue shoes, blonde hair and a face that has seen the inside of the occasional women's prison. Katie Dillinger, the leader of the band.

'Well done, Billy. Now, what have you got to tell us all this week?'

The moustache shrugs along with the shoulders.

'Not sure, really, I've not got that much to say,' he says. 'Youse have all heard my story and . . .'

'I haven't Billy,' says a young woman, not two chairs away from Hamilton's place in the circle.

'That's right,' says Dillinger. 'It's been a while since you spoke, Billy, and Annie's only been here two weeks. Why don't you tell your story again, then when you've done that, just tell us what you've been up to recently.'

Hamilton looks at Annie Webster and nods. Not too keen on having to repeat his story for the fifth time since he joined the group – he's counting – but some women are impressed by it, and Annie Webster looks like the kind of woman he might like to impress. Young, blonde, breasts for Britain. There's no harm in trying.

'Sure I won't bore the rest of you with it?' he says, casting his eyes around the room at the people who have become his friends.

'Don't be daft, Billy,' says Arnie Medlock. 'We're all here for you, you know that.'

Hamilton smiles and nods. A new set of friends he has found at the age of thirty-three. Not many people can say that. And these are real friends, not some fair-weather collection for the good times down the pub on a Friday night. These are people who will put out on your behalf. And Arnie Medlock more than the rest. He gives him another quick nod of acknowledgement, then prepares to go into his past one more time; albeit not for the last. He roots his eyes to the floor, wets his lips, rubs his hands together and takes a deep breath.

'It was about six year ago,' he begins, and tries to divorce himself from the words as he says them. 'I was working in an accountant's in Hope Street, just up from the station. I'd been there a few year, so I was getting

7

paid well enough to be doing OK with myself. Had a wee place up Great Western Road. My motor was all right. Used to go out on Friday with my mates. Shagged some birds, you know how it is . . .' – casts his first glance at Annie Webster, with an attempted roguish smile, but roguishness is out, given the nature of his moustache – '. . . did a bit of this, a bit of that. Had my season ticket for the Rangers . . .'

'We'll cure you of that, if nothing else,' says Medlock, and Hamilton smiles again.

'I had it made, you know. Couldn't have wanted anything else. It'd have been nice if Rangers had been able to get past third-division Maltese sides in Europe, but that aside, life was a big bag of jam doughnuts. But that's the thing, isn't it? You start thinking like that, and you're asking to be shagged. The trouble was, I started having a few problems at work, you know. There was one of those high-fliers there. Graduated a couple of years after me, but the minute he arrived he was angling to be made a partner, just about. In his first year, getting paid less than a fart makes to stink out your trousers, and this bastard was acting like he owned the joint. Course, he got away with it because he was good, I'll give him that, but there were a few of us who would just've loved the chance to knife him in the back.'

He glances apologetically at Annie Webster, who gives him a reassuring look in return, then he hurries back to the narrative, his voice picking up pace so that it is soon blazing a trail through his tale of jealousy, blackmail, revenge and breakfast cereal.

'So, I think I could still have put up with that, or maybe moved to another company, which I probably could've done because I'm no mug with a ledger, but there was a problem. Got into a wee bit of debt, you

8

know. A few too many trips to the bookies; went to see Scotland in a couple of World Cup qualifiers overseas; doing a bit too much smack at the weekends, you know the score. Got myself into a bit of bother with a money-lender called Sammy the Buddhist out Blantyre way. One of the boys in the boozer put me on to him. Seemed like a decent enough chap at the time, but of course, the minute I fell behind with the payments, he developed serious designs on my gonads. You know, threats and all that sort of thing. So, being in a bit of a quandary, I did what any self-respecting accountant would do. I fiddled the books. Did a good job too, mind. Got myself enough cash to pay off Sammy the Buddhist and had enough left over to go to the Juventus game in Italy and get done over by a couple of highbrow Italian opera tarts.'

He looks up, glances around the room for the first time, and gets a few nods in agreement. Few men in this company have not, at some time, tasted the pleasures of an Italian operatic slapper.

'Not bad, you know. I thought I'd got away with it, no mistake. Course, I couldn't have been more wrong. You see, I'd counted without Mr Garden Rake Up His Arse. The bastard digs the ugly out the books, and next thing you know, I'm sat with him in Smokey Joe's All Night Bar for the Criminally Secretive discussing the terms of his blackmail. 'Cause, you see, for all his whiter than white, arse-sucking, holier than thou, I make the fucking Pope look like Reggie Kray bollocks, he was just as much a petty criminal as the rest of us. So he gets down to it, starts taking money off me, and before you know it I'm paying this eejit even more than I'd owed Big Sammy.'

Billy Hamilton leans forward so that his elbows rest on his knees. Now giving Annie Webster his undivided attention. He looks her square in the eye; she accepts his gaze. The air fizzes with tension. He breathes deeply and decides it's cigarette time. Top pocket and his hands are shaking as he takes out the smoke and lights up.

'Just take your time, Billy,' says Katie Dillinger. 'None of us are going anywhere.'

He inhales deeply, letting the smoke out slowly.

'Aye, aye, I know,' he says. 'So, I don't know when it happened, or why it happened when it did, but finally I snapped. I just thought, well, fuck you, Batman. Followed him home one night after the pub, when I knew he'd had a few drinks and the edge would be off – stayed off the lager myself – then waited until the lights were out, broke in at the back, picked the first implement I could find in the kitchen, went upstairs and murdered the bastard. Murdered him. Loved every fucking second of it, 'n' all, I have to admit that. I have to admit that,' he says again, his eyes drifting more thoughtfully back to the floor.

'What did you kill him with?' asks Annie Webster, thrilled by the story, her fingers twitching.

'A box of Sugar Puffs,' he says.

'Wow!' says Webster.

They engage looks for a while, then he turns away and stares at Katie Dillinger, having misinterpreted the look from Webster. Who's going to be impressed by that? he suddenly, and wrongly, thinks to himself.

'Very good, Billy,' says Dillinger. 'And how do you feel after that? Does it bring it all back? Do you still feel anger at your colleague? If you were in the same situation today, what would you do?'

His hands rub together. He feels the rest of the group staring at him. This is what it's all about, isn't it? This is why he's here. It's a relaxed setting, they are all friends, but there's still pressure. The pressure to come to terms

10

with what you did in the past, and every time he talks about it he betrays himself; the fact that he is a long, long way from coming to terms with that past. And it is obvious to the whole room that he still feels anger at Larry Burr. The sarcastic, condescending bastard.

Would he still do the same today? Bloody right he would. He sucks on the cigarette again, almost biting the filter off with his lips. He runs the back of his hand across his mouth. He struggles. He might as well be saying it all, because these actions are speaking so much louder than any words, but he keeps it in.

'My name's Billy, and I'm a murderer,' he says after a while, his eyes once again rooted to the floor. There are a few nods in sympathy around the room. No one claps. The man next to him, Paul Galbraith, Paul 'The Hammer' Galbraith, grips his arms briefly in encouragement. 'You're a good lad, Billy,' he says.

'And what about now, Billy?' says Dillinger, knowing she has to get him talking. 'What have you been up to recently? Do you feel there are any stresses on you at the moment?'

Hamilton breathes deeply and stares at the floor. Back to the present. A brief flirtation with the age-old 'Why am I here?' Would he still think about Larry Sodding Burr if he didn't come to these damned meetings?

'Nothing much. You know I moved to that mob up in Byres Road. Bit of a small concern, but it's all right. At least you don't get arseholes like Burr there, you know. So, I don't know. All right, I suppose.'

'And what about your new colleague?' says Dillinger. 'You expressed some concerns about him the last time, didn't you, Billy?'

Bugger it, he thinks, you remember everything, don't you? The last time he'd just made some chance remark,

11

nothing more. A chance remark about that odious little cretin, Eason, and now she's giving him the POW camp treatment.

He breathes deeply once more. Count to ten, Billy, he thinks. Count to ten. Smoke; deep inhalation.

One . . . she's right, all the same. Two . . . this is why you're here. Three . . . it's not just about coming to terms with the past. Four . . . it's about the present, and even more about the future. Five . . . you're here to make sure you don't do again what you did to Burr. Six . . . there's no way you're going to be so lucky the next time. Seven . . . so be honest with yourself as much as with them. Eight . . . get it off your chest. Nine . . . exorcise your demons, Billy, when you have the support to do it. Ten . . . then sever the guy's testicles first chance you get.

'You're right,' he says, looking up at Dillinger. 'You're right. It's the same thing. I mean, the guy's not some prepubescent genius or anything. He ain't the Mozart of accounting, don't get me wrong.'

'So what is it, then?'

'I don't know. He's got the panache of Homer Simpson; he's uglier than some ugly-looking bird showing her wares in Bonkers on a Tuesday night, with no knickers and more lippy than Madonna; his hair's a mess, he got his dress sense from eastern Europe, and he thinks just because Abba are in these days, it's cool to like the Brotherhood of Man. I mean, the guy could not be less of a threat. And I realise that that was the problem with Burr. Even before the blackmail started, I felt my position threatened by him. But this guy. I don't know. He's a total Muppet.'

He shrugs his shoulders as he looks around the room. Looking for someone to provide the answer.

'Analyse it, Billy,' says Dillinger. 'We can help you,

but you know that answers to this kind of thing have to come from within. Only you can tell what the problem is. Only you can ask yourself if you think you might do to this man Eason what you did before.'

He nods, looks at her with eyes wide.

'Oh, aye, I think I might. That's the trouble. I think I might kill him.'

'But why?'

'I don't know. I suppose he just gets on my tits.'

Dillinger nods her head this time. 'Very good, Billy, tits are good. If you can admit that's all it is, then that's the first step. The guy annoys you. Now you have to address that annoyance. We can't all go around killing people just because they're annoying. You have to address that issue. That's why we're all here.'

She takes her eyes off him and looks around the room. The same old faces, fighting the same malignant spirits they have all fought for years. From 'The Hammer' Galbraith, to Socrates McCartney, they're all in it together.

'Has anyone else got anything to suggest? I know we've all been there.'

Arnie Medlock clears his throat, but Annie Webster is in first with a question. Her own story is a vastly different one. A much deeper psychosis. This is not something with which she can associate.

'Did you not get counselling and that before you got released from prison?' she says.

Billy Hamilton looks at her, slightly surprised.

'I never went to prison,' he says.

'Oh. Did you get off on some technicality or something? I've heard about those.'

Hamilton doesn't know what to say. There are a few awkward glances passed between the group. He looks to

13

Dillinger for help, and she rides in on her pleasure-beach donkey to his assistance.

'Billy's one of our Unknowns,' she says to Annie Webster.

'How do you mean?'

'He's never been caught. That's why you're sworn to secrecy when you join, Annie. Some of our group have served time for the crimes and some have never been apprehended. At least those few have realised that they've done wrong and are here to make sure it doesn't happen again.'

She turns back and stares at him with a little awe.

'So you're wanted by the polis?' she says.

Billy Hamilton shrugs.

'Not really. I mean, they've no idea it was me who did it. They thought it might be someone at the firm, but there were about forty of us there queuing up to do the guy in, so it didn't really help them. It was like that scene in *Airplane* where there's a big line of folk waiting to smack that screaming woman about, only I was at the front and no one else got to have a go.'

'Oh.'

Annie Webster looks around the room. Oh well ... She hadn't realised, but it is fairly obvious. Five months now since she committed her crime, five months since she strangled Chester Mackay. The police have been following her around ever since, but they haven't got anything on her yet, and they never will. But strangely, despite her own case, she has assumed that the rest of the group have all served time. Like The Hammer and Katie and Sammy Gilchrist. But they hadn't covered this point the previous week; obviously just hadn't come up. She swallows hard and tries to decide if this makes any difference. Are the ones who have never been apprehended any more dangerous than the ones who have served their time? Feels a tingle of excitement at the thought. The thrill of danger. She is among more than thieves.

Her eyes fall on each of the group one by one and each time she wonders, and each time she knows that the person at whom she is looking knows what she is thinking; trying to decide whether or not they are a fugitive from justice.

At last she is ready to speak. The question is there, yet still she hesitates.

'Come on, Annie,' says Katie Dillinger, 'say what you're thinking.'

And to a man and woman the collective of the Bearsden chapter of Murderers Anonymous watch closely this newcomer to their midst. They are all here to be judged, regardless of whether or not they might like it.

'Right,' she says, swallowing. Might as well get it out there. It's not like it's an obsession of hers, or anything, but she's curious. For over a year now there's been nothing else in the papers, and where else might he turn up but here. It would be perfect for him. Perfect. And it's not too often that you get the opportunity to meet a legend.

'Eh, I don't suppose one of you is Barney Thomson?'

2

larry bellows sings the blues

'Hey, hey, hey,' says Larry Bellows, smile wider than the moon, slapping his hands on the desk in front of him. 'It's got to be said, folks, they're a nice pair. Hee, hee, hee.'

And off go Burt Keynolds and Pamela Anderson to general audience whooping, applause, delirium and star adulation. Burt turns and winks, Pammy laughs, and the two guest seats beside Larry await their next victim. Larry settles back in his chair, shaking his head. Waits for the general audience mayhem to calm down to a few rogue claps and whoops. Leans forward.

'And hey, she's got a real fine set of bazookas on her 'n' all, eh, folks?'

Further uproar; as ever. Bellows leans back and discreetly presses his finger against the side of his nose, hoping to dislodge any cocaine which might have been caught up in the general turbulence of his nasal hair. (Still four and a half minutes till the next commercial break.)

He smiles some more, the audience whoop and cheer. And off-stage, his next guest stares at the floor and waits. Mouth a little dry, the feeling in his stomach more general discomfort than butterflies.

At last, several *Quiet Please!* prompt cards having been held aloft, the audience settles down into an expectant silence. Larry leans forward, the smile goes, his brow furrows, and he switches from David Letterman to Ed Murrow. The look that gets him Emmy nominations every year. (Yet to win one . . .)

'Listen, folks,' says Larry, sucking in his audience, 'tell ya what. We're gonna get a little more serious now, that's the truth. For there's a fella just arrived in this country for a lecture tour, and he's got some folks in an almighty stink. Some saying he shouldn'ta had a visa, some saying he shoulda been locked up the minute he stepped off the plane. Well, hey, you know me, folks, I'm a fair-minded guy, I like to listen to all sides. And here we are, about to hear the story direct from the horse's mouth. Ladies and gentlemen, you all know who I'm talking about. Direct from Scotland, England, Barney Thomson, ladies and gentlemen, Barney Thomson.'

The audience erupts. Whoops, applause, cheers, jeers, catcalls, proposals of marriage, a cacophony of over-reaction. A few seconds' wait, and then the reluctant star steps out into the limelight. Like a rabbit. Looks at the audience, wide-eyed and furry-tailed. Can see lights and angry faces and excited faces, mouths wide in anticipation, contorted in anger. All for him. Doesn't realise that the audience is always like this whether the guest be Elvis, Hillary Clinton, Winnie the Pooh or Mr Ed.

And so he stutters across the studio, takes Larry Bellows's hand, minces round the front of the desk and sits nervously down into the seat closest. He is aware of the sweat on his brow, the tremble upon his lips.

Eventually the clamour dies to silence. Bellows places his hands on the desktop, takes in the audience, camera and Barney Thomson with an all-embracing, concerned smile.

'Hey, Barney, how does it feel to be Stateside at last?'

Barney stares at his host. Feeling quite lost in this unfamiliar environment. Knew he should have started with Ally McCoist. Can see behind the scenes at everything that is lost to the viewer. Stunned by it all. Stunned to near silence. And, to boot, a tricky first question.

'Don't know,' he says at last. 'Awright,' he adds at a mumble.

Bellows smiles and nods his head. Looks at the audience; doesn't let his eyes say anything just yet.

'Great.' He leans beneath his desk and lifts up a hardback book, which he then holds to the camera. Zoom in, onto Barney's serious face on the cover, under the words *Forty-Three Ways to Bloody Death – A Barber's Story*. 'Right, folks, what we have here is the autobiography of this man they call Barney Thomson. A barber, a writer, and, some might say, a murderer. We can all reach our own conclusions, but here we have the man himself to tell his side of it. So,' he says, turning to Barney, 'are you a murderer? Do you belong on Death Row with the scum and the sleaze and the slime? Are you the evil, deranged serial killer of the media, or are you just some poor sap sucked into a turbulent whirlpool of death out of which you've been unable to escape?'

Barney freezes. Another hard one. Swallows. Thinks. Slowly.

'Don't know,' he says.

Bellows nods seriously.

'Right,' he says. Already realises that he is going to have to do all the talking. Which is fine. Gives him more opportunities to be Dan. And that'll be Rather, as opposed to Desperate or Marino. 'Let's start with your mother. A serial killer, right?'

Barney nods. An easy one.

18

'Don't know,' he says. 'Ah suppose.'

'She killed six people in all. Five men, one woman. Chopped up the bodies and kinda hid them in her fridge. Right?'

'Aye, Ah suppose.'

Bellows shakes his head.

'That's a pretty goddam weird thing to do, ain't it?'

Barney shrugs.

'Don't know.'

'I mean, you must be like really embarrassed, or something?'

'Don't know,' says Barney.

Bellows smiles – this time a small knowing one to the audience – shakes his head and looks at his desk. Still holding the book towards the camera.

'Then you accidentally' – does the inverted comma thing with his left hand on *accidentally* – 'killed your two work colleagues. One with a pair of scissors and one with a broom. Right?'

Barney shrugs. Becoming ever more hunched, with arms folded. A psychologist's dream.

'Ah suppose, aye,' he says.

'Your mother died, and you had to dispose of the eight bodies. And the way you tell it in this here book, now, and listen to this one, folks, is that there were four Federal officers on to your case, and just as they were about to bring you in they all just kinda like killed each other in some weird *Reservoir Dogs* typa shoot-out. Am I telling it straight, barber fella?'

'Don't know,' says Barney. 'What's *Reservoir Dogs*?'

A particular section of the audience whoops and cheers. Some laugh. Bellows holds up his hands. This is serious now.

'Right, let me get this straight,' says Bellows, reading

19

from the monitor. Hadn't known the first thing about Barney Thomson until two minutes ago. 'You thought you'd got away with it, but then one of the bodies turned up, and you fled to some monastery in the north of England to get away from the Feds?'

'Scotland.'

'Right, like I said, England. But if it wasn't just the damnedest thing, there was a serial killer there too and this fellow just happened to murder thirty-three monks.'

There are extended oohs and aahs from the audience. There's no such thing as coincidence. Not on the Larry Bellows show.

'Aye,' says Barney.

Bellows shakes his head and gives his audience the knowing look once more. This is shootie-in. There's nothing easier than turning the audience against a guest who won't open his mouth.

'Well, if that ain't just the damnedest thing, eh, folks? And the way you tell it, barber fella,' says Bellows, 'is that a coupla Feds caught up with you at this point, and they let you clean go 'cause they knew you'd done nothing wrong? Like, is murdering your work colleagues in cold blood legal in England or something?'

Barney's head withdraws a little farther into his shoulders. The sweat beads on his brow, he is aware of the redness in his cheeks. A low rumble of disapproval starts to come from the audience.

'Scotland,' he mutters.

'So you killed this serial killer at the monastery, after he'd bumped off all these other fellas – honest and true men of God, I might add,' says Bellows, looking at the audience, and the low whoop of disapproval grows, 'then the Feds just upped and let you go. Seems to me to be kinda strange, barber fella, I have to say. What next?

That was about ten months ago, right?'

Barney shrugs and his head almost disappears. Slouching right down, hoping the camera won't be able to see him.

'Don't know,' he says. 'Just been walking the Earth and getting in adventures. Ye know.'

Bellows finally places the book flat on the table. The noise from the audience dies away to silence.

'You mean,' says Bellows, 'like Cane in *Kung Fu*, like Jules was gonna do in *Pulp Fiction*?'

'Don't know,' says Barney.

Bellows smiles and nods. Time to wrap up. Almost a commercial break, almost time to reintroduce some nose therapy.

'Seems to me, folks,' says Bellows, 'that this fella here is just a plain murderer, no more and no less than that. And he's been getting away with it far too long. Far too long. Seems to me that the time has come for this fella to face some retribution. Seems to me it's time for this fella to get the punishment his crimes deserve. What d'ya say, folks?'

Barney retreats farther into his shell. Looks at Bellows. Waits for the audience reaction, but they are silent.

'Right, folks,' says Bellows, 'that's all for now. Rejoin us in two minutes, when we're really gonna get down with the latest sounds from Celine Dion. See ya, folks.'

Somewhere Barney can hear the interval music, but the audience remains silent. No whoops, no cheers, no jeers. He stares at the desk. Half an eye on Bellows, but now that the interview is over, Bellows is no longer interested. He can begin to forget about Barney Thomson, and as soon as the drugs kick in – about fifteen seconds from now – he will have completely forgotten the last five minutes.

Barney feels a chill, rubs his hands up his arms. Doesn't yet dare look round at the audience. Takes their silence as hostile. Can feel their eyes burning into him. One pair in particular. Malevolent eyes, wishing him nothing but ill. Eyes that take as read what Bellows has just said about crime and punishment. It is time for Barney to face the music.

Bellows gets out of his seat and bends down behind his desk. Barney can see the back of his head, can't see his hands. The draught around his shoulders gets colder. Feels a spot of rain on his head.

The hair on Bellows's head changes colour. Black to grey. His jacket goes the other way. Grey to black. Barney straightens up and sits back. Swallows. Can feel the tentative tentacles of terror teasing his testicles. Up his back, hairs on his neck standing. Turns and looks at the audience, and they are gone.

The seat is gone from under him and he is standing looking at Bellows a few yards away. But it is no longer Bellows. It is a minister, crouched before God, praying. They are in a church, roof leaking, the pews worn with time, unkempt from misuse and the dripping of water and the attentions of rats and mice and insects and spiders. The windows are broken and more rain enters this benighted house of God from every side; and wind howls through the church, rattling the few fittings left intact.

His world has altered in seconds, but still there is equal discomfort.

Only one window remains as it was, and Barney looks up at it. High above the altar, large red and brown stained glass, in the style of the eighteenth century, a bloodied Jesus looking down upon his flock. His face is tortured, the eyes filled with hatred, cheeks hollow and dark, the mouth etched in a sneer for all eternity. *I shall*

22

look upon you and you shall be damned, he says, and as Barney looks he knows it to be true.

And below this embittered and resentful Son of God kneels the minister that once was Larry Bellows, his hands clasped in supplication, neck bent to the whims of the Messiah. Low words escape his mouth, a solemn prayer.

Barney tries to hear the words, and tries to see his face, for he knows that it will no longer be the face of Bellows. However, he can get no closer. And neither can he turn around, for something stops him; yet he knows that he must, for evil lurks at his shoulder, Satan waits to dance upon his grave. But no matter the feelings that suddenly haunt him, the creeping of his flesh, the pounding of his heart, he is frozen. And he knows that whatever approaches him from behind has the blessing of this bloody Jesus.

He can hear it now. Above the low murmur of the cleric; above the storm and the sound of the rain drumming against the roof and splashing on the floor and pouring through the windows; above the wind whistling through the church, what remains of shattered panes of glass, sucked from their fittings, and smashed on withered stones; above it all he hears the shuffling. A steady dragging across the floor, something low and something evil, and it comes his way and he cannot turn to face it.

And out of the corner of his eye he notices for the first time the slaughtered sheep. Hung by the neck, blood dripping from the wound in its side. Dangling above the font, its eyes removed, blood streaming from the sockets. Yet those empty sockets stare at him. They can see behind him and the look crosses the sheep's face. And beyond the tumult of the storm and the shattered church and the shuffling of his fate, he begins to hear the words

23

of the minister, and the prayer aimed at the disapproving Lord.

He realises it is a prayer for him and his lost soul. His heart throbs, his breath stalls in his arid throat. And then it comes, the touch at his shoulder. A shiver racks his body, so violently his neck muscles spasm. There are no words which can save him from this menace, and it waits to offer him up to the demons of eternity. He closes his eyes ...

And Barney Thomson wakes up. Panting, sweat on his forehead, the air rushing in great gulps into his chest. He fumbles for the light and looks around the small, sparsely furnished room which has been his home for over four months.

A dream, it was just a dream. But it is the same dream that he has had for weeks, and as his head settles back onto the pillow, and his mind tries to clear the terror from the reality, he knows that in every recurring dream there is truth or there is portent.

And as ever, when he has woken from this nightmare, he lies awake for some hours afterwards, unable to allow himself the risk of sliding back into the netherworld to which his bloody past now takes. So he stares into the dark and analyses, and he has begun to believe that he is being told by some higher force to return to his roots; to go back to Glasgow, to face what he has run from for almost a year. We must all be judged, and this dream is telling him that it would be better to be judged here on Earth.

And if not that, then what of this whisper for his soul?

3

my name is barney

'My name's Barney, and Ah'm a murderer.'

It is a busy reception desk; two officers behind the counter going about their business; fourteen or fifteen various members of the public, from concerned parents to assorted criminal element, on the other side, awaiting their turn. The man in the green jumper and purple Teflon C&A slacks has finally reached the front of the queue after an hour and a half. But this a man who is used to waiting. Time means very little to him, and so he has sat and listened to the problems of others while watching the occasional drama unfold. Unsure if he is doing the right thing, but if it will rid him of his nightmares, then it must be done.

The desk sergeant continues to write slowly, the laggard movements of the pen betraying a slight trembling of the fingers. After a while he lifts his head and looks at the middle-aged man, two yards across the counter. There is a discernible twitch in the sergeant's eye; his lips drift between a sneer and a smile; a vein throbs in his forehead, another in his neck. Needs a cigarette. He deliberately puts down the pen, then leans forward, the palms of his hands flattened on the desktop. His head twitches.

'Barney?' he says.

'Aye,' says the man in green. 'Barney.'

'You don't mean Barney Thomson?' says the sergeant.

A glimmer of a smile comes to the man's lips, but it dies quickly, as have all his smiles this past year or so.

'Aye, aye,' he says. 'Barney Thomson, that's me. Ah suppose ye'll have heard a' about me, and a' that.'

The desk sergeant nods.

'Oh aye, Wee Man, oh aye. Everyone knows all about you. It'll be you who killed your two work colleagues in the barber's shop, disposed of the bodies of your mother's victims and may, or may not, depending on your point of view, have had something to do with the murder of thirty-four monks in the monastery in Sutherland about a year ago. Am I right?'

'Aye, aye,' says the man in purple Teflon breeks, 'that's me. Mind you, Ah definitely didnae kill any o' they eejits in yon monastery, ye know. Ah was there right enough, but it wasnae me that did it. Apart fi' the real murderer, o' course.'

'Aye, of course,' says the sergeant. And then he says nothing at all, but fixes the man with a disconcerting stare; and neither does he do anything but stay in the same position, his eyes burrowing into the man, like a jackhammer into cheese.

The silence continues.

'What?' says the man eventually. Beginning to feel unnerved. The strength of his conviction disarmed.

The sergeant raises himself up to his full height – some seven or eight feet – then continues his stare from on high. Finally he points a finger back into the depths of reception at another, younger man sitting on a bench; a man with Elvis sideboards and hair that needs cutting by an experienced barber.

'See that wee guy sitting over there?' he says, and the other nods. The man in green noticed him earlier; Sideboards Elvis has been sitting there since he arrived. 'Funny thing is,' continues the desk sergeant, 'that he's Barney Thomson 'n' all. And strangely enough, if it isn't just the kind of coincidence to make you want to slash your wrists in astonishment, but there's another Barney Thomson back here getting interviewed as we speak.'

He finishes, raising his eyebrows as he does so

'What dae ye mean?'

'What? What do you think I mean, heid-the-ba'? Are you that stupid, Wee Man? You're the fifth Barney Thomson we've had in here today. Yesterday we had a couple and the day before that we had seven – two of whom were Nigerians.' The desk sergeant continues to stare across the divide; the man in Teflon wilts. 'You getting the picture yet, Wee Man? In the past year we've had nearly a thousand Barney Thomsons giving themselves up. There isn't a stupid bastard out there who doesn't want to be Barney Thomson. There are sheep who think they're Barney Thomson. My mother thinks she's Barney Thomson. And now it's just over a week before Christmas, so even more of you sad bastard types are crawling out of the woodwork.'

'But . . . but Ah am Barney Thomson. Ah really am.' Voice a little desperate.

'Fine. You want to be Barney Thomson, that's fine by me. You want to show me some ID, then, Bampot Face?'

The man in Teflon pats his empty pockets. The shoulders slowly shrug at the even more contemptuous look winging its way across the counter in his direction.

'Don't have any,' he says eventually, small voiced.

'You don't have any?' says the sergeant. 'That's not much bloody good, is it, Wee Man? You could've made a bit more of an effort, could you not? Even the saddest bastards who come in here make at least a token attempt. Last week we had a wee seventy-five-year-old woman saying she was Barney Thomson, but at least she'd made the effort to score the name out on her Blockbuster video card and write Barney bloody Thomson in crayon across the top. Initiative, you see,' he adds, prodding his head with his forefinger.

'But . . . but Ah am Barney Thomson. Ah've just been away, ye know. Where am Ah gonnae get any ID?'

The desk sergeant folds his arms across the Wyomingesque expanses of his chest. Delves back into his hard stare for a second or two, then shakes his head.

'Very well, Mr Thomson,' he says, 'have it your way. If you'd just like to take a seat I'll try to get around to seeing you some time before I die. But I'm promising nothing.'

'Oh, right,' says the man. 'Right.'

And so, as the desk sergeant turns his attention to another man who has been waiting some amount of time, a man with a duffel bag full of light armour over his shoulder, Barney Thomson, the genuine Barney Thomson among a thousand impostors, turns and walks out of Maryhill police station and back onto the streets of Glasgow.

✂

It has been a strange year for him. Not quite as strange as the year that preceded it – from now on any year that does not see him involved, indirectly involved, implicated in or downright completely innocent of at least forty murders will seem tame – but strange nevertheless.

Set free to walk the Earth and get in adventures with the good wishes of two officers of the Strathclyde constabulary, he has discovered that it is very difficult to settle somewhere far from home. It takes a peculiar kind of man to walk into a new town, penniless and without an identity, and create a life for himself; and Barney Thomson is not that man.

The previous year had seen some sort of epiphany for him, no question of that. It had been his year of awakening. It had threatened to turn him into some sort of vegetable, but he had emerged a stronger man, with an excellent sense of perspective and a firm grasp of the vagaries of the human mind. This year's model is almost a well rounded individual, but still he is not comfortable with strangers; still he is a Glasgow man.

And so, though his year of wandering the Earth has taken him around Scotland, and even briefly into enemy territory south of the border, he has constantly felt the pull to return to Glasgow, City of his fathers, a world of opportunity, a town where a boy can become a man, a man can be king, a king a god, and a god the very begetter of the Armageddon of disillusion, the eviscerator of failure and the gatekeeper to the crucible of realpolitik. (You don't half think some amount of shite while you're walking the Earth and getting in adventures.)

He has contemplated all sorts of ways of going home. New identities, beards, any number of facial or sartorial gimmicks to fool the forces of the law. But there remain shreds of decency and honesty in the man, there remains a feeling that he ought to have faced punishment for his crimes; punishment beyond his own mental torture and physical hardship. And then there are these dreams, about which he has no idea. Night after night, waking in a cold sweat. A talk-show host abusing, a minister, his back turned, murmuring softly for Barney's soul, while all the time Death creeps up at his shoulder. The very thought makes him shiver.

And so he has returned to the very police station from which the forces of the law had emerged to interview and

29

hound him over the accidental deaths of his two work colleagues, and the serial-killing hobby of his mother. He has walked into this demon's lair, he has proclaimed his identity; he has at last done the decent, honest, deed. And now to what end?

Might give it another go at some other station, just to test the water. Might not. Presumably he will get the same reaction. And if they're not interested, then so be it. Fuck 'em.

That's what he thinks as he heads down the street. Nervousness suddenly evaporated, a new insight into life in Glasgow given to him. Everyone says they're Barney Thomson, so no one is particularly going to believe he is who he says. There are more lines on his face than there used to be, a lot more grey hair. He can walk among the masses and no one need ever know. He might look a bit like the bloke in the photos, but then everyone's got a double. That's what they say.

It could just be, he thinks, that he is a free man.

But there are different types of freedom, and it will take more than waiting in a police station for an hour and a half to free him from his nightmares.

Might as well go and visit the wife, he thinks, walking with a little more purpose than of late, up the street. Take about twenty minutes. Doesn't feel nervous, or interested or bothered for that matter, but might as well check out how she's doing. It's not as if she's going to have any friends she can report his homecoming to.

And as he dodges the cars and feels more at one with his fellow pedestrians than for some time, he wonders if the lousy soap operas his wife always watched, such as *Anal Accident Ward B* and *Only the Bald*, will be as bad as they always were.

4

an instance in the life of blue hawaii

He's happy enough, Stevie Grogan, happy enough. Loves his two boys, his wife, God and the *White Album*, approximately in that order. Job's all right, though he can't afford satellite TV – which is just as well from the marriage fulfilment point of view, given the amount of sport he'd watch – and he has to take the family to that Monaco on the Clyde, Millport, for their holiday every year. Jean Grogan hates it, spending all her time cleaning, but the boys will be all right for another couple of years, until puberty kicks in and they want to have sex, smoke drugs and beat up old people, rather than look for crabs in rock pools and cycle endlessly around the island.

Not concentrating as he drives this night, which is nothing unusual. With some unexpected serendipity, which has been absent for most of the rest of his life, he is listening to 'Wreck on the Highway', that Springsteen paean to gloom, heartache, loneliness and desperation. Talking in his head to Jean, trying to explain how he almost slept with one of the plutonium tarts at work, but that he hadn't, so that's the main thing; not the fact that he'd only been thwarted by Plutonium Tart's indifference, rather than his own conscience. Sounds good in his head. Uses his hands to talk sometimes.

Which is what he's doing when the cat runs out in front of him. A cat called Blue Hawaii. One hand loosely held at the bottom of the wheel, one hand nowhere near. His body tenses in shock, his loose hand tugs desperately at the wheel, the other flies aimlessly between gear-stick and nowhere. The open section of road in front careers away from him and suddenly he is heading towards a field; black as black.

Blue Hawaii the cat watches.

Difficult to say if he would have survived if he'd braked hard and early. But something happens. His life flashes before him, and he has his defining moment of clarity, his epiphany, and at once it all seems obvious to him. The insurance policy, the endowment, it is all set up. He is better off to his family dead than alive. A car accident and all these policies will pay up.

He will not go quietly; he will not go slope-shouldered to his grave. He must die like a man . . .

And so, not knowing what lies out there beyond the limited horizon of his headlights, he floors the accelerator. Better to go flat out than to die in some desperate rearguard action. And with that extra acceleration, as the car leaves the road, it partially lifts off, clearing the low wall it would otherwise have smacked into; and consequently hitting a tree, some twenty yards away, more than ten feet off the ground.

The car bends and buckles and falls broken to the ground, where it lands directly on the top of the corpse of Wee Corky Nae Nuts, whose body has lain undetected for over nine weeks.

The car explodes in a stupendous ball of flame, the tree

burns, the bodies burn, the night comes alive with fire. And although the police will eventually be able to identify the corpses of Stevie Grogan and Corky Nae Nuts, and they will know that Wee Corky had been dead for over two months, the cause of his death will remain in ashes, and they will not know to add him to the list of victims of this year's serial killer. A list which is about to begin to grow.

And as the flames taste the cold night air, off goes Blue Hawaii the cat, in search of another victim.

5

my name is socrates

'Good afternoon, everyone.'

The 'hellos' and 'good afternoons' are returned to him from around the room. He steadies himself, tries not to think too hard of what he is about to do. He has been coming to this group for over a year now and has yet to talk. At every meeting Katie Dillinger has asked quietly and without any hint of coercion if he is ready to speak. At every meeting he has balked and hidden behind the jokes and the forced good humour.

Finally, though, he is ready. If any of them asked him to explain what is so different about this afternoon, he couldn't do it; but none of them will, for they have all been there, in that blighted place, where truth will out and the past must be faced. Perhaps it is the proximity of Christmas, the great embellisher of every negative emotion, that multiplier of sadnesses. But for whatever reason, it is the turn of Socrates, and so urgent is the need to talk, now that it has come, that he could not wait for the next meeting and Katie has called a surprise session of the group. Not all of them have been able to come, but there are enough to hear his cry.

'My name is Socrates and Ah'm a murderer,' he says

at last, and the room is filled with applause, and Socrates McCartney smiles and accepts it.

Katie Dillinger clasps her hands and waves them at him, a huge smile on her face.

'Well done, Socrates,' she says. 'Well done.'

He smiles again, but then the applause dies away and he is left with a silence that he himself must fill.

It is all better out than in, and when he finally starts his voice is a rocket.

'Youse have probably a' been wondering for ages how Ah got my name. People usually do. There are two options, o' course. They think it's 'cause o' the philosopher geezer, or if no, 'cause o' the Brazilian fitba' player wi' bad hair and a fusty beard. And ye know, there's a possibility about both, 'cause Ah have been known tae spout some amount o' philosophical shite in my time, an' Ah can also blooter a ba' intae the net fi' thirty yards if Ah've got half a bottle o' J&B down my neck. Even had a trial for Albion Rovers when Ah wis a lad, but Ah couldnae be arsed. Truth be told, Ah was beginning tae think Ah might be a bit of a poof in those days and Ah thought the communal baths might tip me over the edge. So Ah jacked it in and started hanging out in aerobics classes wi' a bunch o' women.'

'Did it work?' asks Paul Galbraith. The Hammer.

'Oh aye, nae bother. Ah think Ah was just confused due tae some post-pubescent crush on David Cassidy in *The Partridge Family*, ye know. Anyway, Ah chucked the fitba'. If it's no for you, it's no for you. There ye are, a philosophical thought tae take home wi' ye the night,' he says, smiling at the daftness of the last remark and being rewarded with a few smiles in return. A brief pause and he is back in the flow.

'Anyway, it's nothing tae dae wi' fitba' and it's

nothing tae dae wi' philosophy. Socrates was a horse that ran in the two fifteen at Ayr on the twenty-third October in 1981. Nothing special about the lad, just a wee horse. Fourteen tae one, bit of an outsider. Now Ah wasnae a gambling man, or anything like that, just had a wee bet every now and again. Never had a problem wi' it. Ah had a friend in the business but, and he used tae sling sure things my way every now and again, ye know. Ah never asked how he knew, Ah never queried his business or the horse-racing business, Ah wasnae interested. So Ah started slowly, ye know. The first time he told me, Ah stuck a wee fiver on. Gradually, as Ah began tae trust the guy, Ah upped the bets. And here's the thing. He was never wrong. Never. By the time it came tae wee Socrates, Ah must've been paid out on more than twenty bets. Ah was never extravagant, ye know, so Ah hadnae made millions, but Ah had a couple o' thousand by then. Spent it a', of course, but Ah was a bit of a lad, ye know. Anyway, Ah meets this bird. Nice enough looking bit o'stuff. Bit o' class, ye know. Ye can tell. Didnae shag me on the first night. Took me nearly a week tae get intae her knickers, so Ah knew she was for me. Decided tae get married, and ye know how it is, one thing led tae another, and it ended up we were gonnae have the biggest wedding since Elizabeth the First, ye know. So . . .'

'She was never married,' says Morty Goldman, a man of compulsive obsessive personality, and the most dangerous in the room. A quiet lad, you might think, however. The sort you'd take home to meet your folks. Bearsden born and bred, unlike some of these other inter-lopers.

'Aye, fine, whatever. Some other rich bastard, then. It was gonnae be huge. But o' course, my dad couldnae afford it, and she didnae even know who her dad was, so where was the money gonnae come fi'? Especially, ye see, since Ah'd promised the lassie a nice house up in these parts, and a honeymoon in Bermuda. She was a' excited, and Ah didnae like tae tell her that Ah couldnae afford a tenement flat in Govan and a honeymoon in Montrose. But Ah loved her, 'n' a' that, so Ah had tae get the money fi' somewhere. So, along comes my mate wi' this horse. Socrates. Good fucking timing, so's Ah thought. Fourteen tae one. What a chance. He gave me three days' notice, don't put the bet on till just before the off, the usual thing. So's in that three days Ah borrowed and collected as much money as Ah could. Put masel' in debt wi' about five different bastards. A' sorts that yese just wouldnae want to mess wi'. The sort o' fucking eejits that make Billy's Sammy the Buddhist bloke look like, Ah don't know, a Buddhist or something. These were bad men. But Ah did it. Got together about ten grand. Suspicious, Ah know, but Ah just thought, sod it. This is my chance, Ah've got tae dae it.'

He stops to take a breath. Some of the more well-heeled residents of Bearsden who populate the meeting have had a little trouble with his accent – they don't get many from Bridgeton in these parts – but they've picked it up as he's gone along. He's coming to the crunch, and they all know what is going to happen next.

'And sure enough, the horse won,' he says eventually, confounding all expectations. 'Ah had a hundred and forty grand, Ah paid back a' the bampot moneylenders, and Ah was sitting pretty. Life was a bed o'roses. Ah was made, ye know. Blinking made. Started calling masel' Socrates in honour o' that fine beast. Ah could've shagged that horse, nae question. Ah could've shagged it.'

A few puzzled looks around the room, the temporary

pause in the narrative finally filled by the inevitable question, voiced by The Hammer.

'What's the score, then, Big Man? I thought you were going to say the horse lost and you killed your mate?'

Socrates shakes his head, and stares ruefully at each member of the group in turn. Now that it comes to it, he is quite enjoying being centre of attention. He's got them hooked. A natural storyteller. He could be on Radio 4. *Book at Bedtime*, wi' Socrates McCartney, he thinks.

'Ah made an arse of it,' he says. 'Ah mean, Ah only needed about thirty grand tae be going on wi'. Ah could've paid for the wedding, booked the honeymoon, and put a down payment on a decent enough house, ye know. But Ah had too much cash, Ah couldnae handle it a'. Ah was twenty-two and Ah couldnae cope. Ah freaked, nae other word for it. Booked masel' a first-class ticket tae Las fucking Vegas and went an' stayed in some posh gaffe. For two weeks Ah played a' the big casinos, shagged hunners o' birds, did a' sorts o' drugs, totally went for it, ye know. Right in there. The big time. Best two weeks o' ma life. Blew the lot. Ah mean, after a week, Ah might even have been ahead o' the game, Ah'm no sure, but by the end Ah'd blown the lot. And o' course, Ah'd walked out on the work without a word, thinking Ah was some sort o' big shot wi' nae need for a job. And Ah didnae tell wee Agnes where Ah was going. So Ah gets back tae Bridgeton, and what dae Ah have? Fuck a'. Ah've lost a' ma money, Ah've nae job, Ah've nothing. Ah huv tae tell Agnes, o' course, and ye cannae blame the lassie, she's fucked off.'

'What exactly did you tell her?' asks The Hammer.

'The works,' he says. 'Ah just went for it. Told her everything. The money, the gambling, the shagging, the drugs.'

'And?'

'She dumped me. Told me to sling my hook, and buggered off wi' my wee mate Billy Milk Teeth.'

'You can't blame the lassie,' says Katie Dillinger.

'Oh, aye, Ah didnae. Ah'm no saying that. Tae be fair tae the girl she did the right thing. Ah'm no saying any different. Not at all. Billy was a decent enough lad, Ah wisnae blaming him either.'

'So what happened?' asks Dillinger.

'She sent her three brothers round to do me in and Ah killed them a'.'

'Oh.'

'Ah mean, Ah didnae went tae. It wisnae as if Ah was blaming them for what happened. It wisnae as if Ah gave a shite, ye know. But they turned up tae kick ma heid in and Ah lost my rag. Went a bit off my napper. Started smacking them aboot a bit, and ended up wellying the living shite out o' them a' till they were a' deid. Felt bad about it, ye know, when it was a' over. Ah'm a bit of a philosopher, like Ah said, ye know, and Ah've thought about it long and hard. Rage, ye see, is just like any other human need. Once it's sated, well, it's done, i'n't it? It's a' a matter o' control. It's like when yer gasping for sex and ye hitch up wi' some stankmonster just for the sake o' it; but as soon as ye've emptied yer sacs ye look at her and wonder what ye were doing. Or when ye're hungry and eat any old mince just tae fill yer belly. It might leave a bad taste in the mouth, and ye cannae believe ye were so hungry that ye needed tae eat some shite like that, but ye did. Same wi' rage. After Ah'd done it, Ah was a bit embarrassed, ye know. Felt really guilty. Even phoned the polis.'

He stops and looks around the room; slowly shrugs. They are all staring at him; some with wonder, some with sympathy. But they are all killers here, and none of them stares in judgement. That is not their game.

'That's it, really. Don't know what else tae say. Got some amount o' years in the slammer. Cannae even remember how many the old bastard of a judge sent me down for. Anyway, got out a couple o' year ago. Thought Ah was OK at first, but Ah have tae admit Ah still feel rage. Ah think the jail's made it worse, ye know. Cannae be sure. They probably shouldnae have let me out, but ye're no gonnae say no, are ye? So when Ah heard aboot youse lot Ah thought Ah'd give it a go. An' yese've been a big help tae me, and a' that. Ah mean, it was a bit intimidating at first, what wi' being in Bearsden, but Ah think Ah fit in. Naw?'

There are several nods around the room. One or two of the company think he fits in like a forest fire in the Amazon, but they nod anyway in case he decides to kill them.

'So why do you keep the nickname?' asks Dillinger. 'Doesn't it always remind you of what happened?'

Socrates shrugs.

''Cause it's a really cool name. Birds love it. Course, most o' the birds Ah hang out wi' have never heard o' the fitba' player, and they're too thick tae know about the Greek bastard, but it still makes me sound a' exotic and foreign, ye know.'

'Do you not think you'd be better off just being yourself?'

Socrates McCartney stares at Katie Dillinger. He rests his back against the chair, and for the first time in his entire life considers that question. Is it not just better to be yourself? It is a question he's heard asked within this group before, but he never thought that it applied to him. But of course it does, and now this baring of his soul, this outing of his past and telling of his secrets, is forcing him to think about it. Is it better to be yourself, laid naked and bare to the world, hidden behind no sophistry and no tricks, than to put up a front, a brick wall of deceit and subterfuge?

'Naw,' he says, after giving it due thought, 'Ah'm a total arsehole in real life.'

And that, a few relevant details concerning the present day and the continuing juxtaposition of rage against relaxation aside, is the story of Socrates McCartney.

6
a new beginning

Late afternoon, the seventeenth day in December. A robin or a bell or a ball behind the door on the advent calendar; a dark chocolate turned white. Still mild and grey, no sign of winter. As Socrates McCartney tells all, Barney Thomson stands on a pavement, staring across a busy road at a small barber's shop.

He doesn't know how long he stands there. People come and go around him; some bump him, some tell him to move, most pass on by and notice nothing. Grey lives on a grey day, no one with time for anyone else. This is life in the new millennium. But Barney feels the beating of his heart and an unexpected dryness at the back of his throat. A barber's shop.

It is now almost a year since he picked up a pair of scissors in anger. He has carried them around with him all this time, but he has been traumatised; no question of that. The shock of the unremitting murder and mutilation has had its effect, and it is many months since he has even thought of barbery, never mind attempt to practise it.

Yet here he is, standing no more than fifteen yards from a shop. He can smell it; the shampoo, the hair oil, the warm air from the dryer, the hair itself. Dirty sometimes, clean others, but never odourless. And he stares at the small sign in the window, which he passed by an eternity ago. *Help Wanted. Experience Preferred.*

Help to do what? Sweep up; make tea; wash hair; or cut hair. He doesn't know, but whatever it is, it is working in a barber's shop. Back where he belongs, in that land of giants.

His head is a swirl of his past and his future. The years in Henderson's before he accidentally killed his two colleagues; the few days haircutting at the monastery, before he became implicated in another serial killer's murders. Great haircuts he has given, disasters for which he was to blame. For every magnificent Lloyd George '23, there has been a Deep Impact or an Ally McCoist (World Cup '98). He has cut hair with which a king would be content, yet he has also dealt enough stinkers to fill several series of *Ally McBeal* law suits.

And he knows not what his life holds for him, for every decision he makes he finds thrown back in his face. He will walk the Earth; yet he could not face it. He will hand himself in; yet the police would not take him. He will go and see his wife; yet she has moved, leaving no forwarding address. What remains?

And so he stands looking across at the small shop which perhaps holds his salvation. He doesn't know what has led him to Greenock. Just looking around for somewhere cheap to stay; saw an advert in the paper; thought he might as well give it a go beside the cold Clyde. And now, settled in his bedsit above a baker's, he has wandered up the street and almost immediately stumbled across the advert in the shop window. *Help Wanted.* It could be his very own motto. And no doubt fate is playing its hand; and to this fate he may as well concede.

43

There is a gap in the traffic and he takes the plunge. Across the road, doesn't stop to think, straight into the shop. Knows he will not be kept waiting, for he has yet to see anyone come or go in all the time he has been stood watching.

He closes the door behind him and takes a moment to breathe in the surroundings. A small thin room. Two barber's chairs against one wall, fronted by the requisite sinks and individual mirrors; an inconsiderable bench along the other. A couple of sad pictures on the walls. Greenock in olden days, when the Clyde bustled with activity; a lone dog on a deserted street.

'Haircut?' says the old man, not bothering to rise from his seat. Expecting nothing Hasn't had to cut anyone's hair since ten o'clock this morning.

'Help wanted,' says Barney.

The old man nods. An interesting face, something ancient and grey about it, but with an uncommon vigour to him. In his seventies, maybe, but maybe not. Could be older or younger. Life in those old eyes, and a face that has seen much. Grey beard, grey hair and thin; very thin.

'What can you do?' says the man. Gives Barney a long look, and there may be the light of recognition in his eyes. Someone who might actually know me for who I am, thinks Barney, but the thought does little to excite him.

'Ah've cut a bit o'hair in my time,' he says.

The old man nods.

'Aye, Ah can see that, son,' he says. 'Ye've got the look. What's yer name?'

Barney hesitates. What if he does recognise him? Maybe he doesn't want to hand himself in after all. Maybe he wants to be free to work in a small barber's shop in Greenock. Now, there's ambition.

44

'Thomson,' he says. 'Barney Thomson.'

A slight smile comes to the old man's face; but the look in his eyes is warm

'The murderer bloke?' he says.

Barney shrugs. 'Aye, Ah suppose,' he says.

The old man stands up and laughs.

'Aye, sure ye are, son,' he says, extending his hand. 'The name's Blizzard. Leyman Blizzard.' Barney takes his hand. A firm grip, cool fingers. A man to trust 'Ah reckon ye're full o' shite, son, but ye've got the job. We'll see what ye can dae. Cannae promise much in the way o' wages, mind, no unless business picks up a bit.'

Barney looks around the shop again. Spit and sawdust. Needs money spent on it, but you're not going to have any money to spend if you don't have any customers.

'How d'ye manage tae stay open?' he asks.

Blizzard shrugs.

'No many overheads, ye know. As ye can probably tell.'

Barney looks around and wonders why exactly it is that he needs help; except for the painting and decorating. Needs the company maybe, and if that's all it is, then perhaps it'll be ideal. For there is no doubt that he himself also needs the company.

'Could dae wi' a bit o' paint,' says Barney.

Blizzard throws a hand up into the air in a 'What can I do, I've no money' gesture, and for the first time Barney notices his fingers. Bent and gnarled, and he wonders how he can possibly cut hair at all.

'Which chair's mine?' he says, after realising he's staring at the old man's hands.

Blizzard shrugs. 'The one nearest the window, if you like. Ah couldnae give a shite masel'.'

Barney is already standing beside that chair, and he looks

at it and rests his hand on the crudely covered suede head-rest. Like magic or fate or some benign conjuration. Or maybe it is evil sorcery. He has come in from the cold, and not only have the police turned him away, he was walked into a barber's shop, been given a job cutting hair and been presented with the window seat. It is as if a higher force is at work. Yet nothing made him come to Greenock; nothing made him walk up this street. That was all of his own accord. So, it could all just be luck.

The door to the shop opens. A customer. Magnetically attracted by Barney, he thinks, in this new contrived reality of his. He itches to once more lift the scissors in anger, but he defers to his boss.

'What'll it be, mate?' asks Blizzard, as the man – Jamie Spencer, twenty-seven; going prematurely bald; married with two girlfriends; financial analyst, whatever that is; already the worse for wear for too much alcohol; nose tending to redness; can run a hundred metres in under twenty-five seconds – closes the door behind him.

'Can ye dae me a Lutheran, Three at the Back, Cloistered Short Back and Sides?'

Blizzard looks at him, mouth slightly open, showing white teeth and a bit of drool.

'That's a fucking haircut?' says Blizzard.

'Aye, Ah can dae that,' says Barney. 'Sit yerself down there, mate.'

Of course, the last time he did it he made a total hash of it; but a bit of concentration and a steady nerve should see him through.

Jamie Spencer eases himself into the chair nearest the window; Leyman Blizzard gives Barney the nod. Smiles to himself, the old man, at this sudden interruption and being immediately relegated in his own shop. But he is not wont to care.

46

Barney flexes his scissor fingers and prepares for his first haircut in nearly a year. Back in the saddle. Suddenly, from nowhere, thrust onto the stage. Once more at the helm. Returned to the Starship *Enterprise*, like Spock in the first movie. Sean Connery in *Never Say Never Again*. Simon and Garfunkel in Central Park. The coelacanth.

He's back.

And all the while, the God of Wonder smiles

7

the unexamined life is not worth living

Statistically most murders take place after the hours of darkness; or, at least, they do in the netherworld of Barney Thomson. Not that Barney will automatically be implicated in the murder that takes place this evening – though there will be some who suspect – some eight hours after the end of the extraordinary biweekly meeting of Bearsden Murderers Anonymous; but inevitably, there will be a coming together. It is his destiny.

Jacob Wellingborough, an average man. Fourteen years in the plumbing trade; married with three children; a part-time mistress whom he sees on an occasional basis; holidays twice a year, once with the family in Spain, once with his mates in the Lake District; new car every second year; season ticket at Ibrox; half-hour drive to work; satellite TV, *News of the World, Surprise, Surprise* and *Club International*. An ordinary man.

The unexamined life is not worth living.

So some people think; one man in particular, as far as this story goes. Someone who cannot bear the ordinary; who cannot countenance the mundane; who quails at those who might disdain originality; who cannot see the merits of an ordinary life. And so he sits at home each night battling with those demons which tell him to challenge that ordinariness; telling himself that life need not be exceptional to be worth living; that life can go on without catechism and analysis.

How many years has he denied the truth and the inevitability of his nature? How many times has he sat with friends, talking through his weakness and the demons that drove him away; and now the demon that has reignited the evil within him, less than a year after his return? The demon that has been the naked, flaming torch to his blistering desire for revenge upon the world? Even the honest hearts of Murderers Anonymous have not been able to help. Because, for all his time in confession and self-revelation, he has never admitted to anyone what drove him to murder in the first place; what pushed him to the edge, then tipped him over into the abyss.

And so Wee Magnus McCorkindale had had to die. And now many others will follow, though their crimes may be insignificant.

Jacob Wellingborough walks out of the pub, says goodbye to Davie Three Legs, Charro and Baldy McGovern. Monday night, Christmas quiz night at the Pea & Korma, another second-place finish behind the Govan Guzzlers (none of whom is from Govan, and all of whom sip lemonade quietly throughout the night). A ten-minute walk to the house. Sometimes he takes the car, because there are never police around this area, but tonight he'd decided to walk. One of the last decisions he'll ever take.

He is thinking of a variety of things as he goes. Fives the next night; can't believe he let Baldy say that Clark Gable had won an Oscar for *Gone with the Wind*; Janice at the weekend, if he can get away from Margaret and the kids; struggling to get the particular doll Miriam wants for her Christmas; couple of awkward calls in the morning; his mind rambles on. Turns when he hears the footsteps behind him. A bit surprised when he sees who it is; stops and waits. Fatally.

'How you doing, mate, didn't expect to see you?' he says.

The killer smiles; fingers twitch on the knife held in his hot right hand, thrust inside his jacket pocket.

'Just been seeing some mates.'

'Right. Excellent,' says Wellingborough.

And so they start walking along together, side by side, with nothing to say. Wellingborough feels uncomfortable. The killer is a little nervous; this is the first cold one in some time. McCorkindale had been in the heat of the moment. And it is wrong – at least he has the conscience to know that.

'Do you know what the capital of Djibouti is?' says Wellingborough to break the awkward silence.

'Djibouti? Don't even know where it is.'

'East Africa. I mean, I knew that, but I didn't know what its capital was, you know. Should've guessed, I suppose. Djibouti's also the name of the capital, you see. No imagination these people,' he says.

'That's funny,' says the killer.

'How come?' says Wellingborough, turning to face his nemesis.

'Because that's what Ah've been thinking about you.'

'What?'

Wellingborough looks at his murderer. A moment's recognition. The dawn of realisation. He sees the knife coming up out of the corner of his eye, but in no way is he expecting it, and so it goes, the sharpened blade, into

50

his back and into his kidneys and through the viscera, so that the point emerges at the other side, breaking the skin of his stomach.

Wellingborough's mouth opens, his eyes are wide, his pupils dilate; a hoarse query escapes his throat, followed by a grunt as the knife is thrust deeper into his body cavity and upwards beneath his chest. 'Why?' his final word, that great philosopher's question; and then he collapses, and the killer chooses, on this occasion, to leave the knife where it is, and among the flashing images that race through Wellingborough's brain as his life soaks away is the first picture he had of the killer wearing gloves and thinking it was odd as the weather is so mild for December, and men don't wear gloves anyway. Not really.

The killer stands over the body until the spasms have stopped, and the last breath has been taken. A quick glance up the road in both directions, and then he disappears into the bushes, so that by the time the body is discovered late on this December night, there will be no sign or trace of the perpetrator of the crime.

✂

He feels the touch of the sheep in the dark. The cold fleece, damp with water and blood, brushes against his face, then swings back into him after he's pushed it away. He stumbles away from it, tripping over something soft. He steadies himself against a pew. And the wind stops suddenly.

He lifts his head; tries to hold his breath, though his chest screams to pant. The roar from the broken windows is instantly stilled, and now in the quiet he can hear clearly the low prayer from the broken lips of the clergyman, and the shuffling coming ever closer from behind.

Can't bring himself to turn, even though he knows in

51

this darkness he could see nothing anyway. A prayer for his soul, that's what he hears; then he becomes aware of the echo of the words, and the low voice behind accompanying the shuffling. Whatever it is behind him, whatever demon creeps up in preparation for laying its hand on his back, it is mimicking the prayer of the minister. Repeating the words, the voice cruel and mocking, a callous burlesque. A prayer for the soul of Barney Thomson, for not only will he die, he is condemned to an eternity in Hell.

Barney screams in impotent terror.

And, as ever, awakes in the night, sheathed in sweat, clutching the blankets, dragged howling from his nightmare before the true nature of the evil can reveal itself.

8

back at the con

'You ever consider Jelly Babies, mate?'

Barney Thomson has considered many things; Jelly Babies not being one of them. He shakes his head, and snips a couple of unnecessary hairs from just behind the right ear.

'How d'ye mean?' he asks.

The bloke currently submitting to Barney's scissors lifts his hands beneath the cape; making it look, to someone with an eye for that kind of thing, as if he has a pair of massive erections.

'Jelly Babies,' he says. 'I mean, think about it. Is that no just the strangest thing. Jelly Babies. You know, they're always there. You eat them when you're a bairn, you grow out of them, and then you don't think about it when you grow up.'

'Aye,' says Barney, 'ye're right. Ye don't think about it.'

'Well, think about it now, Big Man, that's all I'm saying. Jelly Babies. Consider the concept. They are asking you to eat babies. Is that not just a bit strange? You're eating babies. Every bit of them. The eyes, the nose, the arms, the intestines. You know, folk go on about cannibals as if

53

they're like weird people, but there are millions of school weans out there eating babies every day. Maybe the body parts aren't too well defined, 'n' all that, but a baby's a baby, you know. They're asking us to eat babies. You just couldn't introduce something new like that nowadays. They only get away with it 'cause they're an institution. Like mince and tatties, only sweeter.'

Barney stands back and admires his handiwork. His first Jimmy Stewart in nearly a year, only his third haircut in his second day back on the job, and clearly the old magic is still there. Just about finished this one, and he hasn't lost it. Not at all. A firm hand, a steady eye, that's all that's needed.

Unlike some . . .

He glances over at the work being done on the shop's other chair. Leyman Blizzard is doing his best, but this is a haircut from Satan's own factory; the sort of haircut that two months with a bulldozer, three metric tonnes of cement and a brothel full of politicians couldn't hope to salvage. There was a time when he would have looked askance upon such tawdry work, when he would have cast aside the conventions of honourable workmanship and denounced the haircut to anyone who would listen. But that was then. Barney has gained a sense of perspective. He is working on a rainy day in a small shop, on the outskirts of an old city on the west coast of an unfulfilled country, on the edge of a divided continent, at the heart of an insignificantly small planet, in an inconsequential solar system, at the bottom end of a meagre galaxy, downtown in the great Gotham City of the universe. Who cares if he, or anyone else, gives a bad haircut?

He nods at the mince and tatties remark, then stands back from the final snip. His work here is complete. He can send the man packing with a haircut answering to

54

every Euclidean assumption, and turn his attention to the solitary chap in the queue. Although, as it happens, Leyman Blizzard comes to the end of his magnum opus in malfeasance just before Barney, and he assumes he will take the next customer.

'That's you, mate,' says Barney, 'all done.' Not before time, he thinks. Jelly Babies had been the end of it, but what had gone before had ranged far and wide and touched upon almost every topic in the Barbershop Handbook.

The man looks in the mirror, somewhat surprised. There is yet much in his repertoire which requires airing, not least the bare bones of his thesis on Lysenkoism and its applicability to ghetto culture. All his mates have heard it and they all tell him to shut up the minute he opens his mouth, but barbers have no option but to listen. But he's happy enough with the results, so he rises from his chair as the cape is withdrawn, hands over the required money, sticks a cheeky wee fifty pence into Barney's hand, and is gone; murmuring as he goes strange thoughts on the demise of Spangles.

Just ahead of him goes Leyman Blizzard's customer, the Hair of Horrors upon his shattered head, all sorts of condemnation and humiliation awaiting him, his haircut set to be the concubine to reprobation, and Barney purses his lips and thinks nothing at all.

He and the old man look at one another, each with a common understanding of the other's abilities. And Leyman realises he's made a good decision.

'You take the next customer, son,' he says.

'Ye sure?' asks Barney. 'You were done first, boss.'

'Naw, naw, on ye go, on ye go,' he says, and the customer, his heart singing with triumphant relief, steps up to Barney's chair. A young man, due to go on a surprise last-minute date with the object of his affections, and desperate not to look like a complete idiot.

Barney does the thing with the cape and the towel at the back of the neck, and can feel The Force returning to him. Just like the good old days. Except nowadays he can make a reasonable job of cutting hair. He's back. He's refreshed. This is his Elvis NBC Special. He ought to be dressed in black and be surrounded by babes.

'What'll it be, son?' he asks.

The lad looks at him, considers again what he is about to do.

'I want tae look like Elvis,' he says.

A sign.

'Thin Elvis,' says Barney, 'Ah assume fi' the fact that ye're thin?' Sharp as a button.

'Aye,' says the lad. 'Thin Elvis. Like he looked in *Girls, Girls, Girls*. Make me look like that.'

Barney has never seen *Girls, Girls, Girls*, but he can cope. And so he sets to work with his scissors, a comb, some shampoo, a hairdryer, a Euro-size can of mousse, two litres of olive oil, a half a kilo of fettuccine and a certain degree of panache.

Leyman Blizzard sits and watches; doesn't say much at first. The lad says nothing, being altogether too nervous. He has heard tell that Wee Jean McBean, a girl of moist reputation, will forgo any sort of lovemaking preliminaries – dinner, dancing, presents, desperate pleading – for an Elvis look-alike. If this haircut goes well, he's in there and he knows it.

'What did ye think o' the haircut Ah just did, son?' asks Leyman Blizzard after a while.

Barney glances over at his new boss, remembering to stop cutting hair as he does so, something he wouldn't always have done in the past. He considers his answer, and thinks of this: there are two kinds of time in life.

There's a time for candour, and then there's a time for bollocks. This, thinks Barney, is most definitely, with bright, spanking nobs on, a hundred-piece orchestra playing 'Ode to Joy', and a herald of exultant angels singing hosannas upon high, a time for bollocks.

'It was brilliant. A fine piece o' barbery. Hirsutology fi' the top drawer. A haircut o' stunning eloquence. Pure magic.'

Leyman Blizzard rubs his hand across his beard and nods his head.

'Thought it was a load o' shite masel',' he says.

'Oh,' says Barney.

'Cannae cut hair tae pee my pants,' says Blizzard, and the young lad looks at him out of the corner of his eye and thanks some higher force that he did not have to submit to his scissors. 'Not since a long time passed. You might just be the man tae save this shop, son. That was a good job ye just did there. A Jimmy Stewart. Ah can just about manage one o' them masel' these days, but not much else.'

'What happened?' asks Barney, although he knows the answer. It happens to them all. Eventually the steadiness goes, the hand–eye co-ordination is lost, and even the most basic aspects of barbery become a trial.

'Just the usual, son,' says Blizzard. 'Just the same shite that happens tae every bastard when they get old. Ah've been doing this job for near on fifty year. Now Ah'm washed up. Ah'm finished. You know who Ah am? Ah'm Muhammad Ali when he fought Larry Holmes. Ah'm George Best when he played for Hibs. Ah'm Sinatra when he did the *Duets* albums.'

'Jim Baxter when he went back to Rangers,' says the lad.

'Aye, that's me awright. At a dead end. Ah'm Arnold Palmer; Ah'm Sugar Ray Leonard; Ah'm Burt Reynolds.'

57

'Steve Archibald when he signed for Barcelona,' says the lad.

'That was at the peak o' his career,' says Blizzard.

'Aye, but he wis still shite.'

'Fair point. Anyway, Ah'm all o' those people, all o' them. Ah've got about three regular customers left and one o' them's so short-sighted the daft bastard cannae see what a mess Ah'm making of his heid. Ah don't know ye fi' Adam, son. Ah just know yer name, and ye might be that bloody murdering eejit who disappeared up in the Highlands, 'cause they say he could cut a mean hair or two, Ah don't know, but ye look tae me like a hell of a barber. Ah'll up yer wages if Ah can, and help ye out wi' the Jimmy Stewarts, and Ah'll leave the rest tae you. You're the boss. How about it?'

Barney looks over at Leyman Blizzard. The expression on his face betrays his astonishment. And as he stares at the old man, almost a tear comes to his eye. How many years in Henderson's did he search in vain for such recognition? How many times in the distant past at that shop did he complete some masterpiece, only to see his work ignored, his genius disregarded, so that eventually his confidence had gone and he had become the bitter pursuivant of mediocrity. And now, after just three haircuts, there is a man willing to reward him for doing a good job. It is as if he's found the father figure he has been missing all these years.

'Ah'd like that very much, Mr Blizzard,' he says. 'That'd be brilliant.'

'Stoatir,' says the old man. 'And ye can call me Leyman.'

They exchange a glance. A special bond has been created. It as if he were Skywalker to Leyman Blizzard's Yoda. That is, if Yoda had been absolutely shite at cutting hair.

'Here,' says the lad, having found his tongue with the denunciation of Steve Archibald, 'is your name Barney Thomson?'

Barney nods, now flowing smoothly through the Elvis *Girls, Girls, Girls*.

'Aye, it is,' he says.

'Bit of a coincidence that, is it no? I mean, you being a barber 'n' all?'

Barney Thomson looks down at the lad, and takes a moment. He turns to Leyman Blizzard, looks around the small barber's shop which has become his new home – the two chairs, the small bench, yesterday's newspapers and five-month-old *Sunday Post* supplements, and no concessions to Christmas but for the picture of a former Spice Girl, naked but for a discreetly placed bit of tinsel, on the cover of the *Mirror* – has a glance out of the large windows of the shopfront at the miserable December rain sweeping in off the Clyde, then looks once more at his customer. A shiver eases its way down his spine. All this time stranded in some sort of pointless emasculation, thinking that his only real choice was to hand himself in and face the vicious music of public scorn, when it has proved the simplest thing in the world to walk back into old ways. The simplest thing in the world. He's back doing what he always loved; he's got the same name; he's changed in all sorts of ways, but still he's the same man; and yet he might as well be someone completely different.

'Not really,' he says. 'Actually Ah'm the real Barney Thomson.'

The lad catches his eye in the mirror to see if he's being serious, then smiles.

'Aye, right,' he says, 'I bet ye say that tae a' the birds.'

59

9

a name of kings

Jade Weapon opened fire with her submachine-gun, riddling the bathroom door with holes and pumping the Russian agent, cowering behind, full of hot lead.

'Come on, Malcolm. Do you really want to be in there all day?'

'Ah want tae be in here for the rest o' my life, 'n' a' that. Why don't youse just leave me alone? Ah want tae get some sleep.'

'Your mum and dad are really worried. You don't want to do that to them, do you?'

'I've made yer favourite, Malcolm! Mince!'

'Ah hate mince!'

Detective Sergeant Erin Proudfoot turns round to Malcolm Reid's mother and waves at her to keep quiet. Matters are at a delicate stage. At any moment, he could flush his sister's pet hamster, Huey, down the toilet. This is no time to be talking of mince.

Proudfoot looks at her watch. She has been here for nearly half an hour. Called out to a domestic; could have been anything. Assault; battery; arson; noisy neighbours; murder, even; or it could have been ... a noxious fourteen-year-old, locked in the bathroom, threatening to flush his sister's only pet down the lav if he didn't get to go to Big Angus's party on Friday night. Turned out to be the last on the list.

It was never like this on *Cagney & Lacey*, she thinks. Well, maybe in one episode.

What would Jade Weapon, star of the erotic crime thrillers with which she has been filling her spare time at the office, do? Kill a few people; shag some others; cause mayhem and damage, and be home in time for gin and tonic and a three-in-a-bed sexfest. But Jade Weapon never has to deal with people like this. The mundane, real world. The world that haunts us all.

'Look, Malcolm, it's not about the hamster. Just let Huey go and then we can talk some more,' she says. Mrs Reid grips her by the arm as she says it; in support. Can't believe I'm coming out with this crap, Proudfoot thinks to herself.

'Naw!' he shouts, and there is an edge to his voice. Margaret Reid gasps. She knows the tone. The same tone he used just before he tipped his sister's maggot collection into a fish-pond.

'He's getting serious,' she says frantically to Proudfoot.

Proudfoot glances over her shoulder. Delivers her best 'Back off or I'll arrest you for being a bloody idiot' look. Margaret Reid recognises it, for she has in the past been arrested for being a bloody idiot, and backs off.

'Ah'm no going anywhere till she says it's awright for me tae go tae the party. Big Angus gives brilliant parties. She's got one more minute, or the hamster gets it. Ah'm serious.'

One minute or the hamster gets it. Fuck me, thinks Proudfoot. It's come to this. I know what Jade Weapon would do, she thinks. She'd boot the door in, kick the

61

stupid little twat's head in, then ram the damned hamster up his backside.

'Come on, Malcolm. It's not even about Big Angus's party, is it?'

She can almost see him thinking through the bathroom door. 'What d'ye mean?' he says.

Fine. So maybe it isn't about Big Angus's party. It doesn't mean she actually has a clue what it is about. But then, not in a million, bazillion years, doubled, could she even begin to give the remotest, tiniest, pygmy-sized shit about it. There are flies so small they're invisible under an Eiffel Tower-sized microscope that do bigger shits than I care about this, she thinks.

It has been a long year for Erin Proudfoot, since she and Joel Mulholland set the notorious Barney Thomson free, and then engaged in the angry hostilities of romance. A bloody case, the mental scars of which dominated the few months of their desperate, passionate, bitter relationship, when everything from marriage to suicide was considered.

Six months now since Mulholland imploded and disappeared up the west coast somewhere – not a card or a letter – leaving her behind in solitary meltdown. Still she sees her psychiatrist four times a week; still her psychiatrist tells the superintendent not to put her anywhere near real criminal activity; and still he lies to her about it, and she imagines she's in better mental health than she is.

Occasionally she ponders on Mulholland's whereabouts, but she has made no effort to go after him. She knows he's gone a little – or completely – insane himself. She's heard tell, but just rumour and gossip around the station. But whatever feeling was there is now gone.

And so there have been a couple of flings in the interim, but her scars have brought to her an intensity that her lovers can't handle. Buxton was one, another of the CID sergeants. A few evenings, then one night, and she'd scratched his back so that the sheets were soaked with blood; and that was that. Then there was the idiot she'd met outside the Disney shop in the St Enoch's centre. He'd thought he was picking her up, while all the time it was the other way about. Again he'd been quick to her bed, but when her nails had been unleashed and she had cried 'Havoc!' and let rip the dogs of war, he had crumbled and cracked and off he'd gone, tail between his legs to mourn the death of femininity.

'It's about your parents, Malcolm. I know that.'

'What d'ye mean?' says the mother. 'What d'ye mean?'

Proudfoot looks at her and shrugs. 'He's a teenager,' she says. 'It's always about the parents.'

'Might be,' comes the small voice from the bathroom.

The mother gives Proudfoot a concerned glance, then looks pleadingly at the blue, fading to grey, bathroom door.

'We love ye, son, we really dae.'

'How can ye, Maw, ye called me Malcolm? Ah mean, what kind o' name is Malcolm? It's a crap name.'

'That was yer faither,' she says.

Proudfoot rolls her eyes. *Beam me up, Mr Worf, and take me away from here for ever.*

'It's a name of kings, Malcolm,' she says. 'A name of kings.'

There comes a hefty pause from within. The wheels are in motion; smoke appears from under the bathroom door.

'Who?' he says eventually. 'What kings were called Malcolm?'

She holds her head in her hands. If I had a gun, she starts to think, but she has been told four times a week for the past year to fight these thoughts. You won't rid Sutherland from your mind by killing people yourself, she keeps being told. Maybe, she thinks; maybe not.

'Malcolm I, Malcolm II, Malcolm III. They were all called Malcolm.' Daaaawh . . .

'Who were they?' he asks. His mother looks at Proudfoot as if she is mad, and she's not far off. 'Ah mean, what country were they kings of?'

'Scotland, Malcolm, they were kings of Scotland. A long time ago, maybe, but that's the pedigree of the name your parents gave you.'

'Pedigree? Ye mean, like the dog food?' says Malcolm.

Proudfoot stares at the floor. Imagines the newspaper reports of what might transpire if she were armed. *Crazed Police Sergeant Sets Hamster Free as Mother and Son Die in Hail of Bullets.*

'It's a beautiful name, Malcolm. An ancient, regal, royal name of kings.'

No immediate riposte. She can hear him thinking. The good and the bad of emerging from his hideout running through his mind. And then, after the pause, the inevitable.

The lock clicks, the door to the bathroom slowly swings open, and Malcolm Reid stands framed in the sunlight which streams through the bathroom window. It highlights wisps of hair around his head; it almost looks as if he has a halo; he is dressed in a long white bathrobe; on his face is the fustiest of fusty little goatees. He stands with his arms spread at his side, the palms of his hands facing forward; staring at his mother.

'Is that right, Maw?' he says. 'Is that right? Did you name me after the kings?'

'Where's Huey?' she says in response, as he emerges farther from the light, and the halo fades.

64

'He's under my bed,' he says. 'Ah was making it all up. Ah never even had him in there. Was Ah really named after a king, Maw?'

'Ye little bastard!' she starts.

Time to go, thinks Mulholland, and she is already on her way down the stairs. If there's going to be a domestic assault, she can let it happen; then if someone gets called out to it, it won't be her, because they don't let her near anything physical.

'Ye were named after yer Uncle Malcolm, and he was a bloody eejit 'n' all!' she hears Margaret Reid cry as she reaches the bottom step, and with more words of anger in the air, she is at the front door and out into the street.

She stands for a second looking up at the high, grey clouds, the sun poking through in inappropriate places. Takes a moment, has a few thoughts. One day at a time, one pointless crime at a time. Crime? Not even that. When was the last time she was let anywhere near a crime?

And with that sad thought, she is on her way. It's just another day in late December, getting close to the time of year when salt is viciously rubbed into the wound of being alone. And in less than an hour she will be back on that other pointless, endless job they have had her on for over five months. One of three officers tasked with tracking the movements of a killer on whom they have nothing; a desperate bid to claim a success, among so much failure. And so, night after night, drowning in bars and sitting outside houses, and looking through binoculars, and not for a second can she imagine that she will ever discover anything they can use.

Not for a second.

10
eureka!

Later in the afternoon, on Barney's second day of cutting hair, and it is as if he has never been away. Indeed, it might even be the case that this new, well-balanced, egalitarian Barney Thomson, no longer living in fear of detection, is even more a whizz with a pair of scissors than his bitter former self. There has been a slow but steady flow of customers through the door, as if sensing his arrival – *Hire him and they will come*, the voice in the field might have said to Leyman Blizzard. Blizzard is siphoning off the easier cuts, or the cuts that don't really matter – the Jimmy Stewarts, the skinheads, the children – leaving Barney with the bulk of the more complex work; from the Jimmy Tarbucks to the Mesolithic Preternatural Pot-boilers, and from the Chris Evans '96 to the Gargantuan Liberace Crevice Creepers; and it has even been slightly sunnier in Greenock than normal for late December; that is to say, the sun shone for approximately four minutes just after lunch.

So, it seems, life could not be better for Barney. He is striking up a rapport with customers based on shared interest and intelligent conversation; he can go the pub every night, or just choose to sit in front of the TV without having to watch the kind of mindless soap opera that used to have Agnes slobbering in anticipation – although he'll probably watch the episode of *Return to Beluga Babe Boat* when Tray and Pesticide fall out with Condom; he might even visit Cappielow Park on a Saturday afternoon to watch Morton's continuing struggle with reality.

And naturally, being so content with his lot, having everything he could possibly want, with no need for anything else in his life, Barney is as miserable as shite. Human nature, you see. To always want something more.

'Ye ever see *Eureka!* with Gene Hackman?' asks Leyman Blizzard, as they discuss the matter. Just gone four o'clock, currently no customers of which to speak. They chat between themselves, and Barney values the words of wisdom from the old man.

'Naw, naw, didnae see that,' he says. Never even heard of it.

'Good film,' says Blizzard. 'Anyway, Gene Hackman's a gold prospector. That's what he does, that's his life, doesnae know anything else. For years and years he trawls slowly through Alaska, or one o' they cold places, miserable as fuck, not finding a bloody sausage. Then suddenly, one day, bugger me wi' a pitchfork, if he doesnae suddenly come up wi' the biggest gold find in the history of mankind. Bloody masses o' the stuff. Mair gold than you could stick up your arse. Instantly makes him the richest man on the planet. Anything he wants. Huge mansion, boats, planes, all the women he can eat, the works. And guess what?'

'He's miserable as sin,' says Barney, catching up with the analogy.

'Exactly. Miserable as a bull wi' nae dick in a field full

67

o' cows. Ends up dying, the daft bastard. And ye know why? 'Cause it's a' about not getting what ye want, 'cause as soon as ye dae, there's nothing left. Ye have tae leave yersel' needing mair than you have or you just die. Ah'm telling ye, son, ye have tae be wanting for something. It's human nature.'

Barney sits in his barber's chair and stares back at himself in the mirror. He can recognise all those changes in himself from two years previously. He looks older, a few more grey hairs, but there's something a bit fuller and more confident about his face than before. Whereas he used to look like a scarecrow, now there's a bit of the Sean Connery about him. So he likes to think. A bit of the hard bastard.

'Ye might be right, Leyman,' he says. 'Ye might be right.'

The door opens, and a cold breeze follows in the first customer for twenty minutes. The man removes his coat, sticks his hat on a peg – the only time he ever wears a hat is to the barber's, so that he has something with which to cover the evidence when he leaves, in case it's a nightmare – and turns to face them. The barbers, in turn, go into their new routine.

'What'll it be, son?' asks Blizzard before the man has been ushered to a seat. One of the easier ones and Blizzard will take charge, having regained a certain amount of confidence working next to the master; one of the harder on the list, and Barney's the man.

'Could you do me a Zombie?' he asks.

Barney nods. No bother, and this is one for him.

'Aye, fine, fine. Why don't ye sit down there, mate. Sit down.'

Leyman Blizzard winces at the thought of what might have happened if he'd had to make the cut, then buries himself in that day's *Evening Times* Headline: 'Heeeeeeeeeere's Barney! He's Back as Milngavie Plumber Put to the Sword'.

Barney does the usual with the cape and the towel, lifts a comb and a plant spray gun, and gets to work. The Zombie is the latest in post-modern, retro-club Louisville chic, and Barney has never executed one before. He's seen the pictures, however, and is confident.

'Haven't seen you here before,' says the customer, Davie Whigmore, twenty-six, late of Claverton and Sons, now peddling low-budget window replacements for Arthur Francis Ltd.

'Naw,' says Barney. 'Just started yesterday. Just moved intae the area, ye know. No been here long at a'. A coupla days, that's me.'

'Oh, aye, where've you come from?' says Davie Whigmore, wondering why anyone who had the choice would move to Greenock.

'Well, here an' there, ye know,' says Barney. 'Ye might have heard o' me. Ah'm Barney Thomson, ye know.'

Whigmore looks Barney in the eye in the mirror, then turns around – narrowly avoiding serious injury – and looks more closely at his face.

'Aye, you do look like him, now that you mention it, mate,' he says, assuming the position once more. 'Didn't notice it when I came in. So, you must be on the run, then?'

'Aye, aye. Well, Ah was, Ah suppose, no sure about now.'

'Pretty cool, though, i'n't it?' says Whigmore. 'I mean, you're like the Fugitive, or the Incredible Hulk. Or the A-Team even. Fleeing from justice. Flash bastard, eh? You must get hunners of women?'

Barney shakes his head. Leyman Blizzard stares over the top of the newspaper.

'None so far,' he says.

'Oh, right. Too bad, mate.'

'It's never gonnae happen,' says Barney. 'Apart from the obvious, that Ah'm an ugly bastard . . .'

'Don't know, mate, there's a bit of the Sean Connery about you.'

'Aye, well, whatever. Apart fi' that, no one believes me. Ah mean, dae *you* actually think that Ah'm the real Barney Thomson?'

Whigmore laughs.

'Of course I don't, mate. You think I'd let you anywhere near my head with a pair of scissors if I thought you were the real, actual, slash-'em-as-soon-as-look-at-'em Barney Thomson? No way.'

'Ye see?' says Barney. 'Ah've got a major credibility problem. Ah look like the guy, Ah'm fully prepared to admit tae being the guy, but nae bastard believes me because there are so many crackpot heid-the-ba's out there who aspire tae be me. Very strange.'

Whigmore nods, nearly putting the Zombie in jeopardy. Fortunately, the barber doing a Zombie has a certain amount of leeway.

'I suppose you're right. That's what it's all about these days, i'n't it? Credibility. I mean, the Big Man's going tae have a hell of a job if there's ever a second coming. I mean, imagine some bloke turns up and says I'm the Son of God 'n' a' that. Who on earth's going to believe the guy? In fact, let's face it, there are probably hunners of guys every year saying they're the Son of bleeding God, and they all end up in asylums and stuff. Can you blame the doctor who commits them? Course not. What's he supposed to think? But what if

70

the real Son of God has actually made his comeback already and some eejit stuffed the guy into a loony bin? It's bound to happen.

'So, I can see your point, mate. If you are the real Barney Thomson, and that's not to say for one second that I think you are, no one's going to believe you.'

'Exactly,' says Barney. 'Exactly.'

Whigmore settles back more easily into his seat, having said what must be said; starts to think of some incontrovertible truths. Everywhere you go in life you find people pretending to be someone they're not; from the big lie like the man cutting his hair as he sits, assuming the identity of another, so that they can impress or make themselves the centre of attention, to the more subtle variety, where one might betray one's own personality to cover some excess that one doesn't want shown; right down to the more petty stuff which is purveyed every week in every bar in the country, such as men hitting on women; *Here, love, Ah'm a big mate o' Ewen McGregor's, ye know, and Ah'm going over tae Hollywood next month tae help him shag some women.*

Lies, lies, everywhere you go.

Barney thinks nothing much at all, as he tries to do most of the time these days. Just running through his mind is some vague musing on why it is that he is so unhappy, and what it is that he really wants from life. If not this, what he actually has, then what can it be? Or is the old man right? Are you automatically condemned to misery the instant you get what you want? Is that the penalty you pay for achieving your goals?

And so the day goes as it winds its way to an inevitable conclusion. And all the time, in the endless tussle of inconsequence inside his head, he tries to ignore the memory of the dream that haunts him; and the dread of the future which deep down he knows lies at the heart of his unease.

11

and to them were given
seven trumpets

Sometimes the group gather at a bar for the evening. Eleven murderers out in public. Katie Dillinger always worries on these occasions, because some of them can be a bit boisterous after a few pints of heavy; but they're not schoolchildren, and she can't stop it happening if they decide to do it. Always considers it best to be on hand, so that she can be the United Nations peacekeeping force to their volatile local difficulty.

They are all in attendance this evening, building up to a state of excitement. For this is the week of their Christmas retreat; two days in the country, away from judgemental eyes, where they can be themselves, as far as that can go; murder being right off limits.

They are perched around a large table, consuming one end of the bar, in a standard 4–4–2 formation. Dillinger in goal, then a flat back four of Billy Hamilton, Ellie Winters, Annie Webster and Sammy Gilchrist; four strung across the midfield, in Fergus Flaherty, Bobby Dear, Paul Galbraith and Morty Goldman, and the two showmen up front, Socrates McCartney and Arnie Medlock.

The men are jostling for position. They are going away for a weekend where there will be three women to eight men. An ugly imbalance to please no one – except the women – so tough times lie ahead. It is early days and there will be much work to be done once the weekend starts, but now is a time for points-scoring and unobtrusive denunciation of the opposition.

As ever the great topics of the day have been discussed as the evening has gone on. Should the Old Firm apply to join the English Premiership or a North Atlantic league and leave the rest to get on with it; was Edward G. Robinson a woman; would Bart Simpson make a good captain of the US Ryder Cup team; global warming, myth or nightmare; cornflakes, mundane drudgery or breakfast cereal to die for; the Sixth Commandment, and did God really mean it to be interpreted the way it has been; was Richard II really a poof; milk or plain chocolate; Jim Bett, mug or magician?

Galbraith has something to say to Katie Dillinger; uneasy about saying it, because there is not a lot of truth in what he will say. And they all know that Dillinger can tell a lie from a long way off.

The truth is, he has better things to do with his weekend than spend it with this mob. And Dillinger may just be expecting him to make a move on her and bring some competitive element to her yearly rendezvous with Arnie Medlock. Delicacy will be required, and he has pressures from Sophie Delaux to consider. And all sorts of other issues.

First of all he has to disengage himself from Bobby Dear, a man who could be dull for Europe.

'People who take one sugar,' says Dear, 'are poofs. That's what we used to say in the army. No sugar is fine, that's a definite statement. Five or six sugars, that's a definite statement. But one or two sugars. Absolute shite. Wishy-washy, can't make up their minds. Shite, I say.'

'Sorry, mate,' says The Hammer Galbraith, 'got to have a word with Katie, you know. Be back with you in a second,' he adds, as a monstrous lie. *I'd die rather than come and talk to you again, you boring fart*, might be nearer the truth. Bobby Dear nods, sulks a little.

Galbraith makes his way around the table, clutching his seventh pint of heavy. Thought processes are still working smoothly, but there's always the possibility of a breakdown between brain and mouth.

Stops to listen for a second to Socrates, who has upped, moved back down the wing, and is chatting to Ellie Winters. Giving her the usual line, thinks Galbraith, but it's always impossible to tell whether he's making a move or whether he's just a decent bloke.

'So what do you do, if you're not a philosopher or a footballer, then?' asks Winters. Hoping that this will induce the reciprocal question, for she loves to tell of how she makes her living. Socrates takes a swig from his pint, then digs into his inside coat pocket and produces a card. Hands it over, with a roguish smile on his lips. And so Winters feasts her eyes upon it and buys into the Socrates McCartney legend.

SPIDER-BE-GONE INC.
Socrates McCartney
for all your spider removal needs

Also: Unwanted pests, bugs, vermin &
snakes
24 hr service
Tel. 0898 985 7898
e-mail: spiderbegone@bug.com

Winters looks quizzically at him. A smile comes to her lips, for she is an intelligent woman and can already see the potential.

'You remove spiders?'

'Aye.'

'From where?'

Socrates shrugs. He knows he's cool.

'Fi' wherever spiders get tae. Which is pretty much everywhere really, i'n't it?'

'So, like if somebody's got a spider in their bath they call you up, and you go and remove it?' she asks, still a little incredulous that such a service exists.

'Aye. Ah get five or six calls a day and at least one o' them's a bath. Ah turn up, put the spider into a wee carton, take it outside and release it, and Ah'm on ma way.'

She shakes her head. 'And how much do you charge for that?'

'Ten pound call-out. Then a fiver for the first spider, and three quid thereafter. Special discounts for big jobs like garden sheds and attics.'

Ellie Winters is beginning to find Socrates McCartney attractive. Despite his nose. And despite the fact that she's not really into men.

'So some woman phones you up if there's a spider in the bath, and you charge her fifteen pounds for the all of two seconds it takes to remove it?'

Socrates finishes off his pint with a spider-be-gone flourish.

'There,' he says, 'you've hit the nail on the heid. Women. It's always women. Nae bloke's ever gonnae have the neck tae call me out, even if they're scared o' spiders. Nae bloke's gonnae let his bird call me out if they're in the house. So it's aye women on their own who give us a call. Think about it,' he says, tapping the side of his napper, 'it's the biggest phobia in Britain. There are about a gazillion spiders out there, and most o' them find their way intae someone's house at some stage. It's perfect. And, o' course, the best bit is that these birds are usually so grateful that Ah've rid them o' their pest that they give us a shag. Ye know.'

Socrates smiles. Winters smiles too, shaking her head.

'You serious?'

'Aye, hen, it's brilliant. The perfect job. Ah get paid good cash, and Ah get laid at least twice a day. Brilliant. Mind you . . .' he says, rising to head off to the bar.

'What?'

'Spiders give us the willies. The bath ones are awright, 'cause ye just stick a glass over the bastard. But see garden sheds, Ah fucking hate them. Another vodka. hen?'

Winters smiles, a move which enhances the small, pale hairs along her top lip.

'Aye,' she says. 'Another vodka. No ice.'

'Right, hen,' says Socrates, and off he goes. The hunter-gatherer.

The Hammer smiles. Socrates is all right. In his way. Time to talk his own brand of bullshit.

Dillinger is politely listening to Billy Hamilton's thesis on how Britain and Ireland could have won the Ryder Cup in 1987, and maybe another few times as well, without the addition of the European players. Not even sure what sport the Ryder Cup is, Dillinger, but is nodding in all the right places.

Galbraith leans over her, completely ignores Billy Hamilton. He could crush wee Billy like a paper cube. Doesn't care if he's annoyed at him.

'Sandy Lyle, brilliant player, brilliant. Faldo couldnae

lick his arse, even now,' are Hamilton's last few words on the subject.

'Here, Katie, can I have a word?' says The Hammer.

Billy Hamilton attempts to give him a Robert de Niro, but with the foosty moustache and insipid eyes, it's more of a Terry-Thomas.

'Sure,' says Dillinger, delighted to escape. 'Sorry, Billy, I'll be back in a minute.'

Not a chance.

'Aye, right,' says Hamilton, and his moustache wilts.

The Hammer and Dillinger wander over to the bar, away from the crowd. Arnie Medlock and Sammy Gilchrist explode in near-violent argument over the nature of Wordman's Theorem, but they ignore it and lean against the sodden bar. Brush away the beer and the peanuts, and the detritus of urine from unwashed fingers.

'What's up?' she says.

The Hammer nods, lips clenched. Look her in the eye and you might get away with it.

'Got a few things to do this weekend,' he says.

Dillinger's eyebrows plunge together.

'What are you saying?'

He shrugs, lifts his pint and waves it around a little.

'This and that. Stuff, you know. And the bastard is us going on Saturday and coming back on Monday. Just can't get the day off work.'

'It's Christmas Eve!'

'You know what it's like at that place.'

'So you're not coming?'

He shrugs his shoulders and shakes his head. Then nods it a little.

'Pretty much,' he says.

'Paul?' she says, a little pained. She can be cool, she can achieve her air of aloofness, she can be judgemental,

78

but she still has feelings same as every other human, and a lot of those feelings are for The Hammer. A good man; brutal, perhaps, but always a good bet on the weekend away in case tempers fray and the true nature of some of their crowd emerges. 'I thought, well you know . . .' she says, and lets the sentence drift off.

The Hammer shrugs again. Stay firm, he thinks. Just bullshit.

'Just got things to do, you know. Sorry, love, but that's the way it goes,' he says.

'What are you doing, then?' asks Dillinger. Can tell there's something else going on in there. None of this lot ever tell the truth.

The Hammer shrugs. Can no longer look her in the eye. Quickly downs the rest of his pint. He doesn't owe her anything. He has vague feelings for her, but he can afford to lose them. And, of course, if the worst comes to the worst, he can always murder her. It's not like he hasn't done it before.

Drains the glass, rests it in a pool of sludge. Arnie Medlock drunkenly yells something about Wagner's antagonistic interdependence with Nietzsche; someone obscurely puts George Harrison's 'Behind That Locked Door' on the juke-box; across the bar punches are thrown in a discussion on Paul McStay's overall contribution, or lack of it, to Scottish football; outside a car smashes into a lamppost; overhead, a plane, destined to crash into the side of a Spanish mountain after a near-miss with an Air Afrique 737 flown by the pilot's brother-in-law, roars quietly through the night sky.

'Got to go, babe,' he says. Puts a small piece of paper in her hand. 'Here's my name for the Christmas draw. Ye better give it to someone else.' Cheekily leans forward and kisses her on the lips, doesn't look her in the eye, and is gone. The Amazing Captain Bullshit, that's what he was known as at university. Until the incident with his ex-girlfriend, after which he became the Amazing Captain Bloodbath.

Katie Dillinger watches him go. Curious and moderately hurt. Looks like me and Arnie Medlock this weekend, she thinks.

She turns and surveys her merry men and women. Arguing, chatting, flirting, pointing, shouting, talking, posing. A flawed bunch who she will lead away for a weekend in an isolated house in the Borders; and as she surveys them, a shiver runs up her back and suddenly she feels a cold draught of dread and a vision of blood and of a slashed throat comes to her, and is gone in the time it takes to lift her glass and nervously swallow the remnants of her fifth vodka tonic of the night.

✂

Number three. Or number two, as the police might think it, for it will be some time before they realise that Wee Corky Nae Nuts had been murdered by the same man. The killer is keeping better count, however. For the moment. Seven is his intended number. A good number, seven. Seven seals.

The same thing for supper every night now for two months. Home from the pub, then Spam fritters, chips and mushy peas. The pleasure of it is beginning to wear off. He has only been able to finish them these past couple of nights owing to the wine with which he's washing it down. A New Zealand chardonnay. Strangely it doesn't recommend on the label that you should drink it with Spam fritters, so he's thinking of writing to the vineyard and getting them to change the wording. *A light, fruity wine with excellent length, firm thighs and a hairy arse, with overtones of strawberries, lime and mince.*

Delicious as an aperitif, or as an accompaniment to fish, chicken, salad, Spam fritters, chips and mushy peas. Buy it or we'll break your legs.

That'd do the trick.

He swallows the remainder of the bottle and heads on out into the night. It has turned a little colder, and there is light December rain in the air. A jacket, certainly, but he still doesn't need a jumper. Might not even need the jacket in fact, if it wasn't that he requires somewhere to conceal the knife. Not sure yet of his intended victim. Might be male, might be female. You just never know until it happens.

Moderately disturbed by himself these days, since this psychotic urge has been reawakened. Sometimes, however, you just have to follow through on your urges.

And so he gets a lonely bus to a different part of the city, and in this dank night he will see another lonely figure plying a desolate trade and, with a smile upon his face, he will move in for the kill.

✄

And in the small hours of the morning, as the killer makes his way home on an even lonelier bus, and as the body of Jason Ballater lies slumped in a bloody mess against the wall of a public WC; and as the rain falls softly against the bedroom windows of the city; and as the night weeps for the departed and all the souls who will lose the fight for life, Barney Thompson awakes from a nightmare, the prayers for his own soul still ringing in his head, the spectre of death still standing at his shoulder, his heart thumping, pains across his chest, sweat upon his furrowed brow.

12

and that's all from caesar's palace

Feet up, eyes closed. If it was a warm, sunny day, the air filled with luxurious summer smells, the occasional bug buzzing by, and if some bikini-clad überchick was running at his beck and call, fetching cold beers and endless packets of Doritos, while performing a vast array of indescribably erotic things to his body, then it would be high up in the top ten list of things to do when you're dead.

But it's Scotland in December, so you take what you can get. It's not too cold, he's got a cup of tea and a ham, cucumber and mustard sandwich, and he's on his own; which, while not as good as hanging out with a bikini-clad überchick, is way up on being with some cretinous idiot who irritates the ham sandwich out of you. Which just about classifies everyone Detective Chief Inspector Joel Mulholland knows these days, such ill-humour has he been in these recent months.

The river rolls by, water splashing against rocks and rounding up twigs and leaves to sweep them downstream; a variety of fish loaf about, avoiding the meagre fare on offer at the end of Mulholland's line; a zither of wind rustles what leaves remain on the trees; clouds occasionally obscure the sun, before passing on their way. Somewhere overhead a plane heads west, carrying on board, by some strange coincidence, Mulholland's ex-wife, although he is not to know it. It is some seven months since they have had any direct contact, all communication between them now being conducted through, on the one hand Weir, Hermiston, Jekyll & Silver, and on the other Goodchap, Neugent, Turkey & Bratwurst.

Generally there are two or three ways you can go when nearly thirty people under your protection are murdered, and you are allowed to view most of the mutilated bodies along the way. There is the way where you throw yourself back into your work, doing whatever minor tasks the superintendent will let you near. There is the way where you go completely off your head, wander around the streets, naked bar the pair of underpants on your head, singing the first eight verses of 'Old Shep' ... Or you can go quietly insane, get transferred to some sleepy backwater, and spend your days fishing and doing paperwork on whatever local youth has chosen to fall into the river the night before after drinking too much gooseberry wine at his Uncle Andy's fiftieth birthday party.

Sergeant Erin Proudfoot opted for the first on the list. It was the only way for her, and she has been rewarded with every trivial task coming the way of Maryhill police station for ten months; from the theft of some old granny's thimble collection, to missing cats and stray libidos, she's seen it all.

Mulholland tottered between the other two. A few months of intense romance with Proudfoot and then, with the breaking of any other day, but a day on which reality finally kicked in, he went gently off his head. Over thirty men dead, a police officer downed among them, he'd had to view the sort of carnage that Genghis Khan would have winced at. He had taken it out on Proudfoot – love by any other name – and when at last he had edged towards quiet insanity, he had been posted, at his request, to the requisite sleepy town in Argyll, to fish and sleep and eat and occasionally solve some innocent crime. Not that major crime doesn't happen in Argyll, it's just that none of it is put the way of Joel Mulholland.

So they have gone their separate ways, these two, but they have this in common. They are both in counselling, and will be for some time to come; unless destiny plays its hand, as it has a tendency to do.

Not that Mulholland gives much thought to counselling as he feels a gentle pull on his fishing line; in fact, he doesn't think about much at all. The past is there to be dredged up four or five hours a week by Dr Murz, and not at any other time. And if he is required to face that past in order to return to normality, then, he occasionally opines to the doctor, who needs normality?

The tug on the fishing line is a little harder. Might have something, he thinks, as he tries to rouse himself from the waking dream; a dream which, as usual, has dark edges and strange, evil creatures poised to enter at any moment he lets his guard down. Eyes slowly open; a man stands in front of him, fingers wet from where he has been tugging the line.

Mulholland stares for some time. Nothing worse than being interrupted when you're in the middle of nothing at all, he thinks. The other man looks around them at the trees and the river and the blue sky; there is a light smell of wood burning in the air, and despite the mildness, the promise of a crisp early evening.

'Very treeie around here,' says Constable Hardwood.

Mulholland closes his eyes, trying to drift back into that world of non-demons he has just left.

'Arboreal, Constable,' he says. 'The word is arboreal.'

'Aye,' says Hardwood. 'And there's a lot of trees 'n' all. Reminds me of a place my dad used to take me fishing when I was a lad.'

'Oh aye,' says Mulholland, eyes firmly closed, his netherworld receding all the time. 'Where was that?'

'About fifty yards along the river there,' says Hardwood, pointing.

'Har-de-har-har, Constable,' Mulholland says. 'You want to tell me what I can do for you?'

Hardwood smiles at the closed eyes. There was a time, not long after Mulholland arrived, when he had been in awe of the man. There was a bit of a glint of madness in his eye and stories were legion of the affair at the monastery, as if he himself might have had something to do with all the murders. But over time Hardwood and the rest of the station have come to realise that Mulholland is merely shell-shocked, not mad. Harmless in his way. Although you can never be completely sure; that's what Sergeant Dawkins says.

'You're wanted,' says Hardwood.

'I'm fishing.'

Hardwood nods his head, and stares around at the trees. Doesn't know the name of any of them. They're green, and in the winter the leaves come off; that's the limit of his knowledge. Trees aren't his thing.

Constable Lauder says that Mulholland threatened him with a knife not long after he arrived, but no one really believes it. And if it is true, then so be it, because if anyone deserves to be threatened with a knife . . .

'It's important,' says Hardwood.

'Don't care,' says Mulholland, eyes firmly shut.

Hardwood nods again. Beginning to wonder what to do next. On the one hand he has the perhaps not psychopathic but at least a bit strange Joel Mulholland; while on the other he has Superintendent Cunningham, a woman who eats men's testicles for breakfast. And lunch.

Tough call. He balks.

'You're still here, Constable,' says Mulholland, eyes closed, the taste of ham, cucumber and mustard in his mouth.

'Aye,' Hardwood says.

'What could you possibly want now that I've sent you on your way?'

Hardwood doesn't move. He knew Mulholland would be like this; he has been told to get him under any circumstances.

'You really are needed, sir,' he says, knowing that it isn't enough. He'll need more than that to persuade the shell-shocked victim from his fishing perch.

'Don't give a hoot, son,' says Mulholland. 'Go back and tell Geraldine that she can stick her head up her arse. You can help her if you want; you have my authority.'

Hmm, thinks Hardwood. That wouldn't be a bad idea, but I don't think I'm actually going to suggest it to her. Not today, at any rate.

The fishing line is tugged again; a sharp pull. Mulholland snaps. Eyes open, he sits up, filled with the instant rage to which he has been prone for months. Does not even try to contain it.

'Bloody hell, Constable, I told you to fuck off! It's my day off, I've got nothing to go in for, so would you just get out of my face? Leave me in peace and tell Geraldine she can go and piss in her shoes. I'll see her in the morning.'

Hardwood laughs; inwardly. The guy's not mad, he thinks, he's just an obnoxious little heid-the-ba'.

'That wasn't me, sir,' he says.

'What?'

'The line. I didn't tug the line. It was a fish.'

There is another tug at the line, Hardwood nowhere near it. As ever with his explosions of anger these days, Mulholland feels instant regret; and as ever, it's ruined the sound basis for his argument and put him a couple of goals behind.

It's time, he thinks, leaning forward and rubbing his forehead, that Murz started earning her money. He doesn't need counselling a few hours a week, it should be all day every day for the next twenty years. And so he ignores the jumping line.

'Sorry, Constable, that was bad. I'm just a bit of an idiot at times.'

'That's all right, sir,' says Hardwood. Maybe not such a heid-the-ba' after all. A sucker for an apology. Has been known to let off the odd criminal if shown the right amount of contrition.

'So what's the score, then? Why's Geraldine so keen to see me? Wanting into my pants, is she?' says Mulholland, as he hauls himself from his seat and begins to wind in his third fish of the day; three fish he will never get the chance to eat.

'Likes 'em younger than you, sir,' he says.

Mulholland laughs.

'Right, Constable. About your age, by any chance?'

Hardwood smiles and says nothing. Mulholland shakes his head.

And so it goes; he begins to get his equipment together, fishing posted to the back of his mind. Soon he will have been dispatched back to Glasgow, to be once more commissioned to follow the trail of Barney Thomson; and to be once more landed in the dark heart of a murderer's lair, to taste the putrid flesh.

'Whatever it's going to be,' says Mulholland, 'I'll bet it's a load of pants.'

'Aye,' says Hardwood, knowing no more than Mulholland. 'No doubt.'

13

the clothes-horse of senility

Barney steps back and looks at the hair from a different angle. It's not going well. In fact, it's downright ugly. There have been more successful invasions of Russia in the last two hundred years than this. It is time for retrospection, and perhaps even damage limitation. The Tyrolean Überhosen is one of the most complex haircuts ever to come out of Austria, and only three or four barbers outside the general Anschluss area have ever been able to master it. And for all his greatness, for all his communication with the gods of barbery, for all the angels fluttering their wings at his shoulder, and for all the elves weaving necromancy into the very fabric of his comb and scissors, rendering household plastic and steel into wondrous instruments of sortilege and legerdemain, transforming him from the journeyman barber of his past to the thaumaturgist of the present, turning water to wine by the agency of the theurgical jewels of his workmanship, Barney Thomson isn't one of those three or four; and he's making an arse of it.

It's a tough haircut, no question. Ask any barber in Britain to perform it and they will quail at the very mention, for the line between success and failure is a fine one, and the consequences of that failure are disastrous. Of all the law suits brought against barbers in Great Britain over the final twelve years of the twentieth century, more than half were as a direct result of a failed attempt at a Tyrolean Überhosen. See a man wearing what is obviously the first hat he could get his hands to, on a warm day when no headwear is required, and it is a sure bet that under that ill-fitting hat is a failed attempt at this haircut of which only kings can truly dream.

Why do men take the chance, many have wondered, but only those who have never seen the finished article in all its glory. It is questioned only by those who have never seen a man, bedecked in a perfectly executed Tyrolean Überhosen, strolling through town, with more confidence about him than Muhammad Ali when he fought Sonny Liston (or anyone else for that matter), men in awe of his every word, desperate women tearing frantically at his trousers, and the sun shining down upon him while rain soaks everyone else in his vicinity.

The barber who can execute the Tyrolean Überhosen is a wealthy man, for he can command a huge fee for every cut. And so Barney has dreamed of this day. Twice before, at Henderson's so very long ago, he had been asked for the cut, but never did he have the confidence to agree to do it. Not with those others in the shop just waiting to pass comment; not with his confidence shattered, and even the simplest Frank Sinatra '62 causing him problems. But today he has been offered the chance of his shot at greatness, and such is his confidence, such is the air of indefatigability about him, the all-conquering hero of hirsutology that he believes himself to have become, that he has taken it on with barely a second thought, and hardly a trembling finger.

Twenty-five minutes in, however, and it is, as previ-

90

ously reported, getting ugly. It's not happening the way it's supposed to; the cut itself is uneven, the hair is not sitting as it should; the razor has buzzed unnecessarily long in his hand. Of course, not every head of hair is right to be turned into this cut, and this is indeed such a head of hair. Even Gert Struble, the famous late-nineteenth-century barber-cum-philosopher from Salzburg, would have been unable to successfully transform this head; and, of course, Barney knew of this limitation, but bravado forced his hand.

'How's it going, mate?' says Wolfie Hopkins, not long returned from a walking holiday in the Tyrol and keen to emulate all the gigolos living it up at the expense of a variety of fabulous women.

Barney hesitates. There's a time for candour, etc., etc. This is a new, more-confident-with-the-customers Barney, however. Is there any point in lying? He can hardly cut the guy's hair down to nothing; he's got more hair than Barney the Bear, a bear he once saw in a zoo; and the jug of water treatment will be completely lost on the bloke. Perhaps it is time to cut his losses.

'Ah have tae be honest wi' ye, mate. Ah don't think it's going too well, ye know. Ah'm sorry, but Ah just don't know what else Ah can do.'

Leyman Blizzard looks over from where he is struggling through a Zeppo Marx. He's never even heard of a Tyrolean Überhosen, and he's not about to think critically.

Wolfie Hopkins purses his lips and nods his head. He can tell already, even though there is obviously still some way to go. He's not a fool, Wolfie Hopkins, he knows the difficulty, he knows the consequences, he knows that his hair is probably not suited; and he also knows that if the barber is sensible and pulls out in time, there are still

91

other, albeit less attractive, options open to him.

'That's awright, mate,' says Wolfie. 'Is there anything else you can do?'

Barney breathes deeply and takes a further step back. Suddenly feels relieved. The haircut isn't happening, he'd been foolish to start it in the first place, but at least the customer is being realistic.

'Might be able tae dae ye a Lionel Blair,' he says.

Wolfie Hopkins laughs. 'You've got to be joking, mate. No way. Never.'

'Aye, aye, right enough. Don't want tae leave ye looking like that, eh? Whit about a William Shatner or maybe even an Estonian Eleemosynary Euclidean Short Back and Sides?'

Hopkins turns around. 'Bloody hell,' he says, 'that last one sounds flash. What is it, exactly?'

'Basically,' says Barney, wondering how he can word this so that it lives up to its name, 'it's a short back and sides.'

Wolfie Hopkins stares into the mirror. The dream has gone. He knows not that he currently sits in the chair of the finest barber in Scotland, but he doubts anyway that any other barber in the country would be able to give him the cut he desires. Sometimes it makes sense just to sit back, take what's coming to you, and go with the flow. Two days to the office Christmas party, and he is as well taking the safe option at this stage. It's not as if he desperately needs great hair to get the women anyway. He can always rely on his charm, his impressive good looks, and if all else fails, his horse-sized genitals.

'Aye, that'll do, mate,' he says. And Barney, breathing a sigh of relief, gets down to business.

✂

Late afternoon in the shop. Getting dark outside. It is

about the time that people are beginning to think of packing up work for the day; that the latest Glasgow killer is beginning to wonder about his next victim; and about the time that Joel Mulholland is heading back to Glasgow, to once again face the reality of police work and murder investigation.

Barney is working steadily through a Burt Lancaster '65; Leyman Blizzard is giving a young lad a Jimmy Stewart even though he asked for a Jimmy Floyd Hasselbaink; while one customer sits and waits, reading that day's edition of the *Evening Times*; headline: 'Thomson Strikes Again, City in Grip of Fear'. Barney has seen these headlines, of course, and such is his sense of defeat at the hands of inevitability that he is not in the least surprised that some murderer should have kicked off a killing spree within a few days of his return to the city. He would almost have been surprised if it hadn't happened. But he doubts that anyone is going to turn him in, so disbelieving are all his customers that he is who he says. He might have alibis for the evenings in question, he's not sure. There's a fair chance that when the murders were committed he was sitting in the Paddle Steamer, bored stiff, listening to the bit about how Leyman cut Elvis's hair in 1961 and got some of the King's earwax caught under his fingernail and didn't wash for a fortnight. Although perhaps he was sitting in front of the television at home, with no one to vouch for him but Les Dennis or Peter Sissons.

There is a healthy debate on adverts taking place; or at least, the sort of debate where all the participants are on the same side.

'Load of pish,' says Barney's Burt Lancaster, 'and pretentious pish at that. But that's no the main thing. You want tae know what the main thing is?'

93

Barney nods; at a delicate stage, adjacent to the right earlobe.

'When was the last time you saw an advert where the man in it didnae look like a total wank stain on the pants of society? Eh?'

'Aye,' says Leyman Blizzard, 'what he said!'

'I mean,' Burt Lancaster continues, 'every single advert you get these days where there's a bird and a bloke, the bird's as cool as you can get, and the guy's a flipping idiot. You know, if there's two folk eating breakfast cereal, and one of the cereals is a stunning bit of stuff, while the other's a load of shite, gives you haemorrhoids, and makes you look like a total arseface just 'cause you're eating it, you can bet that it's the bird who's eating the new packet of Just Perfect, or Fucking Stunning, or New Fibre Wheato-Flakes or Some Packet of Shite that Makes You Shit Like a Horse and No Want Lunch until aboot Three in the Afternoon. And if it's a motor, it'll have some stupid name like the new Fiat Pants or the Renault Smug Bastard, and there'll be some bird who's all racy and chic and gorgeous who'll know all about the car and know how tae drive it, while the poor slob of a bloke'll just be sitting watching the fitba', and would much rather be in his Wartburg, and the implication'll be that the bloke cannae drive properly 'cause he's got nae dick. Nae dick, I tell ye. It absolutely rips my knitting.'

'Rips *your* knitting?' says Jimmy Floyd Hasselbaink. 'The ones Ah hate are those domestic ones where the bloke's a total knobend and the bird's got tae show him how tae dae the washing up, or put the washing machine on, or turn on the telly or wipe his arse. It's appalling.'

'Sexist,' says Burt Lancaster. 'Bloody sexist. You couldnae get away wi' doing it the other way about.'

'Naw,' says Hasselbaink, 'ye couldnae. Adverts are all just dominated by women these days. Ye cannae fart without there being some advert for tampons or Canesten or washing-up liquid, or some other women's shite like yon. Shocking.'

'Canesten?' says Leyman Blizzard. 'Did he no use tae play for Morton?'

'Ye know why it is, though?' says Barney, ignoring Blizzard.

'Why?' say Hasselbaink and Lancaster in unison.

'It's because these advertisers know that women are more susceptible tae these things. Ah mean, let's face it, most o' the stuff ye get advertised on the telly's a load o' shite, right? They tell ye something's gonnae make your teeth whiter than white, or make ye more attractive, or make your shoes shinier, or some shite, whatever, but it's all a load o' kiech. Like yon Twix advert fi' a while back where some bloke would take a galumphing great bite out o' some other chocolate bar, jamming the bloody thing so far back down his throat he couldnae breathe, then some eejit would take a minuscule bite fi' a Twix and then start prattling on about how brilliant he was because he had so much o' his bar left, and that the other guy was a wanker. It was all a load o' pish.'

'So?'

'Well, ye see, women cannae see through all that. They're nae as astute as us men. They're more susceptible tae the ad man's bullshit. Men have smart, intuitive, clear-thinking, rapier-like minds. Women are just stupid. So the ad men have tae pander tae women's stupidity, knowing that men are too sage to be fooled by them. Too sage,' he repeats.

Burt Lancaster, Jimmy Floyd Hasselbaink and Leyman Blizzard stare into the mirror, thinking deeply upon what

Barney has just said. Sounds about right, they think Sounds about right.

'Wait a minute,' says Blizzard. 'Wisnae Canesten the guy that went tae the Rangers and got his leg broken?'

14
don't dum-de-de-dum-dum

'Ah've thought of a good advert for that crap you drink,' says Barney to Leyman Blizzard.

Blizzard downs the dregs of his neat whisky and lays the glass back on the table.

'Good for you, son,' he says. 'Ye can tell me a' about it after ye've got me another.'

Barney shakes his head. 'Jings,' he says. 'Ah wish ye'd stop drinking that stuff as if it was lager. Ye've had about five o' them and Ah'm still on my first pint.'

'That's 'cause you drink like a pussy,' says Blizzard, and Barney finishes off the rest of his pint in one gulp as some concession to peer pressure, then heads for the bar.

They are in Barney's new local; the bar that has been Blizzard's home from home for sometime. The Paddle Steamer; ten minutes' walk from Barney's flat, and where he now finds himself for the third night running. The occasional game of dominoes, but mostly they sit and talk, reliving great haircuts from the past. In Blizzard's case this consists entirely of his insistence that he cut Elvis's hair when he stopped at Prestwick on his way back from Germany in 1961. The story usually comes between his fifth and sixth doubles, but sometimes earlier. Barney hasn't heard it yet this evening; it is due.

'Pint o' Tennents and a double for Leyman,' says Barney, and the barman nods and goes about his business.

Barney looks around the bar as he waits. Sees the same old faces. Only the third night and already it is as familiar as anything he's ever known. The faded wallpaper, the one-armed bandits, unchanged in the corner since time began, Old Jack the barman, and the occasional barwoman, Lolita. This is his new life; and if it already seems mundane and overly familiar after three evenings, what will it be like after a few years? A decade? Or worse, will he still be here when he's eighty-five, telling some younger man in the bar how he once cut Billy Connolly's hair before he became famous.

He exchanges money and drinks and heads back to the table. Blizzard is leering attractively at a woman fifty years his junior at a nearby table.

'Stop that, Leyman,' he says, as he sits down, 'you're frightening her.'

'Bollocks,' says the old man, 'she fancies me.'

'Aye, in yer dreams.'

Blizzard downs half the drink in one go then lays the glass on the table.

'Right then, son, tell us about this brilliant advert ye've got. Though Ah don't know why ye're telling me, 'cause it's no as if any bastard needs tae persuade me tae buy it.'

'Right,' says Barney, remembering to take a hefty gulp from his pint so that Blizzard doesn't think he's a girl, 'here we go. The Teletubbies are driving along the road in a motor, right?'

'Who the fuck are the Teletubbies?'

'Ye know, they stupid bastards on the telly. Ye know.

98

Four big fat bastards, o' different colours, 'n' a' that. One o' the blokes has got a handbag.'

'A handbag? A big, fat, funny-coloured bloke wi' a handbag? What kind o' shite dae you watch on the telly, anyway?'

'Help m'boab, Leyman, every bastard's heard o' the Teletubbies. Anyway, they're a' driving along in the motor, when all of a sudden they hit something in the middle of the road and they crash.'

'They hit what? What kind o' thing are ye gonnae just get in the middle o' the road?'

'Ah don't know, something. A pheasant, or some shite like that.'

'A pheasant? Ye really think ye're necessarily gonnae crash just 'cause ye hit a pheasant?'

'Fuck, awright, then, they hit a lamppost. That better?'

'A lamppost? In the middle o' the road? Where the fuck are these people?'

'Christ, Leyman, ye're a cantankerous old bastard. Right, a bloody huge dog runs out in front o' them, they swerve tae avoid it, and they hit a lamppost at the side o' the road. How's that?'

'Aye, that seems plausible. Don't think that's gonnae sell ye much whisky, though, is it? Whit's yer slogan gonnae be? *Drink This Shite and Ye Might Crash Yer Motor and Die?* That's brilliant, son. Think you should stick tae yer day job.'

'Naw, they havnae been drinking yet.'

'So why dae they crash the motor, then?'

''Cause o' the fucking dug!'

'Oh aye, aye, right enough. Right, on ye go. There's these four weird-looking bastards wi' handbags in a motor. Tae avoid hitting a dug they drive intae a lamppost. Got ye. What happens next?' Leyman says,

99

finishing off his sixth double whisky of the night.

'Right. They a' die, except the wee one, the red one, ye know.'

'The red one? One o' them's red?'

'Aye, and she doesnae die.'

'She? Ah thought they were a' blokes?'

'Naw. There's a coupla blokes and a coupla birds.'

'So it's one o' the birds who's got a handbag? Nothing wrong wi' that, son. Ye made it sound sinful.'

'Naw, it's one o' the blokes who's got the handbag.'

'How come?'

'Ah don't know, dae Ah? Bloody hell, Leyman, stop getting on my tits and let me finish. So they're a' deid, right.'

'Ah thought the red one wisnae deid?'

'Aye, right, they're a' deid except the red one. Right?'

'Right. But Ah think ye better get tae the point, 'cause Ah'm beginning tae think yer talking a load o' shite.'

'Right. We switch tae a couple o' months later, and the wee bastard's sitting in a bar quaffing double whiskies. Pissed out her socks, so she is. And she keeps downing the doubles in a oner. Then she slams her glass down on the bar, and says tae the barman, "Again, again. Again, again."'

Blizzard stares across the table, looking a bit bemused. There is a loud cheer from around the dartboard, the sound of lager filling a glass from a malfunctioning tap. The woman Blizzard had been eyeing up slaps her hand viciously across the face of the man sat across the table from her, before he gets up and heads to the bar. Somewhere there is the vague sound of arguing over the exact consistency of Jupiter's atmosphere.

'What the fuck are ye talking about, son?' says Blizzard eventually.

100

'Ye've got tae watch the programme,' says Barney. Ah mean, Ah've only seen it a coupla times masel'.'

'Load o' shite, by the sounds o' it. Right, son, tell ye what. You away and buy me another coupla shots. Ah'm gonnae have a go at this bird that's been giving me the eye while her shag's at the bar. And if Ah blow out, when ye get back Ah'll tell ye a' about the time Ah cut the King's hair. Rare story, that one. Rare.'

Barney rises once more from his seat. Not that bloody rare, he thinks to himself, as he heads off across the pub.

✂

'What are you saying, son?' asks Leyman Blizzard.

Barney stares across the table. There are all sorts of different ways in which drunkenness manifests itself, no question about that. Leyman Blizzard's is fairly harmless. He doesn't get aggressive, he doesn't slur his words, he doesn't get maudlin, he doesn't marry someone he shouldn't, he doesn't pick fights just for the hell of it. What does happen is that he talks incessantly about Elvis.

'Don't,' says Barney. 'Just don't keep telling me about bloody Elvis. Ah know ye cut the bastard's hair. Ah know ye told him he should stick to rock 'n' roll and that if he'd listened tae you he'd still be alive today. Ah know a' that. Give us a break, will ye?'

'Are you saying that Ah've told ye a' this before, is that it, Mr Fancy Pants Haircutting Bastard?'

'Aye, ye told me last night, and the night before that. And ye also mention it in the bloody shop every time some idiot with black hair walks in. Just give us a break. Could ye no have cut John F. Kennedy's hair tonight or something?'

'But Ah didnae cut that bastard's hair. Ah cut Elvis's hair, didn't Ah no?'

'Aye, so ye've said.'

101

Leyman Blizzard holds his hands up in some sort of weird, drunken gesture; waves them around a little; nods his head.

'Awright, son, awright, ye may have a point. But face it, at least Ah'm pissed when Ah start going on about the King, and at least it's a true story. You, on the other hand, are always sober and havnae shut up about how you're Barney bloody Thomson since you got here.'

Barney does the 'Penalty, ref!' gesture and shakes his head.

'What dae ye want me tae say, Leyman? Ah am Barney Thomson, Ah cannae help it. Ah am who Ah am.'

'There ye go wi' yer cod philosophy. Why don't ye hand yersel' intae the polis, then?'

'Come on, Leyman, Ah've tried that. Ye know Ah've tried it. They're no interested. The second lot Ah went tae Ah even suggested they do a DNA test on me, and the bloke told me tae clear off. Said they'd run out o' money tae dae DNA tests 'cause they'd done so many in the past year. What can Ah dae, Leyman? Ah'm stuffed. And you're stuck wi' me.'

Blizzard swallows the last of his fourteenth and final whisky for the night – a man who knows his limit. He shakes his head, reaches across the table and grips Barney by the hand. Barney feels a little self-conscious and hopes no one's looking; just in case, you know . . .

'Ye'll be the saviour o' my shop, son,' says Blizzard. 'Ah cannae imagine it without ye now. Ah hope ye're gonnae be here for years tae come. Ye're a good pal, 'n' a'.' And he takes his hand away as he says it, allowing Barney to feel more comfortable and appreciate the sentiment. Needed, liked and respected. What more could he really want? 'Just a coupla bits of advice,' continues Leyman, and Barney is not entirely sure he wants to hear them. 'First of a', ye've got tae get yersel' a shag, Big Man. There are plenty o' women out there, ye've got tae get stuck in, ye know?'

'Right.'

'And another thing. Don't know if this is for you, or no. Might be, might not. We'll see.'

He does an exaggerated thing with his hand while he pauses, indicating maybe, maybe not. Barney leans forward, although he doesn't know why he's that inter ested. When is advice from drunk men ever even remotely applicable to this planet, never mind the situation to which they're referring? Barney is not to know that this advice will seem strangely relevant, will seem like the perfect foil to the uncertainties over his past and will ultimately plant him firmly, once more, in the nest of vipers.

He strains to hear above the cheering coming from the dartboard area.

'Ah know somebody who knows somebody else,' says Leyman, lifting his eyebrows.

'Aye?' says Barney, when nothing else is immediately forthcoming.

Blizzard taps the side of his nose in an exaggerated manner; winks excessively; nods his head. And then slowly collapses onto the table, so that his face lies in among the whisky swill, his mouth is squashed open and his nose is bent to the right.

Some other time, thinks Barney. Some other time.

15

and you only live twice

Once more back where it all began. Joel Mulholland sits across the desk from Chief Superintendent McMenemy, as the old man reads the only folder remaining on his spartan desk. One late December morning, still the weather outside that nothing, grey, mild, humourless weather that pollutes Scotland for much of the year. And Mulholland sits there and watches the old man, with nothing, grey, mild, humourless thoughts on his mind. Has no idea why he is sitting here; cannot even begin to care; and has already decided that if he doesn't like the sound of what he's about to be told, he'll tell McMenemy where he can stick his job, and where he can stick the entire police force. Although, after several hours of thought on what it could be that requires his presence in front of the self-styled M of the Strathclyde police, the only reason he can imagine for his summons is so that M can tell him that he's not wanted any more. That makes sense. He's a wash-out, and he knows it. Couldn't give a hoot either. He's got enough money in the bank that he can afford to go to some pointless little village some-where, settle down, and live a life of trundling nothingness ... for at least a fortnight. After that, when he's run out of cash, who knows what he'd do. Rob banks maybe.

M raises his head and stares seriously across the old desk at Mulholland. The clock ticks high up on the wall, cars skitter past outside, somewhere a woman bites noisily into a bar of chocolate she saw advertised on television at the weekend. McMenemy's eyes search Mulholland's face for any sign of spirit, but he can find nothing. He has heard, of course, what he's been up to. Weekly reports have come back to McMenemy from Murz and Cunningham. He knows the state of Mulholland's mind; and he thinks he's found the perfect way to get him out of it. Expects, as he sits, that Mulholland will know exactly why he is here; and couldn't be more wrong.

'It's been a few months, Chief Inspector. How've you been?' he asks at last.

Mulholland shrugs his shoulders. How is anybody? he thinks. Is anyone ever as bad as they say they are, or as good as they think they might be?

'All right,' he says, trying not to dwell on introspection, as much of the last year has been.

'Done some work up the west coast,' McMenemy says, half-question, half-remark. He knows everything Mulholland has worked on this past six months, and knows that little of it will have had any meaning or interest to a man such as he. His wife has gone; his life too, and to a place from where it will be very difficult to retrieve.

'Some,' Mulholland replies; and doesn't even bother to think of the little he has done. A few cases, one arrest; only surviving up there as a favour from Cunningham to McMenemy, repaying an old debt.

'How do you feel?' McMenemy asks. 'Ready yet for

some real work, or do you think you need a little longer where you are?'

He knows full well the answer to that question. The soft touch is not working. If he leaves Mulholland where he is, he'll never get his officer back. He's not the best man he's ever had, but he was a good detective, and there are few enough of them around. He has decided there might only be one way to bring him round. Shock tactics. Put him back in the same situation as before, and see how he reacts. If he fails, and fails to the point where he even loses his life, then what have the police lost as a result? Nothing at all, for they do not have him at the moment. And should he succeed, and they get their man back, then it will have been justified. A bit like M sending James Bond after Scaramanga in *The Man with the Golden Gun*, thinks McMenemy. Bond is washed up, has been brainwashed by the Russians, and might as well be dead. If he gets killed by Scaramanga, then so be it. If he kills the greatest assassin on the planet, then he's proved that he's back.

Mulholland is my Bond; and Barney Thomson his Scaramanga, thinks M, in one of his more ridiculous thoughts of the past fifty years.

Mulholland weighs up his answer to the last question. Does not feel like being honest about it, and decides to hold off from the bitter whims of veracity for a little while longer.

'Not sure, sir,' he says, while thinking that if he's ordered back up to Glasgow now, he's heading to Oban and catching the first boat to some remote island where crime is a thing of the future.

McMenemy nods and clasps his hands in front of him. He knows how to read one of his officers, and he can read Joel Mulholland. Maybe this will indeed be to push him too far.

'You'll have seen the newspapers, heard what's been happening in Glasgow these past couple of nights.' More of a statement than a question.

Mulholland stares at his boss, trying to think. Besides the blatant act of not caring, there remains the semblance of integrity and the need to at least give some sort of an answer. So he tries to think if he's heard anything of the news or of anything mentioned at work in the past few days, but there's nothing there. The way Cunningham had spoken implied that there were things going on that he should know about, but he barely ever paid her any attention anyway, and yesterday hadn't been any different.

McMenemy has waited long enough for an answer. He clears his throat, opens the drawer at his right hand, and takes out a remote control for a video and television. He indicates to Mulholland that he should turn around to watch the TV just behind; then fumbles with the buttons to get the whole thing rolling.

Mulholland turns and watches as the screen jumps to life and the creaky closed circuit video footage rolls. A man stands at the counter of a police station, engaged in muted conversation with the desk sergeant; a policeman whose body language suggests some apathy.

They watch for a couple of minutes, until the man turns away from the desk and walks out of the police station, the sergeant hardly even knowing where he has gone. McMenemy shuts the television down and waits for Mulholland to turn and face him, and it is some time before he drags himself back around from the blank screen.

What has just gone through his head? Even he does not know. Not even a jumping of his heart when he first saw the man, so dead is his mind to everything that went before.

'Recognise him?' asks McMenemy.

Mulholland breathes deeply. The old man hasn't so much as toyed with his pipe since he walked in but he can smell it all the same. It is in the fabric of the room. And when he does eventually decide to go, or is kicked ruthlessly into touch, it'll take years for his successor to rid the place of his smell. And he can remember one time long ago thinking that the old man would be there until he himself had risen through the ranks and was ready to take his place.

'Barney Thomson,' he says. 'Good old Barney. What was that all about?'

'Decided to hand himself in,' says McMenemy.

'Right. Got him at last,' says Mulholland, wondering why the man couldn't just walk away and start a new life when he'd had the chance.

'Not as such,' says McMenemy. 'The desk sergeant let him go, didn't get an address. Apparently he tried to offer himself up to a small station in Partick later the same day, but they're being hush-hush about it. Embarrassed as hell, same as us.'

Mulholland laughs and shakes his head. Bloody typical. The Glasgow polis at their finest.

'Looked like Sergeant Mullen, to me. He had his reasons, I suppose,' he says, and McMenemy shrugs.

'These things happen. There hasn't been a crackpot lunatic within a hundred miles of Glasgow who hasn't handed himself over in the last ten months, claiming to be Barney Thomson. There's even been a book published about it. *Fifty-Seven Ways to Make the Police Think You're Barney Thomson*. Quite funny actually, though I wouldn't say that in public. So, of course, when the real thing turns up, our man was so pissed off about all the other idiots that he let him go. A constable spotted him on the tape a couple of days later. You're about the only man here who's seen him in real life. You can confirm it's him, can you?'

'Looks like him.'

'Exactly. And we let him go. If the press ever find out they'll have my testicles on toast, so it's mouths shut. Of course, I've had Mullen's testicles on toast, but there's no way I'm standing for any of that business with my own testicles. Which is all the more likely in view of what's happened this week.'

Mulholland raises his eyebrows. Here we go again drifts through his head.

'He's at it again,' says McMenemy. 'There've been another couple of murders in the city. West End as usual. The bloody city's shitting its pants again. I can't believe it. Bloody nightmare. Why me? Why can't the bastard go and plague some other district of Glasgow for once, or Edinburgh, even? There're plenty of decent people in Edinburgh he could murder.'

Mulholland smiles. Good old Barney; a fool for anything.

'What makes you think it's him?' he says. Leaves it as a smile, but inside he's laughing. They're just back where they were a year ago, when every crime, no matter how absurd that it should so be, was blamed upon Barney Thomson.

'Good God, it has all the hallmarks of the man. He's known to have been in the area for a few days, and all of a sudden there are bloody murders all over the place. It follows the man around, and eventually you have to stop thinking that it's all coincidence. The man is a killer. A killer, I say!'

The smile has not left Mulholland's face. Time to use it.

'Bollocks,' he says.

109

'I beg your pardon, Chief Inspector?'

'Bollocks all the same. Barney Thomson never actually murdered anyone in his life. He accidentally killed his work colleagues, and that's the end of it. He's no more of a murderer than you or me, Superintendent. He's nothing. He couldn't hurt a bloody fly, even if he wanted to. Why can't you just leave the man alone?'

'Chief Inspector!'

Mulholland shakes his head, then relaxes back into his seat. Has said what he had to say. If the old fool wants his officers to spend their time chasing shadows and ghosts and false reputations, then that's fine by him. As long as he's not one of those officers.

'Your condition appears to be even worse than I was led to believe, Chief Inspector,' says McMenemy. 'Barney Thomson is the most feared criminal of the last hundred years. I had hoped the prospect of going after him once again might get your juices flowing, but I fear I may be wrong. He escaped you once, and if you still had it in you, and it appears that you may not have, I would have thought you would be determined to bring him once more to justice.'

McMenemy stares deeply into his eyes again, then stands up and turns and looks out into the gloom of late morning. The streetlights are on, cars are streaming past on the road outside, pedestrians fritter by, many in fear of the killer who once again stalks the streets. He still intends sending Mulholland out on the case; these last few words more intended shock tactics.

Mulholland watches the old man's back. Barney Thomson. Death does seem to follow the man around, but he's no killer. And the man had saved his life, no question about that. If it wasn't for Barney Thomson he wouldn't be sitting here now.

110

It'd seemed like a good thing at the time.

Not that he's about to tell McMenemy that he chose to let him loose. This past half year of introspection has given him a strange sense of perspective, but not so strange as to allow him to happily confess to such an indiscretion. On the one hand, it'd been the right thing to do. On the other, there's no chance on Planet Earth that McMenemy would see it that way.

'For what can I take your silence?' says McMenemy without turning round. 'These are troubled times, Chief Inspector, troubled times. The people of Glasgow are living in terror. Good and honest men cannot walk the streets for fear that they might be struck down by this Satan of the West End. We, the citizens of this great city, stand as one, petrified to the point of dilatoriness, frozen in inertia, waiting for some hero of the hour to come forward and seize the day, to reclaim the city for the common man, from this vampire of justice. Barney Thomson sucks the very life-blood from us all, Chief Inspector, and we are all haunted by him. He has left this station bereft of qualified officers and I, indeed we all, are desperately in want of one fine man to emerge from the swamp of inactivity, the fen of fecklessness and the quagmire of trepidation to lead us to the New Jerusalem of salvation, where men and women can walk along the avenues of hope, with heads held upon high and in the great and certain knowledge that they will live to see the next day dawn, that they will watch their children grow old, and see their dreams become the corporeality of hope, the very verisimilitude of the redemption of the soul.'

Mulholland nods.

'I think I missed some of that,' he says. 'Could you repeat it?'

McMenemy turns around. Not used to such flippancy

111

when he has waxed as the poet of the force. Prefers a little more awe in his officers. Mulholland may just about be too much of a loose cannon. However, he knows that loose cannon are often the only ones capable of hitting the target. Certainly they are in the world of cliché and soundbite which he inhabits.

'You think this is funny, Chief Inspector?' he says.

'No,' replies Mulholland. 'No, I don't.'

'What, then? You're not saying much for yourself.'

Mulholland looks at the man of whom he once lived in fear, or at least once held a healthy respect. Now there's nothing, and he feels a certain desire to unload the truth.

'Go on, Chief Inspector, might as well spit it out. Say what you're thinking.'

Might as well ...

'Two things,' says Mulholland, and such is his lack of spirit these days that his heart is not even in his mouth as he says it. 'Firstly, Barney Thomson is absolutely, definitely, no questions asked, sure as a fucking dog is a dog and mince is mince, not the killer. Maybe he's back in Glasgow, and maybe he's not, but there's not a malicious bone in his body. He's weak, he's a bit slow, he's nothing special, but he certainly isn't a killer. Just not a chance. Not a chance.'

McMenemy nods.

'Very well,' he says. 'You seem quite concerned. Perhaps then you would care to find the real killer, if you so stoutly believe that Thomson is innocent? Anyway, you have something else to say.'

'You talk the biggest load of shite of anyone I've ever met in the force.'

McMenemy looks down from his position at the window. He considers this for some time, during which he takes his seat once more behind the desk. Not for a second does he take his eyes from Mulholland, and not for a second does Mulholland retreat from the stare. All sorts of male hormones are flying. This is the stuff of cinema.

'Of course,' says McMenemy after a while, 'you're right. How'd you think I got to be chief superintendent?'

'Ah.'

McMenemy stares at his detective and wonders if he is right to be doing what he is about to do. Instinct is what it's all about, however, and he used to have it. He used to have it in spades, and that's really why he got to where he is. And right now his instinct says to go with Mulholland.

'Son,' he says, 'you can try and wind me up as much as you like, but you're on the case. And if you refuse, I'll send you back to Sutherland. I hear that monastery's started up again. Right?'

Mulholland looks across the chasm.

'Right,' he says.

Right.

And Mulholland's eyes sink down to the carpet, and even though he may not in actuality be heading back to Sutherland and the terrors of the year before, that is where his mind now takes him, as it drags him kicking and screaming back into the miserable past.

16

the reason why some people get murdered

Barney wraps up his fourteenth cut of the day. Leyman Blizzard has just finished his third. It is a dull day down the Clyde, as it is in the centre of Glasgow. Dull but mild. There are a lot of frogs in Greenock, and the spiders are large for the time of year. And the people, generally, unhappy.

Two Jimmy Stewarts and an Anakin Skywalker for Leyman; he'd botched the latter horrendously, but in doing so had made the lad look much less of an idiot. And four Claudio Reynas, a David Ginola World Cup '98, a double chicken burger with cheese, a Cary Grant (Dyan Cannon retro), a J.R. Ewing, two Frank McGarveys, a lamb biryani, a Cardassian Forehead Transmogrifier, and two Des Lynams for Barney.

The final Claudio Reyna hands over his cash. A crisp, shiny ten-pound note for a £4.50 haircut. Barney heads towards the till.

'Keep the change, mate,' says the bloke, pulling on his Nike Rain Protection System.

Barney raises an eyebrow.

114

'You sure, my friend? That's a big tip.'

Manny Jackson gives Barney a long look. Knows there's something familiar about him, but can't quite place it. This barber has an honest face, mind, and that means a lot to Manny. That, and he's just given him a magnificent haircut. Deserves every bit of the tip.

'No bother, mate,' he says, glancing at himself in the mirror. The wife is going to be delighted. And the girl-friend. And her girlfriend will probably like it as well. (Yes, a man who admires honesty, Manny Jackson.) This haircut will keep him going for a month. 'Worth every penny,' he adds.

Barney shrugs. Not in the mood to be appreciated. 'Thanks a lot,' is all he says.

Manny Jackson delivers a parting smile, then walks out into the drab, sullen December day. And immediately, as has happened to every one of Barney's dream haircuts this day, his hair is pummelled by the wind coming in off the Clyde, and the style utterly laid waste.

(And as so often happens in life, the best-laid plans and most fevered dreams of Manny Jackson will also be brutally laid waste, when late this very day he will meet his death at the hands of Mrs Jackson, who for too long has suffered in silence the fate of the betrayed wife. The concerned reader need not fear for her plight, however, as she is destined to find a jury only too willing to be convinced by her pleadings of justification.)

Barney turns to Leyman Blizzard, who is slowly working his way through the *Mirror*. Headline: 'Thomson Expected to Reduce Global Population by 50% in Next Twenty Years'.

'Nice o' the lad, Ah suppose,' he ventures, devoid of enthusiasm.

Blizzard nods and looks over the picture of four

semi-naked women and the article on how four semi-naked women can be good for your sex life.

'Big tipper?' he asks.

'Five fifty,' says Barney, and Blizzard lets out a low whistle.

'Magic,' he says, then tries to return to reading the paper, while Barney goes about the meticulous business of sweeping up the hairs from another hirsutological triumph.

Blizzard seems distracted, however, and Barney himself feels ill at ease. Sometimes his dreams come to him early on in the night, so that should he manage to get back to sleep, he might wake in the morning and feel nothing for it. But this morning he had woken just before seven o'clock, panicking, heart thumping and full of dread, body clammy and hot, the sheets already sodden. He had turned on all the lights and the television, he had leaped into the shower, he had had his breakfast. But none of it had helped, and fourteen haircuts later he remains filled with unease. He has never before had recurring dreams, but this one feels like it is closing in on him. When he allows himself to think about it for too long during these bleak waking hours, he can feel the hand close around his guts. Real fear, that's what it is, and he can't place it, not at all. And it is odd, for he knows he no longer fears death. So what could be worse than that? What could truly be a fate worse than death?

No more customers await. A little after 3.45 in the afternoon. A slow time, until perhaps the odd straggler arrives late in the day. Blizzard, typically these days, finds that he cannot muster the concentration to read the paper for longer than a few seconds at a time and decides to rejoin Barney in conversation. Barney sweeps the floor. Knows every hair on the back of the head of the minister in the dream.

'Ah was gonnae tell ye something last night, was Ah no?' says Blizzard.

Barney can't really remember. Wonders if he's about to hear about Elvis again.

'Not sure,' he says.

'Aye, aye Ah was. It's something that a bloke in here told me once. Thought it might be just the thing for you, what wi' you being a serial killer 'n' a' that.'

Barney looks up. The door opens. As it does, when you don't want it to. A young man enters: mid-twenties, grey eyes, sharp nose, verdant moustache haunting his top lip, Plasticene smile, head beautifully adorned by a recently executed Sinatra '62; Gap suit, dark grey, collar-high neckline. This is not a man who has come for a haircut, and the barbers look at him warily.

'Hello there,' says the intruder.

They nod guardedly in reply.

'Bit grim,' he says. 'The weather, I mean,' he adds, getting no response.

'What can we dae for ye?' says Blizzard. 'Ye're no here for a haircut.'

Adam Spiers smiles broadly.

'I like that,' he says. 'Sharp. You know what's what. You can recognise who's a customer and who's not a customer. You may be old, but at least your brain isn't turning to sludge the way it does with some people the second they hit sixty. I like that. I think we can work together. You're sharp. Very sharp. I like that.'

They look at him. Barney clutches onto the brush as if it might be a useful implement – he has, after all, used such an instrument in the act of manslaughter. Blizzard's mouth opens slightly; a droplet of saliva waits to roll from his bottom lip.

'What are you selling?' he says.

117

'Selling?' says Spiers. 'Selling? I'm not selling anything. I'm here to help *you* sell. I'm here to help you turn this small business into a multinational hirsutological concern. I'm the begetter of your dreams. I am the Wishmaster. I'm the Bottle Imp, without the bad shit at the end. I'm Robin Williams in *Aladdin*. I'm Robin Goodfellow, I'm Puck, I'm a hobgoblin, a flibbertigibbet, a leprechaun. I'm everything you ever wanted.'

'What the fuck are you talking about?' says Blizzard. Suddenly he has the concentration to return to reading the paper.

'Let me introduce myself. I'm Adam Spiers and I work for Magpie, Klayton, Parmentle and Clip. Pleased to meet you both.'

'A lawyer?' says Barney. This is it. This man is a lawyer. He's heard about Barney and he's come to represent him because he knows the police are about to close in.

'A consultant,' says Spiers.

They stare at him.

'What dae ye mean?' says Blizzard after a few seconds' concentrated staring. 'Who dae ye consult?'

'You,' says Spiers. 'I consult you. You ask for my help, I give you advice on how to run your business, you pay me lots of money, then I depart, leaving your business stronger, fitter, better managed and healthier than when I arrived.'

'So ye're an expert in barbershops, then?' says Barney.

'Don't know anything about them,' admits Spiers, stating one of the consultant's fundamental principles.

'So you're gonnae ask us how we run our business and charge for it at the same time?' says Blizzard.

'Basically.'

'Right. Fuck off.'

Spiers smiles and shakes his head. Looks around him, quickly assesses the situation of this unfamiliar environment as only a highly paid consultant can, and sits down in one of the barber chairs.

'No, no,' he says, still smiling, 'you don't understand.'

'Ah think Ah do,' says Blizzard.

'No, you can't possibly. Just give me a couple of minutes of your time.'

'No.'

'You see, we at Magpie, Klayton, Parmentle and Clip are dedicated to the service of our customers.'

'Piss off.'

'I mean, look around you. Clearly you have a fine little shop here. You've got your chairs and your mirrors and your five-month-old *Sunday Post* colour supplements. All very good. But where are your customers? Where's your output, where's your input? Do you have a management structure in place? You need properly laid down channels of communication between your staff. A chain of command from one level to the next, so that the ideas that prosper in the fertile undergrowth of lower management will not be lost.'

'There are two of us.'

'You need targets. Soft targets, hard targets, stretch targets. You need to take a blue sky approach. You need buzzwords. I mean, have you got any buzzwords? We can make some up for you. And there's more. You'll need to establish an Integrated Project Team, where all aspects of your business are catered for.'

'An Integrated Project Team?' says Blizzard, looking round at Barney. 'What language is this guy speaking?'

'Fluent wank,' says Barney.

'You need to look to every facet of your concern to see where you can make savings. There is nothing which

119

can't be done better, faster and cheaper. Through us you would have access to barbershop best practice. You'll be able to see the latest management techniques from outside industry. We'll teach you to facilitate meetings, map your processes and organise problem-solving and team-building sessions.'

'Map our processes?' says Blizzard. 'Map our processes? What the fuck are you on about?'

Adam Spiers opens his arms in an expansive gesture. I'm getting close, he thinks. Another couple of questions and I'll be able to start charging them.

'What jobs do the two of you do? You cut hair, right? So, do you both cut hair in the same way? Does one of you cut hair more quickly because he uses a different method? If the other was to change, would you be able to make savings? So, we'd help you to facilitate a meeting where you would map the process of cutting hair. What's the first thing you do? What next? Do you use a razor first, or the scissors? Do you wet the hair? Do you use a blow dryer? What kind of shampoo do you use? We go through all of that and, at the end, so that no one feels compromised, we have a clean-up session where we make two lists, one under a happy face and one under a frowny face. We see what we've achieved and what problems have to be addressed.'

They stare at him as if he's an alien.

Which he is.

'Am I making sense?' says Spiers. 'We're talking the latest in Experio-Millennium Consultative Indoctrination. We're talking buzzwords, we're talking maturity model frameworks, we're talking baseline assessments.'

'You're talking shite,' says Barney.

'That's a good point. Let's park that under a frowny face and come back to it. Shite, that's a good point. But what you have to ask yourself is this. Do I want to run my business as if it was a dodgy little barbershop in Greenock, or would I rather it was run as a staggeringly successful multinational corporation, like Boeing or Pizza Hut? We at Magpie, Klayton, Parmentle and Clip have advised Microsoft, we've advised Tesco's, we account for more than eighty-five per cent of the annual budget of the Ministry of Defence. We're huge. We have the knowhow to transform this small shop into a cross-continental, barbetorial conglomerate. You could be the McDonald's of the barbershop business.'

They are still looking at him as if he's an alien.

He stares back. He's used to this, but it doesn't mean he won't get their business. Sometimes you get this reaction, but they're still complete suckers for a good sales pitch and the promise of extra cash. Everyone on the planet is a sucker for extra cash.

'What planet did ye say ye were from, again?' says Blizzard.

'So what we're talking about is a maturity model framework within a best practice, baseline assessment scenario. You'll need critical success factors, strategic objectives, key performance indicators and an overall vision. You'll need to develop management plans, human resource plans and a definition of the skills gap. You'll need a mission statement. Everyone's got a mission statement these days. How about *As God be our witness, we, the honest and true barbers of Blizzard's Hair Emporium, do solemnly swear to deliver the finest haircuts on Earth, in as short a space of time as possible. And all at low-cost prices.*'

Blizzard sticks his fingers in his ears, starts waving his head around and humming 'Nessun dorma'.

'You'll start with a matrix of functions and accountability,

121

on which you'll be able to judge your hard and stretch targets against your query resolution. We're talking plenary sessions, we're talking empowerment, we're talking multi-divisional sanctioning, we're talking cross-integration fertilisation, we're talking triangulated post-nineties matrix differentiation, we're talking . . .'

'You're making this up,' says Barney.

'What?'

'Ye're no just talking shite, ye're actually just making it up as ye go along. When ye're a barber ye spend yer life listening tae shite, and ye can recognise it fi' fifty mile. And you're full o' it.'

'You can think that if you like, my friend, but the fact is that if you don't employ a consultant in this forward-thinking day and age, you'll be left behind. Make no mistakes. Analysts predict that by the year 2015 the only businesses left will be those employing a full-time consultant. Don't do it and you're dead.'

'And how many o' those remaining businesses will themselves be consultants?' asks Barney.

Spiers stares at him then pulls a notebook from his jacket pocket. A wafer-thin computer notebook. Thinner than any panty liner. He flicks it open, taps in a few numbers, looks up and smiles.

'About seventy-three per cent,' he says.

Blizzard has stopped wailing. Barney smiles.

'So in fact, the best way for any business tae survive is for them tae move intae the consultancy world?'

This gives Spiers some pause. He looks at Barney and thinks he recognises a rare intellect. A man at the peak of his mental powers; or, at least, at the meagre hilltop of his mental powers.

'Aye,' says Spiers, 'I suppose that might be the case.'

'So really, rather than us dae a' this crap about matrices and shite like yon, we really ought tae just become consultants? Blizzard and Thomson, we could call ourselves. What dae ye think o' that, Leyman?'

'Sounds like a load o' shite tae me, son,' says Blizzard, 'but Ah'd go along wi' it. It'd be better than sitting here listening tae this heid-the-ba'.'

'Perhaps,' says Spiers, 'we at MKPC might be able to give you a consultation on how to consult?'

'Ye mean,' says Barney, 'that the consultant consults another consultant for a consultation on how tae consult?'

'Aye, we do it all the time. That's why there's so many of us.'

'Right. So how about if *we* give *you* a wee consultation on the cheap, just as a practice run.'

'*You* give *me* a consultation?' says Spiers, breaking into a condescending smile, from which his face will likely never recover. 'All right, why not?'

'Right,' says Barney. 'My advice to you is this. Fuck right off. Do not pass go, do not collect two hundred pounds, don't even stop tae go tae the fucking toilet. Just get the fuck out o' this shop before Ah stick this broom up yer arse. Ah've killed someone wi' one o' these before, ye know.'

Spiers's condescending smile travels a little farther to the outer reaches of his face.

'I don't think you fully understand,' he says. 'We're talking about multidisciplinary, interdepartmental, cross-purpose . . .'

'Fuck off!' says Barney, grabbing Spiers by the arm. 'That's a multifunctional, nae questions asked, nae shite, final and irrefutable offer.'

He opens the door and shoves Spiers out into the street.

'I obviously caught you at a bad time,' says Spiers. 'I'll be back next . . .'

123

Barney slams the door closed and pulls the Venetian blind. He turns back to Blizzard, who is watching him with an amused look. Barney considers his actions of the last two minutes and how his heart has not even picked up a beat. Two years ago he couldn't have had an argument with a feather duster. Now he's telling people they're talking shite, threatening them with a broom, and throwing them out of the shop. And more than that, thinking nothing of it. So that unseen dread and misery still rest on his shoulders.

'Very impressive, son,' says Blizzard.

'Thanks,' says Barney, as he slowly walks back to his station and begins again the cheerless task of sweeping up.

'Ye've obviously got a knack for this kind of thing. A wee bit of a mean streak behind that placid exterior. Maybe ye are that murdering bastard after a'. Good on ye.'

'Thanks,' mumbles Barney. Isn't that just going to make all the difference in the world?

'Oh aye, I was gonnae tell ye about this group,' says Blizzard, after a couple of minutes' attempting to drag his previous thoughts into the present. 'Ah know a bloke who knows a guy. Think Ah might be able tae get ye someone's phone number. Ye know. Seeing as you're a serial killer 'n' a' that.'

Barney looks up; stops sweeping.

'What kind o' group?'

'One o' they self-help groups. Ye know, for folk that've done the kind o' shite you done.'

'A self-help group for killers?'

Blizzard shrugs.

'Aye. That's whit the bloke said. Think Ah know where Ah can get hold o' the bastard.'

Barney stares at him. A group of like-minded people. People who might know what he is thinking. Maybe that might be worth it.

'Aye, awright,' he says. 'Ye never know, eh?'

'Right,' says Blizzard. 'Ah'll see if Ah can get ye the number.'

'Aye,' says Barney, and once more returns to his sweeping.

Blizzard rustles the paper. Already beginning to forget the last conversation. His mind the same tangled mass of pointless information as anyone else's.

'What dae ye make o' these four birds,' he says. 'Would ye shag any o' them?'

17
ride a pale horse

There are two kinds of men in the world. There are those who are crap at sex; and then there are those who have never even had sex. So thought super-spy Jade Weapon, as she lay back on the cool grass of a Kingston summer's evening. The three men attending to what they believed to be her erogenous zones were making a lousy job of it, and she couldn't wait until she got the green light from Walter Dickov, watching the action via satellite back at HQ in Geneva, to take the three of them out.

'Come on, Walter,' she said pointlessly to the humid night. As usual, she could hear him, but had no link-up to speak back to the bastard.

'Who's Walter?' said the abject British agent, the best that M16 could manage, as he thrust manfully, barely touching the sides of Weapon's disinterested sex hole.

'Walter?' she said, between the panting breaths of her sexual assailant. 'He's a guy with a dick. Unlike you three women.'

'Yeah, right,' said the British agent, as he continued to trudge away.

'Come on, Walter, you bastard,' she said once more to the night. 'You must've seen enough by now, for God's sake.'

And so, at last, it came, the crackling voice in her ear.
Eliminate the spies. Those three words that fired her
sexuality much more than any man she had ever met
could. Although, of course, she had heard tales of Walter
Dickov, but he was just a voice to her. She knew the
rules. They must never meet.

Jade Weapon grabbed the throats of her two mammifer-
ous assailants and, with a gentle tweak of her thumbs,
killed them both instantly. The other agent looked up with
an air of British curiosity.

'Time to die, Dickless,' said Jade Weapon.

'Don't mind if I finish,' said Bond. Jeremy Bond.

'Didn't even know you'd started,' said Jade Weapon,
as she closed her thighs firmly around the weak ribs of
the British agent, and squeezed the little breath out of him
that was required, within ten seconds.

Men are so weak, she thought, as she sat astride her
fifteen-litre Harley Davidson, fired off a volley of bullets
from the side-mounted machineguns, just in case there
happened to be any men watching from the nearby forest,
then tore off across the hills and mountains to where her
boat waited at the other end of the island.

✂

'God, I wish I could be like Jade Weapon,' mutters Erin
Proudfoot quietly. Cool, smooth, fit, quick-thinking,
testicle-crushingly confident, horny as hell and breasts
like a behemoth.

She leans back in her chair as she reads. Feet perched on
the desk. Tea break. The report on the four missing teddy
bears in Byres Road can wait. As can the phone call to the
woman who thinks her husband has been abducted by the
Federation of Alien Presbyterian Churches. And both of
those are ahead of the student locked in the basement of the
QM Union, reputedly transmogrifying into an insect.

The noise of the station goes on around her, but no one speaks to her these days, not unless she speaks to them first. A bit of a mad glint in her eye, that's what they all think, and so they tend to be wary of her. Even Detective Sergeant Ferguson has retreated from the sexual innuendo which he once permanently employed.

If I were Jade Weapon, she thinks, I could easily take care of guys like Ferguson.

'Busy as ever?'

Proudfoot keeps staring at the book. She stops reading, but her eyes don't leave the page. A voice from the not-so-distant past, but it might as well have been twenty years ago for all that it matters now. Still, for all the lack of feeling to which she aspires, for all that she would be as cool and unemotional as Jade Weapon, her heart immediately starts thumping voraciously, her throat goes into a dry panic, and ants start crawling up and down her spine. All that kind of stuff.

She looks up at him eventually, hoping her face does not betray her emotions. He hasn't changed, but what has she been expecting? Massive weight loss? Eyes like black holes and hollow cheeks? Bela Lugosi?

It has been six months since they saw each other. The last time had been another passionate night, when they had talked as much as made love, when his intensity had been overwhelming, when she had thought he might kill her; yet in the morning his eyes had been dead, and she had known there was something in his head that wouldn't be communicated.

They had escaped with their lives from an infamy of adventure, they had thrown everything of themselves at each other for a few months, and he had been the first to burn out. Just another sad little love story. The momentum of it, the speed with which it had all happened, the fear and the loathing, had carried them through, but once the emotions were spent and at last a day had dawned cold and grey and hopeless, Mulholland had forced them to accept the reality of what had gone before.

'Not much to do,' she says eventually, after some endless eternity of a stare.

Mulholland nods. 'Don't trust you with anything, eh?'

'No, no, it's not that,' she says, 'just don't have much on at the moment.'

'Right. You don't have to lie, Sergeant. I know what it's like. I've been getting the same treatment up the coast. If some Councillor's wife's cat goes missing and they want to stick a chief inspector on it to try to impress the bastard, I'm the man. Otherwise, I get bog all. There are prepubescent constables getting more to do than me. I'm still supposed to be a detective chief inspector, but I'm getting the biggest load of shite that's ever been handed down.'

'You can't have,' she says.

'Why?'

'Because I've been getting that. You're right. I'm not busy. I've got plenty to do, but it's all alien abduction and teddy bears, and spending half my life following some stupid blond-haired bimbo who may, or may not, have killed her boyfriend five months ago It's driving me nuts. Course, they think I'm nuts anyway.'

Mulholland laughs. Has a degree of sympathy with her; as well as all the other feelings packed neatly in his baggage.

'I had to investigate a sighting of Elvis,' he says.

'Robbing banks, was he?'

'No, no, he was sweeping up leaves in Tarbet. The tax people read about it in the local paper and asked us to chase the guy. Thought that if he'd been domiciled in

Britain for the last twenty-three years they'd be able to make a killing.'

Proudfoot smiles. Beats her teddy bears case, although only just. Her heart has settled, she has an unexpected feeling of relief. Some part of her, she is realising, had been afraid that Mulholland would be getting on with his life with no trouble at all, that she would have suffered scars that never touched him.

'And did you get him?'

'Oh aye, aye, I got him easy enough. I mean, the guy sweeps the streets every day. How hard is it to find someone like that?'

'And?'

'Oh, it was Elvis all right. No question. Got him to do a couple of verses of "Long Lonely Highway" just to prove it. The big guy hasn't lost it. Still got a voice like an angel. Brought a tear to my eye.'

'Is he still a fat bastard?'

'No, no, he's thin. And blond. And he's hardly aged, in fact. Looks as if he's about thirty or so. But it's Elvis all right. Who else is going to know all the words to "Long Lonely Highway"?'

'You sure? By the end, Elvis couldn't remember the words to his own name, never mind his songs. Used to hold bits of paper.'

'Aye, but he was fine after he got out of rehab in the early eighties, he said. Hasn't looked back.'

'And now he can sweep roads with the best of them.'

'That's the King,' he says.

'We're talking shite,' she says.

Mulholland nods.

'I hated you, you bastard,' she continues.

He continues to nod. That sounds about right.

'You want to expand on that?'

130

He turns at the sudden clap on his back. Is greeted by a jolly face, not yet sodden with drink, a fresh moustache still struggling to come to terms with the rabid pink skin. Detective Sergeant Ferguson, a smile charging untethered to all parts of his face.

'Boss!' he says. 'Magic tae see ye, Big Man. They let you out o' the loony bin up by?'

'For a limited period only,' says Mulholland, smiling the best that he can these days.

'Brilliant. Good tae see ye back anyway. Ye havnae missed much, mate. The usual shite, ye know. Stabbings like ye wouldnae believe. A' that crap. Barney Thomson's back doing the business. Good on the lad, that's what Ah say. And this place hasnae changed much at a'. The usual sad lot, eh, Erin? Some of us have been doing a bit o' shagging lately, of course. Ye know how it is, eh, boss? You two gonnae start up hostilities again, are ye?'

No answer. Go on, Ferguson, thinks Mulholland. Step in shite and walk it through the house.

'Aye, well,' says Ferguson, 'whatever. Ye awright for a pint the night, mate? Tell you about the seven Chinky birds Ah shagged at the weekend?'

'Love to, Sergeant, but I can't. Got work to do, I'm afraid. They didn't call me back to listen to your crap, high on the agenda though it is.'

'Aye, right, boss. See you about, then. Maybe get together later in the week, eh?'

'Aye, aye,' says Mulholland. Why not? No harm in listening to one man's sexual ravings over a couple of pints for an hour or two. No harm in anything when your mind is so fucked up you require brain surgery.

'Brilliant. See you around, then, eh? Presume you're up for the Barney Thomson business?'

131

'See you later, Sergeant.'

'Aye, right,' says Ferguson, tapping his nose. 'Nae problem. Need tae know, and a' that. Nae bother, mate.'

And off he goes, to spread a little gossip. As you do.

They turn back to one another. The name is out there, but they can both ignore it for a little while longer.

'You were saying?' he says.

'I thought you were a total bastard,' she says.

'But not any more, then?'

She stares at him for a while and he can handle it and stares back. When you're dead inside you can stare out the toughest situations: emotional, physical, violent, they're all within your capabilities. When you're dead inside, you can stare out Lecter.

She's rehearsed this many times, while never thinking she would get the chance to say it. So, of course, when it comes out it sounds nothing like she's intended.

'Why do I have to explain it? That last night, Christ, I don't know. We talked about a lot of stuff. Fuck, we were even going to run off to the Bahamas to get married at one point. Then up you get in the morning, without a fucking word, and walk into the station and get a transfer. Just like fucking that. What a penis. Christ, I just used to lie awake at night and wish you were dead. I dreamed up at least fifty disgusting ways for you to die. My therapist even recommended I get a dummy and stick pins in it.'

'What kind of therapy was that exactly?'

'The right kind.'

'And did it work?'

'Don't know. Did you feel any of the pins going in?'

He tries to remember. He's felt so much pain in the past few months, could he tell if some of it had been physical?

'All of them,' he says.

'Good. Anyway, it didn't do me any good, although it helped a bit after I'd put the doll through a mincer, mixed it up with some Kennomeat and fed it to my neighbour's dog.'

'I definitely remember feeling that.'

'Well, after that I calmed down a little. I suppose I realised that none of it was your fault. We were both well fucked after what happened. Maybe you just had more guts than me to walk away from it. So then I just didn't want to think about you at all. I thought it would be best if I never had anything to do with you again. A total blank, you know. Pretend you didn't exist.'

'That work?'

She shakes her head.

'For a while, but I couldn't stop thinking about you, not when I was trying to be in denial. So then I decided that I should just accept it all for what happened, that life goes on, and if I ever saw you again, then so be it. And here we are, and I'm totally cool about it. Don't really feel anything, except I'm sort of pleased to see you. But not that pleased.'

'Very mature,' says Mulholland, not to know that she's far more perturbed by his arrival that she would have him believe.

'Thanks.'

'I'm still at the hating you stage,' he says.

'*You* hate *me*?' she says, sitting up. Feelings aroused. 'What kind of arsehole are *you*? Why do you hate me? You were the one who left. You were the stupid prick who talked about pitching up at a beach in the Caribbean one minute and who buggered off for the rest of his life the next. Why the fuck should you hate me? What did I do?'

He looks down at her. Has talked this moment through his head many times as well. In none of his rehearsals has he admitted to hating her, so he doesn't know what to say next.

'Don't know,' he says.

Proudfoot shrugs. Lets go of a long sigh and settles back in her chair.

'Maybe I do still hate you after all,' she says.

'Nice to see you back, sir,' says a passing sergeant, whose name Mulholland doesn't remember. A tall woman, hair a different colour from that which he remembers. He nods and smiles and doesn't risk saying anything because the name is gone.

'Eileen Montgomery,' says Proudfoot softly.

'I knew that,' he says. 'Married to Ron, the airport guy.'

Brilliant, she thinks. In possession of all the facts, just a few seconds behind the times. Just like they'd been in that bloody monastery. But then, why should he want to remember anything of this place?

'So what are you going to do about it?' she asks.

'What? Eileen?'

'The fact that you still hate me.'

'Oh.'

There always comes a time. No matter how much fat you chew, or how long you take to pick the last of the flesh from the carcass of the chicken or however long you worry over the decaying tissue of the dead horse or plunder the carrion of prevarication, eventually you have to get down to business.

'You know what they say when you fall off a horse,' he says.

Proudfoot stares at him, and slowly smiles.

'You think you're going to ride me again, do you?'

He raises his eyes. Face goes a little red.

'We're going back to look for Barney Thomson. Or rather, we're going to find the latest bloody killer who every eejit, including our haemorrhoidal chief superintendent, thinks is Barney bloody Thomson, but who bloody well obviously isn't.'

She looks at him and a million things go through her mind. She's been complaining for months about the pointless crap she's been given to do, but does she really want anything harder on her plate? Does she really want some rabid serial killer to chase? And why on earth, when she's been spending her working life on routine observation work that would dim the wits of the dimmest idiot, would they thrust her into the middle of the biggest investigation of the year? Why, if not to be part of Joel Mulholland's therapy?

She takes her eyes off him and looks back to the book which she has never put down. Obviously Jade Weapon is not going to make it to the other side of Jamaica without being apprehended by at least seven or eight assailants. Fantasy, fantasy. Much more intriguing and involving than real life. And so the next words in her head are not her own and they are not Mulholland's. They belong to Weapon. Jade Weapon.

'*Listen, fuckface,*' *said Jade Weapon to the swarthy Italian, who had suddenly leaped onto the back of her motorcycle, 'fuck me or fuck off, but don't fuck with my aerodynamics.*'

18
down among the dead men

'Nice enough guy, ye know.'

There follows a long proto-silence. A clock ticks. A plane passes by overhead, some 33,000 feet above Milngarvie, the low white noise vaguely penetrating the new, but single, glazed windows. Somewhere outside the posthumous, souped-up version of 'Guitar Man' thumps loudly from an open car window. A bird sings. Somewhere a woman screeches as she drags a shaving system she saw advertised on the television last night down her leg, taking an inch-long gash from just above her ankle. The refrigerator hums.

Proudfoot taps the end of a nail on the Formica table-top. *Mission Impossible*. Feels a twitch in her fingers sitting next to Mulholland again. Out of the blue her life has turned upside down; and what is going to happen when they find Barney Thomson, or when they find the real killer, or when Mulholland fails and McMenemy hikes him from the case? Will he vanish back up the coast, having tossed her world and her neatly wrapped emotions to the wind? Fucking men, she thinks, and feels sleepy.

Mulholland hasn't taken his eyes off Allan Watson.

Spaceman to his mates. 'Call me Spaceman,' he'd said to Mulholland when he'd arrived.

'Spaceman,' he says. 'About ten minutes ago now, I asked you to tell me everything you knew about Jason Ballater. Is that it? Nice enough guy? The bloke was thirty-three, you've known him since nursery school, you're shagging his sister and, it would appear, his wife, and the sum total of your knowledge of the bloke is that he was a nice enough guy. Don't you think you could elaborate a little, or are we going to have to break it down into idiot-proof, tsctsc-fly-bollock-sized, *Who Wants to Be a Millionaire*-type questions?'

'Don't know.'

'Don't know. That it?'

'Ah shagged his mum 'n' all. That any good to you?'

Proudfoot takes another glance at him to see if there's any possible reason why all these women might be interested in him, and when it's not obviously apparent she looks back at the table. Pink, with a disconcerting brown pattern running through it.

It's hot in the kitchen, the result of the heating up full coupled with the still mild temperatures for the time of year. She can feel her eyes getting heavy. Here she is, having wanted to be put on a real crime for the last few months, and now she can't even be bothered looking at the suspect. Or whatever he is. Can't stop herself from looking at the investigating officer, however.

'His mum?' says Mulholland. 'We've just been talking to his mum. You slept with her?'

Spaceman barks out an apologetic laugh; does a short bit of hand movement. But his movements are languid; it is hot and soporific, and he's even more tired than Proudfoot. Had a late night at the Montrose. Office Christmas revelry; all sorts of women to make an idiot of himself over.

'Aye, aye, Ah know what yese are thinking. She's a right bogmonster, Ah know that. But ye see, it was years ago, and it was different then. She was awright, ye know. Tits still in about the right place, no so many wrinkles. It was one o' they rites o' passage things, ye know. Like ye get in the films.'

'Rite of passage?' says Mulholland. You can go away for six months, it can seem like years, but nothing changes. People still talk the biggest load of utter bollocks.

'Aye, ye know. Rite o' passage. It was one o' they hot summer days. Ah comes round tae see wee Jason, forgetting that he'd gone off fishing wi' his dad. Ah wis about sixteen, Ah think. Agnes asks us in, and ye know how it is. Ah was rampant, ye'll know that yourself, mate. We a' are at that age.' Proudfoot squints out of the corner of her eye at Mulholland; he ignores her. 'Agnes was wearing just about nothing, seeing as it was so hot, ye know. She bent over, Ah got a swatch of her boobs, she sees me looking, the next thing ye know we're doing the bare bum boogie on the kitchen floor. Magic, by the way.'

Mulholland rests his face against his hand, so that his cheek squidges up and his left eye almost closes. My God! He's forgotten what it's like to interview people. What a load of utter mince.

'She taught me everything there is tae know. It was brilliant, so it was. What tae put in where. What holes are for what, a' that stuff. 'Cause, ye know, women have got about seven or eight holes down there. There's a' sorts o' stuff going on that men just don't know about.'

Mulholland gives in to it. Why not? It's not as if he's going to tell them anything that'll be of any use. He turns to Proudfoot, who has allowed a smile to come to her face.

'Seven or eight? That right?' he says.

'Double that,' she says.

'See!' says Spaceman. 'See! No matter how many times ye get stuck in down there, there's always something else hidden behind some big floppy pink bit that you . . .'

'All right, Spaceman. I think maybe we should get back to the subject in hand.'

Proudfoot looks at Mulholland. Sees the vague embarrassment and allows herself to laugh. First time in months. Light relief. No thought for the nature of the crime they are investigating, for it seems as if that's taking place in some parallel universe.

Spaceman holds his hands up. Despite the fact that he wasn't even trying, Mulholland has got him talking, and now he is prepared to discuss anything. Tongue loosened, got the woman to lighten up, and now that she's smiling Spaceman can see that she's all right. Nice-looking bit of stuff. If he could nail her, he thinks, it'd be a good one to tell his mates. Not that he can tell Jason, mind you.

'All right,' he says. 'He was a poof.'

The smile dies on Proudfoot's face. Not at the information, but at the return to formality; the return to the other universe where people get murdered.

Mulholland straightens up. Eyes open. Mind almost kicked into gear.

'Ballater was gay?'

'Aye,' says Spaceman. 'He was on the game.'

'You serious? He was married, for God's sake. He was thirty-three, he wasn't some spotty youth with no money. He was on the game?'

Christ, he thinks. Does no one lead a normal life any more?

'That was wee Jason, Ah'm afraid. Confused, ye

139

know. Decent upbringing on the one hand, had a good set o' values and a' that stuff. Then on the other hand, he was a raging bum artist. He did it for a bit o' extra cash when he was a lad, ye know, and never really lost the habit. Didnae dae it that often these days, ye know. Knew it was wrong, 'n' a' that, but he couldnae kick it.'

'And his wife?'

'Doesnae know a thing. Ah knew he was doing it, 'cause he'd give us a call and ask us tae cover for him. Ye know. Ah didnae really approve, but seeing as Ah felt a bit guilty 'cause Ah used tae shag his missus on a Saturday when he was at the fitba', Ah used tae dae it for him.'

'And Tuesday night?'

Spaceman shrugs. 'Same as usual. Gave us a call at work. Said he was going down the Pink Flamingo. That was his wee code word for when he was hitting the streets. Anyway, there ye are.'

Mulholland settles back in his chair. Sometimes, just when you're not looking for it, a breakthrough hits you smack in the face. Something that had seemed dead-end and random suddenly has meaning to it, and various different avenues open up in front of you.

'You know anyone else from that side of his life?'

Spaceman reels. 'Arse bandits? Ye kidding me? Ah didnae want tae know any o' that mob, mate. No chance.'

Mulholland rubs his forehead. Stakes have been raised. There is some serious work to be done, and none of it will have anything to do with Barney Thomson. As long as he can get McMenemy to see that. He looks at Proudfoot, but she has swum back into her reserve, and her eyes are once more rooted to the table, her fingers tapping out the beat to *Mission Impossible*. Perhaps she is even less likely to be of use than he himself, he thinks.

140

McMenemy has made a mistake ordering him to do it, and he has made a mistake asking Proudfoot.

'Ah also shagged his aunt, by the way. Dae ye want tae know all about that?'

19

and the beast enters once more the fray

The tall man coughs. It is a gentle, high-pitched cough. Sounds like a girl. He looks around the room, smiling at the others as best he can. The scar between his nose and his top lip hinders him in this. As ever.

The weekly meeting of the crowd, after the extraordinary general meeting called by Socrates McCartney three days earlier. Bloody show-off, Sammy Gilchrist had thought. And here he is now, with his own evil and his own desire to return to ways of old.

'For those of you who don't know me,' he begins, as he always begins, even though they all know him well, even those who have yet to hear his tale, 'my name's Sammy. A few years ago I murdered some total bastard, and I have to admit, as I stand before you all, I want to do it again. Not to the same bastard, of course. Another bastard.'

He breaks off and notices the few knowing nods around the group. As far as they know, of all of them, Billy Hamilton's designs on Mark Eason included, Gilchrist's is the greatest need to repeat his crime. Gilchrist is the

142

one most haunted by the past, and now haunted by the present. The whims and tastes and growing frustrations of Morty Goldman are unknown to them, for when Morty speaks, he never speaks the truth.

'Has she been in touch again?' asks Katie Dillinger.

Sammy Gilchrist scoffs, a noise like a pig's grunt.

'Not her,' he says. 'It's never bloody her, is it? It's always Julian bastarding Cruikshank. That's Julian bastarding Cruikshank of Bastard, Bastard, Bastard, Cruikshank and Bastard, for those of you who don't know. I mean, I hate that guy. No top lip, a moustache that's even more stupid than Wee Billy's here, and those suits that you know cost more than your house. But it's a rational hate, all the same. I can see both sides. The bloke's only doing his job, you know. If it wasn't him it would be some other bastarding lawyer, so that doesn't bother me so much. Really it doesn't, despite the suits and the moustache. It's that bastarding woman that pisses me off.'

'Your ex-wife?' asks Annie Webster. She has never heard Sammy Gilchrist's story, has only heard tell of it from others. She knows there is an ex-wife lurking in the background. But then, there usually is.

'No, no, not her,' he says. 'She's all right. I mean, I can't blame her for what she did. It was my own fault, you know? But I'm sort of ambivalent towards her now. If I see her again, fine. If I don't, fine. You know? If it wasn't for Priscilla, I'd probably never give her a second's thought.'

'Who's Priscilla?' asks Webster. 'That the woman you want to kill?'

'No, no, that's my daughter, you know. Wee Priscilla. Going to be a golfer, I think. A golfer.'

'I'm confused,' says Webster.

143

'Tell Annie your story,' says Dillinger.

'Do I have to?'

'It's good to get it out, Sammy,' she says. 'You know that.'

'What's the point?' he says. 'You know whenever I tell it, it just gets my back up and I want to get out there and kill the bastarding bastard all over again.'

'But that's not what it's about, Sammy. We're all here for you, and you're here for us. When you let yourself down, then you let us all down. Tell your story and maybe we can help you. If not . . .'

'You all know the bastarding story.'

They lock eyes. She could talk for twenty minutes, thinks Dillinger, and she wouldn't get anywhere. Every time she speaks to him, she knows he's getting closer. There are many of those here who she knows she has saved from the act of murder. In fact, since she started the group she's never really lost a member – so she thinks, although she has her suspicions – but of all of them, Sammy Gilchrist is the closest. Closer than Billy Hamilton, with his pointless jealousies, closer than Annie Webster, with her intimacy issues, closer, for the moment, than Morty Goldman and his taste for fine meats, and closer than she herself, and she twitches at the thought.

'I don't,' says Annie Webster. 'I'd like to hear it.'

Sammy Gilchrist stares at her, and gets a warm stare in reply. Billy Hamilton notices it too, and wonders if Gilchrist is thinking the same thing that he thought when he told his story for Annie Webster. And so his mind wanders, and he wonders if maybe he shouldn't just eliminate Gilchrist from the equation, so that when he makes his move at the Christmas weekend there will be no unnecessary competition.

'Aye, all right, love,' says Gilchrist.

Love! thinks Billy Hamilton, and his eyes never leave Annie Webster for the duration of the story, and not once do her eyes leave Sammy Gilchrist. Just a Murderers Anonymous prostitute, he'll come to think, moving from one hardened killer to the next, glorying in the danger.

'It was about ten year ago. I'd been married for about three year. No big deal, you know. We were getting on all right. The odd fight, and all that, but nothing major, and things were about as good as they're going to get. Had a lovely wee girl, just about a year old; I did have to travel through to Edinburgh every day for the work, which was a bit shitey, but that was about it. Used to go and watch the Thistle every now and again, you know the score. An ordinary life.

'So one night me and Janice, that's the wife, are sitting in a restaurant with the bairn. One of these family places, with plenty of weans in, and our wee one, Priscilla, tucking into a plate of macaroni. The name's a bit of a nightmare, but the missus was a big Elvis fan. So I was sort of glad we didn't have a boy. Anyway, there was a wee lassie behind us, about ten or eleven, who caught sight of the bairn, and Priscilla starts up with that goofy smile she had. She's miserable as shite now, of course, but she can hit a three-iron farther than I can. So she starts smiling at the lassie, and this wee lassie smiles back. Priscilla was looking as cute as you like; a wee stunner, you know, absolutely magic, and this wee lassie was obviously besotted with her.

'Anyway, we bugger off and they bugger off, not a word is exchanged. And that's that, you know.'

He looks around the room. They all, Webster excepted, know what's coming; but they are engrossed just the same. The next part never ceases to amaze. Only

145

Billy Hamilton is distracted. Only Billy Hamilton does not stare at Sammy Gilchrist, although his thoughts are all for him.

'So, jump about a year. We're back in the same place. First time since the last, you know. Sure enough, sitting at the same table as before are this wee lassie and her father. No mum, but there's another bairn this time. Really young, you know, maybe just a couple of months old. Didn't really remember them myself, but Janice recognised them. Course, this time Priscilla wasn't bothering her arse. She was two by then, so she was already getting to be bitter and cynical about the hand she'd been dealt. So there's no smiling going on, but the other wee lassie looks happy enough.

'So I wasn't bothering my backside, but this other bastarding bloke comes up and starts chatting away and all that, you know. Nice as ninepence, seemed like a reasonable bloke. The bastard ends up sitting having a drink and all that, and the wife is quite taken with his latest wean and she exchanges names and phone numbers and all the rest of it, and there you are. A pleasant evening had by all, so you might think. Aye, well right.

'The bastard never phones, of course, and we never phone him 'cause we don't really give a shite. We forget about him, and then, a couple of months later, we get absolutely, sure as eggs is sodding eggs, bastarding shafted up the arse something rotten. A poleaxe up the jacksy. And you know what it was?'

He stares at Annie Webster and Billy Hamilton fizzes. So she shows an interest in everyone's story? She puts herself about, sells her favours so easily. A week ago he'd thought she might be the one for him. Now what? She's a whore, nothing more. A tuppence-ha'penny bitch;

146

spread 'em and bed 'em. Billy Hamilton viciously rubs the palms of his hands.

'It was a letter from some big shot lawyer. Julian Cruikshank to be precise. It was a law suit. This bastarding eejit was suing me and the missus. Well, in fact, he wasn't suing me and the missus, he was suing Priscilla. It seems like the previous time we had dinner, their wee girl had been so besotted with our baby that she'd decided she wanted one of her own. So she went off a-shagging. She was ten years old, and she went out to get whatever she could find. Got pregnant within a couple of months to some fifteen-year-old hackbut who'd been on the brain transplant waiting list since birth. She didn't know what she was doing – Christ, she was ten years old. However, the minute they find out she's up the duff, the bloke decides it's all our fault since it was seeing Priscilla that made their wean want a baby in the first place. So he sues her. Priscilla. Sure as you like, can't bastarding believe it, he sues our two-year-old girl for undue influence, and for inciting his stupid little shit of a daughter into getting herself up the duff. Absolutely bloody incredible. What a litigious society we live in, eh? Can you believe it, Annie, love?' he says.

She shakes her head, and their eyes look across the few yards of floor and become one.

'It is incredible,' she says.

Billy Hamilton's nostrils flare.

'I mean, to be fair to his missus at the time, she thought he was an absolute Spamhead. She was mad about the whole bloody thing, apparently. And it turned out that ever since they'd learned about their wean, he'd brought her to the same restaurant every night waiting for us to return. Which was why the missus wasn't there, 'cause she thought he was a moron.

147

'Anyway, some things are stupid, and some things are unbelievably, incredibly, bastarding stupid. That the bastard sued at all was the stupid part. The incredible bit of it was that he won. The court ordered that Priscilla, the now three-year-old Priscilla, had to support this other baby, who was two years younger than her, until she was sixteen. And pay over a hundred thousand pounds' worth of damages to the father for emotional distress.'

'You're kidding!' says Annie Webster.

'Tart!' Billy Hamilton wants to scream, but he doesn't. He simmers instead.

'If I was, love,' says Sammy Gilchrist, 'I wouldn't be here now. So, you know, I did what any father would have done. I knew the bloke was the driving force behind it all, and that the missus probably wouldn't pursue it if he wasn't around. So, I killed the bastard. Took a day off work, waited for him to emerge from his house in the morning, then knifed the guy in the back, as he deserved.

'So that was that. It was broad daylight, a reasonably busy street. I was caught, slammed in the nick, and the bloke's bastarding wife screwed us for everything we had. Janice was broke, so she buggered off with Priscilla to stay with some cousin in Canada. Divorced me in the nick, married her cousin's ex-wife, one of these weird lesbian things, which I'm not even going to try to understand, and now I see Priscilla about once a year. The only decent thing about it was that the judge could see the sense of my actions, and gave me a pretty skimpy sentence. Got out after a few year, and now here I am. Sad, alone, miserable as a bastarding donkey.'

'You poor thing,' says Webster. 'You poor thing.'

'Aye, well, that may be. Anyway, our lawyers suggested we sued him back. Can't even remember what it was he said we should sue him for, but you know what they're like. Self-perpetuating bastards the lot of them. Turn everything to their favour, to give themselves as much work as possible. He said we should sue the father, the mother, the judge, the jury, and the owner of the restaurant. But I wasn't going for all that crap. I just wanted to get out there and get an old-fashioned revenge. You know . . .'

The door behind him slowly opens, and he takes his eyes off Annie Webster for the first time in ten minutes and turns and looks as Barney Thomson makes his first entrance into the Bearsden chapter of Murderers Anonymous.

Barney stands and stares, feeling nervous. Sammy Gilchrist stares back, as do the others. Billy Hamilton, the self-self-self of Billy Hamilton, wonders if this is the Feds come to bust him. But this man before them clearly does not possess the thuggish confidence of the average copper.

'Barney?' says Dillinger. 'Barney Thomson?'

'Aye,' says Barney. 'That's me.'

Glances are thrown around the room. Not 'Oh jings, we have a feverish, rabid serial killer in our midst' glances. More of a 'Here we go again, another Barney bastarding Thomson' sort of a glance, seeing this is the third Barney Thomson they've had visit them in a year. The hardest looks, however, are reserved for Dillinger, as she must have sanctioned the visit.

'Glad you could make it, Barney,' she says. 'Why don't you come in and take a seat. Sammy's telling his story.'

'Aye,' says Barney. 'Aye, right, nae bother.'

And so Barney enters the very midst of the group and takes a seat between young Billy Hamilton and Fergus Flaherty the Fernhill Flutist. They all look suspiciously at him, all except for Annie Webster, who embraces him with a huge smile, and realises that this might be her chance to associate with a legend. Or even sleep with a legend. Barney is embarrassed and wonders, even in his nervousness, if she fancies him. There *is* a bit of the Sean Connery about him, these days, after all. Billy Hamilton decides that he'll probably kill Barney at some point, although he does not yet know if it will be before or after Sammy Gilchrist.

'Where was I?' asks Sammy Gilchrist, not best pleased by the interruption; not when it's another Barney Thomson. He looks at Annie Webster for a reply, but she is too busy staring at the legend across the semicircle. Sammy grates his teeth.

'The law suit,' says Katie Dillinger. She's handled worse than the likes of Sammy Gilchrist in a mildly bothered mood.

'Aye,' says Gilchrist, becoming the second of the coterie to look Barney over with a professional eye. 'The law suit. Christ, I don't know what happened at the time, maybe I should just have sued the bastard. But you know what it's like these days. You can't open a newspaper without seeing the story of some eejit suing some other eejit. A bird suing her ex-husband; a bloke with a bad haircut suing the barber.' Barney winces, decides to avoid eye contact with Sammy Gilchrist. 'Some polis who witnessed a crime suing the chief constable for post-traumatic stress disorder. Surgeons suing health authorities 'cause they're scared of blood, pilots suing airlines 'cause they're scared of flying, priests suing the Church 'cause they cannae have sex. There was even one where some heid-the-ba' crashed his motor 'cause he didnae take his cardboard sun protector off the windscreen, then sued because it didn't say you had to on the back of it.

150

It's just bloody stupid, the whole thing. So I thought, well, bugger that, I'm not suing any bastarding bastard. It just seemed more honest to knife the guy, you know. No fart-arsing about, just a good old-fashioned stabbing. No shite, no law suits, no ridiculous claims for staggering amounts of cash. Honest.' He delivers the last word with a stab of the finger. Not often that murder can be called honest, but in his case he feels it justified.

It takes some of the others back. How honest had they themselves been? And none of them thinks of prior misdeeds more than Annie Webster, who is no longer looking at Sammy Gilchrist, or the legend that is Barney Thomson. Instead she stares at the floor and thinks of Chester Mackay, among others, and of her miserable past.

'So what now?' asks Katie Dillinger. There's nothing any of them says that can make her review her life. She's heard it all before. 'Why has the lawyer been back in touch?'

'Looking for more money, of course,' says Gilchrist. 'Why else? I mean, obviously I couldn't pay everything I was supposed to at the time. So every time I earn so much as a sixpence, the bastard pops up out the wood-work looking for a hundred per cent share in it. And if he hears of me actually spending any money, he shows up with all sorts of criminal henchmen attached.'

'I thought you'd fixed up some deal fi' a couple o' months back?' says Fergus Flaherty.

'Aye,' says Gilchrist, 'I did. But then last week I bumps into that bastarding woman in Marks and Spencer's in Sauciehall Street. Just bought myself a two pound thirty-nine sandwich. That was it. She stops and looks at me, then looks at the sandwich, then bursts out laughing. Laughing! Can you believe it? And so off she trots to her lawyer to tell tales, and the next thing you know I'm getting threatened in the usual manner about how I've obviously got more money than I'm letting on so let's all move along to the nearest bastarding judge.'

A few heads are shaken around the room. Annie Webster looks upon him with a degree of sympathy once more. Even Barney, who does not know the full details of the story, can see the injustice of it. That a man should not even be able to buy a sandwich.

'And you know the worst thing. I found out last week that the bastarding woman is about to get married again to some rich bastarding bastard out Aberfoyle way. I mean, she's probably delighted I killed her husband. The guy was a wank. Now she's just doing me for every single penny she can get, even though she doesn't need any of it. Unbelievable.'

'So why don't you do something?' says Flaherty, an edge to the voice, suggesting exactly what it is that he should do.

'I'm going to,' says Gilchrist.

'Fergus!' says Katie Dillinger. 'Don't encourage him, for God's sake.'

She looks at Sammy Gilchrist and she knows what he means to do. And maybe this time she can see the point. When you've lost everything, and the instigator of your downfall continues to kick you when you're down, what other way is there for you to act? What else can you do? When you have nothing to lose, why shouldn't you commit the ultimate crime?

'You still coming at the weekend?' she says. Their Christmas weekend, and two days in which to achieve salvation.

Sammy nods. 'Suppose so,' he says. 'If I'm not in the nick.'

She lets out a long breath. It is more than just a point-less couple of days away, this weekend retreat. In the past she has saved more than one wayward heart from committing further murder. It is a good opportunity to become more closely involved with her group than the rest of the year allows. The one time when she can devote full nights to the collective. And so, just how far will she be prepared to go during those nights to help Sammy Gilchrist? And if she does everything she can, will there not be others who might fall prey to that bitter bastard, jealousy?

'You've been before, Sammy. It's a good weekend. There are a couple of excellent sessions, and you know it can help you. You can maybe do some one-to-one stuff, to help you get through it. You never know. It's only two days away, Sammy, so don't do anything stupid. All right?'

Gilchrist stares at her for a while. Then stares at Annie Webster, who gives him a reassuring smile. One-to-one sessions. Sounds good, he thinks. Sounds bloody good. And it'll be a long time before there are any more one-to-one sessions after he's killed that bastarding bitch and been nicked. So he can wait. Might, in fact, just take her out on Christmas Eve, when they get back. That'll fuck her family up good and proper. In fact, might just take her family out on Christmas Eve, let her stew in her own misery, then take her out a couple of days later. What-ever. He can wait. See what Katie Dillinger and Annie Webster have to offer. Maybe a two-to-one session . . .

'Aye, all right,' he says. 'We'll see.'

Dillinger can read every single thought going through his head and knows that this will be tough. But this is why she is here; this is why she started this group up in the first place.

Now for another tough nut to crack, or possibly a soft, pointless waste of time.

'Right,' she says, turning and looking into the near-insipid eyes of Barney Thomson. 'Barney. I'll not give you any shite. You're the third Barney Thomson we've had in here in a year. I'm sure all the others are pissed off at me for inviting you along. Persuade us you are who you say you are. Tell us something we don't know. Give it your best shot.'

Barney swallows and nods. He'd expected to be able to sit at the back for a little longer than this, to rest easy in his anonymity, but he'd known that he would have to speak at some point, so it might as well be now.

And so, at last, it is time to talk. The odd brief explanation aside, he has never really told his story. Many times it has been formulated in his head, many times he has yearned for a captive audience. Now at last they sit before him. It is time to open up the doors of divulgence and spit the clotted words of truth onto the fires of revelation. These people expect to scorn him, and so he must persuade them of the veracity of his words and let them all follow him; this Pied Piper of adumbration, this ringmaster of axiomatic necessity, this bedevilled master of ceremonies, this pantheon of verity and rectitude.

'Ah really am Barney Thomson, honest,' he begins.

154

20
so lonely steps

Barney steps into the church, his feet crunching through autumn leaves. He has been here before, but the memory is vague. He has a strange feeling that it should be more familiar than it is. And he pulls his coat closer to him, as the wind howls through broken windows and the door swings and creaks. There should be someone here in this church, someone waiting for him, but he cannot think who it should be. In any case, he is alone.

He looks up. There should be something there. Something evil. Something swinging from the ceiling, its hollow eyes staring at him. But there is nothing but faded and peeling paint, leaves falling in through holes in the roof.

Barney shuffles up the aisle, his feet dragging through the sodden autumn mass. Takes a look behind him as the door creaks again, but it is merely the wind. An old desolate church, and he is alone. And with this realisation comes almost light relief. The dark of night, and nothing to fear. Perhaps at last he is free of . . . and he thinks and looks around the blighted kirk, and cannot remember of what he should be free.

Then, as he reaches the front of the church and stands

beside the remnants of the pulpit, he comes to the point of the evening. And it induces no fear at first, no thumping heart. Just curiosity.

For in the corner there is a television. Small, portable, old. A round aerial forlornly on top, giving an unimpressive picture of a street scene at night. Live, *as it happens* action, that is what he is seeing. So he thinks. And he steps closer.

Volume down low, but he can hear it now that he is near. The click of a woman's hurried footsteps across a wet road. Blond hair, coat pulled tightly against her, as protection against the cold, or against the evil that stalks her. She glances over her shoulder, and from the look in her eye, she can see what comes behind. Barney only has sight of her, however, not of the one who stalks her.

She passes a couple in the street, tries to talk to them, but they are not interested. They walk on, giggling and laughing, consumed with each other; the feral beauty of young infatuation.

And so she walks on, starting to break into a run, but her shoes are not made for running. Barney begins to feel nervous for her, for himself. Perhaps there is also someone behind him. But he does not look round. Eyes locked on the television. Thinks he recognises this place. Near the centre of town, past Anderston, down towards the crane at Finneston. She walks on, hurriedly, in no particular direction. Waves at a passing taxi; the taxi drives on. Not even employed, the driver on his way home; forgotten to switch off the light.

The camera pulls back, and Barney gets his first glimpse of the girl's pursuer. Just the back of his head, but he recognises that in itself. The dark hair, badly combed. The head of a minister. Seen it somewhere before. No more than ten yards away from the woman.

Barney flinches; his mouth is dry. Decides it is time to leave, but he can't. He can't move. This isn't real, and he doesn't have the control he should. And anyway, there is something behind him too that he does not want to see. Perhaps the same man who is closing in on the woman.

The shivers run all over him; his heart thumps truly now. He would turn away, but he is not allowed. The woman breaks into a run, she stumbles, and instantly the beast is upon her. It wields a knife, hand over the victim's mouth to dull the scream, and a vicious slash to the top of the leg. Barney winces and closes his eyes.

A hand touches his shoulder.

Barney Thomson wakes screaming, face bathed in sweat.

21

a bigga bigga bigga hunka metal

The crane looms large, casting a dull shadow in the half-light of morning. The Finneston Crane. Monument to the recumbent past; grand testament to the flourishing Glasgow of old; as majestic as the rooftops of Florence, as architecturally precise as the Eiffel Tower. The very begetter of the soul of this great city; the physical manifestation of the strength and purpose that lie at its heart.

A big hunk of metal. And at its foot lies a body, red coat stained darker red with blood. The fourth victim of this year's serial killer.

The murder had featured a few stages. Stabbed in the leg as a foretaste; an aperitif. Gagged and bound, but conscious. While Cindy Wellman had watched, the skin had been stripped from the top of her thigh to more than halfway down her leg. This had hurt, and she'd fainted three times. Each time, however, her killer had woken her before continuing. He had thought of using the skin to strangle her, but it'd snapped seconds after he tightened it around her neck. So instead he thrust it deep down her throat, thus suffocating her in a matter of a few, frantic, thrashing seconds.

Creative, but disgusting. As is much of modern art.

Having committed his crime, the killer had made his way home for a relaxing cup of tea, a few minutes' pointless late-night television, and then a good night's sleep. He had, he would admit if he were to confess to anyone – which he will not – even disturbed himself a little with this crime, and intends not to repeat it. Sometimes convention isn't so bad. Next time he'll go back to the more straightforward stabbing scenario.

The body had been discovered – in the usual manner – by illicit lovers at half past three in the morning. Two men, by chance, both firmly in the closet; one a bank clerk, the other a well-known Premiership footballer, and so an anonymous call had been placed to the authorities, and the police think there might be a lead in that call, when there is none.

The body still lies where it was discovered, five hours earlier. There is the usual crime scene. Yellow tape, fencing off the area. More officers than is necessary. The ghouls of the press and public as close as they can get, trying to see what all the fuss is about. Two plainclothes officers moving within the crowd, on the basis that forty per cent of murderers, taking pride in their work, will return to the crime scene after the event. A helicopter circles overhead. Squad cars come and go, head off to round up the usual suspects. Somewhere a woman bites into a chocolate pretzel she saw advertised on the television last night.

Mulholland and Proudfoot stand and stare. The cadaver is finally being placed into the removal bag, everyone who needed to look and prod having had their turn; every clue that could be garnered from the position and substance of the body as it lay having been so.

159

Proudfoot is white, blood having retreated inside to mix with the haunting of her stomach and her heart. She is being taken back down a long black tunnel to the events of the previous winter, and everything she saw then is returning to torment her.

Mulholland feels nothing. In his way he is a lot less ready to address the demons of the past. Still hiding from it all, and it is possible that he will never emerge from that hiding place. Maybe it will penetrate his consciousness in ten, twenty, thirty years' time. (If he lives that long.) Or maybe he will take all the feelings of terror, desperation and inadequacy to the grave. Whatever; as he watches the victim of the most vile of murders being enclosed in the Big Bag, he feels nothing. Nothing at all.

'Well,' he says, 'that's not something you see every day.'

Proudfoot barely hears him. One of the medics gives him a *From Dusk till Dawn* look; the other is as tied up as Proudfoot in horrors of the soul, and does not notice.

'What?' she says eventually. Takes so long to speak that Mulholland has almost forgotten what he said. He shakes his head and says nothing.

A small boat passes by on the Clyde, those on board craning to have a look at the activity. Seeing nothing, they go on their way, but they will later tell anyone who will listen that they were there and they saw everything. She was naked, with a copy of *Jekyll and Hyde* stuffed up her bottom . . .

The two detectives glance at one another and then look around. Activity everywhere, and none of it to any end; that's what they each think. Finally their eyes settle on the water, and the grey Clyde coldly flowing past. Another bleak day, the colour of the river. And there they stay, for neither knows of any point in rushing to their tasks. The immediate work is awful and bears no relation to solving the crime. Inform the relatives; speak to the press. Perhaps there might be some clues to be gleaned from the former, but unlikely at the moment of revelation. *'Your daughter's dead. What were you doing at midnight last night, by the way?'* Can't do it like that. Not any more, at any rate.

Detective Sergeant Ferguson approaches. Looking sombre for once, but only because he hasn't eaten anything in ten hours. They are aware of his approach; only Mulholland bothers to take it in.

'You're in luck,' says Ferguson.

Mulholland raises an eyebrow. 'You mean she's not dead?'

'Better than that. Her parents are dead, so ye don't have tae tell the mother.'

'A blessing of sorts, I suppose,' says Mulholland. 'What about boyfriends, husbands, that kind of thing?'

'She wasn't married, that's about it. Worked at a wee solicitor's up in Bearsden. Got the address.'

'Bearsden, eh? Brilliant. Better start there, then. See if you can get the doc to write her a sick note and we can drop it off.'

Ferguson laughs. 'Aye, right. A sick note. Nice one.'

'It's arbitrary,' says Proudfoot, still staring abstractly across the Clyde. A paper bag floats slowly past; an empty bottle, a packet of cigarettes, a bedraggled cuddly toy, and somewhere a child cries.

Mulholland watches as the body is laid to rest in the ambulance and the doors closed upon it. Ponders on what it must be like to ride in the back of one of those with the deceased, particularly if you've just watched a frightening movie; *The Blair Witch Project* or *The Avengers* (for who could help but be terrified by the sight of Connery in that

161

teddy bear outfit?). Would you constantly be waiting for the zip to be undone and a hand suddenly to appear? If there was an unexpected movement within the bag, would you dare open it? Just in case . . .

'Why d'ye say that?' asks Ferguson.

'Got a feeling,' she says. 'It's nobody he knew. It's just a guy committing murder in an entirely random way. No motive, no reason, just doing it. Might not even know why. He's just out wandering the streets and the mood takes him. The gay bloke from the other night, that's the same. Nothing to do with him being gay. Nothing at all.'

'Right,' Ferguson says. 'Like when ye're driving along the road and ye pass a chippie, and ye get a whiff o' a fish supper. Ye're not hungry, but ye think, what the fuck, and dive in and buy one. Ye usually feel like a fat bastard after it, mind.'

'Then again,' says Mulholland, joining in, 'sometimes you might not go in at all. You might ignore the urge, or you might not even feel it.'

'Exactly,' says Proudfoot. 'And this is our man. He goes out late, for whatever reason, and so he doesn't see too many people. Most of them that he does see, he thinks nothing of. But something hits him every now and again. Something snaps. Some weird, primeval thing. Some memory buried deep in the subconscious, and this vicious, bestial action kicks in.'

'And he buys a fish supper.'

'Right. He buys a fish supper,' she says, nodding.

The three of them watch the ambulance drive off, scattering the assorted officers of the law. The SOCOs are hard at work; every pointless piece of potential evidence is carefully placed in small, airtight bags by rubber-gloved fingers. Every cigarette butt, every piece of broken glass, every leaf, every stone.

162

'What dae ye want us tae do, boss?' asks Ferguson.

Mulholland continues to watch the ambulance go, out of the conference centre carpark, onto the road, up onto the Expressway, until it is lost behind concrete walls and articulated lorries. There's bound to be someone upset by her death, he thinks. There always is.

'How many people at this law firm?' he asks.

'About twenty, Ah think.'

'Better come with us. And grab . . .' and Mulholland's voice tails off as he realises that he can't remember the names of any of the constables still circulating the area. 'Grab someone to come with us. We can do the rounds. Might come up with something.'

'It was arbitrary. We'll get nothing,' says Proudfoot. 'Nothing at all. Unless one of them was with her last night.'

Mulholland nods, but says nothing. Probably right. Doesn't think the chief superintendent would be too impressed, however, if he told him they hadn't bothered to investigate the girl's life, based on his sergeant's hunch that it was a waste of time.

'Come on, Sergeant, let's go,' he says.

And off they meander, to plunder the soul of the investigation.

163

22

love's labours and
barbershop floors

'Ah've been meaning tae ask ye,' says Leyman Blizzard. 'How d'ye get on last night, by the way? Ah presume ye went tae this meeting Ah told ye about, seeing as ye wernae in the boozer?'

Barney sweeps the floor as he thinks of a reply. He's never been particularly adept at formulating opinions – mostly because he's never had any – and so his brain moves in time with his brush as he thinks about the night, and thinks about what he will say and what he won't. And after several minutes he finally comes up with an answer.

'It was awright,' he says. 'Ye know,' he adds as an afterthought.

'Right,' says Blizzard. 'How many folk were there?' he asks, thinking he might get a more definite reply to a more definite question.

Barney sweeps. Doesn't feel like talking. Whatever good may have come out of the evening was instantly taken away by the night. Another night, another nightmare. Different this time; more evil, more truth. More real.

'Ten or eleven,' he says eventually. 'Ah think there were a couple o' folk missing, but that's the way it goes, i'n't it? Ah thought it'd be monthly or weekly, maybe, but they have these blinking things every two or three nights sometimes. Most o' these folk are desperate, apparently. A' seems a bit strange.'

Blizzard nods. A collection of murderers all sitting in the same room? Strange?

'Did ye tell yer story, then? Any o' the bastards believe ye?'

Barney stops sweeping and looks at the old man. The thought of last night gives him a moderately good feeling in among the weight of dread. But how much shall he say to old Blizzard, for he does not want to put a curse upon it?

'Told a bit o' my story. If Ah'd told it all, Ah'd still be there. They were mostly sceptical, ye know, and Ah suppose Ah cannae blame them. There was one woman seemed awright, mind. Ah think she might have thought Ah was telling the truth.'

'Sounds like ye want tae shag her,' says Blizzard.

'What?'

'Ye've got a sudden light in yer voice when ye mentioned her. So what's the score? Good-looking bit o' mince? Big tits?'

Barney sweeps the floor. Feeling a little embarrassed and very uneasy talking about it, although he doesn't know why. Because he's still married perhaps? But then, she *is* a good-looking bit of mince, she has got magnificent tits, and he does want to shag her.

'Ah don't know, dae Ah?' he says from behind the brush. 'Ah don't know anything about tits. Ah don't even know what they're for.'

The old man laughs. 'Away wi' ye lad, ye're full of it.

165

There's no a man jack of us who hasnae spent several years of his life manhandling God's greatest gift.'

Barney stares at him. He tries to remember the last time he even so much as saw Agnes's breasts, and it seems so long ago that it might be lost in the mists of the late seventies. Like the *Starsky and Hutch* episode where Hutch nearly dies; he can't remember much about it, but he'd know it if he saw it again.

Hutch. He'd wanted to be Hutch when he was younger. He'd already been in his twenties himself, with his life going nowhere, and he'd fancied the thought of being some action hero, thumping down arse first onto the top of beat-up old Fords, solving crimes and chatting up women with a reasonable degree of panache. And like so many others in life, he'd done nothing about it, except drift his way through barbery, wasting the best years of his life.

Then finally, a year ago, he'd been given his chance to start that new life and do whatever he'd wanted. And what has he ended up doing? Returning to the West of Scotland, to live in a tiny flat overlooking the Clyde, and to work in a barber's shop . . .

'Haw, son! Ye're daydreaming,' says Blizzard to the glazed eyes. 'Hello! Hello!'

Barney returns, but the feeling of melancholy stays; to walk hand in hand with the feeling of dread.

'Aye, sorry, just thinking about something.'

'So what's the score, then, son? Is she nice? That's easy enough tae answer, is it no?'

Katie Dillinger. There had definitely been a connection there, he's sure of it. It's been a long time, but he can still recognise it. He'd caught her staring at him, even when one of the others was doing the talking. Could have been because he was new, but you never know. And

166

she'd even touched his shoulder before he left. Brought a shiver. And of course, she'd invited him to come along to the pub tonight with them.

'She was lovely,' he says. 'Seemed quite interested in me, ye know. Ah mean, it might just have been 'cause it was my first night and she's the leader o' the group, but Ah'm no sure.' He shrugs and returns to the slow sweep. 'Who knows, eh?' Something tells him that it is too late for these kinds of thoughts.

'So,' says Blizzard, rustling the paper, 'are ye gonnae shag her, or what?'

Barney looks up, head shaking. How the hell is he supposed to know? If a woman approached him, bollock naked, saliva cascading freely from her mouth, nipples like shipyards, proclaiming loudly, 'Take me, Barney, take me, and fill me with your manhood!', he'd still hesitate and wonder if there wasn't some other interpretation to be placed on her actions.

'No sure,' he says. Then he leans on the brush, and decides to open up to Blizzard. If nothing else, it'll take his mind off the hand at his shoulder, the knife hanging over his head. 'But Ah'd like tae, ye know. Ah have tae admit it. She's asked me down the pub the night, 'n' all.'

Blizzard perks up. 'Just the two o' ye? Ye'll be shagging by midnight, son, no doubt about it. Friday night out on the piss, stop for a kebab on the way home, then it's pants off and away ye go. Magic, son. Good on ye.'

''Fraid not, Leyman,' says Barney. 'Most o' the crowd's going. Ye never know, though, eh? Might get in there, Ah might not.'

'Aye, aye,' says Blizzard, looking back at the paper – headline: 'Thomson Ate Too Much GM Food as Child, New Claim' – 'aye, aye.'

Barney looks at him for a few more seconds. The shop

door opens and the first customer for nearly forty minutes walks in. The torpor of a Friday afternoon. They both look at him, as Angus Collins removes his Adidas Cold Exclusion Cloaking Device. Collins stops and looks from one to the other.

'Any chance of a Two-Point Saturated Ukrainian?'

Barney shrugs. Blizzard looks blank.

'Over to you, son,' he says, and delves back into the paper.

And Barney, filled with a strange mixture of expectation and gloom, goes about his business.

23
the peter mccloy

McMenemy stares from his office window at the three youths below. Hanging out on the street corner. Loitering with intent to something or other. Specifically outside the police station to see if anyone will come and do something about it. Which they won't. They guzzle Mad Dog, they hurl abuse and appropriate hand gestures at passing motorists, they verbally assault the occasional passing woman.

The police won't touch them. Not when there's a serial killer to be caught; and people still driving at thirty-five in a thirty zone.

Mulholland waits. Staring dolefully at the desk in front, hands clasped, a couple of fingers tapping gently against the back of those hands. He hums a tune. Is expecting to be told off for not yet having apprehended the killer, be it Barney Thomson or otherwise.

He has had a long day doing the rounds of Cindy Wellman's work colleagues and friends. Knows a lot more about her as a person, but nothing at all about what led to her murder. Out with friends, but parted company while still in the centre of town, to make her own way home. There the trail runs cold, except for a sighting of her being followed by a man they would now like to interview.

He can't concentrate on any of it, however. His head is filled with that obscure sludge which has been there for nearly a year now. Everything much of a muchness – something like the state of the Scottish football squad. A quagmire of mediocrity, nothing rising to the surface. Barney Thomson, fishing, the Thistle, Tom Forsyth's goal in the '73 Cup Final, Melanie, Proudfoot, Cindy Wellman's right leg, Michael Palin in *Brazil*, Scalextric, they shoot horses, don't they?

'How's it going?' asks M abruptly. Still with his back turned, still staring at the three youths; one of whom is unzipping his fly, preparing to put on a show for an approaching female of the species.

Mulholland shrugs, a gesture that is naturally lost on the boss. Doesn't really care how it's going, he thinks.

'There doesn't appear to be a connection between the three victims. Still digging, of course, might get somewhere, but I don't think so. Got a possible sighting of someone seen with Cindy Wellman just before she must have been killed. It's a bit vague, but the computer geeks are putting a picture together. We'll see what they come up with.'

M grunts. Youth Culture 2001 plops his willie out into the open, while passing compliant female prepares to laugh at him.

'Look anything like Barney Thomson?' asks M.

'Couldn't look less like him if it was a picture of a dog,' says Mulholland.

M grunts again. 'Don't know about that. Seems to me there's always been something canine about Barney Thomson.'

'Aye, he's a poodle.'

170

'Something primal; something zoomorphic; something bestial, animalcular and therianthropic. He is filled with some sort of basic instinct. A need for blood, a need to sup on the very essence of the human pneuma, a need for the destruction of the quiddity of kinship that transcends our perception.'

'Or an old Labrador who's lost his eyesight and the use of his legs.'

'Perhaps you should try to get the graphics people to include more of the features of Barney Thomson in the computer image.'

Mulholland finally pays some attention to what the boss is saying. Shakes his head, which is again lost on M.

'It's not Barney Thomson, sir.'

'How do you know?' says M sharply, turning around at last; and consequently missing the action, as the passing woman turns back on the still-leering youths, kicks one of them brutally in the testicles, head-butts another – a precision hit – and punches the last one in his Adam's apple, rendering him breathless and close to death for some ten to fifteen minutes, before going on her way.

'The man seen walking after Cindy Wellman looked nothing like him.'

'But you don't know that it was this man who killed her,' says M quickly, waving an emphasising finger.

Mulholland does a referee gesture. See! says his spirit, you can still get worked up about something.

'So what? The point surely is to speak to the last person seen with her, whether he's the murderer or not. We have to find the guy. What's the point in telling everyone it's Barney sodding Thomson, when it wasn't him seen following her, and it probably wasn't him who killed her?'

M leans forward, knuckles white, resting on the

171

desktop. A bulldog face.

'What's the point? I'll give you the blasted point, Chief Inspector. Everyone in Glasgow knows that Barney Thomson is a deranged killer, and that he's on the loose. And now what? You want me to tell them that there's another killer as well, and there's double the chance of them getting skinned alive or hacked up piece by piece? There'd be panic. Bloody panic.'

Mulholland's mouth is slightly open. You couldn't drive a bus in, but the man is aghast. McMenemy is mad, he thinks to himself, completely mad.

'You listen to me, Chief Inspector,' says M, beginning to foam slightly at the corners. 'You just listen to me. For the purposes of this case, for the purposes of the public and most of all for the purposes of your investigation, you are looking for Barney Thomson. No one else. You got that? I couldn't give a shit if there's another killer out there. I don't want any computer graphics or photofits or descriptions or anything of that sort released to the public, implicating anyone other than Barney Thomson. He is clearly, unequivocally, without a shadow of a doubt, our serial killer. You go after him, Chief Inspector. Him and nobody else.'

Mulholland continues to stare. Toppling over onto the side of incredulity. And so, a few things come to mind. What happens when Barney is in custody and the murders continue? How many members of the public will be duped by the real serial killer, because they are on the lookout for Barney? Those things and bugger you, Spamface, and stick your sodding job up your backside.

But he says none of it. He particularly doesn't say the last one.

'Right,' he says, letting out a sigh. 'Right.'

M slowly sits down, never taking his eyes off

Mulholland. (Perfect positioning sense with regard to his chair. Like a goalkeeper. Peter McCloy, for example.)

'There's a lot riding on this, Chief Inspector. I've brought you back because I thought you could do me a job. Don't let me down.'

Mulholland says nothing. Tasked with bringing the wrong man to justice. Brilliant. He might as well nip out into the street and arrest the first person he sees. Of course, the first person he sees will be a young lad clutching what is left of his genitals.

'You are going to have to enter the belly of the beast, 127,' says M, and Mulholland begins to switch off. 'You must show bravery, stout-heartedness, daring and bravado. You must place your head in the jaws of the lion, and you must not display pusillanimity.'

Yeah, yeah, yeah. And so, as M goes on, Mulholland begins to slide back down into his nest of sludge, and the only coherent thought he can truly manage is that he wishes he were no longer here. And in his head he is standing on a riverbank, wrist flicking, fish jumping at the flies he projects across the water.

24

nine o'clock in the evening, and i can't go to bed, no, no

Jade Weapon stood over the German agent, the steel toe of her red, thigh-length leather boot pressed up against Horst Schwimmer's trembling love-knob. The large machinegun she held in her right hand, which nestled against the inside of her even larger, yet firm, breast, was aimed at Schwimmer's forehead. A forehead beaded with sweat. Yet, as he looked up at her, nervous and expecting to die, he couldn't help but notice her enormous nipples straining against the thin fabric of her Lycra vest.

'Tell me where the formula is hidden or you eat lead,' said Weapon, in the east European monotone she used to cover up her middle-class, suburban upbringing.

'Gotten Himmel,' said Schwimmer. 'Vorsprung durch technik. Franz Beckenbauer, bratwurst, Helmut Kohl.'

With an instantaneous splash of red, Weapon opened fire, pumping fifteen rounds into Schwimmer's face in less than two seconds. His head exploded like a pumpkin. But hey, that's the way it goes.

✄

Erin Proudfoot lets the book down for a second and takes her first sip from the mug of tea which has been going cold on the small table next to her for nearly fifteen minutes. Glances at the clock. Not even nine. The rest of the evening stretches out before her like a great mound of compost. Then bed, and another night of waking sleep, until another bloody day will dawn.

Another night sitting in on her own, miserable as fuck. That's her. Should be down the Bloated Fish, or whatever Friday night dive as should happen along, watching her prey, the pointless stalk she's had on for the last five months. But Anderson, the other poor sap who, along with Crammond, has been dragged into the painful operation, had wanted to change for Saturday night and she'd agreed. Agreed without thinking twice. For she could not know to what it would lead; could not know that Saturday night would turn into a long, long Sunday.

Thank God for Jade Weapon, she thinks. However, there are only two more books to read in the series – *Jade Does Dallas* and *Fast Train to Nowhere* – and then she's finished. Who knows what excitement she'll be able to introduce into her life then?

She takes another swallow of tepid tea, screws her face up, does her best to ignore the feelings of depression and loneliness, and delves back into the novel.

Some days your head gets obliterated into a pulp by fifteen rounds from a semi-automatic. And some days it doesn't.

✄

Another night at the Bloated Fish. Friday, a good crowd in. Not too many of the Murderers Anonymous group, most of them with other matters to take care of before going away for the weekend.

Arnie Medlock, in all his pomp. Katie Dillinger, lips soft and red, hair golden, teeth white like a new pair of M&S pants; a bit of the Georgia out of *Ally McBeal* about her, attractive yet insipid. Billy Hamilton, having turned up on the off-chance that Annie Webster would be here, and being sorely disappointed. (And so Anderson sits outside Webster's flat all night, and falls asleep, so misses her when she leaves, and misses her when she returns three hours later.) Making do with Ellie Winters, a woman of some mystery. Socrates McCartney, in all his new-found, loose-tongued liberalism, chatting to Arnie Medlock, although the chatter conceals a certain amount of contempt. And lastly, Barney Thomson, sat beside Katie Dillinger, toying with his pint of lager. Talking to a woman in an almost intimate situation, for the first time in over three hundred and fifty years. Or thereabouts.

Arnie Medlock keeps a close watch, but suspects that Barney is all sour looks and nae bottle. He won't be any hassle; even though he can hear Dillinger enticing Barney to come with them for the weekend. I could crush Thomson like a digestive biscuit, he thinks to himself, even though he has Socrates muttering about the size of spiders in Bearsden in his left ear.

'Ah don't know,' says Barney. 'Ah don't really feel like Ah'm one o'ye, ye know.'

Playing hard to get. Being coy. Attempting to manipulate the conversation. Displaying self-effacement. Flirting even. All those things at which Barney is really, really crap.

'Come on, Barney,' says Dillinger, running her finger around the top of her wineglass, an act which has Barney

176

twitching in his seat, and which Medlock catches out of the corner of his eye. 'It's the perfect chance to get to know everyone. I won't lie to you. You see, I didn't think we'd be able to fit you in, but we have a vacancy. One of our number's dropped out, last-minute job. Don't know what the lad's up to,' she says, covering up all those feelings of rejection and annoyance which she has done her best to ignore for the past couple of days. She will, of course, never see Paul The Hammer Galbraith again, and perhaps that might upset her even more if she knew. But the future is not for any of us to know.

The wineglass begins to sing. Somewhere distant, Barney is aware of Socrates talking about beetles and Medlock saying that when he was in Africa they had beetles bigger than dogs; while on his other side, Billy Hamilton talks about *Northern Exposure*, telling Ellie Winters that he dreams about Rob Morrow every second or third night, but not in a bad way, while Winters yawns. The pub is full. Evis's 'Blue Christmas' fills the air.

'What's the score, again?' says Barney, giving himself more time. His natural inclination is to say 'no', after all. You have two options: one, spend a weekend in an old house, where every guest is a murderer, or, two, don't. The choice is obvious. Yet, for the first time in centuries, Barney is being led by his penis.

'We meet here at four o'clock tomorrow, and we've got a minibus hired to take us down. Get there in time for dinner, hang out, have a few drinks, then bed. On Sunday, we do what we want in the morning; play golf, go for a walk, lie in bed, whatever. Then usually there's a discussion in the early afternoon, then exchange presents, back into dinner and drinking. Everyone gets drunk, we all have a brilliant time. And the minibus

177

comes and picks us up on Monday afternoon. What do you think?'

Barney nods, takes a small swig from his pint. Doesn't want to have lager breath.

'And besides,' says Dillinger, realising she's got her man, although not so aware that she knows why, 'you have to come. We need someone to replace The Hammer in the exchange of presents.'

'The Hammer?' asks Barney. Unimpressed.

'He's all right, and he's not coming anyway. But we each pick a name out the hat and have to buy a present for that person. So you'll have to take The Hammer's place.'

And she fishes around in her coat pocket and hands Barney the small piece of paper.

'That'll be yours. I haven't looked at it,' she says.

And Barney takes it, and wonders what on earth he would buy one of these delinquent idiots, and would they kill him if they didn't like the gift and discovered who'd bought it. And so he reluctantly opens up the crinkled piece of paper, reads the name, and that old rubbery face displays nothing.

'Are you in?' she says.

Barney looks up, eyes slightly brighter than before, but otherwise no change to the face. Yet choirs of angels have suddenly broken triumphantly into a chorus of hosannas; a raucous cascade of sparkling fireworks has exploded in the night sky, whites and purples and reds and greens, an orgiastic eruption of colour; a thousand-and-one gun salute has just been fired from the barbican of a magnificent hilltop castle; the gods have risen as one and are cheering Barney's name as if he were one of their own. For Barney has drawn the name Katie Dillinger, and he has his golden opportunity.

'Aye,' he says, sipping nonchalantly from his near full pint. 'Why not?'

✄

Mulholland stares at the bottom of his fifth pint of Tennents. Drinking too much since he got back up to Glasgow, but it's only been two days, and he knows he's pretty close to walking out on McMenemy and his ridiculous search for Barney Thomson. He can head back up north, forget the police, forget Barney, forget McMenemy, forget Erin Proudfoot and her pale face and dream lips, and spend his days up to his waist in bollock-freezing water trying to catch fish that have long since headed down to the African coast for a bit of warmth.

Maybe he'll go on with the counselling, but if he's ditched the police, they won't pay for it any more, and there's no way he'll be able to afford the eight-million-pounds-a-minute fees of Murz and her crew. Maybe he could date Murz and get his counselling for free. She may be fifty and a bit hairier than you'd like in a woman, but there's still something about her.

He delves into the bottom of a packet of crisps and comes up with crumbs. Lifts his glass, stuffs the empty packet back inside and heads to the bar. Elvis on the jukebox. *You saw me crying in my beer* . . . Mulholland can hear him singing.

Quiet pub, doesn't have to wait. A large-breasted barman approaches.

'Pint of Tennents and a packet of salt and vinegar, please, mate,' he says.

And the barman goes about his business, and Mulholland wonders if it wouldn't be better if perhaps he were just to die.

✄

And later on this night, the killer will sit at home and

179

drink beer and eat pizza. And he will watch a video of *Silence of the Lambs*, and he will reckon that Lecter is a complete pussy and that he could take him out with one swish of a knife.

Fava beans, my arse.

25

the stankmonster, the plain jane & the sophie marceau

William Stanton squints up at Barney, as he puts the finishing touches to an exquisite Special Agent Dale Cooper; which will nevertheless leave him a laughing-stock among his mates. Special Agent Dale Coopers are out. Stanton is slightly distracted, even though he is in full flow on one of his pet subjects.

'Aye, I'm telling you, that's what it says these days. And another one. Have you seen it, on the top of milk cartons? A big sticker that says *Keep in Fridge*? I mean, what kind of delinquent Spamhead is that aimed at? Who needs to be told to keep their milk in the fridge? Eh?'

Barney is uninterested. Blizzard reads the paper. Barney shrugs. Stanton attempts to catch his eye.

'Keep in fridge. What a load of pants. You know what that says to me?'

Barney shakes his head. Not really paying attention. Another night has passed when he has awoken screaming. Mind in some sort of turmoil.

'That says that they think I'm a fucking idiot. That's what it says. I'm going to sue, that's what I'm going to do. It is. I'm going to sue them for disparaging my intelligence.'

Blizzard glances over. Barney stands back and surveys the finished product. Hasn't been concentrating, but he knows he's done a good job all the same. This haircut will go far. Reaches for the rear-view mirror and lets the bloke have a look.

Stanton does not pay attention. Accepts the cut, but looks quizzically at Barney. There is recognition in his eye. Perhaps he realises that he may just have had his hair cut by a celebrity. Barney lays down the mirror and starts the decloaking operation.

'Keep away from fire, that's another one,' says Stanton, not even listening to himself. 'On every bit of clothing you get nowadays. Who's that aimed at, eh? *Where will I put this jumper while I'm not wearing it? Em, let me see, in the drawer or in the fire? Em, not sure really.* I mean, for goodness' sake, what a load of shite. Bloody bastards,' he adds, handing over the cash, and regarding Barney with some curiosity.

Barney doesn't notice, heads to the till. Stanton decides to indulge his inquisitiveness.

'Have I seen you before, mate?' he asks, reaching for his coat.

Barney shrugs, turning back to him and handing over the change.

'Probably in the paper. Ah'm Barney Thomson,' he says.

William Stanton nods, takes the change from Barney. Forgets to give him a tip.

'The barber?' he asks.

Barney laughs and indicates the surroundings. Of course he's a bloody barber.

'Aye, but *the* barber?' asks Stanton.

'Aye,' says Barney. 'Ah'm *the* barber. Tried handing masel' in, but they're not interested. Just don't believe Ah am who Ah say. There ye go.'

And he reaches for the brush and starts to clear up. Blizzard takes a little notice, but not much. Reading the personal ads. 'Woman. 65. Moustache and large lump on her face. Weekly change of pants. Likes mince. Seeks barber from Greenock, mid-80s.'

'There you go, who'd have thought it. I've had my hair cut by a legend. Wait till I tell Denise,' says Stanton. 'And did you really murder all those nuns at the weekend, like it says in the paper?'

Barney laughs softly and resignedly again; shrugs his shoulders.

'Do I look as if I murdered any nuns?' he says, looking up.

Stanton shakes his head.

'Suppose not,' he says. 'Suppose not. Right, thanks anyway, mate. Stoatir of a haircut, by the way.'

Barney acknowledges the compliment, and bends once more over his brush. The bell tinkles, and Stanton is gone, out into the mild drudgery of another late December day. Three days before Christmas, and the promise of ill-cheer and untold misery in the air. And presents; lots of presents.

Barney sweeps; Blizzard reads the paper. Barney contemplates the dream of the night before, Blizzard wonders about the exact nature of the big lump on the face of Mrs Clean Weekly Pants.

'Oh, aye, Leyman,' says Barney, looking up. 'Ah nearly forgot. Ye don't mind if Ah nip off a bit early the day, dae ye? This mob Ah've joined are going away for the weekend, ye know, and they asked if Ah wanted tae go wi' them. Ye don't mind, dae ye?'

183

'A weekend, eh? Where're ye off tae?'

'Down south, somewhere, ye know. Jedburgh, Kelso kind of a way.'

Blizzard looks at him. Being deserted by his new friend already. Another night in the pub on his own. All thanks to the lure of womanhood. It's always the same.

'Thinking wi' yer dick, son, are ye?'

Barney doesn't even bother laughing it off. Mind on other things, the dream removing all thoughts of Katie Dillinger, so that he had awoken this morning in quite a different mood from that in which he'd gone to bed.

'Aye,' he says. 'Ah suppose. Ah've got tae buy her a present, 'n' a'. Ah was pleased at the time, but now Ah've no idea what tae get her.'

Blizzard nods and sucks his teeth.

'Can Ah give ye the benefit o' my years o' experience, son?' he asks.

Barney smiles – a sad smile, for he is troubled – and rests on the end of his broom.

'Aye,' he says. 'Go on.'

Blizzard lays down the paper and points at him.

'It doesnae matter what the fuck ye give them. They'll either want tae shag ye, or they won't.'

Barney shakes his head, still smiling. Brilliant.

'Tell ye what ye can dae, son, though. Ah'll tell ye what does work.'

'Go on.'

'They aye open up for a bit o' poetry.'

'Poetry? Get a grip, Leyman. This is the West o' Scotland. She'll think Ah'm a poof.'

Blizzard picks up the paper again and prepares to read about Absolutely Bloody Desperate from Kirkintilloch.

'Ah'm telling ye, son. Poetry's the thing. Give 'em a nice poem, and their legs open up like ye're pulling a

184

zipper. Nae bother. A zipper, Ah say.'

Barney laughs and bends to his work. Poetry. Where's he going to find poetry at this short notice? Unless he is to write it himself.

And before he can even begin to wonder what might rhyme with 'shag you', his mind is once more enveloped by the dark dreams of the night before, and the far-off face of his nemesis.

'You see, there are three kinds of women.'

Barney nods. Gerry Cohn is in full flow.

'There's your common-or-garden stankmonster. There's your Plain Jane. Then there's your no badlooking bit of stuff. You know, your Sophie Marceau or your Uma Thurman. Ah mean, obviously you can subdivide they three categories to an infinite amount, to be fair, but when it comes to it, you've got those basic three.'

Barney nods. He's not in the mood for the Gerry Cohns of the world. His thoughts are still plagued by the remnants of the dream; and every so often he tries to recapture the face which presented itself to him, and when it does not come, he does his best to not think of it, hoping that it might come subconsciously to mind; and when it does not, he concentrates his thoughts upon it, and so it goes on. And thus he leaves his brain in neutral, as Gerry Cohn does his stuff.

'So, what about this lassie you're wanting to shag, then, Big Man? Which of the three does she fit into?'

Barney lets his brain judder into first. Where does Katie Dillinger fit into all of this? Has she some obscure, subconscious part to play in these recurring dreams and his daily dread? Is it all just an equal and opposite reaction to his optimism over the potential of his relationship?

185

'Somewhere between the good looking and the average, Ah suppose,' he says.

'Aye, aye,' says Cohn, 'I know what you mean. Quite often there's cross-pollination between substrata. That concept makes up quite a part of the paper I'm writing on it for my PhD, you know. Usually the movement's between the Plain Jane and the good-looking bit of stuff ones, right enough. You meet some lassie, she looks plain enough. A couple of months later, you've got to know her a bit better, she seems awright, good sense of humour and a' that, and you want into her knickers. All of a sudden she's in the A-band. It's common. Course, it's just yourself who thinks she's a looker, not your mates.'

'Aye,' says Blizzard from behind the *Mirror* – 'Thomson Butchers Cow in Abattoir' – 'but a stankmonster is aye a stankmonster.'

'How right you are, mate,' says Cohn.

Barney slides back into neutral and tries to concentrate on the dream. He is sure that the minister, the haunting spectre on his knees, praying for Barney's soul, had revealed himself at last. He still feels the shock of revelation, greater than the impact of just recognising someone he knows. But when he'd woken, the face was gone, and all that was left was the terrible feeling of dread; of Death at his shoulder.

'You're looking a bit distracted there, Big Man,' says Cohn. 'You're no obsessing about the bird, are you?'

Barney looks down at the head of hair beneath him. The requested John Lennon (*Let it Be*) is already in danger of becoming a John Lennon (*Sergeant Pepper*), and if he's not careful, it could become a John Lennon (*Some Time His Hair Was Really Short*).

He lays the scissors down on the table, and looks

around the shop. Blizzard reads the paper, the back sports page pointed at him. 'Barcelona Tea Lady on Way to Ibrox in Swap Deal with Amaruso.' He runs the final comb through the hair of Gerry Cohn.

'Naw, it's no that,' he says. 'Just been getting bad dreams, ye know. Feel a bit distracted.'

Cohn nods as he views the final effort. Not too bothered about the retro-slide of his Lennon haircut, but glad it hasn't gone any farther.

'Portent of your own death, that kind of thing, mate?'

Barney doesn't even bother being surprised. He hasn't been surprised by anything for a long time now.

'No sure,' he says. 'Might be, might no be. Hard to say.'

'Sure they're no just a rehash o' the day's events?' volunteers Blizzard, placing the paper down on the bench. Likes nothing better than a discussion on the swings and roundabouts of outrageous ontology; the precincts and harvests of metaphysics.

Barney emits a long sigh as he removes the cape from around Cohn's neck.

'Might be, Leyman,' he says, 'but if they are, they're someone else's day's events, no mine. And Ah wouldnae like tae be the poor bastard whose days they are.'

Cohn stands up and admires himself in the mirror. He's into Wee Senga Saddlebag's pants with this napper, no problem.

'Well, you know what they say,' he says, digging no deeper into his pocket than required, 'if it's no a rehash of the day's events, then it's a harbinger of something. And if it ain't good, then it's bad.'

They stare at one another.

'You can quote me on that last one, if you like,' he adds.

187

Robotic, Barney fetches Cohn his coat from the hanger and places it over his shoulder. Why can't dreams be just that? Isn't that allowed? He's had plenty of good dreams, dreams from which he has awoken to find the harsh reality of normal life. None of those bloody dreams were a portent of things to come, so why should the one with Death creeping up at his shoulder ever happen, recurring or not?

'Ah wouldnae worry, Barney,' says Blizzard, 'we're a' a long time old, my friend. Especially me. Ye've got nothing tae be scared of about dying. No just yet.'

Barney nods and thanks Cohn for the meagre tip. Dying? He's never been afraid of dying, and feels even less so now. So what else can it be?

'The unknown,' says Cohn, as he opens the door to the outside, allowing in the cold wind from the Clyde. 'Now there's something to be afraid of. See you, lads.'

And he leaves them staring at the door. Barney wide-eyed and knowing. He has just seen the light; the obscure truth which fits his ill feeling like an old sock.

'What dae ye make o' that?' says Blizzard.

Barney doesn't answer immediately; lifts his brush and attends to the detritus at his feet, still not looking at the floor. Sensing where the hairs are. The brush his light sabre, the hairs evil agents of the Emperor.

Yeah, yeah.

'The man's got a point,' he says after a while, head still down. 'The man's got a point.'

And so taken with the final words of Gerry Cohn have they been that, though they are both staring through the window at the street outside, neither of them notices Sophie Marceau as she walks past, naked from the waist up, on one of her regular shopping trips to Greenock.

26

giant octopus eats mum of five

Barney props his brush up against the wall, turns and surveys the shop, mentally twiddling his thumbs. Early Saturday afternoon, nothing to be done and nothing to be gained. A Mario Van Peebles has just left the shop, and not another customer in sight. Probably pick up later on, but his heart isn't in it. Not today. Contemplating the haunting of his dreams and the paradox of the possibilities of the weekend ahead. The chance to get to know Katie Dillinger better. The infinite potential of the sleeping arrangements. Well, the two possible sleeping arrangements. One where he gets to sleep with her, and one where he doesn't.

And so, on and on, his mind goes. He's noticed some jealous glances from the others when talking to her, and perhaps he won't be the only one looking to make his move. And if he does get anywhere, what then? It's been a long, long time. Will he still remember? Will he still function in all the appropriate places?

This occupies his mind, alongside the overwhelming sense of foreboding. The weekend looms large with promise, but also with apprehension and unease. A group of murderers alone in a house together. It's almost a joke. Why shouldn't he feel unease? In his way, he will be a man apart.

But it is more than that, this feeling which plagues him. Much more.

'Why don't ye leave, son?' says Blizzard.

Barney is plucked from his meandering mind.

'Sorry?'

'Bugger off. Ah can tell ye've got other things on yer mind, so why no just get on? Go home and pack, or whatever ye've got tae dae for yer big night.'

'That'll only take five minutes.'

'Disnae matter, son. Away and buy the bitch her present, or write some magic bit o' poetry. Ah can see yer mind's no on yer work. Cut a wee bit too much off that last yin's hair, did ye no? Bugger off and Ah'll take care o' things. Working wi' you's given me a lot mair confidence. Hope ye noticed Ah gave some bastard a Brad Pitt (*Se7en*) earlier. No bad, eh?'

Barney smiles weakly and nods. He had noticed. It'd been a stinker, but at least Leyman was more relaxed about these things now. So what if it was a stinker; it'd grow back.

'Ye sure?' he says, avoiding comment.

'Aye, aye, of course Ah am. Nae bother. Just bugger off and leave me tae it.'

Barney smiles, genuinely this time. He's a good man, old Leyman, and there's not many of them left.

And so, he grabs his coat and grabs his hat. Turns to face the old man, and as he does so, taking in the shop, he feels the strangest movement up his back and over his shoulders, so that his entire body shivers, and the hairs creep up on his neck. A cold hand grips his spine. He

190

turns quickly, looking around the small silence of the shop. And as quickly as it came, the shiver dies, the feeling subsides. An end to sighs. He looks at the scissors which lie on the table and does not know that he will never lift them again in anger.

He looks up. The shop stares blankly back at him, as does old Blizzard.

'There's a nice card shop up by there, son. Get a blank one, wi' Christmas shite on the front, one o' they old paintings o' Paris in the snow, or some shite like yon. Then stick yer poem in the middle. Something like, *Ye're the fairest girl, a bonnie lass; I want tae shag yer tits and lick yer arse*. Like yon. She'll be gagging for it.'

Barney laughs, shakes his head. With the words, the feeling goes. Back on his own two feet, but still troubled.

'We're closed on Monday, by the way, eh?' he says. 'Christmas Eve?'

'Monday?' says Blizzard, mock exasperation. 'Bloody hell, son, ye've only been here five minutes and already ye're wanting days off tae go out shagging?' And the warm smile returns and the old man laughs wickedly into his beard. 'Aye, course we're closed. Merry Christmas, son. See ye in the boozer when ye get back. Ho fucking ho, eh?'

Barney turns to go, stops and looks back at the old man. A father figure, created almost overnight. The father he never had. And he is swept up by feelings of warmth and sadness and regret, and he knows not from where any of them come. It is almost as if this scene is a waking dream, and there is a brief connection with his nightmare, and it is gone. His thoughts still troubled.

'Thanks, Leyman,' he says.

'Aye, son, now away and bugger off. Ah'm no in need o' nursing.'

'Merry Christmas.'

'Load o' shite, son, but the same tae you.'

Barney smiles again, turns and is gone. Blizzard watches him go, shakes his head, then lifts the paper. 'Giant Octopus Eats Mum of Five.'

And strangely enough, Barney closes the door behind him and bends his head into the wind at just exactly the moment when Detective Sergeant Best, the recipient of the Mario Van Peebles – watching over the shop and waiting for reinforcements – is forced to answer the call of nature.

✂

Just after midday. Another day into December, another degree off the temperature, but still the day is grey and mild and bleak and nothing. The sort of day for sitting in a pub drinking copious amounts of alcohol. Although sometimes it can seem like every day is for that, no matter what the weather, no matter what there is in life. It's like that. You've got to have something to look forward to, or you might as well spend your time looking at the dregs in a glass, or staring at a silent fishing line, or parked in front of crap TV. There has to be some focus; and when you're a policeman, you've got a huge murder case in front of you, and you're still not focused, you're losing the point.

Mulholland has had the brass section from *Stop the Cavalry* playing in his head all day. Dah-de-dah-de-dum-dum ... dah-de-dah-de-dum ... And on it goes and he's given up trying to get rid of it. He taps the beat out softly on the side of his glass with his wedding ring; drains the dregs of his second pint of lager. Sort of starting at Proudfoot's hands, sort of thinking of how those hands have ventured to several of the most inti-mate parts of his body – he thinks this because men can't help but think of sex every two and a half seconds – sort of thinking about getting another round in, sort of thinking about the case.

He knows he's not giving much lead to the investigation, but then how is he supposed to when the lead he's being given is so hopelessly off the mark? Does M seriously believe that they should be after Barney Thomson? Maybe M himself is the serial killer, that might explain it. Maybe he should indeed be after Barney Thomson, but just doesn't want to accept it because he had him in his grasp last year and decided to let him go.

He shakes his head, rubs his forehead. He ought to just get out, leave it to someone who can do a better job. He's just wasting everybody's time. There must be some young go-getter left in the force who would like to run with it, and resents the buggery out of Mulholland for having been brought back.

There are always issues, that's the thing. Everyone has their own issues. M has his, whatever they are, in looking for Barney; he himself has his own in not looking for him. Whoever else gets brought into the investigation will have their own angle. Everyone has an angle.

'You think I did the right thing?' he says into the space which has been devoid of conversation for some ten minutes. 'Letting him go?'

'You're speaking, then?' says Proudfoot, dragged from her own melancholia. 'Thought the next time you opened your mouth it would be to offer up the next round.'

'Driving,' he says.

'Oh, aye, where're we going, then?'

Their eyes engage, and when he can't think of a reply she looks back into her drink and watches the bubbles rise slowly to the surface. Her mood a combination of being sucked into his gloom and the realisation that she does not want what she's asked for this past year. She doesn't want to be back in the saddle after all, she doesn't want to have to be spending her Saturday evening on suspect-watch, she doesn't want any of it; and so now she has no clue what she wants. Mulholland? Does she want back into the turbulence of that? Fighting one minute, wanting to get married the next. Except there's no fight left in either of them.

'Probably not,' she says, finally answering his question. 'Seemed like a good idea at the time, but it just means we're having to look for him now.'

'D'you think he might be the killer?'

She shrugs and runs her fingers around the top of the glass. There would have been a time when the action was laced with sexual tension between the two; now it's just something to do for a few seconds. Mulholland stares at her hands.

'No,' she says, shortly. 'But if he was locked up, or appearing on chat shows, or whatever, we wouldn't have to be chasing him now, would we? We might be able to concentrate on the real guy, not some two-bit jessie who can't even stick a fork into a mushroom without feeling guilty.'

Mulholland's shoulders drop another micro-inch. That was about the size of it. It'd been a good idea at the time, but now they were lumbered with it. There was someone out there to be caught and their hands were tied.

He becomes aware of the television playing quietly in the background, a few desperate souls at the bar watching. The early afternoon news, a report on the hunt for this year's serial killer. It drifts through the usual details, including a review of all the murders, an overview of the suspects (total – one), and a rundown of the key police officers involved. Mulholland looks away when he sees his own face on the screen, accompanied by McMenemy's words that his men are on it twenty-four hours a day.

'Macaroon bars.'

He can feel a few pairs of eyes on him from the bar; can imagine the thought processes going on within those heads.

'Macaroon bars. Get your macaroon bars here. Macaroon bars.'

He glances at Proudfoot, but she hasn't even noticed. Takes a quick look up and catches the eye of a woman sitting at the bar, already staring at him. Imagines there's something accusatory in her look, so turns away. Fuck 'em. It's McMenemy's problem. He can spout all he likes, but when he's got his force looking for completely the wrong man, then it might as well be a gazillion of them on the case for two gazillion hours a day, they're still not going to catch the real killer.

'Macaroon bars!' says the macaroon bar salesman, walking through the pub. A little more feeling this time. He carries a full box of macaroon bars, and has been walking the streets and pubs of Glasgow for nearly two hours now. 'Macaroon bars, get your macaroon bars here!'

The landlord gives him the once-over, decides not to eject him. These fly-by-night macaroon bar salesmen come and go with the wind; and it's not as if they take any of his crisps and peanut business, wouldn't even if they were to sell anything. Which they never do.

Mulholland can't help but hold the gaze of the woman at the bar. Evelyn McLaughlin, as it happens; on the lookout for a certain type of man. He gets a strange feeling that something is about to happen; a peculiar and

195

vague sense of foreboding. He stares at her for a little while longer, but her expression is blank, the eyes give nothing away. Mid-twenties perhaps. Black hair, waxed eyebrows, intensifying the apparent *Culloden* look which might lie beneath the banality of the stare. Banal and bellicose at the same time; Mulholland never has been much good at working out women.

'Macaroon bars! Get your macaroon bars here!'

He looks around the bar, trying to identify the possible origin of the unease he is feeling. Proudfoot stares into her drink, the customers – Evelyn McLaughlin excepted – drink their pints and watch TV and talk aimlessly of momentous topics, while the macaroon bar salesman plies his trade in ever-increasing, powerless frustration.

'Macaroon bars! Get your macaroon bars here! Macaroon bars!'

Mulholland toys with his drink, unable to pick the source of his disquiet, finally lifting the near-empty glass to his mouth to finish it off. He becomes aware of Evelyn McLaughlin approaching, waxed eyebrows in full flow. He warily looks at her as she comes to rest beside him. Proudfoot gives her the time of day, seeing as she's got nothing else to think about.

'Macaroon bars! Get your macaroon bars here! Some cunt buy one. Macaroon bars!'

'Here,' says McLaughlin, as the macaroon bar salesman grudgingly gives up the ghost, barely giving enough time for the quality of his advertising campaign to take hold, and makes his way out into the street, 'you that bastarding polis that's just been on the telly?'

Mulholland looks at her, a quick appraisal to see if there might be a knife or some other implement tucked away in the foliage of her clothing. A tight red dress, nothing much showing except the usual array of fat.

He nods his head. A subdued sense of ill feeling all because he's about to get subjected to a volley of verbal abuse from some brain-dead thicko.

'Well, how come ye're no out catching that bloody Barney Thomson, then, ya bampot? This you on it twenty-four hour a day, is it? Magic that, i'n't it no? Sitting in a fucking boozer wi' yer bit o' skirt and a pint o' heavy?'

'It's lager.'

'Lager? Well, that's awright, then, i'n't it, ya polis bastard.'

She places her hands on her hips and they stare one another out. Proudfoot contemplates the thought of being Mulholland's bit of skirt, and decides she couldn't care less. She's been called worse.

'That all ye've got tae say for yersel', ya bastard?'

'Just about,' he says.

She snorts, pig-like. Very, very attractive.

'Anyway,' she goes on, 'that's no why Ah'm here. Ah don't really give a shite whether ye catch that wank or no. Ah mean, Ah'd be delighted for him tae kill maist o' the bastards Ah know.'

'Kind words,' says Mulholland. 'I'm glad you appreciate that the average police officer needs some serious thinking time.'

'Aye, right, ya bastard. Anyway, what Ah'm really here for is tae say that me and my mate Elsie have got a bet on about who can shag mair folk off the telly by Christmas. That bitch is about six aheid o' me, seeing as she shagged the entire Motherwell team in the space o' a couple o' hours. So, seeing as ye've just been on the box, Ah wis wondering if ye'd like tae shag me, or whit. Ah mean, Ah'm no interested in foreplay or orgasms or any o' yon shite. Two seconds' penetration'll dae, and ye're in my book. We could go intae the bog, and ye'll be back here wi' yer miserable bird in less than a minute.'

Mulholland almost smiles; first time in months.

'This is my wife, I'm afraid. Can't do it.'

'Yer missus? This soor-faced pudding? Ah could give ye a much better time, even if it was only for two seconds. Ah bet she hasnae shagged ye in about six months.'

Good guess, thinks Proudfoot; damn near spot on. And she nods.

'See what Ah mean? Nae wonder ye're a miserable cunt, married tae a pun o' mince like this. Come wi' me, Big Man, and Ah'll show ye a good time. Suck a melon through a straw, me. Throat like a vacuum cleaner.'

Mulholland smiles and nods.

'Put like that, hen, I'm tempted. Twenty-four hours a day, though, that's me. Always on the job. Couldn't even spare you that two seconds.'

'Aye, well, whatever. Think ye're full o' shite, whatever ye say. When ye find yon bastard and ye've got mair time on yer hands, then give us a call. Having said that, don't bother if it's after Christmas, 'cause ye're an ugly bastard.'

And so the lounge bar überchick makes her way back to her Bacardi Breezer, and Mulholland can continue the great weight of thought needed to decide if he should get in another round.

'She's got you pegged,' says Proudfoot.

'Watch it, Sergeant.'

The door to the bar swings open, then rocks closed behind the weight of Detective Sergeant Ferguson. He approaches Mulholland, eyeing up the vixen in red as he does so.

'Nice bit o' stuff at the bar,' he says, arriving at the table.

198

They view him as they might a small child.

'You used to police the Thistle home games decades ago when they were still a decent enough outfit and used to get on the telly, didn't you?' says Mulholland.

'Aye, why?'

'Oh, no reason. What is it that brings you steaming into the bar?'

'The boss is just about to get a round in, if that's why you're here,' says Proudfoot.

'A round? Wouldnae mind a pint, but Ah think we better get a move on. There's been a sighting o' Barney Thomson. Some geezer phoned in tae say he'd had his hair cut by the bloke in a wee shop in Greenock.'

Mulholland lets out a long sigh and shakes his head.

'No news of the real killer, then?' he says.

Proudfoot grabs her bag and coat. Something to do at last, although she feels no hint of tension or excitement. So what if they've found Barney Thomson, she thinks; as does Mulholland.

Out they go, into the grey gloom of early afternoon. Mulholland can smell the cigarette smoke from his jacket; he can taste the bitter remnants of the lager on his tongue. Beginning to need to go to the toilet. The ordinary scene around them as he gets into the passenger seat of Ferguson's car seems less ordinary today. It is somehow challenged, as if at odds with itself. But really, it is he who is at odds with it, and the weight of the world sits uneasily on his shoulders. There is something not quite right. Some weird Jungian thing going on. (That'll be Freddie Jung, used to play outside right for Stenhousemuir.)

'What's the score, then, Sergeant?' he says.

Ferguson cuts up the only Rover 75 sold in the last six months, and pulls out into the flow of traffic.

199

'Bloke goes in for a haircut, an Agent Cooper, apparently.'

'That's a little more information than I needed, Sergeant.'

'Ah'm setting the scene.'

'I know what a sodding barbershop looks like.'

'So, the guy goes in for his Agent Cooper. Not the film version Agent Cooper, but the TV show Agent Cooper.'

'Thought it was the same?' says Proudfoot, already beginning to doze in the back.

'Whatever, Ah'm just reporting what Ah was told. Ah never watched that shite. Anyway, the bloke does a good job. The guy thinks he recognises him, asks him who he is, and he quite happily admits to being Barney Thomson.' Mulholland gives a sideways glance. 'So, he goes home and calls the local Feds. They're a keen lot, and obviously wi' nothing better tae dae, so they send one o' their plods along tae get his napper seen tae. So the guy gets his hair cut by Thomson, asks him a few questions, and again he readily admits tae who he is. Which, let's face it, ties in wi' the fact that he was giving himself up a' over the shop. So the plod leaves wi' a stoatir o' a haircut – a Mario Van Peebles, no less – and waits outside for the cavalry.'

Ferguson steams through the traffic, towards the confines of the westbound M8.

'So, have the locals moved in?'

Ferguson snorts.

'Have they bollocks. They're a' shitting their breeks, which is fair enough. Waiting for you two, by the sounds o' it. They're watching the shop, waiting tae see if he makes a move.'

'So he doesn't know they're on to him?'

'Doesnae know shite.'

200

Mulholland shakes his head, then winces and extends his braking foot as Ferguson nearly drives into the back of a green Peugeot.

'What are they going to do,' says Mulholland, once they are back in the clear, shooting up the middle lane of a dual carriageway, 'if he makes a move before we get there? Cake their pants and see if the Scouts can follow the guy?'

Ferguson shrugs. Got a couple of mates on the force down there. All in it together. Can tell that Mulholland is no longer a team man; if, indeed, he is anything at all.

'Cannae blame them, really,' he says. 'That Thomson's a murderous bastard. Mad as fuck, they say.'

'He's a big poof.'

'He's still a mad bastard.'

'If he's mad, it's only because we won't leave him in peace to cut hair. And all the time we shit our pants about this guy, and go careering off across the country looking for him, the real killer is pishing himself laughing at us wasting our time. There's better things to be doing than this, Sergeant, and the local bloody plods can't even be bothered their arse going in and arresting him.'

'What about you!' says Ferguson, as he heads slowly up the slip road onto the motorway. 'You were sitting in the pub.'

'Shut up, Sergeant. I get enough lip from this one,' he says, indicating the back of the car.

They both glance behind. Proudfoot's head is resting uncomfortably against the rear window. She sleeps, the smile of the curiously perturbed on her face.

They turn back and Ferguson accelerates into the midst of the flow. And off they go in search of Barney

Thomson, to the exact little barbershop on the edge of Greenock where he has been working this past week; and which he walked out of some half-hour earlier.

27

been going down this road so long

The car pulls into the side of the road. Apart from the twenty or so grown men and women secreted in inadequate hiding places or attempting to blend in with the crowd, it is a perfectly normal afternoon scene. A grey day, the suggestion of rain, cars coming and going, pedestrians doing their thing.

Ferguson has had the heat up higher than necessary, the music down low. Proudfoot has slept soundly; Mulholland has stared dumbly at the passing grey day, contemplating his bank account. Can he afford to jack in the job and spend his days fishing? A life on the river-bank, watching the water trundle by, bugs buzzing above the water, and fish nibbling at the surface, has got to be worth the trade-off of having no money coming in. He's been in the service for fifteen years, so there'd be something of a pay-off from this bloody lot. Eat the fish he catches. Go out all day and so use few utilities. Nae mates, family all gone to the big football terrace in the sky, so no phone calls. He could live on buttons.

But then there is the issue – and it is an issue – of

Proudfoot. Can he bring himself to leave her again? Ought he not really to ask her to come with him? They could argue on a permanent basis. They could wind each other up. They could enrage each other, and press all the other's buttons. They could drive one another to the point of violence. All that, and they could have masses of sex.

Ferguson turns off the engine. Springsteen is cut off in mid-stride; the last line and sudden silence filter through to Mulholland. He snaps from his myth of El Dorado; a fish, some fourteen pounds at least, snapping frantically on the end of his line, Proudfoot saying not bloody fish again for dinner. He looks at the sergeant, glances behind at their sleeping beauty.

'*I'd drive all night again just to buy you some shoes?*' he says to Ferguson. 'You don't half listen to some amount of shite, Sergeant.'

Ferguson shrugs. 'Always thought it was quite poignant, masel'.'

'Poignant? You? You wouldn't know poignant if it bit your arse. You thought it was poignant when Alan Rough played his last game for Scotland.'

'Ah'm hurt,' says Ferguson.

'I bet you are,' says Mulholland. He turns round and taps Proudfoot on the leg. Gets that mild shock from physical contact. A remnant of the past, or the underlying flicker of interest. He ignores it. 'Wake up, Sergeant, the evil monster awaits.'

Proudfoot stirs, drags herself uneasily from her dreams of disembodied hands and midnight killers.

'Right,' she says, taking in the surroundings. 'I'm on it.'

They get out of the car, another three Feds to add to the ever-increasing collection. There are some in uniform, crouching behind cars; some in plainclothes milling around, pretending to look in shop windows, mingling with the crowd, yet still standing out a mile. And that crowd continues to grow, as grandstanders and gloaters add to the throng. Something they can tell their grandchildren about might well be on the verge of happening.

'You know who's in charge?' asks Mulholland.

'Ye see,' replies Ferguson, 'Ah've never been sure about it. Is it that he's driven a' night once before tae buy her some shoes, and he's saying he'd do it again? Or is it that the last time he drove all night it was for some completely different article o' clothing, and he's saying that he'd also be prepared tae dae it tae buy her shoes. Ah'm no so sure. What dae ye think, Erin?'

'You talking about Springsteen?'

'Aye.'

'I think he's a wank. I'd shag him, mind.'

Mulholland stops and holds up his hands.

'Would the two of you shut the fuck up? Who's in charge, Sergeant?'

Ferguson smiles and flicks open the notebook. It's that DCI thing, where they're obliged to be impatient and surly with their sergeant. None of them did it before Morse came on the telly.

'An Inspector Hills.'

'Thank you. You may continue your discussion.'

Mulholland approaches the nearest uniform lurking behind a car, surveying the situation as he goes. The small barber's shop is directly across the road, the view inside largely obscured by a blind.

He aims his badge at the uniform. 'Inspector Hills?' he says. No mood for civility.

Constable Starkey, a woman of some infinite depth, completely wasted on her chosen profession, indicates two men standing outside the door of a small grocer's, pretending to be interested in tomatoes. And Mulholland turns away without a word.

'Hills?' he says, approaching.

'Aye,' says the taller of the two. A good man; honest face, broad shoulders, firm handshake. Someone to rely on in a crisis. 'Graeme Hills. You must be Chief Inspector Mulholland?'

'Aye.' He briefly contemplates introducing his sergeants into the fold, but decides not to bother. This isn't going to take very long. 'What's the score, then, mate?'

'Got the report an hour or two ago,' says Graeme Hills, arms crossed. 'The guy seemed fairly certain it was him. We got one of our men to go to the shop, on a purely customer-orientated basis. Got a lovely Mario Van Peebles off the bloke, by the way. Anyway, it's Barney Thomson all right. Talked quite openly about it. Our man said he seemed almost sad.'

Mulholland breathes deeply. Looks across at the shop. Can't be bothered with any of this.

'So why didn't he arrest him?'

Hills does a thing with his eyebrows.

'We're talking Barney Thomson here, mate. Our guy was alone and under strict instruction to wait for back-up.'

Mulholland nods. Fair enough, perhaps. He'd had his own reservations about Thomson until he'd discovered his true nature. However, that doesn't excuse everything, he thinks, looking at the accumulated masses.

'And what do these three or four hundred officers represent, if not back-up?'

Hills does something with his mouth, shrugs his shoulders.

'We're not armed. We thought it best to wait for you, seeing as you've direct experience of the bloke. Got the place covered. Can't really see into the shop properly, but there's no way he's getting out without us getting him.'

'I'm not armed, either,' says Mulholland.

Hills does something with his cheeks.

'That's your call, Chief Inspector. You know how to deal with him. We've got no experience of him.'

Mulholland gives him his best Morse face. Waste of bloody time, he thinks.

'So why haven't you got this road closed off, if you think he's so dangerous?'

Hills points up and down the road in a completely aimless gesture. 'And alert him to us?' he says. 'He knows nothing of us being here. We're sharp, discreet and smooth. There could be three hundred polis out here and he wouldn't have a clue. My officers blend in like trees in a forest. They're the SAS. They're the Pink Panther. They're Pierce Brosnan in *The Thomas Crown Affair*. They're Sean Connery in *Entrapment*. We can move in and get him any time.'

Mulholland continues to look unhappy; Ferguson nods in a 'seems reasonable' gesture; Proudfoot looks across the road at the shop, wondering if it really is Barney Thomson in there. Why should this be any different from any other hoax they've had in the past year?

Mulholland shakes his head and turns to Ferguson. 'Right, Sergeant, me and Proudfoot will go in, you wait just outside the shop in case he makes a break for it. Your discreet Pink Panther-type unarmed, scared heroes got the back covered, Inspector?'

'Of course,' says Hills.

'Brilliant. Right, let's go.'

'But you're not armed,' says Hills to Mulholland as he walks away. 'Shouldn't you wait for some armed back-up?'

Mulholland looks over his shoulder.

'Have you called any?' he says.

'Well, no,' says Hills.

And Mulholland shrugs and steps out into the road, saying, 'Come on, Sergeant, you joining me, or are you just going to stand there gawping at the pavement?' to Proudfoot as he goes.

Proudfoot wanders a few steps behind, taking oblique notice of the traffic. Face to face, once again, with Barney Thomson. She remembers a year earlier heading north to hunt for him, full of fears and trepidation and terror. And now . . . now she vaguely wonders what she's going to have for dinner.

Hills watches them go. He's heard tales of Mulholland and Proudfoot; great odysseys that paint them mad as hell. And here's confirmation. Walking unarmed into the lion's den, the stench of alcohol on their breath. These maverick cops are all alike.

✂

The door to the shop opens; Blizzard looks up as the man and woman enter. Man with a great shag of black hair, and might well be here for a cut. No idea about the woman. But he can tell that this is not business; at least, not his business.

'Ye're not fucking consultants, are you?' says Blizzard, with a casual charm.

Mulholland shakes his head and produces his badge. Proudfoot looks around, and realises that she's never before been inside a barbershop. Then it occurs to her that she couldn't care less about it, and stares at the old man. And they both notice the obvious absence of anyone

208

remotely resembling Barney Thomson.

'Polis,' says Mulholland to back up the badge. 'We're looking for Barney Thomson.'

Blizzard grumps.

'Thought you'd be by eventually,' he says. 'The lad buggered off about forty minutes ago. I noticed your lot gathering outside like a pack of hyenas. Stupid wankers. Anyway, he's gone till after Christmas.'

Mulholland's shoulders drop another inch or two. Proudfoot switches off. It's still the same old story.

'Who the fuck are you?' says Mulholland, vaguely annoyed at the old man; can't think why.

'Blizzard,' says Blizzard. 'Leyman Blizzard. And don't talk tae me like that, or Ah'll kick yer arse.'

'So if you had Barney Thomson working in your shop, why didn't you report it?'

Blizzard sits back in his seat. Straightens his shoulders. Always hated the polis.

'What was the point? He's a nice enough bloke, and there's no way he's the killer yese are looking for. And besides, he's tried handing himsel' in and yese wernae interested. And you just watch yer tone, laddie.'

Mulholland has no argument. Barney is not the killer they're looking for, no question. And the police do look stupid turning up here, mob-handed, to arrest the man when he's already tried to hand himself in and been turned away. Good thing the public in general don't know about it.

'Where'd he go? Where does he live?'

'He's away for the weekend somewhere. Don't know where. Why don't yese just leave the bastard alone?'

And Joel Mulholland stands and stares at the floor, at exactly the same mark as Erin Proudfoot, and neither of them can think of an answer. Why don't they just leave him alone? And why don't they just walk away from this bloody stupid investigation?

And old Leyman Blizzard says nothing, and waits for them to go.

210

28

now ye need not fear the grave

Mulholland has refused to sit. Knows what is coming, already aware of what is in his head to do. McMenemy is on the prowl, stalking the few yards between his desk and the window, head bent to the ground, looking at the pattern of the carpet. Trying to control his burgeoning rage. Eyebrows knotted together, teeth set hard. A man on the verge of a verbal explosion.

Mulholland is not far off the same.

'Will you sit down, Chief Inspector?' McMenemy barks one more time. 'Sit down!'

Mulholland purses his lips.

'I'm not staying,' he says dryly, teeth gritting.

McMenemy stops his endless backwards and forwards charge and engages his eye. The Klingon warbird decloaked and about to unleash photon torpedoes. Of course, those Klingon warbirds are pussies.

'Damned right you're not staying! Damned right. You let the man go from right under your nose. My God! He's a monster and he roams our streets free, because of you! You had him in his shop and you let him go!'

Mulholland moves forward and presses his hand against the desktop.

'He was gone by the time I got there. It was the bloody local plods who let him go. And you know why? They were so shit scared of him because of the press and the likes of you, making the guy out to be a shit lot more than he actually is. Watch my lips, sir. He's not the killer.'

McMenemy points a finger, arm outstretched, from no more than three yards across the desk.

'Don't you "watch my lips" at me, my boy. This is it for you, Sergeant Mulholland. You can report for front desk duty on Monday morning, and consider yourself lucky you're not busted all the way down. You should be plodding the damned streets for your incompetence.'

'*I'm* incompetent? You're the arsehole chasing after a big, mild-mannered bloody jessie!'

McMenemy's pointing finger wilts a little. His nostrils flare. Eyes widen, then slowly narrow as he lowers his arm. From the side of the room comes the low hum of the fish tank. Cars outside cruise at forty-five in a thirty zone. There is a distant tantrum of a Salvation Army brass band breaking heartily into 'Good Christian Men, Rejoice', and the tune starts playing in Mulholland's head. Aware of his own breathing; can hear McMenemy's breath, thick and clogged through his nose, lips clenched shut.

Now ye hear of endless bliss, Jesus Christ was born for this ...

'What did you just call me?'

The words snap out into the room. Cold, short, violent.

McMenemy pulls his shoulders back and stares at Mulholland, waiting for the answer. Not the answer as such; waiting for an apology. But Mulholland does not quail. The word was so easily said. He has had enough, and it is time to go. And if you're going to go, you might as well be Al Pacino in *And Justice for All* ...

He takes another step towards him, and places both hands on the desktop. Leans closer.

'I called you an arsehole. And you know what, Chief Superintendent? You know what? I was right. You are an arsehole.'

Straightens up, waiting to see the reaction. Had rolled the word *arsehole* around his tongue, as if it were a Cuban cigar. If you're going to burn your bridges, you might as well do it properly. So, in fact, he's not finished.

McMenemy rises to his full, intimidatory height. A good six three in his socks, and no mistake. Looks down on him, face begins to snarl. An easy-going man, really, turned to madness.

'Get out of my office, Mr Mulholland, and get out of my station. You're finished, boy. Absolutely finished. I should have listened to Geraldine Cunningham. You're a useless waste of space. A has-been. You might as well have died in the monastery last year, 'cause you're good for nothing. Get out, get out! And do not darken the door of this station again. Do you hear me?'

Mulholland starts to turn, but he has been given even freer rein than he thought he had. Points a finger himself, but more after the manner of a defensive back who's just sacked the quarterback.

'You know what you can do?' he says.

'Get out, right now, before you make this even worse,' says McMenemy.

'You know what you can do?' Mulholland repeats. 'You can fuck your job.' Starting to warm to his subject. A few steps away from the desk, pointing at his boss. His ex-boss. Getting serious, annoyed, flustered, excited. A great weight of frustration and anger to burn off before he walks out for the last time.

'Get out!'

'What are you going to do?' he says, starting to laugh. 'Call the police? Eh? Is that it, you stupid, ignorant bastard? Well, you can fuck your job. And you know what else? You can fuck you, and fuck the station. And you can fuck your post of chief inspector. You can fuck Glasgow, fuck Barney fucking Thomson, fuck the real fucking killer, and you can stick your fucking job up your fucking fuckhole, you stupid fucking fuckbag. All of that stuff. Fuck it all.'

Final words uttered in triumph, a small piece of spit sent flying through the air in front of him. And McMenemy stands and stares, and strangely the anger is gone, and slowly he sinks down into his seat. And when he speaks again the voice is low and cold, and filled more fully with malice than at any time in the past twenty years.

'Leave, please. Now. And be assured, Chief Inspector, that this matter is not over.'

Mulholland breathes heavily. Face flushed. Loved every second of it. Knows from past experience that his voice will have travelled out from within these walls. He will be a hero! Word will spread, and they will all know him as the brave visionary he most certainly is. Either that, or the stupid, burned-out idiot.

'Yes it is,' he says in a low voice, and turns to the door. Quick snatch at the handle, door open, and he is gone out into the wide world of the station, where business goes on as usual for a Saturday afternoon, and a few look at him as he goes by, and care not whether they ever see him again

Walking quickly to get away from it all, and within half a minute Joel Mulholland is outside in the mild but bleak midwinter. A hint of rain in the air and he pulls his jacket close to him.

Stops and takes a moment. Turns and looks back up at the old building and immediately starts to think of Erin Proudfoot. And so, as he begins to wander the streets aimlessly, contemplating his new life, he can do little but think of her and what she will be doing as he slides rapidly into the oblivion that awaits him.

part 2
i'll be your buzz lightyear

1

on córdoba's sorry fields

The minibus travels the slow roads of the Borders bereft of first, second and fourth gears, all of which departed in a robust judder somewhere south of Peebles; so that every time they come to a tight bend, the driver can go no lower than third, and the bus shudders round the corner in a series of vibrations and jerks, spilling drinks and causing general mayhem with elaborate hairstyles; while providing those women bedecked in tight underwear a little more pleasure than they would otherwise have anticipated.

The rain comes down in great crashing torrents, and Bobby Ramsey leans forward and peers into the dead of night. Only seven thirty, as he heads towards the final short stretch of labyrinthine turns and convolutions, but it is black all around them. Occasionally a dark grey hill is evident against the night; a light in a farmhouse window set back from the road; and rarely another vehicle passing them in the opposite direction, for no one is going where they are going.

Barney has sat in silence on the way south, staring dolefully at the sight of Arnie Medlock, making moves – he assumes he's making moves – on Katie Dillinger.

He'd hoped to get the seat next to her, but he hadn't had the confidence to breenge in and take control of the situation. And so he had dithered, Arnie had won the prime seat, and Barney had ended up next to Bobby Dear, the wealthy accountant type, from whom Barney has never heard a word.

So he has stewed in his own jealousy, attempting to hear above the roar of the diesel engine and the conversation of the others what is being said. Feels ridiculously like a spurned lover, even though he has no claim on this woman. Can imagine himself doing a variety of vicious things to Medlock, even though he had, until an hour ago, thought him to be a perfectly pleasant bloke. Yet he cannot be all that pleasant, or he would not be part of this group. Barney cannot see himself as one of the others; does not even consider that some of them might be as feckless as he himself.

He looks out at the rain and the passing hedges and walls and trees, beyond which the darkness holds its secrets. He has been contemplating engaging Dear in conversation, but for all the mild-mannered-accountant demeanour to the man, he can recognise the killer's guise that lurks behind that kind face. Still, he joined the group to talk to this kind of person, not to become embroiled in romance. That's an entirely unexpected subsidiary element.

As the minibus lurches around another corner he can see and hear Dillinger laughing, then leaning towards Medlock and whispering something in his ear, which has them both heaving with hilarity.

Barney seethes. Feels that strange anger and discomfort that comes with envy and suspicion, and which has replaced his nervousness over the weekend's potential, and the foreboding brought on by the premonition of his own wake.

220

Bites the bullet.

'Nightmare weather,' he says, nodding. Looks at Bobby Dear to see if it's registered. Dear, only slowly, becomes aware that he is being addressed.

'Talking to me?' he says at last. A Piccadilly Scot by the sounds of it, thinks Barney. Has heard tell of such creatures, but you don't get many of them in Partick.

'Aye,' says Barney. 'Nightmare weather.'

Bobby Dear stares at him. Has something of the comfortable, cardiganed Richard Briers about him. Except, of course, that these days Richard Briers is as likely to play a bad guy. So behind Dear's placid exterior lurks a heart of pure evil, thinks Barney.

'You think this is bad?' says Dear. 'You should have seen it in the Falklands in '82. Makes this look like the desert. And we had the Argies shooting at us.'

'Soldier, eh?' says Barney. Sharp as a button.

'Commissioned, if you don't mind,' says Dear. 'Was a lieutenant-colonel in the Highland Fusiliers. Bloody murder that campaign, bloody murder.'

Says *lieutenant* like an American. Barney doesn't notice. Already wishing he hadn't opened his mouth. Wondering at the Pandora's box he might just have opened up for himself. What if he gets stuck with the bloke all weekend? Two complete days of old soldier's stories. Oh ... my ... God.

'What happened?' asks Barney. Knows from experience that you have to attempt to keep control of the conversation. Ask questions, and try to take the talker in the direction in which you want him to go. *What happened*, he thinks, mapping out the questions in his head, followed by *How did you get here*, and then *What can you tell me about Katie*, because he could talk about her all night.

221

'What do you mean, what happened? We won, you idiot. Kicked some Argie arse, boy. Didn't you watch the news?'

Barney feels stupid. Wonders how he can impress upon him what he'd actually meant by the question, but then can't think what that was.

'So how did ye get here, then?' he asks, attempting to regain the control he's lost by the previous question.

Bobby Dear breathes in deeply and Barney waits for another verbal assault. Out of the corner of his eye he can see Dillinger's mouth no more than an inch from Medlock's ear, lips moist, and he wishes he could cut that ear off, violently and painfully.

The bus swerves around an unexpectedly tight corner; Billy Hamilton 'accidentally' sways into Annie Webster's lap, his hand brushes her thigh, and both receive a quick pulse of excitement.

'Damn fool question,' says Dear, 'but I might as well give you an answer. Your lot are always too bloody thick to work these things out for yourselves. A bit mundane, I'm afraid, compared to some of these stories the others come out with. Reckon most of them are making it up, mind. Couple of these blokes have never killed anything other than time. That's what I think. And you yourself, I suppose, your story's pretty fantastic, if you are who you say you are, and half the things you read in the paper are true.'

'They're not.'

'Dandy. Glad to hear it. Thought it was a load of Argie's bollocks. Anyway, I met a girl in the seventies. Usual thing. Eyes like pools, voice like an angel, tits like the Himalayas and a plum duff sweeter than a toffee apple. Brains too, apparently, that's what they all said, though I never spotted them myself. You can lead a woman to water, but you can't make her think, that's what I always say. Anyway, married her, of course, because that's what you did back then. Nowadays they just screw 'em and spend the next eighteen years dodging the CSA. No, no, that wasn't for me. Did the right thing. Made an honest woman of her. Showed her a thing or two, 'n' all, I reckon. No question. Showed her the world, yes indeed. Germany, Cyprus, even managed to get her down to Egypt for a month or two. Showed her the world.'

Barney's mouth drops open a little. He can tell. He might possibly just have made the biggest mistake of his entire life. He has turned the key, and opened up this great sarcophagus of tedium, a momentous Ark of the Covenant of monotony, a humungous golden chest of dreary wonders. He could be here for days. He could be stuck listening to this bloke for ever. He could die.

'Know what she did? I went off to fight for Queen and country. Didn't really agree with it myself, did I? I mean, it was that bloody woman engaging in flagrant electioneering, let's face it. Handed over Hong Kong easy enough, didn't she? I mean, who gives a stallion's bollocks about the bollocking Falklands, but off we went, poles up our arse, to fight for justice and all that bollocking nonsense. Anyway, while I was away fighting the evil horde, the bloody woman screws my best mate, Old Jock McAllister. The wife, I mean, not Thatcher. I get back and she tells me she's leaving me for the old soak. Pissed off, I don't mind telling you, I was pissed off.'

'So you killed them?'

'Bloody right, Barney Thomson, bloody right. Bullet in the back of the napper for them both. Deserved everything they got. Waited for the RMPs, and handed over my revolver. Wore my Union Jack boxers throughout,

223

'cause I did it for the Queen just as much as I shot all those bleeding Argies. And let me tell you, I shot a few of them.'

Barney's eyes have glazed over. Maybe this is it. Maybe this is why he's had that grave sense of foreboding. Because he's going to be stuck for the rest of his life listening to this man. Could be he'll start inviting himself round for tea in the evenings; coming in for a haircut; coming along to the pub. God, Leyman will be cheesed off.

But the future has other things in store for Barney Thomson, and the minibus jumps and stalls and jolts to a halt. Dear stops mid-flow, in the middle of a description of what he'd said to his wife as an explanation for her murder. Other conversations come to a premature end and a few tired or bored heads are lifted.

The minibus has stopped in a large driveway facing the house that will be their home for the next two nights, and each of them gazes with curiosity at what is betrayed to them by the headlight's beam.

Bloody hell, thinks Barney. Just like *Psycho*, thinks Morty Goldman. *The Shining*, thinks Arnie Medlock. Must be murder to clean, thinks Katie Dillinger. Fanny magnate, thinks Billy Hamilton. *Dracula!*, thinks Fergus Flaherty. This must be worth a packet, thinks Socrates McCartney. Good divisional HQ, thinks Bobby Dear. *Play Misty for Me*, thinks Annie Webster. Fucking scary, thinks Sammy Gilchrist, you could murder somebody here. Going to be a lot of spiders, thinks Ellie Winters.

'Big fucking house,' says Socrates McCartney, in awe.

And it is, it is a big house. Four storeys high, conical towers at each corner, high, sloping roof in the centre of the building. A massive wooden front door awaits them.

No one adds to McCartney's reasonably accurate

224

comment. What else is there to be said? And they each stare in wonder at this magnificent late-seventeenth-century monstrosity, stuck away in the heart of the Borders, buried behind hills and woods and the low mist that hangs in the glen through almost half the hours of daylight.

Katie Dillinger swallows, but she is impressed. They'd said on the phone that it was an imposing place. And she's glad there's a housekeeper and that they won't have to clean up after themselves.

'Right,' she says, turning round; and despite his immediate trepidation at seeing this place, despite the vague feeling of association with his recurring dream, Barney's first thought is of relief that Dillinger is no longer talking to Arnie Medlock, that he might now be able to redress the balance. 'This is it. Grab your things and pile out. Make sure you don't leave anything 'cause Bobby isn't staying here with us.'

Bobby Ramsey glances over his shoulder at the mention of the name, but the look says nothing. Bloody right I'm not staying here, he thinks. Bloody right.

And so this motley crew, this testament to the ill effects of bad life choices, this Garibaldi of insouciance, this plethora of criminality, this belligerent bastardisation of immoderate human behaviour patterns, begin to collect their belongings and troop off the bus. And Barney faffs and prevaricates and lets others go before him, in the hope that Bobby Dear will move on and latch on to some other poor sod.

He collects his bag, and slides himself out of the bus, into the pouring rain, last of all. And they each scamper the short distance to the doorway and the great stone awning that protects the front of the house.

There are no lights on, there is no sign of life. Dillinger takes the lead and lets the huge brass knocker

225

explode in sound upon the door; and the noise mingles with that of the rough diesel engine and Bobby the Bus Driver lurching into third gear and staggering away back up the drive. And with the bus goes the only light that was available to them, and they are left alone in total darkness. And so Dillinger knocks again and they wait, the rain cascading all around them.

They feel the cold now, in the midst of this downpour; a few shivers rack bodies, a few glances are cast out into the dark of night. But these are murderers all, and there is little fear. Barney shivers too and looks at Dillinger, jacketless and cold. I can offer her my jacket, he thinks. It'd be cool, smooth, cavalier, errant and romantic. The act of a chevalier.

'Got stuck with old Bobby, Ah see,' says Socrates McCartney, talking softly in Barney's ear.

Barney turns. Hesitates.

'Sorry?'

'Stuck with old Bobby on the bus. See you made the mistake of talking to him,' says Socrates.

Barney nods. Is about to excuse himself – although he suddenly feels self-conscious about his chivalrous act – when from nowhere Arnie Medlock swoops towards Dillinger, jacket outstretched, to the rescue; and gets an affectionate touch of the arm in gratitude.

He who hesitates ... Barney sighs – ever his lot – and turns to Socrates.

'Aye, well, ye know,' is all he can be bothered saying.

'Bit of a boring bastard, eh?' says Socrates.

Barney smiles ruefully, but feels condemned to defend him, in the usual British manner.

'Don't know,' he says. 'Seemed all right tae me, ye know. Interesting story, fighting in the Falklands and a' that.'

'That what he told ye?' says Socrates.

Barney looks at him. Here we go. Out of my depth again, he thinks.

'Bollocks, was it?' says Barney, in a world-weary way. Why does he always end up with the nutters? Of course, if you're going to join a murderers anonymous group, what do you expect?

'Total,' says Socrates, as finally the great wooden door swings open, and a small, neatly dressed woman waits to greet them. 'Murdered a family o' seven in Ayr 'cause they wouldnae let him use their phone after his car broke down outside their house.'

'Ah,' says Barney. 'That sounds more like it.'

'Works in Edinburgh wi' some big stock market mob. Lives in Bearsden. Rich, post bastard. Serial liar, though, that's his problem. Give ye another story tomorrow, soon as look at you. He *was* in South America, mind ye. Argentina '78, wi' the rest o' the sad bastards who thought we were gonnae win the World Cup. That's what really turned him intae a headcase. Tragic, so it was.'

And with that, the further education of Barney having been promulgated, Socrates lifts his bag over his shoulder and marches after the others into the house. And Barney stands on the periphery of the pouring rain, the last of the crew, and wonders what on earth he'd been thinking about.

Back in the minibus, Bobby Ramsey slows as he reaches the end of the drive and the turning back out onto the main road. He is surprised to see a car now sitting opposite the exit, a lone figure inside staring back past him at the house. But he couldn't care less as he shudders away up the road, and has forgotten about the car almost before he has come to the next turning.

And inside the car sits Detective Sergeant Crammond,

who, with a slight smile, lifts his phone and dials the number back to the station. The smile grows with the ring.

'DS Proudfoot,' says the voice. Bored. Reading bloody Jade Weapon probably, thinks Crammond.

'Erin,' he says, 'just phoning up to completely shag your weekend, mate.'

2

barney sings the greens

'Aluminium-free deodorant. Ah mean, have ye ever heard o' such pish? Aluminium-free deodorant. That's what they're selling these days. Ah mean, who the fuck knew there even was aluminium in deodorant? Eh? Did you? Did you know there was aluminium in deodorant?'

Barney suddenly realises he's had a question fired at him and turns slowly to Socrates.

'Sorry?' he says. 'Oh, deodorant. No, no, Ah didnae. Maybe they mean the can.'

Socrates McCartney spears a piece of deep-fried scampi, which is resting on a divan of lettuce, then waves his knife in Barney's direction.

'The can? Here, Ah hadnae thought o' that. So ye mean there's nae can. It's deodorant in a bag? How would that work?'

Barney is distracted. He is in a good news/bad news situation. They are at dinner and he's managed not to be sitting next to the psychotic Bobby Dear. That's the good news. Unfortunately, he's at the other end of the table from Katie Dillinger, who is once again receiving the close attentions of Arnie Medlock.

The man is a smooth-talking, smart as they come, cool,

dressed to the hilt bastard. Barney doesn't stand a chance against him. Unless he is to kill him, of course. That'd make all the difference. And when the police showed up, there would be no end of suspects. Barney could be in the clear.

'Don't know,' he says absent-mindedly, toying with a piece of scampi himself. Never really liked scampi, Barney Thomson. More of a crab man.

'Maybe,' says Socrates, 'ye like get yer bag, bung it in the oven for a couple o' minutes tae warm the deodorant up, stick it under yer arm, then let the air out and it a' drifts up tae yer pits. What d'ye reckon?'

'Sounds about right,' says Barney.

'It's just pish, though, i'n't it?' says Socrates. 'It's everything these days. Ye cannae drink coffee or eat butter, ye cannae lie under a sunbed, ye cannae even let yer weans watch *Tom and* fucking *Jerry*, for God's sake. Supposed tae be too violent. Ah mean, whit a load o' pish that is. Ah've been watching *Tom and Jerry* since Ah was three, didnae do me any harm. It wisnae like Ah ever thought ye could stick a frying pan down somebody's gullet and think they'd be awright two seconds later.'

Barney gives him an awkward sideways glance. 'Ye did murder three people, though,' he says.

Socrates polishes off the remainder of his starter and takes a satisfyingly large swallow of cheap Bulgarian white. Dry, with a gravelly texture, lemony overtones, fruity underbelly, a long nose and a rare skin condition.

'Suppose ye might have a point,' he says. 'Anyway, Ah always thought that wee Jerry was a pain in the arse, myself. Vicious little bastard. Vicious.'

They are arranged around the table for maximum effect, with regards to the situation of eight men and only three women. Arnie Medlock has free range at Dillinger, with Barney left to stew in his jealousy and pent-up testosterone more than three seats away. Annie Webster has Sammy Gilchrist on one side and Billy Hamilton on the other, and is constantly being dragged between the two. And just to keep them both on edge, she continually sends enticing looks the way of the legendary Barney Thomson – who has so far completely failed to notice. He did catch her eye once, but he thought she was having trapped-wind trouble. Meanwhile, Ellie Winters is surrounded by Bobby Dear, Fergus Flaherty and Morty Goldman, all of whom are vying for her attention; although Goldman is only doing it in a strange, silent, non-interactive kind of way. They all suppose themselves in with a chance, and despite Winters' general dislike of the opposite sex, fifteen glasses of wine and she could be anyone's. Of the assembled company only Socrates is uninterested. Or perhaps just playing it cool.

The dining room is hung with huge pictures of boring men in red riding jackets, and austere women with that 'I've been standing here for fifteen hours in this enormous sodding dress; I'm starving, I'm dying for a pee, I could kill for a Marlboro Light, and I can't wait to be emancipated' look on their faces. The cornices have been carved by master craftsmen of old – craftsmen for whom angels sang and elves wove spells of necromancy and magic, and who were smoking large quantities of drugs. The sideboard is bedecked with crystal and silver, the dining table is large and opulent, the drapes are thick velvet, the fireplace is sixteenth-century Venetian, a chandelier hangs above the table, 173 lights sparkling in opalescence. A Christmas tree, decorated as if by Cary Grant in *The Bishop's Wife*, shines in the corner.

'Fucking flash gaffe this, i'n't it no?' says Socrates, for he is a man who needs conversation.

'Aye,' says Barney after a while, the question again taking its time to penetrate.

'Ye seem distracted, mate,' says Socrates.

Barney nods and pushes the remainder of his starter away from him. Arnie Medlock is on the verge of success. He can tell. The two of them are almost snogging. If they start that up, Barney might as well go home; a walk to the nearest bus station, however far it is, in the pouring rain, and he could be gone. No problem.

'Fancy our Katie, dae ye?' says Socrates, following the doleful look of Barney across the great expanse of the table to the far side of the room.

Barney is no longer one for bullshit and lies. Not after all he's been through.

'Aye,' he says. 'Ah do.'

'Well go for it, then, Big Man.'

Barney turns to look at Socrates, gestures up the table at the two of them, Dillinger whispering some seeming affection in Medlock's ear, and shrugs his shoulders.

'Ach, don't you worry about that, Big Man,' says Socrates. 'Medlock's full o' shite. Always makes his move every year, never gets anywhere. Reckon Katie's a lesbo myself, which doesnae dae you much good either, but at least Medlock willnae be feasting on her the night, know what Ah mean? So Ah think ye just ought tae breenge in there and take control. You're a hard bastard, mate, are ye no? Ah've read a' about ye in the papers.'

Barney gives him a sideways glance. If only he knew. But then maybe he'll get more respect from these people if they believe all that nonsense.

'What about Medlock?' he says. 'What's he doing here?'

Socrates snorts into his wineglass.

'That big poof. Shagged a couple o' farmer birds, their

blokes came after him, and he did the business. Cut one o' the guy's testicles off, then left the bloke bound and gagged in some deserted house in a scheme on the edge o' Springburn. Couple o' council workers found him six months later. Arnie had stemmed the flow o' the guy's blood fi' his gonads, so he died o' starvation or some shite like yon.' Barney swallows. 'And he just clean chopped the other guy's head off wi' an axe. He'd just been watching *Highlander* apparently, so he was intae a' that stuff. Then he mashed up the bastard's body and fed it tae the pigs.'

Barney swallows again.

'And how long'd he get?'

Socrates finishes off his wine and reaches once more for the carafe.

'Arnie? Bastard's never been caught. Who knows how many more he's killed? So Ah'd watch him, Ah suppose, but Ah still reckon he's a total poof.'

'Oh,' says Barney. That's all right, well.

The large wooden door leading towards the kitchen swings open, and Miss Berlin, housekeeper to the weird and dishonest, enters slowly, ready to clear away the plates.

A brief description: short, strong, old, grey hair, bespectacled, could crush a man's bollocks with a snap of her fingers. In her younger days she used to lift whole cattle and put them into the back of lorries. A hardy country gal, with the strength of ten men, hairy armpits and terribly robust underwear. Could shag like a horse, mind.

The chatter and laughter continue as she clears away the remnants of the scampi à la lettuce. Men hitting on women; women being coy with men; men pretending not to hit on women; women pretending not to notice that

233

men are hitting on them; men pretending that women are hitting on them and not the other way about; women attempting to hit on men in a passive-aggressive, non-sexual, fudged-outlines kind of a way; men looking on in seething jealousy and impotence as bastards like Arnie Medlock steal their birds. The usual roundabout of a Saturday night cattle market. Miss Berlin has seen it all before, and knows that inevitably it will end in tears. Or even murder.

Socrates quickly downs his third glass of wine as he surveys the scene. A new man since he got his murderous past off his chest. Relaxed, confident, more chilled than a '93 Australian sauvignon blanc which has been in the fridge for a fortnight.

'Might have a go at one o' the chicks myself tonight. Ye never know, eh? Ah'll leave Katie tae you, mind ye, if ye're gonnae get wellied in there. Ye are gonnae have a go, right?'

The big question. When it comes to it, the biggest question of all. Love is involved.

'You finished?'

Barney looks up at the clipped tones of Hertha Berlin. Voice like a skelped buttock, she awaits with a handful of plates. Tone of voice which means that what she said actually translates into 'So you hated my food, then, did you, you bastard? Well, I'm coming into your room in the middle of the night to either garrotte you with my nose hair or disembowel you thoroughly with a blunt instrument'.

Barney swallows.

'Aye,' he says. 'Finished.'

The new, improved, low-cal, sodium-extracted, warp-enhanced, plutonium-enriched, caffeine-inhibited, aluminium-free Barney Thomson is still intimidated by a strong woman, and in part he wilts. But she rudely lifts his plate from in front of him and is gone in a whirr of legs, plates, arms and a long-since-faded blue rinse.

'What about the old bird?' says Socrates, smiling and leaning towards him. 'Would ye shag that?'

Barney screws up his face. To tell the truth, such is his infatuation with Katie Dillinger, should Madeleine Stowe walk in, unfettered by clothing and morals (and taste), he would pass her on to the next poor sap.

He is about to attest to the negative when he sees the inevitable unfold across the table. The horror, oh! the horror, he thinks, becoming frighteningly, pretentiously poetical.

It almost happens in slow motion. There is laughter, there is arm-touching, there is an obvious connection. The words of Socrates McCartney had meant nothing to Barney. He knew there was something between Dillinger and Medlock; knew it, absolutely dyed-in-the-bollocks knew it.

As if watching a slow-mo replay on *Match of the Day*, analysed from twenty different angles by Alan Hansen, it unfolds before him in frightening detail. The laugh, the grin, then the lasting smile, the touch of the arm, the lean forward, and then the soft kiss on the side of the cheek. And not Medlock kissing Dillinger, for that could be almost acceptable; almost part of the whole hitting-on thing. It is her, the Desdemona, the harlot, the siren of enticement, who leans forward and plants her soft red lips onto Medlock's cheek, and then leaves them there for that second or two longer than is normally required by Chapter 5, Paragraph 3, Sections 5a through g of the Department of Environment, Transport and the Regions Official Charter on Cheek Kissing.

And Barney feels it as sure as if it is his cheek that is

being kissed, or his cheek that is being crushed to a pulp with a battering ram, along with his heart. His mouth closes, his eyes half shut, his shoulders wilt, and the potential of the weekend dies like an animal downed by a sniper. He might as well go home. And first thing tomorrow morning, that is exactly what he is going to do.

Socrates sees it as well, and rests his hand quietly on Barney's shoulder.

'Too bad, mate,' he says. 'Too bad.' Barney does not respond, for what is there to say? 'Looks like he's gonnae get his fill o' her, no mistake,' says Socrates, continuing. Barney stares into the mire. 'Yep, he's gonnae be up tae his armpits in that baby tonight. Goes like a tank, apparently, that's what a' the other guys who've shagged her say. Old Arnie's gonnae be pumping away like a piston for most o' the night.' His words begin to penetrate. Barney gives him a look. 'Lucky, lucky, lucky,' says Socrates. 'Yes siree. It's all-night action for Arnie. The old studster's hitting the back o' the net, nae question. The Big Man is in there, pure in there. Shag-a-roonie. She'll be lying on her back when he comes,' he adds, beginning to break into song.

Barney breathes deeply and sits back in his chair. The laughter continues; Dillinger holds on to Medlock's arm with ever greater tenderness. Barney eyes Mrs Berlin and decides that he just isn't desperate enough. It's Dillinger he wants. Or wanted, for Arnie Medlock is getting his way.

I could kill him, he thinks. Fucking kill him.

And with his jealousy and his seething resentment, he means it. Absolutely, he means it.

'Lucky, lucky, lucky,' says Socrates. 'Lucky guy.'

236

3

punch drunk

It was one of those days when it seemed the whole world was on the streets. It was hot, so that your shirt stuck to your chest and your armpits smelled like they'd been napalmed.

But not Jade Weapon's armpits. They were smooth, delicious and fragrant, and smelled of sex.

'Who's she shagging this time?'

Proudfoot looks over the top of the book. Mulholland looks tired; older, she realises suddenly, than when they first started working together last year. Hadn't really noticed in the last couple of days. Lines on the face; not yet any grey hairs, but all in the eyes. They have seen too much. And in that moment, it also occurs to her that she sees the same thing when she looks in the mirror. They have both seen enough misery and death to fill anyone's boots, and unquestionably it is time to get out before they see any more.

A blinding flash of light, but perhaps it'll lead to nothing. She's never just acted on these things. Usually blinding flashes of light are gone when you wake up the next morning, and it's a bastard if you've acted on it the day before.

'Oh, everyone,' she says.

Mulholland smiles. Wearily; time to go.

'Where've you been?' she asks. Nearly two hours since she got the call from Crammond, and she has spent the time concocting the stories she will use to explain why she is so late. Flat tyre, called out to something by the chief, couldn't be arsed, dum-de-dum.

'Just walking,' he says.

'In Maryhill?'

'Way beyond. Ended up at the university. Walked through the grounds and some of those dodgy tree-lined avenues. Past all those prepubescent students. Some of them looked about seven, for God's sake. And they're all holding hands and snogging and practically having sex and smoking God knows what. Little bastards.'

'You're getting old,' she says.

He laughs and shakes his head. A sad, resigned movement. Resigned; that's appropriate.

'Aye, I suppose.'

They look at each other. Tired eyes, and they recognise the look they share. A few days of indifference have followed several months of loathing and ignoring. But now even indifference seems pointless.

He shrugs his shoulders again. Maybe he and Proudfoot could have been something, he thinks, but there's no point now. Not with all the baggage they carry around with them. What kind of relationship would they be able to have?

'I'm off,' he says.

'Where to?'

'Back up north, I suppose. Do a spot of fishing.'

'Right. You're off off?'

What is that feeling that's just stabbed at her unfeeling soul?

238

'Aye. McMenemy ripped me to shreds, so I told him to fuck off. And I resigned, so I won't be going to the plods up there either.'

'I heard a few of them talk about it, but I wasn't sure whether it was true.'

He smiles.

'It was a dream. You know how you go through life thinking that someone or other higher up the food chain is an idiot, and you always think it'd be nice to be able to tell him to fuck off? Everybody thinks it; everybody wants to do it, but no one ever does, 'cause you know you're going to get the push. You just can't do it.'

She smiles broadly, nodding. Absolutely right. She'd even wanted to tell Mulholland that, while wanting to sleep with him at the same time.

'But you did . . .'

'It was beautiful in there. I just went for it. Threw it all at him. Mostly just said the word *fuck* at him for a couple of minutes, but I managed to get in the odd insult as well. It was beautiful. I shall take it to my grave.'

The smile broadens across his face; and it's genuine. The glory of release, of being free of what has ailed him for years; combined with the temporary insanity of not caring what comes next.

'You should smile more often,' says Proudfoot, suddenly; and his smile lessens but does not die. She shakes her head to cover up the intimacy of the remark, quickly changes the subject. 'What are you going to do now, then? Just fishing?'

He stares at her for a few seconds, lost in the thought, then shrugs.

'I suppose. Not sure really. I'll do that for a while, then who knows? It's not really a job, fishing, is it? I'll

239

be all right for a bit, then I can start panicking when I run out of money.'

'Aye.'

And there the conversation ends. A lot more to say, no words to say it in. In his harmless way, Barney Thomson has taken another couple of victims, but life is like that. It gives, it takes away. It leaves broken promises and broken hearts in its wake.

Something like that.

Another shrug from Mulholland. Time to go and break all ties with the past, regardless of how painful the break might be.

'Got to go. Get up there tonight, be up early for the fishing tomorrow.'

She stares at him; her eyes drift to the floor.

'Right,' she says. 'See you.'

'Aye.'

He stands and looks at her. She lifts her eyes and looks back. Jade Weapon rests uneasily in her fingers. What would Jade do? Apart from shag him and kill him? So much crap has gone before, yet still they are fettered by convention and discomfort.

He turns to go. The Jade Weapon inherent in Proudfoot comes out.

'Why don't you come with me tonight?' she says; instant butterflies, dry throat.

He stops, slowly turns back to her. Gives her the look.

'You going somewhere interesting?'

'Down to the Borders. This bloody woman I've been following for the last few months. Apparently she's gone away for the weekend. Crammond called me a couple of hours ago to come and take over, so I really ought to be going.'

'A couple of hours?'

240

She smiles and shrugs. Hair moves across her face. Lips red. Mulholland stares into the depths of the old familiar gold mine.

'Well,' she says, 'the guy's an arse.'

Mulholland laughs again. Softly. Thoughts of going away for the night with Proudfoot charging around his head. And longer than the night, perhaps. With the sudden release and freedom has come revelation. Hasn't he just been thinking about this for the last four hours, wandering the avenues and cloisters of the university? Spending time with Proudfoot. Spending his entire life with Proudfoot, maybe. God, who knows? Mind like a jar of pickle.

'So what about it?' she says, feeling more confident at the absence of an instant refusal. 'Bound to be fishing down there.'

Mulholland stares at her, lets his thoughts untangle.

'Aye, all right,' he says at last. 'Why not?'

Proudfoot stands up and takes her coat from over her chair.

'Your enthusiasm has me soaking,' she says.

'I always did have that effect.'

Proudfoot lifts Jade Weapon, throws her arms into her coat and follows Mulholland from the office. A few remaining desk officers watch them go – the office is already buzzing with Mulholland's soon-to-be-legendary denunciation of McMenemy – then the door is closed behind them and they are gone.

✂

Sitting in Mulholland's car much later, heading south on the concrete part of the M74, left turn at Moffat. Not much to be said between them, neither worrying about the impetuosity and inevitability of what they are doing – throwing themselves once more into the heart of a

241

relationship. The rain sweeps across the hills and lashes the motorway; artics fly by in the outside lane, travelling too fast and throwing gallons of spray into the air. Old Fiestas trundle down the inside lane doing less than forty. Cars with full beam flash by in the opposite direction. Services promising expensive petrol and all-night accommodation flash by on their left. A silence grows between them, yet it grows into nothing at all, for it is not awkward in nature. Proudfoot dozes, and ponders the do's and don'ts of making a certain dramatic move. Mulholland listens to Middle Elvis, volume low, and barely audible above the concrete. 'Guitar Man'. Quitting your job and heading off into the unknown. It's all there. Chucking in your life, walking away, and hoping you're lucky enough to find a four-piece band somewhere looking for a guitar player.

'So this is it,' he says to break the silence, without remotely intending seriousness. 'You and me back on. Is that what we're talking here?'

She stirs and stares into the darkness, and wonders why Elvis didn't just tell the Colonel to go stuff himself.

'What do you think?' she says as an answer.

He shrugs in the dark.

'Don't know. I mean, I was in love with you before. You were a pain in the arse, and I hated the way you ate cornflakes. And if I'd had to listen to 'At My Most Beautiful' one more bloody time, I would have stuck the CD player up your backside. And you do talk some amount of utter pish. But you know, I thought I was in love, and I haven't stopped thinking about you since God knows when, so, well, I don't know.' Runs out of things to say. Being too honest. Not sure where his tongue was going to take him. 'Your turn,' he says, to get out of it.

She nods her head. Has forgotten in the muddle if she

242

listened to REM as much as she did just to annoy him. And she hates cornflakes.

This is it. Chance to throw in there the thing that she had been honestly waiting for him to say six months before. No reason why she cannot say it herself.

'We could get married,' she says, taking the plunge. But then, why not? That's what you do when you're in love. She loves him, no question. It's the equal and opposites thing. To hate someone as much as she's hated him, she must love him as well.

He laughs; bit of an ugly laugh.

'Married?'

'Aye.'

'Why would we want to do that?' he says.

'Don't know,' she says. 'Something to do.'

'Bit of a crap reason to get married, Officer,' he says. 'You've got to get to know each other, spend more time together, understand one another, all that stuff. You need all of that.'

She shrugs sleepily. 'I know you perfectly. You're an unemployed, miserable, grumpy bastard. What else is there to know? We've spent plenty of time together, we've both been traumatised by the same thing, so we understand one another, and we've shagged so we know we're compatible in that respect. What else is there? And we were talking about it six months ago and for a night it seemed like a good idea. You just buggered off and blew it out the water. So what if it's taking a bit of a chance? Let's face it, you tried it the right way with your wife and it was crap.'

A well-constructed argument.

Mulholland nods. 'Aye, well, I suppose you might have a point.'

She rests her head against the seat belt, attempting to

243

make herself comfortable enough for sleep. Closes her eyes.

'That's settled, then. We are going to the Borders after all, so we can nip along to Gretna,' she says, and yawns. Sleep will soon come.

'Settled, then,' he says. And stares ahead into the spray from a passing fuel tanker and immediately starts to think of something else.

And on they drive into the night, while Crammond stews. Not knowing the danger that will come from this chance decision. For how is anyone to know the future? Unless you are Barney Thomson, and the future comes to you in dreams.

4

into the river of night where the waters run cold. hey! hey! hey!

The post-dinner period on the first of two nights for the Murderers Anonymous group Christmas weekend. A time checking out the opposition, and perhaps laying the foundations for a more fruitful night the following evening.

The men are in splinter groups, eyeing up their romantic adversaries, eyeing up the women. The three women are grouped around a table in the corner of the large billiards room, downing copious amounts of wine, and laughing louder and longer as the evening drifts into Sunday morning.

Arnie Medlock has been at the snooker table since just after dinner, taking on all comers and beating each of them by a mile. Excellent safety shots, good long potter, comfortable around the cushions. Only a hesitancy with the rest and an uneasiness with regulation pots into the centre pockets have prevented him making it as a pro. That, and a tendency to insert a snooker cue into the anal

245

passage of anyone who beats him. The pros just don't go in for that kind of thing. Mostly.

Socrates sits with Fergus Flaherty and Billy Hamilton, the latter two discussing their chances with Ellie Winters and Annie Webster respectively. As do Sammy Gilchrist and Morty Goldman, united by a desire to infiltrate the bedclothes of a different woman. Morty is unimpressed by Sammy Gilchrist, however; extremely unimpressed. Morty is beginning to think certain things. Bobby Dear is the current victim lying down to Medlock on the snooker table, and all the while Barney sits alone. As is his wont.

His mind is involved in the normal male pursuit of wondering how he's going to manage to get a woman into his bed; and equally contemplating the usual male likelihood of total failure.

He doesn't stand a chance of moving ahead of Arnie Medlock. The guy is smooth, funny, built like a 747 and uses the snooker cue as if it's an extension of his penis. All evening he has been casting smiles and winks the way of Dillinger from the table, as he has brushed aside the opposition; and every time she has met his eye and coyly smiled back. And not once has she looked the way of Barney, and he feels quite out of place. He is here to befriend and bed Katie Dillinger, and he has as much chance of it as he does of running naked through a vat of molten steel and coming out with all his chest hair intact.

He ought to pack up his troubles, go to bed, then make a move first thing in the morning. He belongs back in his studio flat in Greenock, or sitting with Leyman in the pub. A lonely Christmas, and then back to work and he can slide easily into his box and stay there till he dies. Romance isn't for men like Barney Thomson. Never was, never will be. Loneliness, unhappiness and cold fish suppers on windblown promenades, that's his lot in life.

He gets to give other men the haircuts that help them go out and get women. He's a giver. A provider. He's a slave to the demands of others; the polemic that drives the male soul. He's Kirk Douglas in *Spartacus*. He's Geordi La Forge in *Roots*. He is the downtrodden, the browbeaten, the subjugated, the depressed and the demoralised. He's India before independence. He's Russia under Stalin. He's thinking pish.

Time for bed; and to get away from this torture.

He rises slowly, wanders around the small group. Might as well say goodnight to the instrument of his torment. Glances at the old clock on the even older mantelshelf. Almost one o'clock. He has suffered this agony for nearly four hours since dinner. Time to put himself out of his misery, because no one else is showing any signs of leaving. This could turn out to be a very long night, and it's the last place he wants to be.

'Ah'm off, then,' he says, standing above the select group of three women. 'Feeling a bit tired, ye know.'

They look up at him, mid-giggle. Pissed, all three.

'Barney!' says Dillinger. 'Don't be daft. We're just getting going. Why don't you stay?'

This plea is accompanied by the requisite giggle from Winters.

Barney hesitates; but he's not stupid. He can tell the discolouring effects of alcohol from several yards off. He would love her to mean it, but he's not seventeen. He knows that to stay is just to subject himself to more torture.

'It's all right, Ah'll just go tae bed, thanks. It's late.'

Ignores the giggling Winters; smiles at Dillinger. A resigned 'I would've liked to have slept with you but I know I can't compete with Arnie Medlock, so I'll just go to bed myself and leave you to it' smile. And suddenly

247

Dillinger looks a little more serious, and returns the smile. A compassionate 'if you're sure you have to go to bed then OK, but really I understand, because frankly, Barney, even though I think you're a nice enough bloke, I wouldn't touch you with a stick, you've got to understand that, and besides, Arnie's hung like a donkey' smile.

He goes. Catches Arnie Medlock's eye on the way out, and does his best to return the goodnight. Closes the door behind him, and now he is alone in the great hallway of the house. Sudden quiet, the chatter distant. Grand stairs leading away to his right; enormous paintings hung randomly – a harvest table, laden with food; two wild dogs feasting on a felled sheep; a large faded port scene, with acres of greeny-blue water and few boats. And he climbs the stairs. Faded red carpet with brown pattern.

Arnie's a nice enough bloke, he can see that. It's just jealousy playing its demonic part which is turning him against the man. But truth be told, none of these people are for him, and this group is not for him. He really ought to go the way of the other two Barney Thomsons they've had this year and move quietly on.

A floorboard creaks beneath his feet and he gets a shiver at the sound. And from the shiver, induced by a sound of his own making, he suddenly gets the sensation of where he is, who he is with. In a large, old house, where everyone is a murderer.

He swivels quickly, and does not know where it comes from, but suddenly the vision of the old church is in front of him. Silence but for the wind. The cleric on his knees. The one-eyed, bloodied sheep. The hand at his shoulder. Cold. A touch running along his back.

He turns hurriedly, looks back up the stairs. Straight into the eyes of an old painting; a maid, high white

248

collar, hands folded in her lap, on a rocking chair. It seems to move.

And the vision of the church is gone, and once again he can hear the sounds of chatter and laughter from the billiards room. He starts to climb the stairs again, past the old maid, who watches him go. It is dark at the top, and he must get to the second floor.

He wonders if the old housekeeper sleeps up here, or if there are old-fashioned servants' quarters down below. Stops as he gets to the top of the stairs and stands on the first-floor hallway. Looks along the long passageway, the ends of it disappearing into darkness. Not sure who is sleeping where, but knows that Dillinger is on his floor. And so what about that?

He shivers again, and starts to make his way to the second floor. Looks up, and can see nothing at the top. A tentative climb, past pictures of stern figures in seventeenth-century dress. Hunters and officers and ladies with their hands neatly folded in front of them. They watch him go.

A floorboard creaks. Not from Barney's foot. He stops at the halfway point; swallows and does not breathe. Waiting for another sound; his heart thumps. He waits for it to come again. Couldn't tell where it came from. His eyes grow accustomed to the dim light, and he can see into corners. Ornaments on tables. Old carvings and faces of evil.

Another sound, this time a definite movement from below. A swish of a footstep along a carpet. Then nothing. He has to let his breath out, draws another. Looks behind him, but he's sure no one followed him out. And the sound had come from along the corridor. Probably the old housekeeper. Going to the bathroom. Something like that.

The unknown. There's something to be afraid of. That's what the customer in the shop had said, and he was right. Barney climbs the stairs to the next level, determined now not to look back. That's the classic fault they always make in films. Walk one way, looking behind them, and when they turn, thwack, they've got a serial killer in the face, and they're Shreddies.

He gets to his floor; the stairs lead farther on to a horribly dark third floor. Now definitely aware that there is someone below. He can feel it and the sensation is growing. As in his dream. The sure knowledge that something is behind you. He looks along the dark corridor of the second floor. His room right at the end. Should go to the bathroom first, but he just wants to get into his room, turn the light on and lock the door.

Another noise from down below, another sliver of sound, and this time he is drawn to look. Nothing. The dead eyes of ancestors look mournfully up at him and wonder at his concern. He turns back, half expecting to find a killer in front of him. The passageway extends sullen and menacing ahead.

Eyes ever more accustomed, he sets out. Past old, warped mirrors, into which he dare not look. Paintings of battles at sea and horses on the hoof; men at arms and women with their hands folded neatly in their laps. The sensation of someone at his shoulder, having gone with the quick look round, returns and begins to follow him along the corridor. Head down, he dare not look back. Imagination running riot. Sees no demons behind him; just killers and their contorted faces and their knives.

Can't tell what he's running from. Substance or imagination? He's faced killers, he's seen some horrible things. But this is real evil he imagines; the evil of his dreams.

250

And now the noise behind him is constant, a shuffling along the old carpet. Barney walks past paintings of angels, past an old ottoman, past a straight-backed chair, in which someone must have sat long ago, the cover worn.

He waits for his name to be spoken. To find out the truth of it; one of the others toying with him, a demon, or something worse. A shuffle, footsteps on the carpet, thinks he can hear breathing. Key already in his hand, regretting that he locked the door. Heart hammering, head muddled, stomach gripped, almost in a run. Gets to the door, starts to hum some bizarre tune to cover up the sound. *Brazil*. Key fuddled in the lock. *Daaaaaah, dee-dah-dee-dah-dee-dah-dee-daaaaaah*.

The noise from behind stops. The key clicks in the lock. Not for a second does he think to look round, and he is in the room. Light on, the door slammed shut, the key fumbled back into the lock and turned. A brief moment of exhausted exhalation, then a look around the room to see what lies in wait for him. Another classic of the movies.

And the room dully stares back at him, the centre light dimmed by the dusty cotton shade. Pale pink, ornate bedspread, dull paintings of animals and men at supper on the walls.

He can still feel it outside. Something. A presence. He backs away from the door into the centre of the room, then looks around, finds the wall lights, and goes around the room putting them all on. As much light as possible. Imagination still running riot, feasting on his uncertainty and renewed lack of confidence.

It is waiting for him. Something out there; something malevolent. Something even worse than the roomful of killers downstairs.

251

He checks under the bed, then takes the large comfy chair and moves it into the centre of the room, from where he can see the door and the window. And into this he sinks, wide awake, regretting that he ever came here; but for the first time in several hours, not obsessing on Katie Dillinger.

For there is something else to think about. Something strange, something evil.

5
the sixth bottle

'I bet your house is crap anyway.'

Mulholland looks around at Proudfoot's red lips, before allowing his gaze to drift down to her breasts. Suffering from the effects of an on-going eleven cups of wine. A light, fruity Australian; exuberant, polished, friendly and clean shaven, with a hint of strawberry and subtle undertones of kerosene and the fourth series of *Blackadder*. Proudfoot is only marginally behind, as she downs her ninth cup, and fills it up again with the remainder of their fifth bottle. Quite enjoying the attentions of his eyes; wondering vaguely what will happen next, when knowing full well that neither of them is so much as capable of removing their clothes.

Three o'clock in the morning. Sitting in a cold car outside the seventeenth-century mansion that is home for the weekend to the Murderers Anonymous Bearsden chapter. Stopped off in Jedburgh for some supplies on the way in, just to take longer and to annoy Crammond even more. (Crammond's annoyance ameliorated by the presence of a DCI.) All that was open was an off-licence. Mulholland couldn't decide whether to buy one or two bottles of wine, so bought five.

And so they sit outside the house in the middle of the night. Would be as well finding a B&B, but both avoided making the suggestion. Hardly likely that Annie Webster will be going anywhere now; and if she did, neither of them would be in any state to drive after her.

'We could always have movie sex,' says Proudfoot, before Mulholland's fudged brain can get round to objecting to the previous remark.

'Sex?' he says. Thinks about it for a while. 'What?'

She takes another long draw from the cup. The wine, she would have to admit if asked, has been tasting bitter these last few cups, but somehow, at three o'clock in the morning, it doesn't seem to matter.

'I was just sitting here thinking, well, I'm feeling quite horny and you're looking at my breasts.'

'I'm not looking at your breasts.'

'You're looking at my breasts.'

'I am not!'

'You are absolutely looking at my breasts. Look, you're doing it now.'

'No way!' he says, gesturing wildly, looking at her breasts.

'Sure you are. Anyway, I was just thinking, I could do with a shag. But then I thought, bugger it, look at the state of us, we couldn't even get our clothes off, never mind manoeuvre into the back seat, never mind actually fuck.' A pause. Mulholland looks at her in that distractedly perplexed way of the utterly pissed. 'See what I mean?' she says.

'Haven't a clue what you're talking about.'

'Movie sex. You know in movies when they're in a fully-clothed clinch, and then the next thing you know, boom!, they're shagging. No one's taken any clothes off, there's been no fumbling around to find the right hole, 'cause you know, we've got seven or eight of them down there. It's just straight in there and off they go.'

'What?'

'Movie sex. And it's worse at the end. When do you ever see someone go to the bathroom after movie sex? They just roll apart and nod off, or both immediately pull their clothes on. What's going on? Either the guy's got a dripping condom to get shot of, or the bird's got a pint of the stuff cascading down her thigh. See what I mean?'

'I haven't the faintest idea what you're talking about,' he says, reaching for the empty bottle and tipping the last few drops into his cup. 'You're pissed.'

'So are you. Which is why we can't have real sex.'

'I'm not looking at your breasts.'

'I didn't even mention my breasts.'

'Anyway,' he says, last of the wine into his mouth, 'you're getting away from the main issue, which is that you're trying to change me already. It was inevitable.'

'What?'

Proudfoot starts looking around the back seat for the sixth bottle, which she was sure Mulholland had mentioned, but which she never actually saw.

'That remark about the house,' he says. 'I bet it's a crap house. We only decided to get married two minutes ago and already you want to change my way of life. It was inevitable. Inevitable, I say.'

'You're definitely pissed.'

'Whatever,' he says, waving an explanatory hand. 'You're all the same, you birds. Get your hook into a bloke and you're off. Change that, change the next thing. Get a new house, ditch all your mates, can't go to the pub any more, get a nose job, start wearing different clothes, don't like your motor, disown your relatives, change your job, don't shave so often, you're not shaving

255

often enough, blah-de-blah-de-blah-de-blah. Change this, change that, watching too much footie on the telly. You're all the same. Bloody bastards. Go to the toilet, get the shopping, do fucking the next thing.'

'And you're not bitter about your divorce?' she says.

'Lose weight, clean the motor out more often, don't drive so fast, can't go fishing any more, on and on and on and on and on. You're all the same.'

She turns her back on him, and leans more into the back seat area, searching among the empties for the sixth bottle.

'What're you doing?'

'Looking for the sixth bottle,' she snaps back at the tone that comes her way.

'There is no sixth bottle.'

'You said you bought six!'

He holds his hands out.

'See? See what I mean? Now you're even changing what I said in the past. You're Stalin, that's who you are. Stalin.'

'Oh, shut up,' she says. She turns back and slumps down into the seat. Pulls her jacket more tightly around her. 'You don't half talk some amount of shite, you.'

'I won't stand for this,' he says, sitting where he is, numb from the waist down. And up.

'Look, why would I change you?' she says. 'You don't have any mates to give up, your family are all dead, you're way too ugly for a nose job to make any difference, you don't have a TV, and I don't give a toss about all that other stuff. So shut up and stop talking shite.'

He stares through the darkness and the intoxicating effects of two and a half litres of wine.

'Fuck,' he says, before attempting to get another micro-litre of fluid from the cup. 'You must really love me.'

She shakes her head and yawns. Suddenly feels very tired and very drunk. Late at night, surrounded by empty bottles, and cold and darkness. The burst of energy in search of the mythical sixth bottle having completely drained her.

'Like I said, you're full of shite,' she says.

'And you've got brilliant tits. Can I get a shot of them some time?'

The words 'I don't think they'd fit you' have not quite escaped her mouth and Mulholland has collapsed into a heap on the steering wheel. She smiles at something, although she couldn't explain what, then reaches out and touches his hair. Lays her arm on the dashboard, rests her head upon it, and within ten seconds has joined him in sleep.

✂

Three o'clock in the morning. The revelry over for the night. Strangely Barney had set the tone and the others had drifted off to bed in his wake. They had gone in ones and twos, but even the twos had split up when the upper floors had been reached, and tonight all these people sleep alone.

A few disappointed souls, but there remains ample time to jostle for position tomorrow. And, of course, one more night, when deeds will be done, agendas set and promises kept or broken.

Arnie Medlock had been the most disappointed of the lot, having considered his union with Katie Dillinger inevitable. But she had made her excuses, and he had been left alone; as alone as the others. Death and taxes, he had ruefully mumbled to himself, on finally retiring to his room. That's all you can rely on. But it's not somewhere he hasn't been before, and he is confident of the following night's success. Disappointed, yet sanguine, Arnie Medlock.

And so the house sleeps. Most in their beds, Barney in his chair, from where he can watch the door and the window. But not, however, the secret door built into the wood panelling beside the bed. His back is to that.

The house sleeps, but for one. A lone figure, walking through the dark. Along corridors, searching out secret doors, down dark passageways. Never been here before, but a long night of searching has revealed every hidden doorway, every hidden passage, every concealed flight of steps or alcove, every area of the house blocked off for some clandestine use more than three hundred years previously.

Eyes adjusted, he visits each of the bedrooms in turn. Does not know into whose room he is about to walk until he is there; then he stands over the bed and watches the breathing of every potential victim. And none awakes to him. None concedes to a sixth sense.

He lets the tip of his finger run along the cheek of Katie Dillinger; he touches the hair of Annie Webster and considers that at another time he might have had a chance with her; might even have forced her. He gently kisses the lips of Ellie Winters, and she stirs and tastes the night air, then shuffles in her sleep, and ends up all the way over on her other side. And he watches her for another fifteen minutes, hand always on the knife in his jacket pocket, before he leaves, to follow another directionless passage.

He stands over Barney too, for a short time. A little more circumspect here, as his is the only room with the light left on, and he does not blend so easily into the dark. A few minutes, then he is gone.

And then, half an hour later, Barney awakes in terror, the vision having visited him again in the night; but this dream even more forceful, the stage having shifted to a

258

large house, with old paintings on the walls, and the minister on his knees, supplicant to a vengeful God, praying for Barney's soul. And once again Barney sees the face, and once again that face is gone from his memory the instant he awakes. Sweat on his forehead, heart pounding, mouth dry.

So Barney sits in his seat, eyes wide open, and waits for the dawn. And all the while, this year's serial killer does the rounds of the house, lurks in damp and dirty passageways, dances with the rats and stands over each of the members of the Murderers Anonymous Bearsden chapter.

6
the african dawn

Proudfoot awakes, feeling just about as awful as it is possible for one single person to feel. Draped over the dashboard in the same position, all aches and pains and uncomfortable joints, yet with an empty bottle of Australian white now clutched curiously to her chest. She lifts her head and immediately a high-velocity train starts sweeping through it. One, two, three, up and out of the car, bent over the side of the road, and vomiting violently over the wet grass and general shrubbery.

A full two minutes before the retching is over, her stomach settles, and she has a temporary respite from nausea. She looks up, hands on her knees, throw-up on her shoes, face covered with sweat, panting, and sees her surroundings in daylight for the first time.

The car is parked off the road, no more than six inches away from the drop of a few feet into general bog. All around enclosed by trees, so that her immediate world is small. The aroma of rain on the forest and earth. Fresh and cold, the first hint of the chill of winter in the air. Beautiful. Across the road is the driveway up to the house; the bleak mansion sleeps quietly in partial obscurity. Then she finally notices that Mulholland is no longer in the car and her head hurts so much she can't think straight as to where he might have gone.

Back into the car, searches her bag for something to help with a headache, and comes up empty. She closes the car door and winds down the window, lets her head fall back on the headrest, does not even attempt to clear the growing fug in her head, and falls asleep in less than half a minute.

✂

The late night has taken its toll of early morning risers at the weekend retreat. No one gets up early on this Sunday. All except Barney Thomson, who hasn't slept since waking in a cold sweat at just before four o'clock.

He had waited for the dawn, from his position of uncomfortable terror, then, when he'd been satisfied that the night had been vanquished and the vampires put to sleep, he had ventured out to plunge himself into a steaming shower.

And so now he makes his way down the stairs that had caused him such terror the night before, past the same old paintings. In the half-light of a grey early morning, they look more miserable than menacing, more despondent than intimidating. Wretched souls and sullen soldiers; distracted dogs, painted with the stilted strokes of an amateur brush. Barney is no art critic, but he can tell. Painted for a hobby, not for commission, most of these.

As he reaches the bottom of the stairs he can smell breakfast, the glorious pungency of fried bacon, and he wonders who else has managed to drag themselves up at this time. Despite the night before, he has his first thought of the day of Katie Dillinger. Hopes it will be her who is up, and that she and Medlock have not spent the night together. Still, it is his intention to leave early today. He's not trapped here. Maybe even before he has

261

to see any of them. Except the breakfast king.

He winds his way through stuffy rooms and short corridors with uneven floors until he finds the kitchen and the origins of the magnificent aromas. Opens the door with little confidence, for his self-assurance is gone.

Hertha Berlin stands at the cooker, administering to a panful of frying breakfast goods. A man Barney has not seen before sits at the table, large jaw encircling a roll packed with every available morning enchantment. Sausage, bacon, black pudding, egg and mushrooms.

'How you doin' there, fella?' says the man through his breakfast bite. Mid-sixties maybe, bit of a paunch, distinct American accent through the food.

Barney looks bloody awful. Unshaven, worry lines, whole ISO containers under his eyes, the look of the haunted man. His eyes themselves would say it all, never mind the face.

'Fine,' he lies, 'just fine.'

'Surprised tae see ye up,' says Berlin. 'After the time you lot went tae yer beds, I thought it'd be lunch-time before I saw any of ye.'

'Why are ye making breakfast, then?' says Barney, taking a seat at the large kitchen table. Presumes breakfast will be served in the dining room, but for one of the first times in his life, he is glad of human company.

'I'm just feeding my man here. He likes a big breakfast. Got tae keep him well fed for all his duties, ye know. Ye'll be wanting something yerself, I expect,' she says.

The smell finally penetrates. Barney is the Ravenous Bugblatter Beast of Traal.

'Ah'm starving,' he says.

'Right. Dae ye want yer food in here or will ye be eating in the big room?'

262

'Oh, here's fine,' he says. 'Ah don't really feel part o' that mob.'

The handyman raises his eyebrows and takes another large bite from his breakfast roll. Hertha Berlin plunders the fridge for more food to heap into the frying pan. Every part of her bustles between fridge and cooker; the frying pan pops and sizzles.

'Aye, well, Ah'm no surprised. Right funny-looking lot, if ye ask me. I said that last night, did I not?'

'Sure,' says the handyman, spitting a small piece of sausage onto the table, 'sure you did, honey.'

Hertha Berlin starts piling food into another roll.

'No that we havenae had some strange folks staying here in the past. They Southern Baptists, they were a right weird bunch. And they devil worshippers fi' up Coldstream way, they were a queer lot. Whit kind o' group are you, anyway?' she says, laying the roll in front of Barney.

Just in time, Barney remembers the code, and the word *murderers* does not pass his lips.

'Hm, we're barbers,' he says, uttering the unsurprising first thing that comes into his head. 'Barbers, that's us.'

Hertha Berlin bustles, the handyman raises his eyebrows as he polishes off his second roll and settles back to wait for this third. Will have to get on with a bit of plumbing soon, however.

Barney loups into his sandwich and decides he'd better change the subject.

'Either o' you walking about at one o'clock this morning?' he says, a little more casually than he feels.

Looks at the table in discomfort as he says it, so misses the glance that passes between the two.

'We live in the houses at the bottom of the road, barber fella,' says the handyman. 'You heard someone at one in the morning, must've been one of your other barber folk.'

Barney nods. Stares at the table. Fuck.

It was the minister. He can feel it. The minister who keeps infiltrating his dreams has followed him down here, and in this house full of killers he will be the obvious first victim. That's what the dream means. He will die horribly. In fact, that's what the past two years have been pointing to. All this death and visceral carnage to which he has been subjected must have had a point; and this is it. He will die and die in a grotesque manner; his soul condemned for ever to damnation; the very essence of his being cast asunder to wail for eternity in the belly of infernal Hades; destined for all time to suffer the persecution of the damned in the fiery pit of Erebus. His soul will be a bloody carcass on which the dogs of war shall feast; his heart will be torn from his chest, ingurgitated by the beasts of fury, then spat out onto the playing fields of retribution; he will ride the black horses of the apocalypse and be tossed from his mount, head first into the crematorium of shattered illusion, where his very qi will be raped and plundered and tossed to the winds of abomination.

'This is a bloody good roll,' he says, to break the chain of thought.

'Damned fine,' says the handyman. 'Damned fine.'

✂

An hour later, still early morning, still nothing much stirring the house but for the staff and the lost soul of Barney Thomson. He pulls the zip along his bag and prepares to head out into the cold of morning and the twenty-minute walk to the nearest bus station; and the projected five-hour wait, as this is the Borders and decent public transport is something that happens to other regions of the country. That is not his concern, however. He needs to get out, that's all; doesn't care about the wait.

Puts on his jacket, lifts the bag, out of the room and door closed behind him. Minces along the corridor, head down, dejected. About to walk into the rest of his life. No hope of romance, no hope of anything different. For all the crap and the drama and the murder and the adventure of the last couple of years, here he goes back to barbery and abject poverty of spirit. Nothing changed.

And anyway, why should he expect anything more? How many sad lives out there are blighted by disappointment? Millions of them. Absolute millions. Why should he be any different? He's just a guy. A bloke. A wee man. A shmuck. A duffus. He's the kind of guy John Steinbeck used to write about. He's Garth out of *Wayne's World*. He's nothing. He could be in an Ingmar Bergman movie. He's Woody Allen without the jokes.

A door opens behind him, but he walks on. Doesn't care who it is; which one of this bloody awful crowd this is going to turn out to be. Probably Medlock, sex all over his face, with a comforting word in Barney's ear. *Never mind, mate*, he can hear him saying, *she was never going to be yours anyway. I'm way more interesting* and *I can shag like a bulldozer*.

'Barney?'

The word stops him like a bullet in the back of the head. That soft voice, delicate and succulent, smooth as a non-stick pan. And slowly he turns, throat dry, expectation suddenly pumped up from the deflation of less than three seconds ago.

Katie Dillinger stands at her door, still attired for the night. Looking a little rough, but gorgeous with it. Up all night with Arnie, he presumes, and the hope begins to fade again before another word is said.

'Where are you going?'

Barney shrugs. Cat got his tongue.

'Don't know,' he says. As eloquent as if he were sitting next to Larry Bellows.

She steps into the corridor. Wearing dark green cotton pyjamas. Dishevelled. Bit of a gap opened up between the buttons, so that Barney has the merest glimpse of the smooth curve of a breast. Tries not to look. Swallows. Shakes his head. Stares at the carpet. Can see breasts in the carpet just as much.

'You don't have to go,' she says. 'I know you feel a bit out of it, but today should be a good day. You can get to know us all a bit better. Should be all right.'

He looks her in the eye. Already knows that the decision is made for him. Just no way that he could say no to this woman.

'Just ... Ah don't know,' he says. 'Just feel like Ah should leave.'

She steps towards him. The gap in the pyjamas closes and Barney's swift look is too slow to catch another glimpse, so he stares at the floor again.

Bare feet across the carpet. She stands in front of him, puts her hand to his chin. Lifts his head so that their eyes engage.

'I want you, Barney,' he hears her say. 'I want your huge cock to fill me up like a marrow.'

'What?' says Barney.

'I want you to stay, Barney,' she says. 'You'll have a good day then go back up with us tomorrow.'

Barney stares again. Not trusting himself to say anything. Best just to nod and shut up, as her hand falls away and he loses the electricity of her touch.

'All right,' he says. Utterly capitulating. Nothing to go on but a look and a touch. For all he knows Arnie could

266

be snoozing quietly in her bed as they speak. He is as completely vulnerable to women as every other man on the planet. Just as he'd been thinking a couple of minutes ago. He's no different from anyone else.

She smiles and backs off.

'I'm glad,' she says. 'I'll see you at breakfast?'

And Barney nods and watches her retreat back into her room. And he stands in the corridor and looks around at the grey light of day and wonders. Finds himself staring at a painting of a woman, grey beyond her years, sitting slouched in a rocking chair, before a great hearth; eyes looking at him with contempt. *You're all the same*, she says to him. *You haven't got a single principle that doesn't take second place to the contents of your pants.*

'Fuck off,' mumbles Barney at the carpet, and walks slowly back up the corridor to his room.

7

my friends, these clowns

Tempers are becoming frayed. Angry words exchanged, fists clenched, jaws protruded and, in some cases, bottom lips stuck out. It is ever the way at their annual Christmas get-together, and Dillinger has often pondered the wisdom of including the session in their weekend event.

Discuss: The Morality of Murder.

It is why they're all here, after all, the only thing that binds these people, the only thing they truly have in common. So why not get down to the nitty-gritty, cut the bullshit of exaggerated storytelling, and discuss what it's all about? It's Christmas, so they can have free rein to admit that they enjoyed what they did, and that they'd do it again if they had the opportunity. An extension of what they do week in, week out, but the circumstances, the surroundings and the time of year combine to let tongues and minds roam free.

Of course, it's not the subject matter which really sets the tone of tension. It's the testosterone and oestrogen flowing in great fluid quantities. Gallons of the stuff, swishing about inside each of them, as they jostle for position with members of the opposite sex. There was one year when there had been equal numbers, and apart from the fact that none of the men wanted to go anywhere near Peggy Penknife, the Paisley Penis Punisher, there had been limited discussion, a nod and a glance at the convention of present exchange, and then off they'd all gone to each other's bedrooms for some fearsome love-making.

This year is altogether more complex, however. Eight men, three women. A recipe for treachery, jealousy, lies, deceit, bedlam, uproar and possibly even murder; given the company. Rather nice to be one of the women, thinks Dillinger, but as the leader of the dysfunctional bunch, she knows to not let things get out of hand.

So, it's Arnie Medlock and Barney Thomson, looking to make a move on her; and she knows which one she's going for tonight. Sammy Gilchrist and Billy Hamilton are shaping up for a fight over Annie Webster. And Ellie Winters has the attention of Morty Goldman, Fergus Flaherty and Bobby Dear; the last of whom actually wouldn't have a chance if he were the only bloke in a room full of eight million slabbering women, despite his cash. And, of course, that leaves Socrates, the wild card. Yet to show his hand. Or any other part of his body.

The discussion is nearing some sort of peak of intellectual debate; the very zenith of the brilliant criminal mind. Billy Hamilton and Sammy Gilchrist, vying for the mind and body of Annie Webster; who, if truth be told, would have them both at the same time, and would then kill them. Seeing as that's her thing. Though she hasn't confessed to that much in the meetings. A girl with intimacy issues.

'Away you and shite in a poke,' says Hamilton.

'Shite in a poke?' says Gilchrist, pointing a finger.

269

'Ah'll shite you in a poke!'

Both perched on the end of their seats; the others watch distractedly. Kind of enjoyable, the whole show, but they have their own arguments in which to become embroiled.

'What does that actually mean?' says Hamilton. 'Eh? You're just full of it, Big Man. Full of shite. And I'll tell you this. I've had enough of you and your bloody moral high ground. The bloke brought a ridiculous law suit so he deserved to die. All that shite. You're just a murdering, low-life, brain-dead scumbag, same as the rest of us.'

'Speak for yersel', ye little bastard,' says Fergus Flaherty, the Fernhill Flutist. 'There's nothing wrong wi' me.'

Of course, this last line is from a man who murdered the entire family next door, using nothing but the flute of the youngest son, who had spent several weeks practising non-stop for the Twelfth of July. A bloody rampage, and he had taken out the boy, his two brothers and the mother and father, all inside fifteen minutes. With a flute, remember. It had been messy.

'I agree with Billy,' says a quiet voice, from a large, comfy chair pushed a little farther back than all the others.

The explosion on Billy Hamilton's lips is temporarily averted. The sneer of Sammy Gilchrist is calmed. The fizzing tension in the room is turned to curiosity. For Morty Goldman rarely speaks.

They all turn and look at him. Morty Goldman. At official group meetings they have heard him talk but the once, when he'd brought his story into their lives. Here is your classic skin slicing off and wearing it, keeping women locked up in a cellar for months, stalking, bug-eyed, serial-killing lunatic. And for all the hardness and strength around the room, each of them finds Morty Goldman a little intimidating. Except for Barney, who finds him spectacularly intimidating, having been told his story the previous night by Socrates McCartney.

'Why is that?' asks Dillinger, to break into the almost shocked silence.

Morty points a finger at Gilchrist, and even this seasoned killer feels a chill at the look. Goldman is your classic combination of Jack the Ripper, Darth Vader, Genghis Khan and Bill and Ben the Flowerpot Men.

Mainly, thinks Goldman, because I have to say something. Otherwise Ellie Winters will never notice me.

'Mr Gilchrist does indeed take an unwarranted moral high ground. This ethical masturbation of his really is rather tedious. His is a self-righteousness born of unnecessary benevolence to his own misdeeds of the past. We've all been victims of absurd law suits, but that's hardly justification for murder.'

'What about you?' explodes Gilchrist. 'You skin-slicing-off weirdo fuckhead?' Too late, he remembers to whom he's speaking.

Morty Goldman parades a tortuous smile, the likes of which most of the group have only ever witnessed once or twice. Shows no teeth.

'I'm not pretending that what I did has any ethical superiority. It was cruel, disgusting and really rather unpleasant. I ought to have gone to prison for my crimes, I know that.' *Ought* to have gone to prison? thinks Barney. Bloody hell. And he starts to question his decision to cede to his penis and stay. When you decide to do something, you should just do it. Bugger the wait for public transport and the possibility of romance. Yet here he is, still prevaricating, a sucker

271

for one nice word from Dillinger. 'That's why I'm here. But at least I'm not pretending to be something I'm not. At least I'm not claiming some sort of honourable code as justification for my murders. At least I don't,' continues Morty, and the voice has taken on a sudden immediacy, a sly quality, tending to evil, and bones are chilled, 'pretend to be some sort of arse-wiping Jedi knight, fighting the forces of evil on behalf of humanity. You're just a stupid prick, Gilchrist. A fucking stupid little prick, and one day you might well get what's coming to you. One day soon.'

You can hear a piece of tinsel drop.

The fire dully roars and sharply crackles in the hearth; the tree sparkles, green and gold in the corner; outside, a buzzard cries and a mouse scurries beneath some shrubbery; somewhere the handyman bites massively into a quadruple cheeseburger with relish, humming the opening lines to 'I Got Stung' as he goes.

'Why don't we just calm down?' says Arnie Medlock. The voice of reason. 'Maybe we should give this a miss and get the housekeeper in. Have some drinks and food and think about opening the presents. We're here to enjoy ourselves.'

Sammy Gilchrist and Billy Hamilton, the two principal protagonists, stare at the carpet and nod. Don't meet Medlock's eyes as he looks at them. Morty Goldman has a steady gaze, however. Steady. The desire to impress Ellie Winters has gone. He is aware of all the old feelings again. The bad feelings.

'Fucking Medlock,' he says.

Arnie Medlock is not a man to be intimidated. Even so, this is a card-carrying, skin-wearing psychopath, not a regular, run-of-the-mill hard man.

'Watch it, you,' he says.

272

Morty Goldman sneers.

'Fucking Medlock,' he says again. 'Think you're hard? I've eaten guys like you for my breakfast. And I mean eaten. You're nothing, Medlock. You're a pathetic, sexually inadequate fuckwit. No wonder gorgeous Katie here didn't sleep with you last night. No dick, no brain, no heart, no balls. You in a nutshell, fuckwit-face. You're nothing.'

Arnie Medlock stares across the rich tapestry of the carpet. His face twitches. A vein throbs in his neck. He bites his bottom lip, hard enough that he can taste the blood. Looks round at Dillinger, seated between himself and Socrates McCartney on the large settee. She does her best to placate him with a smile, while they both wonder how Morty Goldman knows that they did not sleep together.

With the timing of one of the better episodes of *Star Trek – The Next Generation*, the door opens. Hertha Berlin, brandishing tea and Christmas cake.

'I thought you might like some tea,' she says. 'And there's a cheeky wee half-bottle of Johnnie Walker in the pot to keep you going.'

They watch her as she comes in, an intimidating array of eyes pinning her down. And in this heightened atmosphere of draining tension and tangible aggression, there is more than one person viewing Berlin as a potential victim. Hertha Berlin is not daunted, however. Seen worse than this lot, she reckons, although that is only because she thinks they're barbers.

The tray is laid on the table, she clinks around with a few cups and saucers, then turns back to face them.

'Would there be anything else, now?'

'No, thank you, Miss Berlin,' says Dillinger. Still marginally in charge of the proceedings. 'That'll be all.'

'Right, then. Enjoy your tea.'

And off she goes. Hertha Berlin. A woman of secrets.

And there the tea sits. Still tension hangs over them like a thick North Sea haar. Still no one wants to be the first to talk, lest Morty Goldman threatens to turn them into soup. Still the fire crackles and the Christmas tree sparkles. Morty is enjoying his sudden emergence as the group loon and leans back in his comfy sofa, eyeing each of the others slowly and in turn.

'Aw, fuck this,' says Sammy Gilchrist, 'Ah'm going for a walk. Cannae be bothered with a' this shite.'

Up he gets, the tension shattered, and some are relieved.

'It's pouring, Sammy,' says Dillinger.

'Don't give a shite,' he throws back over his shoulder. To the door and out, and he immediately feels the weight lift from his shoulders when he steps from the room, and worries not about the effects of leaving Annie Webster to the pointless charms of Billy Hamilton for the next couple of hours.

Dillinger stands up. This is supposed to be an enjoyable weekend, and there's no point in sitting here in silence for the rest of the day.

'Come on, Annie,' she says, 'give us a hand, will you?'

And Annie Webster nods and lifts herself out of an ancient comfy seat, then Fergus Flaherty says, 'Big Sammy's probably just away tae pish up a tree,' because it's the closest thing to a joke he can think of, and it gets a laugh, and the tension is gone; and Morty Goldman retreats to his shell. For now.

Drinks are served; someone switches on the CD player and 'Have Yourself a Merry Little Christmas' fills the room; the crowd eats cake and breaks off into small groups to chat about Sammy Gilchrist and Morty

Goldman and the weather. And no one notices when ten minutes later Morty Goldman sneaks out through the door, and is gone into the midst of the rain-strewn day.

8

the magnificent hugh rolanoytez extravaganza

Like some sort of Brad Pitt, Mulholland takes to his fishing with a reverential relish. Treat the river with respect and it will respect you. The river is your friend. It may be your friend, but it also your god. The river controls you and holds you in the palm of its hand. It can give, but it also takes away. Do not betray the river or you will die. All that stuff.

He is in the middle of it, waders clinging to his legs, water up to his thighs, the bottom of his jacket dipping into the cold. Not happy, but content in that freezing cold, miserable as shite, grumpy, hungover, depressed, angry, buggered kind of way peculiar to the Scots. A cold day at last, as winter rears its head. Rain stopped finally. Casting his fly short distances, snagging it on the riverside grass every time he tries to extend the pitch. Has been at it for nearly six hours and has caught just the one fish; the younger brother of an extremely small fish that he failed to catch.

Mind still in gloop, he does his best to focus. Fishing gear in the back of his car. A walk for a mile or two, found a petrol station, bought a sandwich. Got into conversation with the Sunday best wee woman in the shop. Was directed to the closest river, and ignored the instruction about there being no fishing for salmon allowed at this time of year, not that you can fish for salmon on a Sunday in any case, so, son, you'd better think twice or Big Alec will be after your testicles.

Could do with tea and food, but has now been standing in the water, using the same bedraggled fly, for nearly two hours. Focused has become mechanical and one-track.

And so he can't see the eyes in the undergrowth, the body cowering behind the trees. Watching the fishing line fizz and snap behind him, and wondering if the line would be strong enough to pull around Mulholland's neck, to tighten, and to strangle the life out of him. He can tell Mulholland is distracted in what he does; wondering whether it would be possible to steal up on him, grab the line and do what must be done; or whether he should step free of his hiding place, make himself known and then take him. Or he could drown him, or hit him over the head with a rock, or throw a heavy stone at him from a distance; although he never did have much of a throwing arm.

So many choices.

And as he stands and thinks and peers through the remnants of winter leaves and the bare protection of trees, another option presents itself. For down from the road and along the bank comes Erin Proudfoot, and the killer lowers himself farther into the undergrowth and imagines the sweet taste of a woman.

'Mulholland!'

She looks out across the water. All of ten yards. A still day, barely a zephyr bothers the last of the leaves and the

277

bare branches. The water is slow and it bubbles and trundles on by. No background noise from any nearby road, no planes overhead. Still, calm, cool winter's day. Grey cloud. Peaceful.

A slight noise among fallen leaves, and Proudfoot turns. Stares into the shadows of the trees and sees nothing. Assumes a bird or a rabbit.

'Mulholland!' she says again. 'Brought you some tea.'

He turns, dragged out from the mire. As his head swivels, he looks right into the killer's eye, it briefly registers and then is gone by the time he sees Proudfoot. The memory of it leaves him vaguely troubled, but what he saw is gone.

'What?' he says.

She holds up a bag. Food, tea, everything you might want after having been fishing for hours.

'Thought you might want something to eat. Brought you some tea.'

He stares at her for a while, brain not yet out of first. The fly lies limply in the water. A couple of fish swim by underneath. 'What a joker,' one of them says, 'using a mayfly in December,' and by the time the other has thought of a reply, he's forgotten what was said in the first place.

'Just stick it down by the bag,' says Mulholland. Continues to look at her for a while, then turns and resumes his aimless flicking of the line across the water. Trying to remember what transpired between them the previous night, but can remember nothing. Only knows that he awoke with them both slouched in the car, the dregs of several bottles of wine surrounding them. Anything could have been said. Still remembers the decision to get married, however.

'Piss off!' she calls out, though they are close enough

278

and the water still enough for her not to have to shout. A brief contemplation of leaving him to it, and taking the food back with her, but decides to be more pig-headed than that.

He turns again.

'What?' he says. 'What now?'

'Come and have something to eat, you ignorant bastard. You must have been here ages. I've not got this stuff together just for you to completely ignore me. I'm going to be your wife, remember, so put the bloody rod away and come and get something to eat.'

He turns away, gives one last pointless toss of the fly into the water, a toss treated with disdain by the river life beneath, and then he turns and wades back to the bank. Proudfoot busies herself with unpacking her bag.

In the trees the watcher is fascinated by the last line. Stumbled across these two, quite by chance, but he knows well who Mulholland is. Supposed to be out hunting him, and here he is, inadequately hunting fish instead. And they are to be married. Slowly he begins to creep through the damp leaves and twigs, to get nearer and listen to what is said. Never miss an opportunity, that is the killer's code.

'When did you wake up?' she says.

Mulholland starts to struggle out of his waders.

'About seven, I think. Still dark, anyway.'

'And have you eaten since then?' asks Proudfoot. Annoyed at him, but mostly for not looking after himself. Taking the whole marriage thing seriously. This is her man.

'Bought a stack-load of food from the petrol station down the road,' says Mulholland.

She removes the plastic lids from two cups of tea, and the steam rises into the cold December air.

'That's funny. The woman I spoke to in the shop remembers you buying a sandwich and a can of Coke, and nothing else.'

He lays out a jacket and sits on it. Raises his eyebrows at her.

'Checking up on me, eh?' he says.

'I am a detective.'

'Right,' he says, and lifts one of the teas. Just a sip in case it's too hot, and then a longer gulp. Just right and it hits the spot; can't beat machine tea. Melanie's tea always tasted like socks.

'So you reckon we're still doing this marriage thing, then?' he says.

She bites into a closed-face, triangular-cut, white bread, disencrusted cheese and smoked ham sandwich, with cucumber, lettuce and tomato and a light spreading of mayonnaise.

'Why? You changing your mind?' she says through the food.

He shrugs and takes a bite out of an open-faced, square-cut, heavily crusted, wholemeal Belgian pâté sandwich, with a thin garnish of fresh cucumber. He waves it at her.

'Good sandwich, by the way. You choose 'em or were they all that were left?'

'My choice.'

'So we are compatible. Maybe I will marry you.'

'So what, have you changed your mind?'

He watches the river, cold and grey. How many days since they'd stood and watched the Clyde? Three maybe, that's all, and not much has happened in between, yet it feels so long. Time slowing down. That's what happens when you step into gloop. Or shit.

'It just seems kind of stupid,' he says after a while.

280

Sadness in his voice, and it is deep felt.

She munches her way through the sandwich. Follows his gaze into the river. Thinks exactly the same things that he does, except for one. So what if it is stupid?

'Everything's stupid,' she says. 'You standing in a river for God knows how long. That's pretty stupid. Life is stupid. You coming down here in the first place. Whatever. It's all stupid.'

He distractedly nods his head. Feeling depressed again, good sandwich or not, and she joins him in his melancholy.

'I must've said a couple things last night,' says Mulholland. 'Sorry if I offended you.'

Her turn to shrug.

'Doesn't matter if you did. Can't remember what you said anyway. Expect I was talking pish 'n' all.'

The river rolls on by. The sun momentarily makes an appearance before once again being swallowed up by the layers of cloud. There is a noise in the trees just behind them. Mulholland barely notices, Proudfoot turns slowly and sees nothing. Assumes birds or rabbits.

'You want just to go back to Glasgow?' she says. 'I don't know how long this bloody group are going to be here. It's not as if I can barge in there and check out what they're doing.'

'When you off duty?'

'Not till midnight.' She shrugs. 'Fuck it, maybe I should just come off duty now. I've left my post, after all. I mean, she could nip out while I wasn't looking and go and kill somebody, and I wouldn't give a shit.'

Mulholland laughs softly. 'Fine words for a police officer,' he says.

He turns and looks at her. Her face is colourless with the cold and he notices for the first time how poorly she

281

is dressed for the weather. Her lips are soft and pale, her hair touches her cheeks. And in this grey light, she is beautiful.

'Sorry, Erin,' he says, removing his jacket, 'I'm being a pig.'

She starts to protest, but he holds it towards her and she gratefully takes it from him and slips her arms inside. She can feel the warmth of his body, gets the faint smell of him. And for all that she's hated him for the last six months, you can only hate what you can love, and she has missed him.

'Stay with me,' he says, and she closes her eyes to savour the words. 'Phone them up tomorrow and tell them where they can stick their job.'

She drains her cup of tea to give that air of calm. 'You think? Are you sure you want to be with me?' she says. Tries to keep a level head. Here she goes, carried away on nothing but a little tenderness. If she were Jade Weapon, she'd shag him breathless, karate-chop him to his neck; then toss him to the fishes.

Then his hand is extended to hers, the first genuine moment of tenderness between them, so that neither of them notices the slight movement in the bushes behind, the small noise of someone scrambling over damp ground.

He leans forward and gently kisses her on the lips. A short touch, then pulls away, his hand still on hers, the other rested against her cheek. With the warmth of his jacket around her and of his hand on hers, her heart melts.

'You've got smoked-ham breath,' he says.

She purses her lips then breathes out massively over him.

'You're right, you are a pig,' she says.

And he laughs, she joins him, and at last there is some light in their lives.

And well away from the riverbank, out of earshot, the footsteps stride more confidently across wet ground. As off goes the killer to sabotage Proudfoot's car, and the radio in the car, and thereby lead the happy couple along the road he wishes them to walk. To lead them to play their part in the magnificent extravaganza which has quickly formed in his criminal head.

9

liz taylor? she's a woman.
no question

'And Cary Grant, he was a woman, yes siree,' says the handyman. As ever, Hertha Berlin is spellbound with his tales of Hollywood in the sixties. 'Steve McQueen, there was another one.'

Berlin pours him another cup of tea. Glad to be away from the strange crowd in the lounge. Raised tempers and voices. It is ever the way with the Christmas crowd, when expectations are up and more drink than normal is consumed. She prefers the midweek bookings, with companies sending their people on team-building events. Everyone is hacked off and grumpy and expecting to be miserable, and consequently much less bother as a result.

'Did ye know anyone else famous?' she asks.

'Sure, honey,' says the handyman, cramming his mouth full of pancake. 'I knew 'em all. Jimmy Stewart, Eastwood, Newman, Ann-Margret, Liz Taylor, the lot of 'em. Bobby Mitchum, he was a big friend of mine.'

Berlin shakes her head and sips quietly from her cup.

'It must seem terribly mundane being stuck here in the south of Scotland, after a' that fuss,' she says.

The handyman looks at her and considers the statement, and reckons that it is worth a decent answer. It is something he has given much thought to these past twenty-three years. Trading in the glamour, the women, the drugs, the parties, the booze, the handguns, the television sets and the celebrity pals for a quiet life, from which he knows he will never escape.

'Mundane's just what you want it to be, honey,' he says, and she nods her head, even though she doesn't know what he means. Helpfully, and unsurprisingly, since he's a talker, he elaborates. 'Hell, everything's mundane if you do it often enough. You make movies all your life, it becomes mundane. You have twenty number-one records; mundane. You snort enough cocaine offa naked women' – Hertha Berlin blushes – 'that becomes mundane too. Sure, this might be mundane now, but it was fresh when we first started, and now it's good mundane. I like it. Keeps me young. I'm telling ya, honey, physical-wise, I'm a lot better off now than when I first got here. Ain't that the truth.'

Hertha Berlin finishes her tea and tops up her cup. Has to pour some more for the handyman at the same time.

'Thing is,' he says, 'look at those folks upstairs. Maybe they've got money, maybe they ain't, but there ain't none of them happy. Not real, down-to-the-damned-socks happy. Just a-trundling through this and a-trundling through that. Most of them ain't going nowhere. You just need to stop every now and again and look at your life, know what I'm saying, honey? That's what I did in '77. Realised I was in a world of hurt, and I got on outta there. But these fellas, they don't know shit. There was an old fella in Greece by the name of Aristotle, and you know what he used to say, honey?'

Hertha Berlin lowers the cup from her mouth and licks

some tea from her lips; wonders if it still makes her look as alluring at seventy-one as it did fifty years before.

'Ah sure don't,' she says, in a strange amalgam of accents.

'The unexamined life is not worth living. Yesiree. That's what that good fella said. And no doubt about it, he had a point.'

The handyman crams another biscuit into his mouth and stands up. Washes it down with the last of his fourth cup of tea. Brushes the crumbs from his jeans and nods his head.

'Gotta go clear that drain out back, honey. I'll be an hour or two, I expect, 'cause that little fella's gonna cause me a lotta trouble. I can feel it. You'll have my supper ready about seven?'

Hertha Berlin nods, standing herself and already beginning to clear away the dishes.

'Aye, aye,' she says. 'Chicken casserole the night.'

The handyman smacks his lips.

'Sounds delicious, honey,' he says. Grabs his coat and his hat. 'See ya later, alligator.'

'Bye,' says Hertha Berlin.

Door open and then out he goes into the cold. She stares after him for a while, wondering how it is that you can be seventy-one and have the same sort of mad infatuation that you get when you're fifteen. Aren't you supposed to grow out of that kind of thing?

The words to 'Love Me Tender' quietly begin to escape her lips, and Hertha Berlin goes about the business of washing up and getting the dinner ready.

10
tidings of comfort and joy

The fire crackles and spits, the tree sparkles in the corner. The gang of chums is gathered around the tree drinking Hertha Berlin's coronary-inducing Christmas punch, waiting for the annual present exchange. The presents are all present and correct, it's just one of the participants who is missing. Sammy Gilchrist has yet to return after leaving the previous meeting. They had had to wait for Morty Goldman as well, but he has been back for some twenty minutes now.

Conversation is low, but the alcohol is flowing and the mood is improving. Chances are, they mostly think, this could be a good night. One or two of the inmates who see themselves failing in their love quest are already thinking of calling on a couple of outside agencies of sex to provide the night's entertainment. Things could be worse. And given the obtuse minds involved, the gift exchange is usually pretty interesting.

Barney waits nervously, the words of his grand venture into poetry going through his head. Wondering if Dillinger will know it was him who wrote it; and wondering how he'll tell her it was him, on the assumption she doesn't work it out.

'You don't think something's happened to him?' says Dillinger to Arnie Medlock. Barney has been watching them talking for the past ten minutes, and has assumed it is far more intimate than it actually is. His own attempt at introductory conversation with her – 'Apparently if you pull a condom over your head you can still breathe for nearly three minutes' – had crashed and burned, and she'd wandered off in search of something more conversationally appetising. Barney needs better lines.

'Who?' says Medlock. He is in his element. Playing the king; the senior figure; the captain; the skipper, the chief, the boss; El Presidente; General Fantastic; Mr Invincible; The Amazing Captain Sperm. Whatever. He sees himself as the godfather to these people, and the Christmas weekend is his turn to establish that position even more. And the worst aspects of it emerge when he gets drunk.

'Sammy,' says Dillinger, slightly annoyed. Fully aware that Medlock knows who she's talking about. Hates it when he does his Al Pacino shite.

'That poof?' says Medlock. 'He's a jessie. Wee Morty just looked at him funny and the guy creamed his pants. He'll be back, the sad bastard, you can count on it. Won't want to miss out on his present.'

Dillinger takes another dive into the depths of her Christmas punch, and bites her bottom lip. Can see the weekend falling to pieces, despite the current revelry and good humour among the inmates.

'What if something's happened to him?' she says. 'I'm beginning to get a bad feeling about this weekend.' And she catches the eye of Morty Goldman as she says it, and his eyes slime away from hers and he stares once more at the carpet.

'Settle down, babe, everything's going to be fine,'

288

Medlock says, then notices her looking at Morty Goldman. 'Don't worry about Morty, for goodness' sake. I can take care of him. He's a bit daft, but he's under control.'

He rests his hand on hers to reassure her, and she feels a sense of relief at the words, and does not know that Medlock could not be farther off the mark. For Morty Goldman is not fine, not by any means.

Barney sees the blatant hand-touching and quails at it. Buggerty shit-farts, he thinks. Bugger, bugger, bugger.

Silver bells, silver bells, lah-de-de-dum-de-de-lah-lah ... So goes Bing Crosby for the eighth time this weekend. The drinks the thing, and none of them is getting fed up with it. And in the midst of the Christmas festivities, the door opens and in walks Sammy Gilchrist. A bit of mud on his shoes, face slightly damp with sweat, hair a bit wet, breathing hard, but trying to cover it up. The appearance of the guilty man about him.

Morty Goldman slings him a sly look, then turns away; the carpet to contemplate. The carpet and other things.

Medlock nods his head towards Gilchrist and Dillinger follows. Relaxes a little when she sees him, and Medlock feels the tension go from her fingers.

'Told you,' says Medlock. 'The big poof was probably out pulling his pudding behind a tree somewhere.'

Gilchrist moves straight for Hertha Berlin's pungent punch. Ladles a glassful, swallows it, goes through the appropriate facial contortions, then pours another glass. He turns and surveys the scene, and realises that everyone is watching him. An antagonistic few words flash through his head, but in the air there's the feeling of Christmas, so he goes for conciliation.

'Sorry about that,' he says. Still a little breathless. 'Just went for a wee walk, and Ah got caught in the rain, ye know. Pishing down like a bastard the now, ye know. So are we doing the presents?' he adds, sitting down away from Morty Goldman, not even looking him in the eye.

'Aye, we are,' says Dillinger. 'Glad you're back all right, Sammy.'

'Nae bother,' he says.

'Poof,' murmurs Arnie Medlock under his breath, to general amusement. Sammy Gilchrist snarls, but keeps his thoughts to himself and takes another long swallow from his second lethal punch. Can already feel it having the required effect on his limbs, head and thought processes.

'Right,' says Dillinger, 'come on, round the Christmas tree. Arnie's going to be Santa Claus.'

Medlock quaffs the rest of his quadruple Lagavulin and heads for the tree. Magnanimous look on his face. Santa Claus. The bearer of gifts. The controller of people's emotions. The Almighty. That's him. And Dillinger potters after him, Santa's little helper. Barney watches in envy.

The annual Christmas present handout. Something childish about it, something alien to the very being of this group, but Dillinger thrusts it upon them every year, and every year they mope and grump, but every year they enjoy it all the same.

So they top up their drinks and they gather round into a small circle. Eleven wise men or women, and they are all overcome by the atmosphere, the lights, the music, the alcohol and the general feeling of goodwill. Even Sammy Gilchrist and Morty Goldman are prepared to lend a hand to the air of geniality. Even the jealous Barney.

Nat King Cole has headed into enemy territory on 'O! Holy Night', and the Christmas tree shimmers.

'Hope I'm going to get loads of condoms,' says Billy Hamilton, and laughs.

'You don't need them for rubber women, Billy,' says Arnie Medlock, and he laughs louder and longer and is joined by the others, including Hamilton, because he's got that Christmas feeling, which only comes this time of year.

'Right, then,' says Medlock, delving into the sack beneath the tree where all the presents have been discreetly placed. 'Ho fucking ho. The first one's for Katie herself. There you go, hen.'

Instant nerves for Barney. A stranger in this crowd, wishing he had left, but here's a good reason to still be here. Wonders if his long-thought-out poem will bring home the goods. Also worried that she will instantly recognise it as being from him and will denounce him publicly in front of the others.

'No, no,' she says, 'I'll go last. Let one of the others have theirs.'

Her protest is greeted with a chorus of disapproval, and Medlock thrusts the present into her hands.

'On you go,' he says. 'Santa says,' he adds, magnanimously.

Dillinger smiles, and begins to unwrap the gift with a certain childish abandon. Barney watches nervously. Feels like a teenager; or at least what he assumes teenagers feel like, 'cause he never felt much like a teenager when he was one.

The paper comes off, and all is revealed.

A box of chocolates. A man of limited imagination, our Barney. Had thought long and hard, had even gone so far as to check out a couple of lingerie shops, but hadn't had the nerve. It's all in the poem, he thinks. The chocolates are mundane, he knows that, but the poetry will sort her out.

She smiles appropriately and seems genuinely pleased. Knowing the sort of thing that the others get up to, she immediately suspects Barney. The conservative idea of a new boy. If he's still here in a year, she thinks, he'll be buying vibrators the same as the rest of them.

'That's brilliant,' she says, beaming. 'Thanks.'

She hasn't noticed the poem! thinks Barney. She hasn't noticed the poem. It's still in the wrapping. Bugger, bugger, bugger. I can't say anything. Shit, shit, shit. Bugger. Should I say? If I say she'll know it was me. The poem! he screams at her using telepathy, but he's no *Star Trek*-type alien, Barney.

Medlock reaches into the bag for the next present. Barney nearly explodes in frustration. The poem! Look at the poem!

'Here,' says Ellie Winters, who from now on will be known to Barney as The Saviour, 'is that not a card or something in the wrapper for you, Katie?'

Medlock hesitates. Dillinger lifts up the wrapper, fishes out the small card and opens it.

'Ooh, it's a poem,' she says, with a little more enthusiasm than she'll feel after she's read it.

'Read it out!' a few of them cry.

Dry throat, Barney holds his breath.

'All right, all right,' says Dillinger. Medlock eyes her suspiciously. Bloody poetry, he thinks. Should he find out who sent it, he'll kill them. Or something like that. And she quickly looks over the poem – and then decides to read it out, despite what it says.

You're nice, you're smooth, you're sexy as fuck;
You're hard, you're strong, you're tough.
I want to kiss you everywhere
And see you in the buff.

And feast my eyes on every inch
Of your delicious body,
And do the kind of sordid things
That Big Ears did to Noddy.

A long silence.

Dillinger looks up, slightly red. Trying not to look at Barney, because this is the sort of thing that none of the others would have written. And she knows all their handwriting . . .

'Ooh,' she says, to no one in particular.

'Fuck,' says Ellie Winters. 'Smooth bastard that, eh? Your luck's in the night, ya bitch.'

'You never know,' says Dillinger, and finally she risks a glance at Barney. Barney stares at the floor. Arnie Medlock fumes.

'Christ!' says Socrates. 'Ah didnae know that Big Ears and Noddy were shagging. Bloody hell. Ye just don't know, dae ye, ye just don't know.'

Without further hesitation, Medlock hands out the next present. Morty Goldman holds out his hand, Medlock gets the feel of a clammy finger, and the show is once again on the road. Dillinger sneaks another glance at Barney and this time he catches her eye. Bright red.

And so the presents go. A large kitchen knife for Morty. A pump-action shotgun for Socrates. False breasts for Annie Webster (and she is not amused). A blow-up rubber woman, with real hair, moving parts and fully operational triple orgasm mechanism for Billy Hamilton (who always gets a blow-up rubber woman). Half a litre of cyanide for Ellie Winters. A working replica 1940s Luger for Bobby Dear. A full set of Davie Provan videos for Fergus Flaherty. Four different types of lubricating jelly for Barney; a present originally intended for the

293

ubiquitous Hammer Galbraith. A range of penis rings and other genital attachments for Sammy Gilchrist.

Round they go, and each is pleased or uninterested in turn, and none of them goes so far as to be upset by their gift. It is Christmas, and for all that the Day of Days is two days away, when it comes it will not match the feeling of pissed relaxation that they each feel now. For Christmas Day itself will either be spent in unruliness with their family, or passed alone in front of the television, succour only to be gained from Jimmy Stewart or Judy Garland.

Arnie saves the most important to last. He always gets an original or limited-edition Conan Doyle. It's a Christmas tradition within the group. A bit of a bugger for whoever picks Arnie's name from the hat, but it is expected of them. He's their spiritual leader, after all, with Dillinger more the secretary and the accountant. Medlock is the one they all look up to, and none of them begrudges him his rare gift.

In fact, this year Bobby Dear, who is not especially fond of the man, has searched long and hard through the bookshops and antique markets of the west of Scotland, and uncovered a near-pristine copy of a 1901 edition of *The Sign of Four*. Not a first edition, but a good catch all the same. He knows Arnie will be chuffed, and despite himself intends to discreetly let slip that it was him who bought it.

Sadly, what is left of *The Sign of Four* lies smouldering under a pile of ashes in the heart of the fire, which spits and crackles.

Arnie lifts his present up to his ear and gives it a shake. Breaks into a broad smile.

'Sounds like a book,' he says, and the others laugh.

He frowns along with the smile, however, because he

had heard a slight movement with the shake and knows that this is no book. Too light as well.

He opens it up. The others look on, vaguely indifferent. Another Sherlock Holmes, and who cares? Most of them have been forced into dingy bookshops on behalf of Arnie Medlock at some time, and each of them breathes a sigh of relief when they don't pick him in the yearly draw.

Arnie holds up his gift. Face like thunder. The others suddenly show a little more interest. Morty Goldman, who has been sitting stroking his knife, suddenly leans forward, eyes lit up. Dillinger holds a hand to her mouth. There is a gasp or two. Frank and Bing break out into 'God Rest Ye Merry Gentlemen'. The fire spits. The Christmas tree sparkles.

And the rough nail on the end of the discoloured human finger which Medlock holds in his right hand glints dully in the light.

He looks quickly up at the others, and none of them shows anything other than shock or at least genuine interest. Here we go again, thinks Barney. Once more unto the breach.

Medlock grits his teeth and looks each one of the group in the eye.

'When I find out who did this,' he says, the voice that murdered at least a couple of farmers menacingly low, 'you're in big fucking trouble. Big trouble.'

And they all look back at Medlock, then glance around at one another. There goes that Christmas feeling.

Let nothing you dismay.

11
frontier justice

An hour later, and the mood is still low. Not all of them in the lounge; splinter groups having headed to the kitchen to plunder vast quantities of food, or made for the snooker room to lose yet another game to Medlock. Barney has waited for his chance; Dillinger and Winters and Webster have been in conversation, the Snatch Batch as Socrates had called them, discussing the distressing turn of events.

Dillinger wants to call the police, but that is not an option open to them. None of the people here present delights in the involvement of the authorities in any aspect of their lives; and, what is more, at least three of them have never been convicted, or even suspected, of their crimes, so the Feds will not be welcome snooping around and asking awkward questions. The severed finger will have to be ignored, or more likely left to Arnie to sort out. Frontier justice, that's what he can administer.

And there's the point of the snooker table, as suspects are brought before him to be interviewed around the green baize.

Morty had been first, as he is everyone's favourite suspect, and he had submitted to the interrogation with a

296

sly and ironic smile. Then Sammy Gilchrist and Socrates; currently Bobby Dear, placid and dour. Medlock is not looking for anyone to confess, he just asks innocent questions in an expert way; and using all his criminal psychopathic knowledge, he knows that he will be able to spot the one responsible when he sees them.

Webster and Winters have gone off to hit the bar, leaving Dillinger on her own. Staring into the depths of the fire, recently puffed up, the wood augmented, by Hertha Berlin; out of whose sight the finger will be kept.

Barney sees his chance; his prey is on her own. The mood may have gone, but still there are points to be scored, opportunities not to be missed. And so he pounces like a wildcat on the slow-moving mouse of Dillinger's distress.

He mooches over, the smooth-talking bastard in his element. Wondering how he can turn the finger thing to his advantage. Wondering how he can put all his experience of bodies and dismemberment to good use. Wondering what he can possibly say to sound mature and sensible, aloof yet concerned, nonchalant yet sensitive to the situation.

He sits down across from her and follows her gaze into the fire. And at first she doesn't appear to notice him. Quite distracted, Katie Dillinger. Running through each of the group, trying to work out which one of them could have done the finger thing; as well as the small matter of whose finger it might be. She draws the obvious conclusion that it has been removed from one of the past weeks' murder victims in Glasgow, and that this new serial killer who haunts the city is indeed one of their own.

'Bit of a bastard,' says the eloquent voice next to her.

It takes a few seconds to filter through. Eventually she turns, sees Barney Thomson; the one of her group she knows the least, the one of her group of whom, if he is who he says he is, she should be most afraid. Except for Morty Goldman, of course. They make films about people like Morty Goldman.

'Sorry?' she says. Doesn't smile at him. Thinking about the poem. *Feast my eyes on your delicious body.* That was it. She's sure it was Barney who wrote it. It'd been embarrassing at the time, but what exactly had he meant by it? And now here he is, sitting next to her like an obedient puppy. She can't see any danger in his face, she has to admit that. With all the others, particularly the real loons like Goldman and Winters, it's obvious and it's out there. In the eyes, the curl of the lips, the general demeanour. Not in Barney Thomson. He looks like, well, a barber.

'Bit of a bastard,' he repeats. Has been using the gap to desperately think of something else to say other than *bastard*, but his mind is its usual blank. More confident now with customers and in all other sorts of situation, perhaps, but still a complete and utter duffus when it comes to women.

'What is?' she says. Furrowed brow as she examines him. Was beginning to convince herself this man was the killer, but as he sits, she can see the gormless look of him, with only the remotest hint of Sean Connery remaining.

'Eh,' says Barney, hesitating. 'The, eh, situation, ye know. A bastard. The finger and a' that.'

'I know,' she says. 'Any ideas?'

A wee tester to gauge the reaction.

'On what?' says Barney. Hoping she's gone off at a tangent, and is asking if he has any ideas who wrote the poem. Or maybe, if he has any ideas as to how the two of them can spend the night. In bed, under the sheets, he begins to think, doing the sort of things that men and women do, although he's not sure that he can quite remember what that is exactly.

'How the finger got into Arnie's present,' says Dillinger.

'Oh, aye,' says Barney. The finger.

Finger schminger. So there's a serial killer among them, he thinks. Bugger it. There's always a serial killer among them; I'm in the mood for love.

'Someone's just having a wee joke,' he says. 'Pretty funny, really, when you think about it,' he adds, smiling. How can he get off the subject and on to more interesting matters such as sleeping arrangements and women's pants?

'You think it's funny?' she asks. Perhaps there is something of the serial killer about him after all. 'It was a real finger, Barney. Someone, somewhere, is missing it.'

'Aye, but they'll have another nine. Ah mean, how many dae ye need?'

Smooth. Very smooth.

She looks at him in a particular way.

'I'm glad you think this is amusing, Mr Thomson,' she says. Mr Thomson! An arrow in Barney's heart, and he can feel the pain as sure as if the metal point had just plunged into his chest.

'Naw, naw,' he says quickly. 'Ah didnae mean it like that, ye know. Honest Ah didnae. Ah just meant ...' God, I don't know. I just meant that I'm a total Spamface, I've forgotten how to relate to women, and I'm a bag of nerves. 'Ah don't know what Ah meant.'

He looks into the fire, and she looks into his eyes. Can see the hopelessness there, and cannot associate the callousness of the words with the pusillanimity in the face. She doesn't know what takes hold of her, or what it

299

is that so dissipates the suspicions of a minute earlier; but here she is holding out her hand, and she gently touches his and squeezes his fingers.

'I understand,' she says.

Zing! Barney looks up at her. At last, suddenly, getting what he wanted, despite himself. Zing! I'm in the mood for love! And a million cheesy-listening songs break out in Barney's head. I'm Errol Flynn, he thinks. I'm Casanova. I'm Cyrano de Bergerac without the noggin. I'm John Malkovich in *Dangerous Liaisons*. I'm Joey in *Friends*. I'm alive! I'm Frankenstein's monster without the chip on his shoulder. I'm Peter Boyle. I'm Boris Karloff. I'm Robert de Niro.

Yet, despite the general goofiness of his thoughts, his face displays nothing, as is ever his way. Still too early to get carried away. And the look he returns to her is as sad as the one she gives him; and he responds to her touch.

Something makes Dillinger turn her head; and there in the doorway to the lounge, wiping his hands free of chalk on a dry rag, is Arnie Medlock. Eyes piercing, a look that could kill. Arnie Medlock; a dangerous man to cross.

Her heart flutters, but she does not remove her hand from Barney's. Their eyes engage for a while, then Medlock turns his back and is gone. Dillinger stares after him, briefly catches the eye of Socrates McCartney, who watches the action suspiciously from a corner afar, then looks back into the fire.

The flames hiss and crunch, and the fire slowly growls and emits small noises as wood slips and logs diminish. Barney's eyes are lost within it, and he has not even noticed the attentions of Arnie Medlock. And Dillinger stares into the fire and feels quite lost. And does not know that she will never see Arnie Medlock again.

300

12

be thou my battle-shield, sword for the fight

It was raining hard. Hard like wet stone and hard like a slug from a .45. The river was rising faster than a lump on a bashed skull and it seemed like it'd been raining for a million years. And in some ways, for Jade Weapon, it had been.

There's only one thing to do when it's raining, and raining hard, that's what Jade Weapon has always thought. Get hold of a man, shag the life out of him, and leave him dead in the gutter, 'cause that's where all men belong. So she grabbed the Turkish agent, tore down his pants and rammed his throbbing wet love-stick into her sopping engorged sex-hole.

Proudfoot tramples through the wet undergrowth that runs beside the road, dripping branches brushing against her face, the rain teeming down through the trees on top of her. Imagining what Jade Weapon would do in these circumstances; and knowing full well that Jade would grab Mulholland, wildly thrash about in a sexual frenzy for ten or fifteen seconds, then strangle him with her thighs.

Mulholland marches ahead, head down, no particular destination in mind. They have just passed the petrol station and found it long since closed, as this year's serial killer had known they would. And they have trudged along the road ever since, now almost four miles from where they had been fishing; and where they had found Proudfoot's car refusing to start, and her radio refusing to work. It hadn't seemed such a long walk for Mulholland in the bright morning, especially given the few miles he'd hitched on the back of a tractor. Had seemed nothing at all for Proudfoot in her car.

Not sure if anything lies along this road before the mansion where Proudfoot's prey is spending her weekend. Vague memories of a house and a church, but neither of them is sure. And so they plod on, aimlessly through sodden grass, with no plan and without any idea or care for their direction. A fine metaphor for both their lives.

Someone knows where they are, however. And he lies ahead and waits, his business already taken care of.

'Bloody hell, Mulholland,' says Proudfoot eventually, deciding it is time to be at least part Jade Weapon. 'Maybe we should just go back and wait at the car. One of these rare bastards who keep driving by and completely ignoring us is bound to stop some time.'

He stops and turns, lets her make up the few yards she'd trailed.

'It's bloody miles,' he says. Not angry, not frustrated. Face a blank look of determination; a determination to not care. 'We'll get there, and if you blow your cover with this lassie you're trailing, who gives a shit? You're quitting the force anyway, aren't you?'

She lifts her shoulders. The rain runs off her hair and down her forehead, and cascades off the end of her nose.

A steady stream of water. She is wearing his jacket, which has long since given up the ghost and is leaking water like the ill-fated seventies prototype PG Tips over-coat.

'Look at you,' she says. 'Standing there in a jumper. You'll catch your death, for fuck's sake. And I'm not much better in this thing. We shouldn't have even started to walk in the first place. Let's just turn back and go and wait in the motor. It's fucking miles to the house.'

He stares through the rain. She looks gorgeous. Cold face, water streaming all over it – vulnerable, beautiful, gorgeous. And somehow unattainable with it, despite their affections of earlier. And if she is vulnerable, is he the one to protect her?

Catch his death? Might be an idea. He could get ill with respiratory problems, be really cool for a few days like Val Kilmer in *Tombstone*, and then die. There's a way to go.

Doesn't say a word. Just turns back and keeps going the way he has been. Proudfoot considers turning back, but does not deliberate long. She can't lose him now. And so off she goes, head down, charging after him. They can go together to that bloodied police station in the sky, in apathy; cold and wet and hypothermic.

Stoatir, she thinks. Absolute, nae questions asked, bollocking stoatir.

'You're being an Advert Man, you know,' she says, drawing up alongside him.

Head down, he doesn't even bother to lift it. Overcome once more by misery, melancholy and grumpiness.

'What are you talking about?' he says.

'An Advert Man. You know what men are always like in adverts. Stupid. Can't put the toaster on, can't work out how to get stains off the carpet. Can't put their under-

303

wear on the right way round. That's what you're like just now. Pig-headedly, blindly, ridiculously, stupidly heading to some place that's bloody miles away, even though you know it's wrong.' Laughing as she says it. Has given in to the rain and the possibility of dying as a result of wet clothes. Starts banging her hand against the side of her head and saying 'daaaaaawwhhh'.

Mulholland shakes his head and trudges on. Ignoring her, although a smile comes to his face for the first time since they left the riverbank.

'And you'd be the Advert Woman, I suppose? Smooth, intelligent, cool as fuck and worth it?'

'Too right. Glad you know me so well.'

Equanimity resumed, Mulholland shivers with the cold. The day is turning to night, the temperature beginning to drop, the rain pelting down. His clothes cling to his skin and he dreams of a hot drink beside a warm fire.

'Why do we always end up bloody freezing?' he asks.

She shivers too, as if being reminded of the cold has increased her sense of it.

'Must be fate,' she says.

Mulholland looks up and stops immediately. Her head down, bent into the wind, she hardly notices.

'There's bloody fate,' he says, as the killer's trap opens up before him, large and inviting. They have walked along the given road, and now they will drink in their salvation, and they are in no fit state to see the lair into which they are about to walk.

She stops and follows his gaze. They have turned a corner, and there in the distance, some half-mile down a long straight stretch of road, is a house, lights in the windows glowing bright.

They stand for some seconds, staring in wonder. Relief, redemption, they are saved.

'Think there'll be room at the inn?' asks Proudfoot, as they begin the trudge down the road, feet squelching noisily on tarmac.

'Don't give a shit,' says Mulholland. 'If they don't let us in we'll arrest them. Got my badge in that jacket pocket.'

'Thought you'd resigned?'

'Aye, I did, but in a "keeping my badge until they officially ask for it back" kind of way.'

'Aye, I think I'll resign in that way as well.'

And on they plod through the rain. Trees at the side of the road thin out, there is no protection at all, and so the rain thunders with unbroken intensity. A wall of water, spanking down in glorious sovereignty, creating pools and small lakes all over. But on they go regardless. The lights get slowly closer, the shape of the buildings ahead becomes clearer.

A large, detached house, late nineteenth century. And the closer they get, the more clearly they can see the spire of the church which lies some few hundred yards behind the house. A classical spire, reaching up into the gloom, atop a large church, hundreds of years old.

Proudfoot sees it first, Mulholland's eyes rooted to the mud and water, and occasionally the beacon of the lights in front of them.

'See the church?' asks Proudfoot.

'Church?' he says without looking up. 'Think you're dreaming.'

'Could mean that this is a manse. They're bound to ask us in and give us a nice bowl of soup.'

Mulholland's mouth hangs open, breathing hard, swallowing rainwater.

'Don't give a shit,' he says. 'It can be a minister, a priest or a bloody hockey-mask-wearing psychopath. I'm going in there, I'm sitting down in front of the fire, and I'm having a cup of tea. Don't give a shit if it's a manse.'

'That's the spirit,' she says, and plods after him through the loch.

✄

Another ten minutes and they find themselves standing outside the door of the Old Manse, as the small sign proclaims. Shoes sodden, clothes clinging to them, still in the belly of the storm.

'Your shoes are soaking,' she says, looking down at his feet.

'Aye,' he says. 'Should have kept my waders on.'

'Aye,' she says. 'Shouldn't have left them behind that tree either. The river'll be up and away with them.'

'Bollocks to them,' he says. 'I'd trade them for a cup of tea at the moment.'

The door opens. A man in his slippered feet stands in the way of the light. C&A slacks, a crew-neck jumper his gran must have knitted for him a long time ago, under which can be seen the edge of his dog collar; a shock of black hair, kind face, blue eyes, white teeth. Young and old at the same time.

'The Lord bless you!' he says, a look of horror on his face. 'What a night tae be out. Come in, come in. Ye can't be standing out there, whoever ye are.'

Mulholland and Proudfoot drip into the house and stand in the middle of the hallway, water pouring off them onto the carpet. Hit by a marvellous wave of warmth, and the smell of home cooking. Pictures of rivers on the walls, thick patterned carpet, stairs leading up into the heights of the old manse. Low lights and an air of comfort.

'What has happened tae ye, in God's name?' asks the vicar. Fussing about, without actually doing anything.

'Ye're no from around here?'

'We were fishing,' says Mulholland. 'Car broke down, and there was no one at the petrol station.'

He can see into the sitting room, where a fire blazes in the hearth. A cup of tea, something – anything – to eat, and a seat beside the fire, that's what I need. Not even thinking of how they're going to get back.

'At the old river way by?' says the minister, pointing in the direction from which they've just come. 'That's a fine distance, indeed. Ye must have been walking for ages.'

He gazes at them for another few seconds; soaked to the skin, water dripping, shoes creating massive puddles on the floor. Mulholland wonders where the wife is; the creator, he presumes, of the wonderful smells emanating from the kitchen.

'Look, ye cannae just stand there, the two of ye. You get yer shoes off, 'cause if ye walk through the house like that my wife'll have a fit, God bless her. Jings! I'll go up tae the bathroom and get a couple of towels and then I'll see about getting ye some clothes.'

And off he goes, mincing up the stairs, muttering about the weather and the night and the folly of fishing. They watch him go, then see about removing their shoes and socks without spreading water over a radius of three or four miles.

'Nice old guy,' says Proudfoot. Wouldn't have been surprised to have been chased from the front door, minister or not.

'Recognise him?' asks Mulholland, voice a little lower.

She looks up the stairs, although he has now disappeared into the bathroom.

'Don't think so. Should I?'

Mulholland shrugs.

307

'Not sure. Just something about him, about the face. Might have seen him before. Maybe on a case, maybe somewhere else, don't know.'

'Everyone looks like someone,' says Proudfoot, getting to the root of most appearance-based relationships. 'Or maybe he appeared on one of those docu-soaps on TV. Everybody else has.'

The minister appears at the top of the stairs again, clutching a great pile of thick, cushiony towels, behind which he minces back down the stairs. Shoes removed and dumped in a pile on the 'Welcome' mat, they watch him come. Wondering what it is that's creating the smell, and hoping they're going to be offered some of it.

'There you go,' says the minister, handing out towels all round. Light pink for Proudfoot, dark blue for Mulholland. Old-fashioned is the Reverend Rolanoytez. 'Now you two get in there in front of that fire and get out of those wet things. I'll go and get the kettle on, then I'll find ye some dry clothes tae wear. If only mother hadn't gone out tonight, she'd be in her element. Still, she's left me wi' a fine rabbit stew for masel', and I'm sure there'll be enough tae go around.'

'Thanks a lot,' says Mulholland, 'we really appreciate this.'

'Don't be daft, laddie,' says the minister. 'Don't be daft. The Lord smiles upon us all.' And off he minces towards the kitchen. They watch him go, then drip their way into the sitting room.

A warm room in every way. Red carpet; walls lined with books and hung with old paintings; velvet curtains; fire roaring and the dinner table set for one, with a small candle burning. And they immediately begin to strip off with no sense of embarrassment that he might walk in on them. They are freezing and this indeed is a godsend.

Clothes off and dumped in a heap, and within a minute they are huddled in front of the fire, wrapped in light pink and dark blue, watching the flames and feeling the warmth and life return to their bodies.

Backs to the door, they don't see the Reverend Rolanoytez make his way along the hall and back up the stairs. Small mincing steps, until he gets to the main bedroom. Flicks the switch and in he goes in bright light, hardly giving a thought to the two visitors downstairs. Except he must find them something to wear, something not too incongruous. The younger ones today, he thinks wrongly, they'll want something they like, regardless of the situation, not just something they can be comfortable in.

'What have we got, then?' he says quietly, and begins to rake through the two sets of clothes drawers. 'What have we got?'

Then he starts to hum a quiet tune as he goes about his business. *Be Thou my vision, O Lord of my heart* . . .

And lying on the bed behind him, the real Reverend Rolanoytez and the dear Margaret Rolanoytez say nothing. Had they just been bound and gagged, perhaps they might have tried to make some noise; if they'd dared. But as an extra precaution against their alerting the outside world, their throats have been slit, and both lie dead; eyes and mouths open, staring wildly up at the ceiling, faces blue.

Waking or sleeping, Thy presence my light.

13

the last supper

For the first time in several years there is a subdued atmosphere at the table, for the Murderers Anonymous Christmas dinner. Not since Malky Eight Feet tried to grab Jenny Four Stretchmarks' boobs over pudding in 1993, resulting in a free-for-all fist fight, has there been such lack of good-humoured revelry.

Around the table set for eleven, there are three empty chairs. And like a team with three players sent off before the end of the match, those remaining are merely playing out time until dinner is over. However, the night ahead in this blighted house, with creaks and noises and ghosts in every corner, does not invite anticipation.

Barney is on a roll and has his wish; a seat next to Katie Dillinger with the added bonus that the one on the other side is vacant, Arnie Medlock having not arrived for dinner. It is a huge round table, elegantly set by Hertha Berlin. Cutlery all over the place and more glasses than you could have claimed at an Esso garage in the late eighties. And around the table from Medlock's vacant chair go Bobby Dear, Ellie Winters, a gap for Morty Goldman, Socrates McCartney, Annie Webster, Sammy Gilchrist, Fergus Flaherty and a gap for Billy Hamilton.

They have waited long for the missing men to show – the Three Wise Men, Sammy Gilchrist will call them after tasting the prawn cocktail – but eventually they have started on the repast and now, in subdued humour, the merriment of Bing and Frank having finally failed them, they munch their way through turkey and roast potatoes, wee sausages, stuffing, a bit of bacon, cauliflower and Brussels sprouts.

Hertha Berlin appears as if by magic. Not too concerned whether all her food gets eaten, for she knows the handyman will polish off anything that remains. Quite pleased, in her way, that there is not the sort of riotous behaviour she was expecting, but is nervous nevertheless. This crowd gives her a bad feeling, and the fact that three of them are missing and out of sight only serves to heighten her discomfort.

'Is everything all right for ye?' she asks the assembled company, while looking straight at Dillinger. At least Dillinger looks a solid sort, she thinks. Honest. She is not to know that Dillinger murdered her first four husbands. A knife in the throat every time. The fourth one cottoned on to the pattern, but too late.

'Aye, thank you, Mrs Berlin, it's fine,' Dillinger says. Barney watches her lips. Pale, red and full. He could kiss those lips. Right here, right now. Lean the few inches across the table and, if his memory serves him correctly, pucker up as if he's drinking a Bud Lite straight from the bottle.

There are a few other nods around the table; a few other comments come to mind, but they all restrain themselves. Except Sammy Gilchrist, released from the presence of Medlock and Goldman, who feels free to air his concerns.

'The prawn cocktail was shite,' he says, 'But the turkey's awright.'

Socrates McCartney laughs; Fergus Flaherty sniggers. There are one or two embarrassed looks around the table. Hertha Berlin gives Sammy Gilchrist her best *Slow Train to Nuremberg* look, the light grey hairs on her top lip glinting slightly in the candlelight. Gilchrist does not wilt, however. Morty Goldman and Arnie Medlock may well intimidate him, but he can still stand up to old women. That's how tough he is.

Hertha Berlin gives it her best, then quickly marches towards the door when she realizes the stare is getting her nowhere. Out she goes, and the door closes behind her with a precise, Germanic click.

'That's 'cause I pissed in it,' she mutters under her breath, making her way back to the kitchen.

Back in the dining room there is an awkward silence, filled only by Bing Crosby, sleigh bells ting-ting-tingling or whatever the hell it is that they do.

'Ah thought the prawn cocktail was nice,' says Barney to fill the silence. 'A hint o' ammonia perhaps, but ye get that wi' fish sometimes.'

'Tasted like pish tae me,' says Gilchrist, and the conversation dies away once more.

And they stare at the table and listen to some pointless line about coffee and pumpkin pie. Good old Bing. The fire crackles; the Christmas tree sparkles in what, to be frank, is becoming an irritating manner; Ellie Winters blows her nose and is caught inspecting the contents of the hankie by a glance from Bobby Dear, who finds it attractive.

'Doesnae look as if there's gonnae be much shagging the night,' says Socrates to bridge the gap.

Another few embarrassed looks around the table. Ellie Winters and Annie Webster stare at their thick slices of roast turkey – covered in Hertha Berlin's own special

312

gravy – and think that just because Dillinger's boyfriend, the seemingly pubescent Hamilton and the mad-as-a-loon Goldman, have disappeared, doesn't mean that there's not going to be any shagging going on.

So Annie Webster murmurs something to Socrates that no one else can hear, just to keep Sammy Gilchrist on his toes, and gradually conversation breaks out around the table. Like smallpox. And each of the inmates reaches for their glass, wine is drunk, and tongues will be made gradually more loose.

'You think they're all right?' says Dillinger to Barney, strangely the only person to whom she feels like talking. Despite the Noddy thing, rather than because of it.

'Who?' says Barney, mind not on the job as usual. Had been wondering whether Fergus Flaherty would suit a Victor Mature or a Tyrone Power '45.

'Arnie,' says Dillinger, slightly annoyed. 'And Billy, and that awful little man, Goldman.'

Barney turns to her, a small piece of cauliflower protruding from his mouth. All sex.

'Are you allowed tae say that?' he says. 'You think wee Morty's awful?'

She frowns at him to keep his voice down and glances around the table. No one notices, however, all conjoined in the old black magic of love. Or at least, no one appears to notice.

'He gives me the creeps,' she says, dropping her voice a little farther. 'I mean, I know it does him some good to come to the group, and I'm afraid of what would happen if we kicked him out, but he gives me the creeps all the same. Can't like everyone, I suppose,' she adds, forcing a smile as she says it.

Barney nods. You can't dislike everyone, that's always been more his way of looking at things. Although there

313

have been times in the past when he's proved that adage wrong.

'Ah thought he was awright,' says Barney. 'A bit weird, but that doesnae single him out among this mob, does it?'

Careless words, and again Dillinger looks round the assembled throng to see if anyone is listening, but once more her look is ignored and the idle chatter of romance shimmers around the table.

'I suppose not,' she says. 'I suppose not.'

And so dinner progresses, on and on, through the turkey and on to Hertha Berlin's Unique Recipe Christmas Pudding with brandy butter, then the coffee and mints and mince pies; or the coffee and mince and mints pie as Fergus Flaherty has always presumed it to be.

Barney and Katie Dillinger get along fine, in a one-sided kind of a way, with one of the parties looking for love, and the other looking for absolution. Socrates McCartney decides to take up the fight and engages Sammy Gilchrist in a battle over Annie Webster, using words as weapons, each trying ever harder to outdo the other with witty throwaways, intellectual debate, and lengthy discussions on the relationship between Titian and tubes; Fergus Flaherty and Bobby Dear, free of the mad intentions of Goldman, vie for the hand of Ellie Winters.

And every now and again, Annie Webster and Ellie Winters exchange a passing glance.

✂

'So,' says the minister, 'are you two young lovers married?'

Both Proudfoot and Mulholland have their faces buried in rabbit stew. Cooked with onions, garlic and mixed herbs in half a bottle of red wine. Slow-cook for four to

314

six hours. Food of the gods. Drinking red wine with it, despite initial hesitation after the night before. All going down like a dream. Mulholland in his dead man's clothes; a pair of slacks, by God!, a sweater and comfy shoes which almost fit. He could be Ronnie Corbett. Proudfoot in her dead woman's clothes could be June. From *Terry and June*, that is, not mad June Spaghetti, who murdered a family of fifteen in Kirkcaldy because they wouldn't let her take a short cut through their back garden.

'Not yet,' says Proudfoot, 'but we're going to be.' Casts a glance the way of Mulholland as she says it, but he shows no reaction to the statement. Up to his neck in *Watership Down* rejects. Might have thought twice about digging in so readily if he'd known that the meal, while being initially prepared by the moderately kind-hearted Mrs Margaret Rolanoytez, had been finished off by a man who has murdered five people in the last week and a half. And that's not to mention Wee Magnus McCorkindale, whose death now seems light-years away. Like the Star Ship *Voyager* or the one-pound gallon of petrol. Remember that? Bastards.

'Any day now,' says Mulholland without looking up, and Proudfoot examines the words and tone in search of sarcasm, but his head is buried in his food, shovelling away like Bart and Homer, and he appears to be serious.

'Oh, lovely,' says the doppelgänging Reverend Rolanoytez, politely picking away at a small plate of stew. Here is a man who has had his fill earlier. 'Where's the service to be?'

'Don't know yet,' says Mulholland, during a convenient gap in the sprint between the plate and his mouth. 'Might go to Gretna.'

Proudfoot slams food into her mouth at an almost equal rate. Impressed by Mulholland's seeming willingness to

315

discuss their betrothal. One minute he's for, the next he's against. That's how it seems.

Men. Bastards.

'You don't want tae go tae that dump,' says Rolanoytez, with unusual vigour. Mulholland looks up at last, colour returning to his cheeks. 'It's for the English and the Americans.' He hesitates to instill the required impression of giving the matter some thought. 'I could marry you here. We've got a lovely church. Beautiful for weddings.'

They look at each other and back to the faker. No doubt, there is God's light in his eye. A broad smile comes to the vicar's face and he clasps his hands together.

'Oh, what a lovely idea,' he says, and the smile broadens, then slowly dies on his lips, but stays in his eyes. 'Ye know, I was wondering what it was that brought the two of you here, because ye know God does not do things for nothing. And now he has spoken. It is kismet, it is the work of the Lord. I must marry the two of you, that is your destiny. That is why God has brought ye to me.'

They take a break from the Great Food Race. They look at Rolanoytez, they look at one another. The smile in his eyes is infectious. A kind man, wishing to spread the light of God into the hearts of others. Proudfoot can feel the tears begin to well up. Daft, but there you are; she always does cry at moderately emotional points in her life. Like during the final episode of *Blake's Seven* or when unknowingly spending half the day with her skirt tucked into her pants. Mulholland looks at her and can see that emotion. Feels it too. Wants to reach across the table and kiss those warm lips.

'All right,' he says, nodding. 'You on?'

Proudfoot smiles through the first tear that has formed.

This is it, they are about to start planning their wedding. She's found her Lancelot; her hero; her knight in shining armour, her Lothario; her recently divorced, verging on middle-aged, moderately psychotic, grumpy sod.

'Aye,' she says, swallowing back the whole tear/emotion/passion thing.

'Right, then,' he says. Turns to Rolanoytez. 'When are you free?'

Rolanoytez licks a small amount of potato from his lips. The smile returns, although this time with a devilish, or psychopathic, edge.

'Tonight,' he says.

An instant. Then Mulholland frowns; Proudfoot looks like a kid who's been offered a pot of paint and a spray gun in the house of a relative she doesn't like.

'You can't do that, can you?' says Mullholland.

Rolanoytez laughs, and it sounds joyous and romantic and adventurous.

'Why not? It will be just wonderful! Seize the day, my children. This moment has been presented to us. Grasp it with both hands and do the will of the Lord.'

Mulholland lifts his shoulders and waves his fork around. A small bit of gravy falls to the floor and soaks into the carpet.

'Marriage licence? Posting banns? All that stuff?' he says.

Rolanoytez raises his shoulders and the smile returns to his face.

'And the Lord said, "There is but one moment, and that moment is now." There would be paperwork to be done next week, but I am God's organ, here to do his bidding. A marriage made in the Lord's house is a true and a just one, and the bonds cannot be broken. Ye will require a couple of witnesses, and the bond can be made.'

317

There is but one moment and that moment is now. Doesn't really sound like Jesus, thinks Proudfoot. More like *Dead Poets Society*. Of course, she hasn't stepped into a church since she was three, apart from during the case of Davie One Nut, who was strapped naked to a statue of the Virgin Mary on his stag night, and had frozen to death by the time he was discovered. And so her doubt passes.

Rolanoytez leans forward, taking the hands of the soon-to-be-happy couple. His face is warm and encouraging and the light of love and hope beams upon them.

'Do it, my friends. Take the Lord into your hearts and be wed before him.'

Getting carried away with it all. As you do. Not sure about the 'taking the Lord into my heart' bit, thinks Proudfoot, but Mulholland looks glorious in the light of the fire and the candles; her James Bond.

'No,' says Mulholland. With infinite finality.

Proudfoot swallows and sits back. Tears threaten once more. For all the shite, when it comes to it, maybe he hasn't changed a bit. The Reverend Rolanoytez senses the immediate intrusion of atmosphere and pushes his chair back, lifts his plate.

'Tell ye what,' he says, voice filled with heavenly concern. 'Why don't I leave ye alone for a minute while ye have a wee chat to yourselves?'

He begins to walk slowly from the room. And in a moment of cheeky psychosis, he winks at Proudfoot, smiles encouragingly, and is gone.

The fire crackles. Mulholland spoons some more stew onto his plate. Head down, he doesn't look at her. Knows what she's thinking, but she is wrong. She's probably wrong. And he attempts to think straight, but the sludge in his head is so thick no clear thoughts can emerge.

318

Feels her eyes burrowing into him. The grace of another few days before the commitment is made is being snatched away. Ridiculously and absurdly, and he knows instantly that this will all be part of the game. Refuse the blistering romance of this, and Proudfoot will assume fear and lack of interest on his part.

'Well?' she says, the word whipping out.

He looks up. Stew on his lips. Tries not to show what he's thinking.

'It's stupid.'

'Why? What difference does it make? I thought you wanted to get married. You wanted to get married two minutes ago.'

'I know. Just not like this. I mean, we'll still have to go to a registrar, won't we? For all his sanctity of God's house crap, that old fart pronouncing us married in the middle of the night probably won't mean diddley-fuck. So what's the point?'

She throws her arms out in beseechment. Losing the emotional self-defence.

'It's romantic, for Christ's sake. That's what marriage is supposed to be about, isn't it?'

'It's stupid. Let's take a few days to plan it.'

'Plan what? There's no family, no friends, no honeymoon, no flowers, no walk down the aisle. What's there to plan? This is it, Joel, you either want to do it or you don't.'

He looks her in the eye. Right enough. You either want it, Joel, or you don't. Doesn't matter whether it's before an eccentric old minister in the middle of the night or in the cold light of day, or if it's before a boring stiff in a suit in a registrar's office. The effect is pretty much the same.

'Look,' she says, not letting him away with further

319

protestations. 'I know fuck all about the law of it, but it probably means something. We'll be married in a church, for Christ's sake, and who would have thought that would happen? Fucking hell, Mulholland, I love you, and you, as far as anyone can tell, probably love me, so who gives a shit if it's the middle of the sodding night, it's pishing down like a whore's pyjamas, and it's probably illegal? Let's just go for it. It's romantic, it's spur of the moment, it's impetuous, it's Jade Weapon. You've walked out on me once before, and if you do it again I'll crush your balls like a dumper truck, you bloody bastard. So let's, for fuck's sake, just cut the crap, stop messing about, and get married.'

Mulholland dabs the stew from his lips. Their eyes lock together. Hearts beating as one.

'That you quoting Shakespeare again?'

Proudfoot's shoulders collapse in an emotional heap. Her impassioned plea greeted by the usual male defence to emotion. A cheap gag.

The Reverend Rolanoytez, who undoubtedly heard every word, returns to the room and sits himself down at the table. God's light still shines in those eyes. He looks from one star-crossed lover to the other; waiting.

'What about witnesses?' says Mulholland, the first to speak.

The Reverend Rolanoytez does not hesitate. The big house lies a couple of miles up the road, and there await any number of potential victims.

'A mile or two up the road,' he says. 'It is some way, but I can give you rainwear to see you through the storm. There is a house of some size.'

'We know,' says Mulholland. Jesus Christ. He looks at Proudfoot, who shrugs.

'Ah, wonderful. There is a party there. A group of

some description, on a Christmas weekend away. I'm sure you could find two of them to share in your joy. You could phone, but perhaps for something such as this you might need the personal touch. I shall ready the church. Turn on the heating and light the candles. I shall prepare everything. Finish your dinner and then set out for the house. I shall meet you at the church at eleven o'clock. Oh, dear Lord, it will be joyous!'

This is stupid, thinks Mulholland. It is all wonderfully contrived, but the policeman in him is completely shot. Why not? he now thinks, at last giving in to Proudfoot's emotion. Why not be stupid? He's still got another couple of hours to back out. Still got another couple of hours to get lost in the woods.

'Let's do it,' he says. Heart of light and stone.

'You sure?' asks Proudfoot.

'Of course not,' he says, starting to laugh.

The smile spreads across her face; tears fall.

And the smile spreads across the face of the Reverend Rolanoytez's killer. For he knows who will return with them from the big house.

He just knows.

14

lesbians roasting on an open fire

Post-dinner, and the mood for the evening is set. Small groups have dispersed around the house, and the usual Christmas spirit has completely gone. Still no Arnie Medlock, Morty Goldman or Billy Hamilton. Annie Webster and Ellie Winters have finally and firmly nailed their colours to the mast. Ending more speculation than usually surrounds the election of a pope or the draw for the first round of the Champion's League, they have chosen to eschew the host of men, who had gathered to slobber at their doors, and are snuggling down together in front of the dwindling fire.

And so the men have gone their ways, suitably chastened and abandoned to all their masculine impotence. Mince without potatoes. They could have reacted by swarming around Katie Dillinger, but they have been warned off by the look on her face – she is clearly upset by the missing three, which is even worse than her being annoyed – and by the presence at her side of Barney Thomson. The evil Barney Thomson. For all these men have heard about the man; they know what he's done in

322

the past, and they are beginning to think that maybe it is his doing that so many of their number have fallen away. Perhaps he is taking them out, one by one. And so, none will cross him, and none will get in the way of his attempted conquest of Dillinger.

Fergus Flaherty the Fernhill Flutist and Socrates McCartney are at the snooker table. Bobby Dear is watching them intently, waiting to play the winner. Developing a strategy. Sammy Gilchrist is sitting in the lounge, pretending to read a book, keeping his eyes on Ellie Winters and Annie Webster. He's heard about this kind of thing – of course he has – but he's never actually seen it done. Wondering if they're going to get stuck in, or whether they'll save it for the privacy of their room later on.

Barney and Katie Dillinger sit side by side on a huge sofa, staring at the dying fire; and in Barney's case, trying not to stare at the Webster/Winters combo.

'This is a disaster,' says Dillinger, breaking ten minutes of silence.

Barney slowly nods his head. He doesn't feel it so badly, but he can see it for what it is. If only he'd known, he could have spent the weekend sitting in the pub with old Leyman, talking about Elvis. Yet he is next to the woman, and this evening has brought them closer. This could still go somewhere, albeit more than likely not this night.

That said, he still fears the night, and if he can spend it in the company of someone else, then he will grasp the opportunity. The walls have eyes, darkness has come, and once the lights go out who knows what walks the floors and skulks in secret passageways? And he knows that his nightmare awaits, for when at last he closes his eyes.

323

He places his hand on top of hers, squeezes slightly.

'Don't worry about it. They'll be fine,' he says. Doesn't believe a word of it; not in his world. Everyone gets murdered in this life, that's how it appears these days.

She lets out a short, bitter little laugh.

'God, I don't know,' she says, but does not remove her hand from his. 'It's always the same every year. There are tensions and doubts and anger. Always. But I usually manage to keep it in check. Or Arnie usually manages to keep it in check. Or The Hammer, but God knows what he's up to. I suppose it was bound to go wrong some time. But if one of this lot have done something to Arnie . . .' and she lets the sentence drift off.

'Arnie can take care of himself,' says Barney, not doubting for even a second that Arnie is dog food.

'I'm scared for him,' she says. 'Really scared.'

Barney swoops.

He places his arm around her shoulder and draws her towards him. It seems so natural, although he has not had such intimacy with a woman in decades. And Dillinger gives in to the comfort and leans towards him and rests against his chest.

Bing Crosby is joined by the Andrews Sisters for some mindless piece of Christmas twaddle, and the two unhappy couples snuggle down in front of the fire.

Sammy Gilchrist watches and wonders and waits.

✂

They struggle on through the rain. Done a lot of walking today and they're both tired, but the meal and fresh clothes have revived them. And now they have waterproof jackets and an umbrella each, and so the relentless downpour does not seem so bad.

'Do you feel swept along by the tide?' asks Proudfoot, to break a long silence.

Mulholland considers his reply. They notice every word, every nuance, he says to himself. Be very careful.

'Aye, I suppose,' is all he can manage. 'And this. Going to a house which is occupied by a known murderer to ask for witnesses to our wedding. How stupid is that? How's it going to look with our lot if Annie pops up and volunteers?'

Proudfoot nods and stares at the sodden ground. Couldn't the minister just have lifted the phone and brought in a couple of his parishioners? Still, she hadn't liked to say. It is their wedding, after all, it seems reasonable that they should do some of the work, some of the asking. Perhaps the minister was worried that someone from his congregation would report him to the Out of Hours Church Use Police.

'Don't care,' she says. 'I'm pretty sure I'm not going back, so what can they do to me? And they can't bring it out in the open because, to be honest, a lot of the stuff we've been up to in the last five months is illegal. I hope she does volunteer. God, who knows, maybe the bloke she killed asked for it. She's seemed nice enough to me these last few months.'

'Aye, but look at your judgement. You're marrying me.'

Proudfoot laughs and takes him more tightly by the arm. Does not notice the tension in response.

'I've never had any judgement,' she says. 'That's why I joined the police.'

'Ah. The perfect officer.'

She laughs again, and at the same moment sees the lights ahead through the trees. The house awaits them. More warmth, and more comfort. She hopes. Never know what sort of crowd they might encounter on a weekend away. Particularly when one of them is Annie

Webster. Immediately feels the possibility of embarrassing rejection. Turning up at someone's house at nine thirty on a Sunday night with an absurd request. Who the hell is going to want to come out on a night such as this? Nervously aware of the tightrope of indecision along which her husband-to-be is walking.

'And I always thought you were in the zone,' he says, to take his mind off the inevitable. 'At least, when you weren't reading crap magazines and listening to shite music.'

'No, not me. I don't think I've ever been in the zone,' she says.

'Me neither,' says Mulholland. 'Unless it was when I scored a hat trick for the Cubs against the 150th when I was nine. Certainly haven't been in the zone since I joined the polis.'

The house approaches; inching its way towards them through the trees. Until, suddenly it seems, it is there in front of them, huge and grey and sombre in the night, at the end of the long driveway. And they walk past where they spent the previous night, an age ago, and begin the trudge down the driveway. Slowing down as they go, as neither particularly relishes the thought of turning up at the house of a stranger. They are enjoying the walk, and maybe there's the feeling that what they are about to do will change things completely, and not just because they will be married.

'Maybe,' says Proudfoot, 'I hit the zone when I shagged every member of the first and second rugby fifteens in one weekend when I was in the sixth year. I was pretty hot back then.'

They walk on. Mulholland casts a sideways glance. Just the sort of information you want to receive on your wedding day. Such shredded emotions as his can't really compute the information quickly enough, however.

'Oh,' is all he says. They walk on.

'I made that up,' she says after a while.

'Oh.'

'Honest.'

'That's good. I don't really think that's a zone, anyway. It's more of a planetary system than a zone. Still, you must have been very proud.'

'I didn't actually do it. I said that. I made it up.'

'Aye, aye, right.'

Their travels bring them to the front door; and in out of the rain under the shelter of the porch, where Barney and his fellows had stood the previous evening. So close to this nest of vipers, this grand house of criminality, that had they been in any sort of zone themselves they might have sensed it. Evil lurks within. But they have both left their police zone a long way behind.

'You still love me?' she asks, as Mulholland rings the bell.

Love? The question comes winging its cherub's way towards him. Who mentioned love? A jokey question, but you know what women are like, he thinks. Laced with meaning.

Does he love her? Is that what this is all about? Charging through the night in the pouring rain to get married at midnight in the company of strangers. If not love, then what is it? Would I die for her? he wonders, for there's a way to judge. Would I give anything for her to be happy? Is she more important to me than life itself; and Partick Thistle? All that stuff.

He looks into her eyes, pale and grey in this dim light.

✂

Not much else to say. Dillinger and Barney snuggled up on the couch, unsure of the horrors that await them in the night. She knows Arnie – at least, she thinks she knows

327

Arnie – she knows he would not just leave them. Something has happened to him, and if Arnie isn't safe from one of their crowd, then neither are any of them. She doesn't know Barney, but she can tell a good and honest man by his face. She will stay with him tonight. If something romantic happens, then it happens, but she's not giving it thought. She needs succour, and Barney is her man.

The doorbell rings, the grating bell slotting nicely in between 'Suzy Snowflake' and 'The Snowman'. Dillinger starts slightly at the noise and sits up. Looks at her watch. Barney sits up with her, while the others in the room ignore it. The Webster/Winters combo is becoming ever more comfortable; and Sammy Gilchrist ever more engrossed.

'Christ,' she says, 'who do you think this is going to be?'

Barney shrugs. 'Probably some o' the auld house-keeper's mates. Come tae drag her out on a Sunday night. Some big Germanic gang o' goosestepping lunatics, off tae invade somewhere for the evening. See if they can hang ontae it longer than they hung ontae Poland.'

She ignores Barney's near-rapier humour.

'I've got a bad feeling about this. Something's not right. I'm going to get it.'

'Just leave it,' says Barney. 'It'll be for the ...'

And he doesn't bother completing the sentence, for she is already scuttling through the lounge and out into the hall. He shrugs and slouches back down into the sofa. Thinks he is unconcerned, but from nowhere the hairs begin to rise on the back of his neck. Suddenly the one-eyed sheep, hung by its neck, swinging in the wind, comes into his head. Sitting with Dillinger, he has

328

managed to push it from his mind, but now it's back. The hanging sheep, the shuffling from behind, the presence of Death at his shoulder. The prayer for his soul.

It all awaits him; and he feels the cold.

How immune he has become to it all, these last two years. Before all this had started, if he had found himself staying in a creepy old house with a group of convicted or unconvicted murderers, and some of them had gone missing, he would've been running. Now it almost seems mundane. But the feeling of doom which has suddenly crept up on him is something to concentrate his mind. He has had it for a few weeks now, and it is nothing to do with his current situation. But perhaps where he is, who he is with, will be the promulgator of events that are the making of the dream. He stands and looks round at the door, knowing that someone will be brought into the house. Doesn't know who, doesn't know what effect it will have upon him, just knows that they will play a part in the unfolding of his future.

His heart beats no faster, for he has become impervious to moments of tension. And perhaps it is time for him to leave this life, for he has no lust for it any longer. Not that he ever had, but at least before he had been stuck in his rut. Now, freed from that and emancipated in the world to do anything he chooses, he has found that freedom is not for him either; yet the thought of returning to his rut is impossible. Not after he has seen what lies outside. Can't stand freedom, can't face the oppression of normal life.

But it is the dread of what comes next, that undiscovered country, which ails him. Once again he feels the hand at his shoulder, and he looks towards the door as it slowly swings open.

Four people walk into the room, and Barney's mouth

opens a little, and at last his heart skips and jumps and picks up a little pace. Dillinger, followed by a man and a woman, with Hertha Berlin bringing up the rear offering tea and Christmas cake to the weary travellers.

Mulholland and Proudfoot quickly take in the room with the well-practised eye of the detective. The Christmas tree, the vanishing fire, the lesbians on the floor, the crazed and demented Sammy Gilchrist, lusting after the two lesbians on the floor. And the well-known, ever so popular, everybody's favourite serial killer, Barney Thomson, showing all his bottom teeth. Not the magnificent sparklingly white teeth of a crap chewing-gum advert, but white all the same. Good teeth. Hasn't had to visit the dentist in seventeen years.

'Bugger me! Barney?' says Mulholland. 'Barney bloody Thomson. What the fuck are you doing here?'

Barney stares into the eyes of the law. They've let him go once, but now that there's a new series of murders in the city and he is once more a suspect, will they be so forgiving? Assumes they must have come looking for him, and is therefore confused by the question. But they're here now, and so is he with his band of happy thieves. The last thing he can do, whether he actually likes many of these people or not, is tell them the nature of their group.

The glum Barney is as confused as ever when put on the spot. And so he says the first thing that comes into his head.

'Don't know,' he mutters.

15

don't suppose it can get any weirder than it already is

Annie and Ellie are overcome by ardour. Two women, a tender passion. Lips meeting in soft caress; pale cheeks glowing by the fading light of the fire. They don't even notice the arrival of the newcomers. Hands held lightly against cheeks, fingers run against the firm outline of a breast. *Jade Weapon opened fire with her World War II Bren gun, riddling the screaming lesbians full of lead. The blood poured from them and soaked swiftly into the carpet, as their voices screamed in tortured agony. If there was one thing Jade Weapon hated more than men, it was lesbians.*

Proudfoot looks quizzically at them. Annie Webster, in the midst of another woman. Hasn't betrayed any signs of that kind of behaviour in the past five months. Not that it changes anything, she thinks. She shrugs, then turns back to Barney Thomson; a man she thought she'd never see again. Mulholland stares at Sammy Gilchrist, but his mind is not switched on and he thinks nothing of him. Yet Gilchrist wilts under the gaze and can spot a polis a mile off. Takes the executive decision to walk casually

331

from the room; then stands barely out of sight behind the door into the snooker room, so that he can hear everything. Including the quiet sucking noises from the amorous couple.

'So would you like some tea or no?' says Hertha Berlin.

They are plucked from their respective contemplations. Still full up from the vast meal they had fed to them; but a cup of tea on a wet night is always welcome.

'That'd be nice,' says Mulholland.

'Cake?'

'Whatever. Anything would be good.'

'Right ye are,' says Berlin, and off she goes, making her way to the kitchen. Where the handyman eats his supper, his fifth meal of the day.

The door closes once more on the small group. *Dum-de-dum*, the usual stuff from the CD player. *We three kings of Orient are . . . dum-de-dum-de-dum . . .* On goes Bing, in his relentless search for Christmas cheer. Bless him. The fire dies slowly, the happy couple smooch, Sammy Gilchrist lurks in the snooker room, where Fergus Flaherty and Socrates McCartney continue to muddle their endless way through a four-and-a-half-hour frame of snooker while Bobby Dear awaits his turn; the clinking of balls drifting through to the lounge.

'You know each other, then?' asks Dillinger.

'Aye,' says Barney, hoping that Mulholland won't explain the situation.

'Aye,' says Mulholland, 'we've had dealings in the past. Small world, eh, Barney?'

'Aye,' Barney says again. Doesn't like to venture anything further.

Polis, thinks Dillinger. Written all over them in letters a gazillion miles high. And she's just let them into the house without so much as a word. However, there's something a bit different about them. Somehow it is obvious that the edge has gone.

'What's the set-up here?' asks Proudfoot. Wouldn't take even a moderate detective to know that there's something behind this odd collection of people. And she may, or may not, be about to throw it all away, but she hasn't lost all that innate ability.

Barney hesitates. Never was much good at handling the police. Certainly not when they have just been thrust upon him.

Dillinger shrugs. 'We're AA,' she says. 'Bearsden branch.' Then realizes as the words are coming out of her mouth that there are signs of alcohol consumption all around the room. 'This is our Christmas weekend away. Just a bit of fun. Have the odd drink. Group policy, and we can all keep an eye on each other. Seems to work.'

Mulholland nods. 'So you're hitting the sauce, Barney?'

Barney stares into the headlights. Eventually says, 'Aye, aye. You know how it is. Bit of a strain all that monastery stuff.'

'Know what you mean,' says Mulholland. 'Downed a few quintuples myself in the last year.'

'So what are ye doing down here, then?' asks Barney.

The door opens and in comes Hertha Berlin, almost unnaturally quickly. As if she had been expecting to serve tea for two. She breezes through the lounge and sets the tray down on the table. Tea, milk, sugar and a variety of cakes and biscuits that the handyman – who is currently devouring a double giant extra jumbo whopper burger with chips, down in the heart of the kitchen – has forgotten to eat.

'Thanks a lot,' says Proudfoot. Vaguely suspicious of

the whole set-up, including Hertha Berlin. Will still drink the tea, however.

There is an odd sucking noise from the happy couple, Bing moves on to *It came upon a midnight clear*, and Berlin strides purposefully from the room.

'We quit,' says Mulholland. 'Well, I quit. Not certain that Proudfoot has completely made her mind up yet.' Swings her a look.

'Sure I have,' she says.

'Oh,' says Barney. Sammy Gilchrist raises an eyebrow. Doesn't believe it.

'And we're going to get married.'

'Oh,' says Barney. 'Ah thought you two were shagging, right enough.'

'Congratulations,' says Dillinger, still eyeing them with a degree of suspicion. Ex-polis, that explains a thing or two. Still, you can't trust them even when they're dead, never mind just because they've retired. She should know; she was married to one. Until she killed him.

'Thanks,' says Mulholland.

'When's the big date?' Dillinger asks.

Mulholland takes the cup of tea that Proudfoot thrusts into his hand, then looks at his watch.

'Tonight,' he says. 'In just over an hour.'

The others look at the clock on the mantelshelf.

'You're getting married at eleven o'clock on a Sunday night?' says Dillinger.

Barney gets the strange sensation of a colony of bugs marching up his back; he shivers and stares at the floor. You don't get married at eleven o'clock on a Sunday evening. This has got to be wrong. It is bizarre, unnatural, and you'd think they'd realize. Or is he only feeling this because he himself is on edge?

Mulholland shrugs; Proudfoot smiles from behind her

cup. Young and in love; and not thinking very clearly.

'Aye,' says Mulholland, 'it's a bit daft, but you have to grasp these moments. We'll tell you about it on the way.'

'What do you mean?' say Barney and Dillinger in harmonic unison. The perfect couple.

'We're getting married at a church a mile or two down the road. Don't have all the paperwork and all that, but we're going to do the religious part and then get the paperwork sorted out next week. The minister's a bit odd, but enthusiastic. All we need are a couple of witnesses.'

And Mulholland casts a glance around the room, and through to the snooker table. Just how insane is this whole thing going to get? Getting married on a whim? Not entirely unreasonable. If he hadn't gone off his napper six months ago, he and Proudfoot would have been going out for a year by now, and might well have been married already. But Barney Thomson as a witness? Just how fucking mad is that? And he looks at the two lovers in front of the fire, and knows he's getting nowhere with either of them. Another glance at the suspicious characters in the snooker room. Looks at Barney and shrugs.

Barney shakes his head. For the first time in his life his brain moves quickly and everything falls into place. Like a punch from the sixties Ali, like a twenty-mile-wide meteor in the face, like a thunderbolt from the gods fired from on high, it hits him. A church, late at night, this strange company he keeps.

He's been wondering all along what the dream meant and what events could possibly lead to it having some sort of significance. And here he is in a strange old house, with a collection of murderers and psychotics, and now two punch-drunk ex-police officers; and they are taking him off to a church in the middle of the night.

335

This is it for him. And his face begins to lose colour as the others stare at him; the smile that had come with the suggestion dying on Dillinger's face as she watches. And the thoughts work themselves out and clarify themselves in his head and he makes his decision. If this is the way things are planned out, then there is nothing else to do but to walk headlong into those plans. Running and avoiding only delay the inevitable.

'What?' asks Mulholland, having watched the thoughts run and gather in Barney's head.

'Nothing,' he says. 'Nothing. You two sure about this? You want the greatest serial killer ever to walk the planet to be a witness at your wedding?'

Mulholland laughs.

'Come on, Barney. You're a jessie. If anyone other than you knows that all the stuff in the papers is shit, it's us. You're a big poof.'

And Barney laughs sadly and shakes his head. A life less bloody ordinary than this has anyone ever known? Weird as damn fuck, right to the end. If the end it is to be.

'How d'you meet the minister?' he asks 'When did you decide to get married? What's the story?' For they cannot surely just be getting married to suit his dreams. They could not have been sent to the monastery in search of him a year ago to end up at this moment. A pishing wet, bleak Sunday in Advent, surrounded by all sorts of psychopaths and ne'er-do-wells.

'No time for the Spanish Inquisition, my friend,' says Mulholland. 'To be honest, and I think I speak for us both, we're a bit fucked up, but we've decided to go for it. Seizing the blinking day and all that shite. Never been a better reason to get married. You coming? We'll tell you everything, such as it is, on the way there.'

Barney stares back. What are his options? Accept his fate, and at least approach it head on, eyes open – even if he doesn't know exactly what he's looking for – or stay here with the merry band of thugs in this house of demons.

He shrugs his shoulders, attempting an air of lightness he does not feel. It is time to face the nameless fear and to accept his fate. A brave man. It is not as if he has run from it these past few weeks; he has merely been waiting for it to show its hand. And now it awaits him, poised like a coiled snake, to strike him down.

'Count me in,' he says. 'Ah owe ye, after a'.'

'Thanks,' says Mulholland. 'Appreciate it, mate.' Then he turns to Dillinger and shrugs at her. 'Sorry, ma'am, don't know your name. But you couldn't come along as well, could you? Don't really want to split up the happy couple,' he adds, nodding in the direction of the Winters/Webster combo, slobbering away in phallic envy.

Dillinger swallows and looks around the lounge. Bing trudges wearily into another bloody Christmas number; the fire wanes; the tree sparkles, the lesbians snuggle on the floor, oblivious to everything, and everyone else is gone. In previous years the second night would be a riotous party – copious drinking, mad dancing, laughter, arguments, ebullience, games, idiocy, *joie de* sodding *vivre*. A party, and a bloody good and noisy one at that, regardless of the low numbers. But this? It seems almost to be admitting defeat to walk out on the evening, but then who is left? Of the other ten, Barney is about to go, three are missing, four have retired to the snooker room, and the two women have very definitely nailed their passion to the bedpost for the night.

She could join the men in the snooker room, but somehow it all seems so pointless. And as she stands and

337

looks around this depleted room, she considers that perhaps she is looking at the end of the Murderers Anonymous group she has run for over ten years.

You're being unnecessarily dramatic, she thinks. However, as it happens, she is not wrong.

'Aye, all right,' she says. 'I'd like that. Haven't been to a wedding in years.'

Mulholland swigs his tea; still too hot for such violent swallowing, and it burns his tongue.

'Brilliant,' he says. 'It's all coming together. We should get going, mind you. Don't want to keep the minister waiting. And it'll give us less chance to change our minds.'

Barney swallows. His life awaits. No time for second thoughts, no time now for repentance. He must face what the future has to offer him. And Katie Dillinger bows her head in similar resignation. This group she has fought so long to keep together has fallen apart before her eyes in just a few short hours. She intends to be back here this night, but somehow it feels as if she is walking away for ever.

'I'll get my coat,' she says. A voice of melancholy, which Mulholland can read despite the strange mental fugue by which he is afflicted. He stops her with a touch to the arm; has no idea of the thoughts and regrets coursing through her head.

'We appreciate it,' he says. And she half smiles and turns and walks slowly from the room.

They watch her go in curious solemnity, her mood communicated to both Mulholland and Proudfoot. A check on their irrelevant good humour. The weight of the night falls upon them and they share the gloom of Barney and of Katie Dillinger and of this house.

'Is there a bathroom I can use?' asks Proudfoot, staring at the floor, the rich warmth of the carpet.

338

'Out there, second door on the left,' says Barney, before Mulholland can ask how the hell he's supposed to know whether or not there's a bathroom.

This time they both watch Proudfoot go; small steps; she is tired. Fingers moving on her left hand, head down. Beautiful, even from behind, Mrs Rolanoytez's coat, too large and old for her, dragging damply on the floor.

'When did ye decide tae get married, then?' asks Barney. Beginning to walk towards the hall in search of his own coat.

'Last night,' says Mulholland.

'Right?' says Barney. 'Stunning.'

Can't think of anything else to say. Mind on other things, his brain pulled in a hundred different directions; yet all of them down.

'So why did you try to hand yourself in?' says Mulholland. 'We let you go, for God's sake. What was the problem?'

Barney shakes his head as they pass out into the hall. Behind them, one of Annie Webster's eyes flicks open to watch them go. She follows them out of the room, then closes it again and delves back into the amorous arms of Ellie Winters.

Annie has relationship issues that can usually only be resolved with a knife.

'Couldnae hack it,' says Barney, reaching for his coat. 'Just couldnae settle anywhere, ye know. Went fi' place tae place, but nowhere seemed tae be for me. So eventually, Ah just thought, bugger this, Ah cannae run a' my life. Decided tae come back tae Glasgow and hand masel' in, ye know. Course, Ah gets back here and no bastard wants me. They a' think Ah'm an imposter. So, what the hell, eh? It's no like Ah give a shite after a' Ah've been through.'

Dillinger appears beside them, coat buttoned, face heavy. About to walk out on the herd. Desert the sinking ship. Get a transfer to Rangers just before your team gets relegated.

'We ready?' she says.

Mulholland is still staring at Barney, thinking about what he's said. Because what has he just created for himself but a life such as the one that Barney has turned his back on. They are different people, certainly, but perhaps the results will be the same. He imagines he can just walk away from life out into the great beyond, and that his days will somehow be filled, but what if every life needs structure? What if his life needs structure? Will he find himself turning up at Maryhill police station in ten months' time asking for his job back? And will they look at him and ask who he is?

'Just waiting for Proudfoot,' he says.

He's getting married. That should give him some purpose. And the doubts set in, and he wonders.

He stares at the floor, the rich tapestry of a sixties brown-and-orange carpet. Frankly, a hideous carpet. The sixties and seventies have a lot to answer for, he thinks, as he lets his mind wander off in positive distraction.

Footsteps. *Les trois misérables* raise their heads and stare at Socrates McCartney. Shaggy and smiling.

'Did Ah hear yese say there's gonnae be a wedding?' he says.

Mulholland nods.

'Aye.'

'Right,' says Socrates. 'Stoatir. Don't mind if Ah join yese, dae ye? Ah love weddings. Think it's got something tae dae wi' the fact that Ah made such a horse's bollocks o' my own.'

Mulholland looks at him and does the shoulder thing.

340

'Sure,' he says. 'Don't suppose it can get any weirder than it already is.'

✂

Proudfoot washes her hands and stares into the mirror. She can see the tiredness in her face, the beginnings of lines and wrinkles which she will never lose. Used to be beautiful, that's what she tells herself these days, although she never thought it at the time. The first sign of grey in her fringe, and the now common signs of defeat and depression in her eyes.

She has lived her life not knowing what she wanted, and it never seemed a problem before. This last year has brought it out into the open, however. Here she is, drifting aimlessly. The odd pointless affair, the continuing pointless job. And now, to be married.

She swallows, splashes more water on her cheeks, then looks at her dripping face in the mirror. Where did you go, Erin Proudfoot?

And although it is within the line of sight of the mirror, she is so suddenly gripped by a peculiar sorrow that she does not notice the tiny panel in the bathroom wall pushed back into place.

Her husband-to-be awaits. And so she reaches for the towel, dries her face, then spends another few seconds looking into the eyes that once she knew. It is time to start the rest of her life. And all she has to do is shake off the burden of melancholy, and she can be happy . . .

And the figure who has watched her these last couple of minutes in the bathroom, who has gazed eagerly upon the soft white skin of her legs, who has licked his lips in anticipation and hunger, who has recognized her for the police officer that she is, makes his way slowly down the secret passageway that runs throughout the house. And he smiles, and his tongue twitches, and he tightly grips the knife in his right hand, and already thinks he can taste the blood.

For he is about to make his move.

16

the sorrow of hertha berlin

'I tell ya, honey, if there's one thing gets up my ass, it's milk floats.'

Hertha Berlin walks in on the handyman, up to his eyes in food and drink. Shovelling away the remains of the day's repasts. A small dollop of mayonnaise at the corner of his mouth, and a milk moustache. He takes another large bite from his sausage burger and points the glass of milk at Berlin.

'You're looking way too serious, honey. Come and sit yourself down and I'll talk to you about milk floats.'

'There's something going on,' she says. 'Something serious.'

He takes another large bite, even though his mouth is still full.

'Sure there is, honey, and it's me eating my supper. Come and join me. Put your feet up.'

She shakes her head and starts to fuss around the room. Something to tell him with which he's not going to be too pleased. Should have discussed it with him before she did it, but she knew he'd talk her out of it. Had to be done. Just had to be.

'Something serious with that lot up by,' she says.

'There's something funny going on.'

'Thing is,' he says, spraying a couple of small pieces of tomato onto the table, 'they obviously just don't spend money on milk float technology in this country. Here we are, the beginning of the third goddam millennium, and we've done all sorts of different shit. There's been men on the moon, there's digital TV, there's electric tooth-brushes – hell, they're even cloning goddam pigs, for Chrissake – but we still can't get a milk float to safely convey five hundred pints of the stuff quicker than fifty goddam yards every three days. Those damned things just clog up the roads. Pain in the ass.'

'Ah really ought tae tell ye something.'

'Course, it's not really the technological aspects of it that's the problem. In the States they've got milk floats can do nought to sixty in under three seconds, without breaking a bottle. The problem is, you people are too damned inter-ested in saving money. That's all you're about.'

Hertha Berlin has started pacing; biting her bottom lip, rubbing her thumb into the palm of her hand. The handy-man bites massively into another burger, even though he hasn't finished the one he still has bits of in his mouth.

'Ye're no listening tae me,' she says, no longer looking at him. On the other side of the kitchen, staring at the cold stone floor.

'Sure I'm listening, honey. I'm just not interested. Those folks upstairs can just keep themselves to them-selves far as I'm concerned. I'm talking about milk floats, baby. You see, you can tell a lot about a country from their milk floats . . .'

'Would you listen!' she suddenly snaps. Tongue like a snake, zipping out. Eyes blazing, with fear and worry as well as annoyance. He does go on sometimes, her handy-man. Her glorious, wonderful handyman.

344

The glorious, wonderful handyman giggles. Shows the pieces of burger bun stuck to his teeth.

'Sounds like you must be menstruating, honey. Thought you were too old for all that shit. Obviously everything's still in fine working fettle, eh? What d'ya say, honey?'

'I've called the police,' she says quickly, just to get it out. Lets the words out into the open and braces herself for the reaction. Should have discussed it before I did it, she thinks and repeats the phrase over and over in her head.

He pauses, ninety per cent eaten burger is one hand, twenty-three per cent eaten burger in the other. A soggy cornflake – Berlin knows that the handyman likes all kinds of things in his burgers – drops from his mouth and onto the table. Some strange liquid concoction that he is intending for his late supper comes to the boil on the huge old Aga which steams away in the corner.

'What? You're kidding me. You called the Feds? Why the damned screaming children of Moses did you call the Feds? You know what you've done? We can't have the damn Feds all over the joint.' He stands up, pushing his chair back from the table. Stretches his hands out in appeal to her, a burger yet in each.

'Ah had tae. There's something no right, ye know?' she says, voice pleading.

'What? What's not right? What are you saying, honey? You called the Feds and said "Excuse me, there's something not quite right, can you come over for a few minutes?" You said that? What?'

'Surely you can see it. They're a funny bunch and no mistake. Three of them have gone missing, ye know that. Ah mean, why come all the way down here fi' the Big Smoke, and then no eat yer dinner?'

The handyman waves a burger.

'You called the police and said that some of our guests didn't eat dinner? That's an offence in this country?'

'It's not just that,' she says. Rattled. Confused. Wondering whether she is going to look stupid when the police arrive.

'What, then? Someone look at you funny? Did you not like somebody's aftershave? What? I said you must be menstruating.'

'There's those two strangers just arrived. Ah didnae like the look o' them. And now there's three fi' our lot left wi' them tae go down tae the kirk.'

The handyman spreads his arms, shrugs his shoulders.

'At last, I can see your point. Going to church on a Sunday. That is criminal.' The calm before the storm. 'What is the matter with you! Who cares if they go to the damned church? I don't care. I don't care if they go to the damned church. Jesus, I'm just a bigga bigga bigga hunka nerves, honey. A big hunka nerves.'

'The phone lines are down!' she says, ever more exasperated. 'Ah had tae use Mr Thornton's mobile.'

'Jeez Louise, baby, there's a storm a blowing out there. These damned lines are always down.'

'There's more.'

He drops his shoulders, lets his expressive burgers fall to his side. He breathes deeply and lets the air slowly out through his nose. Finally gives her the time of day. He does, after all, have a soft spot for Hertha Berlin.

'Go on, honey, I'm listening to ya.'

'One o' the strangers,' she says. 'Ah was listening at the door, and he said that the minister down at the kirk was a lovely man. A lovely man, Ah tell ye, that's what he said.'

'And?'

'Well, everyone knows the Reverend Rolanoytez is a total bastard.'

The handyman is not sure what to do. So he takes a large but unfulfilling bite from one of his burgers. Technically an illegal immigrant, unknown to the taxman, and with more people to hide from than just the authorities, the handyman can do without the unwanted attentions of the police. Not if they are going to start snooping around his business. He crams the last of both his burgers into his mouth, so that his fat cheeks are huge and bloated and misshapen, then pushes his seat away and walks around the table.

'Ighths tgmhhym tghg ghhgh, hchughny,' he says.

Hertha Berlin stares at him, much in the same way as she once stared at Dr Jorg Franks in the heart of the Brazilian jungle. Of course, she had understood what he'd said.

'What?'

The handyman chews quickly on his food, swallowing large chunks of something which could almost pass as meat. Soon finished, he wipes the back of his hand across his mouth.

'It's time to go, honey,' he says. 'I can't wait for these guys. And when the Feds arrive, I'd appreciate it if you didn't mention my name.'

My God, what have I done? Hertha Berlin looks stone-faced across the kitchen at the man she has loved these past twenty years or so. A silent adoration, and now one pointless, stupid act and he is about to leave. Does not even think of rushing to the phone and calling them off, for he has nailed his colours firmly to the mast. Giving her instructions on what to do when the police arrive. Not a thought of asking her to go with him. But then, why should there be? She is an unattractive old woman in her

347

seventies. Older even than her years, after all she has seen. Wrinkled and pale, ugly grey hair and the definite substance of a moustache. Humourless and severe in equal measure, which no lightness of thought or heart will ever be able to penetrate. Why should this man who has been with so many women show even the slightest interest in her?

So for years she has contented herself with what she had. She saw him every day, she cooked for him, they talked. What more could she ask for? There are millions out there who would die for the same privilege. And now, with one thoughtless act, she has tossed it all to the wind.

'Of course no,' she says. Voice stern, as ever.

The handyman nods and galumphs his way to the door, muttering as he goes. 'Probably done me a favour, honey. I shoulda left this place years ago.'

Gets to the door and pauses; her heart flutters in an instant of hope, then leaps as he turns and looks at her. Say something! Say anything. If not you, then I must, she thinks. But words of hope or appreciation or love or even desperation are not her words, and in an instant the moment will be gone.

He nods at her, and cannot think of much to say to this woman who has been his cook for over twenty years. As stern and unforgiving as the first day he saw her. She'd hated cooking every meal she ever had to make for him; that's what he assumes. That's what everyone has always assumed by the cold front to the unbeknown warm heart of Hertha Berlin.

'Thanks, honey,' says the handyman.

Berlin's mouth opens and not so much as a breath is released. The handyman gives her a few seconds and is not surprised by the frosty heart presented to him. And so, with a nod of the head, he is gone.

The door closes, the handle clicks loud in the silence. Hertha Berlin stands and looks at the end of her sad little fantasies and dreams. He will not be gone immediately. He will be down to his house to pack the few essentials she knows he keeps close to his heart. There is time yet to go after him, to tell him everything she has felt for years. But she could sit here for a hundred years and never think of a reason for him to be interested in her.

And so she drops down into the warm seat that he has just vacated, pulls it up to the table, rests her elbows in among the burger crumbs and pieces of tomato, holds her head in her hands and, for the first time in over sixty years, her face wrinkles in emotion, her chest heaves, and she begins to sob.

But no tears come, so she will not even have that release. So many years of suppressed emotion and she is a tangle of conflicting thoughts and passions and jealousies and sorrows. The man she loves is gone, and she cannot even weep for him.

Hertha Berlin hangs her head low.

17

and they walk on in silence, down the road darkly

... four forlorn figures, heads bowed into the falling rain. And Socrates.

Barney contemplating the immediate future, feeling sure that his ultimate fate awaits him. There is a point to every recurring dream, and now it stands before him, arms open, ready to welcome him into its evil fold for all eternity.

Katie Dillinger contemplates the future of her group, which she has moulded and cajoled and inspired for years. On the verge of falling to pieces, or perhaps having already done so. Maybe it was all much more to do with Arnie Medlock than she had supposed. And now that he has suddenly disappeared, all cohesion has gone. He was the glue that bound them together, not herself, as she has always thought. No more Arnie, and the group is dead. She realizes it, as finally and surely as Hertha Berlin has realized that she will never see the handyman again. And that Arnie has been murdered by one of the group, of that she is equally convinced. It is not like him to just disappear. A good man, Arnie Medlock.

Mulholland contemplates the future. Marriage. Every day, more or less, with Erin Proudfoot. A big decision, made as easily as deciding on breakfast cereal. A lifetime of compromise, not getting everything, or anything, you want. Children? Haven't even discussed it, but then don't all women want children? It's one of their things. They all fancy Sean Connery, they want at least ten children, and when they hit sixty they start knitting. Mulholland has them sussed, and now he's about to commit himself to one for the rest of his life. That is a very, very long time.

Proudfoot wonders if she'd like a boy or a girl. Concentrating on the offspring question, because she doesn't want to contemplate the reality of what she's about to do. Commit to someone for the rest of her life. It seems right, but it also seems madness. A romantic story to tell their grandchildren – if they miss out all the stuff about multiple murders – but that's only if they survive together long enough to start a family. What if they hate it?

Socrates minces along the road, wondering what the basic guidelines are in life on hitting on a bird who's just about to get married. Proudfoot, despite the worry on her face, beats Katie, Annie and Ellie any day. Maybe not put together, because Socrates wouldn't throw any of those three out of bed for farting biscuits. But Proudfoot has got to be worth a go. Despite the presence of her boyfriend no more than ten yards away.

So, what the hell. In for a penny, in for a mound . . .

'What's the score then, hen?' he says, dropping in line beside her. Rule 1 of the unsolicited approach. Keep it simple. If that doesn't work, move casually on through the other five rules.

Proudfoot raises her eyes from the road and looks at

him. Wonders what demons dragged Socrates into the bosom of alcohol.

'How do you mean that?' she asks, the interest in him dying as it forms.

'You and the big guy,' he says. 'Ye don't look too happy there.'

'We're OK,' she says.

Socrates hums and raises his eyes. Sees an opportunity.

'Ye sure ye know what ye're doing, hen? Ye're a good-looking bird. Maybe ye'd be better off wi' some smooth bastard than yer miserable friend here.'

'Like you?' she says, smiling.

'Aye, well, aye,' he says. 'Ah'm glad ye noticed. Smooth, erudite and available. That's me.'

'Available, eh?' she says.

'Oh aye. Ah was going out wi' a bird until a few week ago, but it went tits up.'

'Oh aye?'

'Aye. Accused her o' shagging for biscuits one night and she buggered off.'

'Too bad.'

'Ah know. Ah was a bit pissed and my tongue got the better o' me. Told her a few truths. So she kicked me in the ba's, broke my Beatles CDs in half and urinated a' o'er my settee.'

'Vicious.'

'That last one was a bit o' a turn-on actually, but after the toe in the nuts Ah was hardly in a position tae dae anything.'

'Shame.'

'Aye,' he says, and stares contemplatively at the ground. 'Still, Ah was right. She did shag for biscuits. Anyway, the point is, Ah'm free and a' yours. What about it?'

'I'm damp,' she says.

'Really?'

'If I wasn't getting married tonight, I'd shag you.'

'It's no too late,' he says hopefully, and in the dark he can still see the look she slings him, and that is all it takes.

He shrugs and moves a few feet away from her on the road. What the hey, it was worth the asking.

'Blow out with the two women back at the house, then, did you?' she says.

Happy to continue the conversation, despite his take on it. Mulholland walking away in front, she is aware of the darkness around them. The wind and rain in the trees, rustling leaves, and the ghosts of footsteps. The creeping feeling of someone skipping through the forest, watching their every move.

'Just a couple o' dykes,' says Socrates, doing his best at nonchalance.

'Right,' says Proudfoot.

And maybe Socrates doesn't want to talk after all, and his head sinks a little lower, and he drifts imperceptibly away from her, and looks at his feet.

The bare branches of trees rustle in the rain and gentle breeze. The night is suffocating in the intensity of its darkness. And the forest surrounds them, in a way that it had seemed not to when they had so lightly walked up the road in search of the house.

On they muddle, Mulholland a few yards in front, the church and Proudfoot's future getting ever closer. And every step of the way she hears a sound in the woods, and can feel the penetration of eyes into her soul, as surely as she will soon feel the zing of an arrow.

Maybe she's about to do the right thing. The trouble with romance – there's no right and no wrong. Just possibilities. There's got to be a perfect one for every-one, that's what she's always thought. Even Jade Weapon had met the man of her wildest desires and fantasies. Of course, he had been immediately killed by the Bulgarian Secret Service, and Jade had had to personally murder half the population of Sofia. Maybe Proudfoot *is* Jade Weapon, and Mulholland her Spunk McCavern.

And the rest are no different, with various strange and melancholic thoughts in all their heads. Barney finds his life passing before him, but not at a flash. It is all there, like a video on slow rewind. Present day back to birth, a dirge through several thousand haircuts. He doesn't want to think about all this stuff, but it is all coming to him nevertheless. And he can think nothing of it other than it must presage his death, for when else is your life so plainly opened to you?

And, by God, what a bloody dull life it's been until these last couple of years. Perhaps it is better ended. And so his mind takes him back through the years of neglect to the essence of life; dull marriage, back to dull college and dull school. Wasted opportunities, missed chances, lackluster thoughts and insipid actions. And all the while, one grand truth awaits him, when he reaches the end of this bleak odyssey through his days.

✂

Eventually, they come to the manse with the church behind. The house is dark, all lights extinguished to the night. Inside, the bodies of the Reverend and Mrs Rolanoytez begin the long process of decomposition, although they will be discovered later this night before they have gone too far. If only Mulholland would think to act upon the vague suspicions aroused within him by the dark manse, then events might not unfold in the manner in which they will. But he stares at the great house,

354

shrugs his shoulders, and walks on by to the church. Stained-glass windows greet them, illuminated from behind and magical with the light and the rain splashing upon them.

Their pace slows, the church awaits. Should be snowing, thinks Proudfoot briefly, but the thought is submerged beneath all the doubt and concern and confusion that she feels. And the nerves. For she is nervous as she cannot recall being for many years. Puts it down to her impending betrothal; knows, inside, that there is some much greater impending doom.

Mulholland has been a few yards ahead of her nearly all the way. Now he stops and turns, speaks to her for the first time since they left the house. Has a hollow feeling in the pit of his stomach, which he can't even begin to explain. What they are about to do is wrong, but he cannot bring himself to say it. She has been through enough, without him dumping her at the altar. Maybe it will work out; maybe it won't.

'You all right?' he asks.

She meets his eye and does her best to smile. *I feel bloody awful*, she wants to say. This is the man she's going to marry, after all. She should be able to say anything to him. Anything but the truth.

'A bit nervous,' she says, and adds the uneasy laugh.

He holds out his hand and takes hers. Squeezes tightly and hopes he manages to convey emotions other than what he is actually feeling. Wrapped up as she is against the rain, cold face peering out from an oversized hood, he thinks, as always, that she is beautiful. But there must be more to it than that.

'You sure you two want to do this?' asks Dillinger. Barney stands apart, says nothing. Stares up at the church. His life has reached the point to which it had

355

been dragging him back, and he knows. He knows everything. The great wooden doors are closed over, but they will open and behind them will be his destiny. Of that he is now completely convinced.

Socrates huddles against the rain and waits. Looks at his watch. Had expected to be up to his eyes in one of the women by now. His playing it cool would usually have worked. But he doesn't mind. Easy-going, Socrates. Very easy-going.

Mulholland and Proudfoot do not notice Socrates, they do not notice Barney, suddenly detached and staring wide-eyed at his doom. They consider the question, and both know that you cannot answer something like that without giving primary concern to the other's feelings. They look at one another and hope that what is in their hearts gets through, for they cannot say the words.

'Aye,' says Mulholland, 'I'm sure.'

Proudfoot swallows and nods. Why not? How difficult is it to become unmarried these days? If marriage is all that awaits them in this church.

'Aye,' she says. 'Me too.'

Dillinger shrugs her shoulders. Can easily tell that they're making a mistake, but then perhaps all the reticence is due to nerves. They may be as right for each other as any other ill-starred couple.

'Right,' she says. 'Let's do it, then.'

'Aye,' says Mulholland. 'Come on.'

He nods at Proudfoot then turns towards the doors. The women fall in behind. Then Socrates, glad to get out of the rain. Beginning to wonder if he should have a go at Dillinger, despite promising Barney he wouldn't. No honour among thieves.

Barney barely notices them move. Consumed by the hazardous thoughts of revelation.

356

'Come on, Barney,' says Dillinger, walking past him. 'We're on. The happy couple are going to do it.'

Barney looks at them as they walk up the stairs and Mulholland opens the door. He knows who awaits them now, and he knows that these two will not be married. He should say something, he should stop them and face this himself, because he is really the one this concerns. But his tongue is stilled, his head numb, and the two lovers walk into the church, out of the rain and the cold. Socrates and Dillinger walk behind them and Barney drags the pillars of his legs into action and moves slowly up the stairs.

Into the church, eyes locked at his feet in concern, not wishing to face his future. The door closes behind him, then Barney looks up at the others and at the church. The wall of light . . . Had fully expected it to be the church of his nightmares, but this couldn't be farther from it.

A glorious building inside, magnificently lit with ten thousand candles. Not a shadow in the place, as row upon row of small flames fill the huge theatre. Yet the only true illumination of what awaits them comes from the few candles around the door which have been extinguished with the draught.

Enormous wooden beams in the roof; a vast, circular stained-glass window behind the altar, depicting the Penultimate Supper, the one where Jesus predicted that Simon Peter would get a sex change and that Judas would win the Eurovision Song Contest for Israel; ten, maybe fifteen statues around the sides of the church and at the foot of pillars; a majestic pulpit, projecting the preacher some ten feet above his congregation, from where five hundred years' worth of ministers have sternly lectured their flock on the perils of fornication, sortilegy, jealousy, desire and going to watch Queen of the South on a

357

Saturday afternoon. A large Christmas tree sits up against the back of the church, beneath the round window. Fifteen feet high, immaculately decorated, reams of gold and silver cascading in perfect uniformity from every branch; visions of angels randomly dotted among the decorations playing silent tunes on golden flutes. The whole a perfect encapsulation of the beauty of Christmas, and somewhere Bing Crosby lays heartily into 'Hark! The Herald Angels Sing'.

The pulpit is empty. The church silent. The flames of ten thousand candles burn.

'Bloody hell,' says Mulholland, voice in awe. 'Bloody hell.'

The others stare in equal wonder. While Mulholland and Proudfoot have plodded wearily between manse and big house on the hill, their minister has been at the most wondrous work. How could I now, thinks Proudfoot, possibly decline the invitation to wed?

Barney feels the confusion of contradiction, for this is not how his dream goes; this is not what he had expected. This is to be an occasion of light and beauty; a wedding with the blessing of angels. Not the dark, sinister world that he inhabits and which his dreams have promised.

Dillinger says nothing. Her mouth slightly open, her eyes wide, such as they have not been since she was a child. And suddenly the woes of the day are forgotten, for this is some kind of majesty. A wonder the like of which she will never know again.

'Fuck me up the arse wi' a duck,' says Socrates.

Mulholland takes a step farther into the midst of magic. He turns slowly as he walks, taking it all in. There are candles lining the aisle, candles along every pew, candles around every wall, on every surface. Walls of light and

358

flame. He looks at Proudfoot and sees she shares his awe. And so bereft of his police instinct is he that he cannot see the sense of it, cannot see the malign thought behind the enchantment.

'Hello!' he shouts. 'Hello.'

Looks up at the low-level gods, but in the box seats candles burn and nothing stirs. Wooden beams, high above, look dully down upon them. Ropes around two on either side of the altar, and he does not notice them at first. Looks back at the others.

'All dressed up and nowhere to go,' he says.

'Maybe he's gone to get some more candles,' says Socrates.

They continue to look around, the candles still burn.

Barney feels it first. Like the fetid breath of Death at his shoulder. He turns quickly, but sees nothing but small flames. But he senses the presence as if it is running all over him. They are not alone, and whatever haunts this church along with them shares not their wonder at these surroundings. This bloody façade, for there is nothing honest in this light.

'He's here,' says Barney.

Mulholland turns.

'Where?' he says. Then 'Who?' when he sees Barney's face.

And suddenly it happens in a rush of falling flesh and rope against wood.

They turn at the sliver of sound from the pulpit. A click or a cut. Quietly it goes. And from the gods they come. Either side of the pulpit, falling at an equal rate. Two bodies wrapped in rope, which unwinds with the fall from the roof.

Six feet above the ground the ropes tighten and twang at full stretch; the bodies, suspended by the neck, bobble

359

and bounce until, at last, they come to a sad end and hang limply from the roof.

Mulholland stares at them, police brain still to kick in. Proudfoot numb. Barney, with opened mouth, expectant. Had to happen. Katie Dillinger, hand to mouth, swallows, instant shock.

And the bodies of Arnie Medlock and Billy Hamilton, their eyes cut from their heads, throats slit so the blood covers the rope around their necks, swing softly in the still air.

'Cool,' says Socrates.

18
will the real morty goldman step forward?

Morty has fought it off long enough. The inner demons that have raped his mind since those blighted teenage years, and which briefly escaped for a limited period only in the eighties, are now running rampant. All the frustration of a psychosis kept in check is now laid waste. He is unbound, and can do whatever he wants; as if a brace has been removed from around his head. Suddenly, unequivocally, deliciously, he is free, and the real Morty Goldman can at last be welcomed back into the world.

Heccccceeeeeeeeere's Morty! A big hand, ladies and gentlemen, your friend and mine, Morty Goldman. Let's hear it for Morty! Morty Goldman, ladies and gentlemen, Morty Goldman.

Shackles. The news that the police are expected at the house has not remained a secret for long. The conversation between Hertha Berlin and the soon-to-be-ex-handyman overheard, word of the arrival of the forces of Good has spread like wildfire around the few inmates left, and they have each, in their own way, acted accordingly.

The handyman will not go ill prepared. He will leave on foot, certainly, but he has local knowledge and a place to stay, no more than three miles away. A place where another woman awaits his infrequent visits, with a cup of hot chocolate, a plate of toasted sandwiches, a couple of glasses of whisky and a warm bed. The handyman need worry about nothing.

Bobby Dear goes his own way. Imagines himself a military man, well suited to the rigours of outdoor life. He is a man who has served his time for his crimes, but has no desire to further engage the police. He will escape armed with everything someone on the run through open or forested countryside could need. A map, compass, rations, a torch, a hefty pair of boots, a light tarpaulin, matches, a small can of kerosene, some teabags, a condom, a sawn-off shotgun and fourteen large pairs of women's undergarments. And as a result he will survive, return unscathed and unnoticed to Glasgow, where, scarred by the experience, he will kill once more. Although this time he will save his savagery for sheep.

No more need be said.

Fergus Flaherty the Fernhill Flutist intends to go the same way as Bobby Dear. Out onto the open moor and through the forest, for he is a man who has done a bit of walking in his time. However, he is unfortunate enough to be the one who makes the second sighting of Morty Goldman since his disappearance just before dinner.

The first person to see him is Sammy Gilchrist, just after Morty emerges leaping from the secret passageway that leads from the bathroom to the lounge; knife glinting in the fading light of the fire, eyes glinting in the glint from the knife.

Bing is singing some pointless twaddle about how it's looking a lot like Christmas, but in a way he's right.

There's a lot of red around, a good colour for decorations, as Morty flails savagely at poor Sammy Gilchrist. No ordinary stabbing, this is the frenzied work of a madman unleashed. Whipping the knife viciously across his face and body; keeping him alive for as long as possible while he terrorizes him with the weapon, fending off the not insignificant ripostes from Gilchrist; before plunging the knife deep into his heart, and dragging the serrated edge along his chest cavity. There is as much blood on Morty as there is on Sammy. And it is in on this that Fergus Flaherty has the misfortune to walk.

A slightly frenzied look in his eye himself, as he makes final preparations to flee. He opens the door to the lounge, and finds himself not three yards away from a crazed Morty Goldman. Bug-eyed, covered in the blood of Sammy Gilchrist, in the process of hacking off his right arm with the knife. For he intends to stay and feast, Morty Goldman. The police may be coming, but he is happy to while away the hours in prison. There will always be other Sammy Gilchrists; and he will also enjoy this one while he has the chance.

And two is always better than one.

He pounces on Flaherty in an instant, even before the necessary profane ejaculation has escaped his lips. No messing about, no preliminaries. A knife in the face, and then another thrust up under the guts and deep into his chest cavity. Fergus Flaherty, the man who did more for the flute industry than James Galway could ever dream of, is dead in seconds. Yet Morty unleashes the full extent of his venom, and continues to thrash wildly at the body for nearly half a minute, the knife thudding into the chest and face, and the body rising up with the pull of the knife, then bouncing softly on the floor.

Annie Webster and Ellie Winters have missed the fun

in the lounge by a few minutes. Off upstairs to Webster's bedroom to savour the beauty of female flesh. A new experience for Webster – yet she is not surprised – but a familiar onc for the seasoned Winters. For she has long ago dispensed with the services of men. Has not looked at one in anger since she was accosted by three drunken youths outside a club on Hope Street, and had to kill two of them to prevent them violating her. Women, women all the way, and she is much the happier for it.

Annie Webster, however, has intimacy issues. The principal issue being that she feels compelled to murder anyone who sees her naked. Sometimes before the goose is cooked, and sometimes after. She likes Ellie Winters and her tender caress, and so she will submit to the romance of it. So, while Bobby Dear flees and Morty wields his knife, on the second floor of the house, blissfully unaware, Ellie Winters kisses Annie Webster softly on the lips, then moves down her naked body to tease and bite her erect nipples.

Yep, that's lesbians for you.

The house is laid waste. What was supposed to have been a joyous weekend has become a disaster. Morty Goldman let loose, four of the party dead, soon to be joined by another. Dear on the run. Barney Thomson, Katie Dillinger and Socrates about to confront the other evil abroad this dark night. The weekend is utterly destroyed; and there'll be no getting their money back. Not unless they write to *Watchdog*.

✂

All the while, Hertha Berlin sits alone at the kitchen table, unaware of the gruesome events unfolding in the lounge; waiting for the police, her thoughts consumed by her folly, and how the rest of a life can be slaughtered by the simplest of unthinking actions, as much as by any psychopath with a knife.

Her future is bleak and holds neither the comfort of the past twenty years, nor the adventure of the fifty that preceded them. Like that of Anthony Hopkins in *Remains of the Day*, her life has finally been shattered by the inability to express her feelings. But then, what had been the point? At least Emma Thompson had been waiting for the big guy with her legs open. What would the handyman have done had she made any kind of advance? He would have laughed, he would have broken into a chorus of 'Hound Dog' and he would have hit the Jedburgh–Moffat interstate before she could bite her tongue.

There is a slight noise, a gentle movement. So oppressed by gloom is she that she can barely lift her head to look at the door. One of the merry band of morons looking for a turkey sandwich, she thinks. Why can't they just leave her alone? Don't they know that her life is over? Why can't these damned people just look after themselves? Why can't the whole world just go and bugger off?

'Hey, Hertha, honey,' says the deep voice from the door. 'You just gonna sit there, or you wanna take a trip down to the ocean?'

Hertha Berlin looks up. For the first time in decades a smile, an impossible smile, comes immediately to her face. A tear as quick to her eye. The handyman stands, framed in the doorway, jacket on, bag over his shoulder. Sideboards on his cheeks, determined look in his eye. Hell, he knows what he's doing. She gasps, catches her breath, puts her hand over her mouth.

'Come on, honey,' he says, 'don't just sit there looking like some chick at my '68 NBC Special. You gonna come or ain't ya?'

Hertha Berlin stands up. Her chest swells, she looks for her coat on the back of the door. She walks round the table, suddenly shaking, her legs barely able to support her insubstantial weight. She tugs at the solitary pin that holds her bun together, and as her long, smooth grey hair cascades around her shoulders, she stands before the handyman, a woman reborn. Suddenly there is a light in her eye, a beauty in her smile, and the hairs on her top lip fade to nothing.

'Ah sure am, honey,' she says.

And the handyman touches her hair and the back of her neck, sending shock waves of tiny orgasms rampaging through her body. Like a surge of Panzers crossing the border into Czechoslovakia.

'Come on, baby,' he says, 'there's a place I know we can spend the night. A little old lady's gonna have a plate of burgers and a warm bed. And in the morning we can go wherever you want.'

Hertha Berlin pulls on her coat. A woman released. As her arms stretch, her blouse is pulled across her breasts, and the handyman licks his lips.

'Memphis,' she says. 'Ah'd like tae go tae Memphis.'

And the handyman laughs and shrugs his shoulders.

'Wherever you want, Hertha, baby, wherever you want.'

19
fall on your knees

The bodies of Arnie Medlock and Billy Hamilton swing in the thin air of the church, warmed by the flames of ten thousand candles. The blank, black depths of their bloody eye sockets stare down at this elective congregation, rapt in their attention. The ropes around their necks appear to be dragging down the corners of their mouths. Foreheads furrowed, and they blindly scowl at their audience. Arnie in particular, upset at the ruin of a good weekend. And they swing in silence, slowly, in a vague circular motion. They can barely hear the sound of the ropes straining and creaking.

The killer had intended letting his audience stew. That's part of the whole serial killer milieu, the modus operandi, the thing, the standard procedure, the usual technique. A cliché perhaps, but what the hey? Some clichés are there because they're good ideas. Bacon and egg. It's a cliché, but who's going to fight it? You don't say, bugger this, I'm having aluminium with my eggs this morning, just to be different.

However, having said and thought all of that, this serial killer just cannot contain himself. His audience is before him; he is Auric Goldfinger, waiting to explain his plot to rob Fort Knox; he is Jimmy Jones, waiting to denounce the Devil and order his flock to their deaths; he is Genghis Khan, waiting to book his crew on the 10.15 to Constantinople. This is it. The moment that every self-respecting serial killer waits for. His big finish.

And so, announcing himself with a laugh from beneath the rim of the pulpit, a hideous sound which fills the church and reverberates around the flaming walls and statues, a sound which quails the congregation, yet toughens the resolve of Mulholland and Proudfoot – for there is nothing better than to be able to face your enemy – Leyman Blizzard, hair blackened, dog collar hugging his neck, the Reverend Rolanoytez's glasses perched on the end of his nose, raises his head into view.

He stares down at his flock, mocking smile upon his face. There's nothing a madman needs more than an audience. There really ought to be an orchestra playing, but he hadn't the time to fix it all up. 'Ode to Joy' or 'O Holy Night', or something. Something big. And the audience stare up at him and wait.

Mulholland would be the first to act, and is in the process of the quick step forward when Blizzard raises his arms to the rafters and shows the small, loaded crossbow he holds in his right hand. Dillinger takes a step back. Mulholland and Proudfoot stand firm. Socrates smiles. Barney, for his part, knows now for sure that he will die. He is ready to meet it, and he remains steady. What comes will come. That's Barney's take.

'Leyman?' says Dillinger. 'What are you doing here? What's going on?'

The others turn. Mulholland questions with his eyes. Aware that he should know who this is.

'This is fucking brilliant,' says Socrates.

'You know him?' says Barney to Dillinger.

'Aye,' she says, never taking her eyes off the cross-bow. 'He was part of our group. I knew it was going to go wrong with him when he left. I could tell. I always know when they're about to stray.'

'What group?' asks Mulholland

'What about you?' says Dillinger to Barney, ignoring the question, because that is not a discussion she wants to get into.

Leyman Blizzard looks down upon his flock and enjoys their confusion.

'Ah work for the guy,' says Barney. He looks round at him, the old smiling face beaming down upon him. And the relationship goes some way beyond that; but that is for himself and Blizzard to sort out. If he gives him the chance.

Mulholland thumps a theatrical hand off his forehead, closes his eyes, shakes his head. Looks round at Barney then back up at Blizzard.

'Christ,' he says, 'I knew it. I saw you in the fucking shop. Yesterday morning. Grey hair, beard, no glasses.'

Blizzard laughs a dirty old laugh. Sid James without the humour.

'Brilliant, Chief Inspector. I was wondering how long it'd take ye tae work it out. Ah thought ye might have got it a' dinner, but you're obviously too slow. Nae wonder ye havnae caught yer serial killer. Thick as shite, as far as Ah can tell.'

Mulholland turns to Proudfoot and lifts his shoulders. Still doesn't see the extent of what's going on. Shakes his head.

'Sorry love,' he says, 'didn't get it. Brain's in too much of a fudge.'

She touches his hand. Here they are, thrown once more into adversity, and love will out.

369

'Come on, I was there too. I'm as bad.'

Sid James laughs again, dirty and dangerous.

'Ah!' he says. 'Young fucking love. I'n't it no brilliant. Eh? Too bad one o' ye is gonnae peg it.'

Mulholland turns back to the pulpit. No more than ten yards away, looking up into the face of their latest madman. Proudfoot stands beside him, still holding his hand. Barney watches. Dillinger has started to take small, surreptitious steps back towards the door; although, of course, Blizzard notices every movement. Socrates settles down into a pew to watch the action. No more fears the old man's crossbow than he would a bath full of spiders.

'Okay,' says Mulholland. 'What's it all about this time?' Been through too much to feel threatened, despite the crossbow waving maniacally in the air.

'What dae ye mean *this time*?' says Blizzard.

Mulholland holds his arms out.

'We come up against one of your lot every week, just about. There's the loon up in Glasgow at the moment, there was the loon at the monastery last year. There's Barney here. No offence, Barney.'

Barney shrugs. Arnie Medlock and Billy Hamilton swing slowly, round and round, up on high. The ropes creak softly, the candles burn, and it is as if the two of them are no longer there. Two bodies, eye sockets penetrating into the thoughts of everyone in the church, and with the violence of the fall, fresh blood has begun to drip, drip, drip; and they are part of the furniture.

'By Christ, Chief Inspector, you're even slower than Ah gave ye credit for. Ah don't know about this monastery shite, but Ah'm the guy who's killing folk in Glasgow, ya numpty. Me,' he adds, pointing to his chest, 'Leyman fucking Blizzard. God, ye're slow. Fuck sake, ye cannae even find yer killer when he's standing right in

370

front o' ye wi' two deid bodies and a murder weapon in his hand. How stupid are you?'

Mulholland shrugs. Realises he looks a bit thick. Wonders if Proudfoot had worked out the obvious before he did.

'Couldn't give a shit, mate. There are so many serial killers these days it's hard to keep up. Leyman Blizzard one week, some other sad bampot the next. Who cares?'

The Sid James smile dies on Blizzard's face. He lowers the crossbow and aims it roughly in the general direction of the five. Dillinger continues her deliberate back-pedal. Barney waits for an arrow in the throat, because that is the inevitability of it.

'You're full o' shite, Chief Inspector. It's your job tae catch me, so don't come it. Cannae believe the crassness of you lot, sometimes. Taking a weekend off tae shag a bird when there are folk getting shafted a' over the place.'

Mulholland shakes his head, laughs a light, bitter, unamused laugh.

'I'm off the case, Blizzard. I couldn't care less. Go back to Glasgow, mate, and kill another few hundred of them. There's got to be, what, a million or so in the city. They can cope. On you go, you stupid arse, I don't give a shit. I've retired.'

Blizzard stares down at them. Getting annoyed, but keeping an eye on Dillinger, now only a few yards from the door.

'Barney?' he says.

'White man speak truth,' he says.

Mulholland shakes his head, turns back to Barney.

'You know this guy was doing all this crap?' he asks.

'No me,' says Barney. 'No this time. Thought he was just an old bloke.'

'What is it about you, mate?' says Mulholland. 'You

371

keep turning up with these bloody loons.'

Barney shrugs, shakes his head, holds his hands out. The full Italian routine. Tugs at his genitals.

'Nae idea, but it's getting on my tits.'

'I bet it is,' says Mulholland.

'Hey, this would make a brilliant movie, wouldn't it no?' says Socrates. 'A bit o' lesbo shagging and a deranged auld cunt wi' a crossbow. It's just like *Star Trek* or something.'

Mulholland looks at him; shakes his head. Everywhere he turns ... And so, he looks back at Blizzard, still mean and armed up on the pulpit. He has had enough. And despite the swinging bodies in front of him, does not believe for a second that any of them are going to come to any harm. Or perhaps just does not care

'Come on, then, you old arse,' he says up to the pulpit, 'what's the score? You've got us all where you want us, so what's next?'

Blizzard twitches, mouth in a sneer. The crossbow shakes slightly in his hand. His eyebrows knit together, so much more telling black than grey.

'Ye know,' says Blizzard, 'Ah had intended just tae kill the one o' ye. Ye know. Ah was gonnae kill seven folk in all. Seven. It's a good number.'

'Go on, then, Batman,' says Mulholland, his usual tired voice that he reserves for the criminal element at their most narcissistic. 'Why seven? I'm sure we're all interested.'

Dillinger has almost reached the door. Freedom awaits. A quick dash and she could be there in a second. Back out into the rain, run for freedom, and she can concentrate on Arnie's dead eyes and the sadness that will engulf her. And at this door to freedom, she fatally hesitates. A combination of doubt and curiosity. There is something about this madman which grips her; and she fears for the others should she flee. What kind of person is she to get herself out at their expense? A decent, honest woman, Katie Dillinger. And, as usual in this vinegar life, she will pay for that decency.

'Seven!' exclaims old Leyman; different, yet the same as the wee, grey-haired man who was handing out Jimmy Stewarts with a certain degree of confidence only the day before. 'Seven is the number of God, and I am his head executioner. I am the begetter of life and the bringer of eternal misery. I exercise his will. I am our vengeful God incarnate. I shall be king!'

'Jesus,' says Socrates, 'how far up his own arse is this guy?'

'Seven,' continues the mad Blizzard, unconcerned with the comments from the cheap seats, 'is the number o' angels he sent down tae proclaim the New Jerusalem. It's everywhere. Seven Deadly Sins. The Seven Wonders o' the World. The Seven Horsemen o' the Apocalypse.'

'The Magnificent Seven,' says Mulholland, ignoring the last remark.

'What?'

'*Blake's Seven*,' says Proudfoot.

'Ooh, Ah really liked *Blake's Seven*,' says Socrates. 'No that there were ever seven o' the bastards.'

'*The Seven Samurai*,' says Mulholland, voice still flat. 'And *Seven Brides for Seven Brothers*.'

'The TR7,' says Proudfoot. Had sex in a TR7 when she was fifteen.

'Shut it!' barks Blizzard. 'Just shut it, the lot o' ye.'

'The number seven bus from Springburn to Auldearn,' says Socrates.

'Shut up!'

'Celtic beat Aberdeen seven nil last season,' says

Mulholland. 'You're right. It is everywhere. Good choice, you old wank. Couldn't have picked a better number.'

'Listen you brain-dead polis scumbag,' says Blizzard, 'Ah'm warning you. Seven might be a brilliant number 'n' a' that, but Ah'm mair than willing tae make it eleven. The five o' ye just shut the bastard up. Let me finish.'

'Who were the first six?' asks Proudfoot. Voice low and calm. Back to normal. Recognised that he was about to vent the anger they are building within him. Takes a step forward as she says it, and Mulholland joins her in the small movement. If the two of them charge the pulpit from different sides, there's no way he'll get them both with a single crossbow. Assuming, of course, he doesn't have another fifty weapons stashed about his person.

'Ah,' says Blizzard, relaxed and back on home territory. A murderer at ease with his subject matter. 'Glad ye asked. These two numpties, obviously. Then there were the last three in Glasgow, and the first one yese probably don't know about. Ah never saw it in the papers, ye see, so Ah don't know if they found the body.'

'What about the minister?' says Mulholland.

'What?'

'That garb you're wearing. The manse. I'm assuming you killed him.'

Blizzard looks awkwardly at the floor. The crossbow sags a little, and suddenly the arrow doesn't look so sharp.

'Maybe,' he says.

'And his wife?' says Mulholland, going on. 'You left her down the pub, did you?'

'Might've,' says Blizzard, gritting his teeth.

'So in fact,' says Mulholland, enjoying the whole

humiliation of a man with an armed weapon thing, 'you've already killed eight people, and if you take out one of us, that'll be nine. Brilliant, you senile old arse. I mean, nine's a good number too. Let's see. Frank Haffey let in nine goals against England in '61 ...'

'Shut it! Shut it the lot of you.' Crossbow straightened, finger twitches.

'What started you off, then?' says Proudfoot. In again, just in time.

Blizzard looks down upon his flock. Top lip goes like Bad Elvis, but he quickly settles back into Goldfinger mode.

'Don't know who the bastard was, he just asked for it.'

'Go on, Batman, explain yourself. I can see you're just dying to,' says Mulholland, taking another step forward.

Blizzard appears not to notice, but he does. He notices everything. Very old, and sharp as a button, Leyman Blizzard.

'He was dressed as Santa Claus,' says Blizzard.

'Ah,' says Mulholland. 'That makes sense.'

Blizzard sneers; the very name is enough. Santa Bastarding Claus.

'Ah suppose you'll think Ah'm mad if Ah tell ye this,' says Blizzard.

Mulholland holds his hand up towards the swinging bodies, taking another step forward. 'Mad? Not at all. Wouldn't dream of it. This is all perfectly normal.'

Blizzard twitches. Lowers the crossbow to accommodate the encroachment of Mulholland and Proudfoot. Dillinger could be gone for sure now, if she acts swiftly. And she does not, not at all. Rapt, with this grand instance of the psychotic mind.

'As was raised in Glasgow. Got married, the whole biscuit. But Ah was traumatised by Santa Claus in childhood, and eventually it got the better o' me and Ah had tae leave. Started killing folk, so Ah took masel' away. Went tae Cuba where there wouldnae be any mention o' the guy. Forty year Ah was away. Didnae kill anyone. Ah was fine. Then they bastards decided tae start celebrating Christmas, so Ah thought, bugger it, Ah should be awright now, Ah'll just go home. So Ah came back in the summer. Set up a shop cutting hair, thought Ah'd be fine. Come home tae die really, that was me. Then Ah was walking along Argyll Street one day and Ah sees him. Santa Claus. Don't know what happened. Ah just felt the auld feelings, ye know. Ah followed the bloke that night, and Ah strangled him. Felt good, ye know?'

Mulholland has moved forward another few feet. Approaching the pulpit, but he has no idea of how to storm the thing, being as far off the ground as it is. He and Proudfoot are just going to have to take a side each and hope that Blizzard misses with his first shot. And if it gets either of us, he thinks, let it be me.

'I'm just dying to know,' says Mulholland, 'how you were traumatised by Santa Claus.'

The others look on, fascinated. Barney sees part of his life's history unfold. Dillinger has even taken another step or two back into the belly of the church. If only this was a TV show, rather than an actual 'nutter with a crossbow' situation. Socrates kicks back and smiles. He could do with a Bud.

'Ah saw my mummy kissing him,' says Blizzard. Says it defiantly, because he knows deep down that it's a really, really stupid thing to be traumatised by.

''Scuse me?' says Mulholland.

'Ah saw Mummy kissing Santa Claus,' says Blizzard. 'Ah was upset. Ah came downstairs one Christmas Eve, and Ah sees my mother snogging this big cunt wi' a white beard.

Don't know where my father had got tae. He must've been out wi' his mates. Ah was fair upset. Ah thought my parents loved each other, Ah thought Ah came fi' a happy home. That night Ah realised my life was a lie. And if the one thing Ah held dear was a lie, well then, wisnae it a' a lie? Life. The whole thing. Ah could just never look at the big guy again without getting upset. Just got worse over the years, ye know. The bastard. Started killing folk when Ah was about twenty-three. Ye know.'

'You saw your mummy kissing Santa Claus?' says Proudfoot. Another step closer. 'Really?'

'Aye. Too right.'

'Underneath the mistletoe, by any chance?'

Blizzard thinks, but he need not think long. It is still there, etched in his memory. The very scene, every detail clear as if it were last night. The fire dying out; the old gramophone playing softly, the Paul Whiteman Orchestra; a sparse tree, a few presents beneath, presents which he had barely been able to open the next day, never mind play with; the mistletoe suspended from the light fitting; his mother giggling quietly, while tickling Santa Claus underneath his beard so snowy white.

'Aye,' he says eventually. 'Under the bloody mistletoe. Bastard.'

They look up at him. The crossbow wavers. Candles burn, and the bare sockets of plundered eyes look down upon them.

'You're fucking kidding me,' says Mulholland.

Blizzard grinds his teeth together. None of these people ever understands. That's why he hadn't bothered explaining it to the bloody Murderers Group, because what did they know? Soft bastards, the lot of them. Except Goldman. He has a certain respect for Goldman.

'Didn't think ye'd understand,' he says. 'None o' you

lot ever understand the likes o' me. Too good for the lot o' ye, ye know. Aren't we, Barney?'

Barney says nothing. Looks lost. This can't be happening again. Despite the dream, despite the knowledge he was sure he had, it still seems so incredible. Why me? he thinks. Why me?

'Don't you think,' says Proudfoot, 'that it was your father dressed up as Santa Claus?'

The crossbow wavers. Blizzard twitches; the sneer hovers around his face.

'What?'

'Well, there's got to be hundreds of dads who dress up as Santa Claus for their children. They probably knew you were awake, or made enough noise to disturb you, so that you'd get up and see him. What age were you?'

Blizzard swallows.

'Five,' he says.

Proudfoot shrugs. 'See? You were five. It was your dad dressed as Santa Claus for your benefit. Did you ever talk to them about it when you were older?' she says, all the time getting closer, Mulholland at her side.

Slowly he shakes his head. His life flashes before him.

'Naw,' he says, 'Ah never liked tae.'

Almost there. Classic situation for a counter-attack, even with the height of the pulpit to be scaled. Very close, the prey distracted and unsure of himself, as he stares into some vague point in the distance. Mulholland has a hundred words of abuse on the tip of his tongue, but the time is not now. Not yet. A dash round the back, up the stairs, and he can get him.

Close enough, about to move. Proudfoot is poised, waiting on Mulholland's signal. Barney stands isolated, rooted to the spot. Socrates watches their pulpit approach and shakes his head. Much too obvious, he thinks.

378

Dillinger has heard enough. All these sad old men are the same when it gets to it. Just plain daft. And so she decides it is time to go. Another few seconds and it might all be over, but she has waited long enough.

A few quick steps backwards, almost to the door, and then she turns and is on the point of exit. Grabs the handle, door open. But Blizzard is not slow. Sees the movement out of the corner of his distracted eye, does not hesitate. Lifts the bow and in an instant has fired off the arrow. Into her back. Dillinger collapses, falling out of the church into the rain.

'Hey, nice shot,' says Socrates, turning quickly, looking at the stricken Dillinger. I'm definitely not shagging her the night, he thinks.

Barney turns in despair; another down. Mulholland and Proudfoot take their chance, their prey disarmed. Mulholland round the back and up the stairs; Proudfoot, suddenly Jade Weapon, leaping at the front of the pulpit.

And with the door open, the wind and rain howl into the church and the candles start to blink out, hundreds at a time; so that darkness approaches the altar in a calamitous, headlong rush.

It all happens in an instant. Mulholland almost upon him. Proudfoot coming over the wall of the pulpit. Barney rooted to the spot. The church plunging into gloom. And Blizzard reaches for the other loaded crossbow he has on the shelf in front of him, and in a second has it raised and fired into the chest of Proudfoot.

With a thud, it explodes into her ribcage, firing her backwards off the pulpit, so that she falls back and crashes down onto the floor, her head cracking off the cold stone. In the twinkling of a killer's eye the lights are out and Mulholland is upon Blizzard. But he has instantly lost interest. He has had enough of killers, there are no

379

more loaded weapons to hand. He pushes Blizzard to the side, and leaps over the end of the pulpit to land at his lover's side, shouting 'Proudfoot!' as he goes.

And in the dark, Blizzard picks himself up, makes his way down the stairs, looking stealthily around him in the dark as he moves. A moment's hesitation and then out he goes through a rear exit, his escape route clearly established beforehand. His work is done. Ten downed. Anger and psychosis assuaged, amid completion and revelation.

Kate Dillinger lies dead. And alone. To rise to meet her lover Medlock.

Mulholland holds Proudfoot's head, and desperately feels for some sign of life. Heart still going, faint breaths. 'Erin,' he says softly. 'Erin. Don't die on me. Not like this.'

And his heart beats so strongly with fear that it could make up for hers. You don't know what you've got until you lose it, the thought starts thumping into his head. He'd walked away before, but he'd believed he could easily walk back in. But there will be no walking back into this. This could be the end for his bloody fantasy of Erin Proudfoot and happiness.

So when her eyes flicker open, his heart thumps even more, his head floats.

'How *would* you like me to die on you?' she says softly, lips barely moving.

'Oh, Christ, Erin, are you OK?'

The barest smile crosses her lips. The eyes slowly close.

'Course I'm not, you stupid bastard,' she says quietly.

Socrates sits and watches from a few yards away. Begins to smile. That mad, impetuous thing called love. Mind you, he says to himself, she's probably still going to peg it.

Barney watches for a few seconds. But these two are not his business. Not any more. Something else, much grander, much more ominous, awaits him. And so he walks past Socrates without a word, and then past the desperate couple on the floor, Mulholland faced with his own emotion, and heads out the back way on the trail of Leyman Blizzard.

20

the eternal midnight of barney thomson

Barney can feel The Force. It guides him through the trees as he follows the path of Leyman Blizzard. Since the old man left the church he is yet to catch sight of him, but somehow he knows he is going in the right direction; or is being led that way.

There is a thick forest of pine behind the church, mixed in with firs and deciduous trees of various shapes. An ancient wood of the type that it is rare to encounter in this day of forestation, with identical rows of trees in regimented lines, ending in a mathematically precise border. So leaves and bare branches and the spidery touch of fir brush against Barney's face. The rain does not fall with any force within the forest, but everything is sodden and clinging, so that it feels as if there are hands grabbing at him as he goes.

He stops every so often to try to listen for Blizzard's movements, but the noise of the forest in the rainstorm is all-consuming. Leaves in the wind, water pouring through trees, and there is little chance of him hearing anything else.

He does not fear the hand suddenly appearing from the forest; a knife in the face or the crossbow aimed at his head. For he knows there will be a confrontation. It is fated. It is what he is being led to, and before Leyman Blizzard strikes him down, as he is absolutely sure he will do, he will receive some form of absolution. For he knows truly the identity of this man who runs from him, and leads him on at the same time.

After a few minutes the forest breaks, as it is bound to do in this green and pleasant land, where no longer do forests stretch for mile upon mile. Barney stumbles over a low wire fence, then makes his way across open farmland. He is free from the trees, and the rain hammers down upon him, his feet squelch through mud. Every so often he imagines he sees the grand impression of a recent footfall in the field, but he knows he comes the right way regardless of whether he sees any trace of his prey.

He is consumed. Haunted for several weeks, forced back in from the cold, he will face this man who has plagued him. Has no thought for Proudfoot, downed at last, a year after he had saved her life. Little thought for Katie Dillinger, the woman who had galvanized him into coming on this weekend, who had aroused his desire for the first time in decades. Dead, and he will never again feel that kind of desire for anyone.

Eventually he is over another low wire fence, the farmland turns to open moorland, and he is heading uphill through marsh and peaty bog; feet sucked into the ground, occasionally stepping on rocks. And he can feel it getting nearer. The presence. Whatever it is that has lured him into this whole thing, as surely as his feet are being sucked into the ground, is not too far in front of him. It has stopped running, and now waits for him to arrive; to deliver the final damned, crushing blow.

Barney stops and looks ahead. In the pitch black of night and rain he can see vague shapes up ahead; rocks etched against the muddier black of the sky. And as his eyes sweep around the rocks, his heart gives nothing more than a small jump, he lowers his head, and tramps off once more, determined to meet his fate. For just ahead, carved into the dead of night, standing on top of a large promontory of rock, is Leyman Blizzard. Hands held aloft in silent supplication to the gods, dog collar still around his neck, black coat and black shirt matted to his skin in the rain.

Up he climbs, struggling over wet rocks and jagged overhangs. Feet into large pools of water, plunged into bog and plucked out. Hands grasping wet rocks, slipping, jarring thumbs and fingers. But despite the struggle, eventually he closes in on the inevitable.

Up a final grassy bank on hands and knees, wet and cold and frozen to the bone, Barney at last gets to his feet and walks out onto the large rock at the end of which stands Leyman Blizzard. Back turned, still, and it would be nothing for Barney to approach him and push him over the edge, for there is a drop large enough to send a man to his death. And that man could be Leyman Blizzard. One push.

But Barney stands still, waiting for the old man to turn. At last his heart beats a little faster, at last his mouth goes dry and he licks rainwater from his lips to wet his throat. And, at last, no more than five yards away, Leyman Blizzard turns.

Their eyes engage. Not long since they looked upon one another in the church; and, indeed, barely any time since they stood in the shop and Barney thought he had found the last decent man in the whole of Scotland. Only the previous afternoon, and it seems as if it happened a long time ago. A long time ago, in a galaxy far, far away.

'The Force is strong in you, young one,' says Blizzard.

Barney squints into the rain. 'What the fuck are ye talking about?'

'Ach,' says Blizzard. 'Ah'm just having a bit o' fun.'

Barney's mouth drops a mile or two. He shakes his head, and suddenly he feels very, very sad. That could've been his mother talking. These two were obviously very well matched.

'Fun? Ye just murdered three or maybe four people. Ah saved yon police lassie's life last year. And for what? So you could do her in? And the woman, Katie. She was awright. She didnae have tae die. Why, Leyman?'

Blizzard shrugs. The storm rages around him, his long, dark coat unbuttoned and free to be blown in the wind. He holds his hands out in appeasement.

'Sorry about that, son. Ye know, Ah didnae want tae kill her. Ah knew ye were intae her pants. That's why Ah took out they two bastards.'

'What?'

'Medlock and Hamilton. They were both after her. Hamilton was angling for that other bird, but I overheard him talking to himsel' last night. He was intae yon Katie no end. So Ah thought if Ah got rid o' them, ye'd have a clear road, ye know?'

Barney looks quizzically through the storm. The wind picks up, a great gust howls past them, and momentarily he loses his footing. Does not come near the edge. Straightens up, finds himself another step or two closer to Blizzard.

'Ye did that so Ah could get intae her pants?'

'Aye,' says Blizzard, smiling. 'Ah thought ye'd appreciate it.'

Barney laughs. After all, it has come to this. One final stupid conversation at a cliff edge on a dark and stormy night, before he will inevitably be pushed to his death.

'Brilliant, Leyman. Absolutely stunning. Ye wanted me tae get intae her pants, so ye killed her. Brilliant. What were ye thinking? At least now she won't be able tae say no? That it?'

Blizzard shrugs. Takes a step closer to Barney.

'Ah didnae mean tae kill her, son. It a' happened so fast. It was just a blur, ye know. Ah didnae mean it.'

Barney shakes his head. This is bullshit. All the terrors, all the nights waking screaming, all his trials, for this. Another ridiculous conversation, like every conversation he ever had or listened to in a barber's shop. A fitting end. Two guys talking shite. Every barber should face it. Serendipity; the word could find no better use than this.

'So which one of us did you mean to kill?' says Barney. *As if I don't know.*

Blizzard raises his eyebrows, rubs his chin. There, he thinks, is a good question.

'No sure, son' he says. 'One o' the polis, Ah suppose. Ah mean, Ah know they're no that bad, and Ah didnae realise they were off the case, but Ah mean, polis are polis, after a'. Never had any time for them. No time.'

Barney shakes his head. The time of revelation is near. It is obvious who this man is; has been obvious since he first saw him. And with that revelation will come the certain end. That's what has been foretold; that is the omen which has been shown to him. His mother had been mad; his mother had lived a lie all her life; his mother had finished that life by murdering six innocent people. It makes complete sense that his father should also be a mad murderer; that he should have disappeared early on in his

386

life, and that his mother would lie about his death; and it makes sense that he should return now, to presage the end, and indeed to cause that end.

There is a symmetry there, he supposes. Your mother and father bring you into the world; it almost makes sense that they should ease your way out of it. (Not that that could work with successive generations, but this is a piece of philosophy in its infancy.) His last two years have been murder, principally through the actions of his mother. A normal mother would have had him turned over to the police after the first manslaughter; and a normal mother would not have had six dead bodies in her freezer. And now, after these two hellish years, it will all be ended by his father, whom he thought dead, and with whom he is to be reunited on a wind- and rain-blown cliff top, above a desolate moor, at midnight.

'They were good people,' he says, delaying the inevitable. Funny how it is, that even though he has accepted what will be the circumstances of his own death, he still chooses to put it off.

Blizzard shrugs. Takes another step closer.

'Good schmood,' he says.

And now they are no more than a few feet apart. Barney looks into old Leyman's eyes, and realizes that it is like looking into a mirror. All these years he has thought his father dead. In retrospect he has thought it odd that his mother had let neither him nor his brother attend the funeral; that there had been so little fuss and no visitors; that she had kept them away from people for so long. His father hadn't died at all, but run off. And these last two years he has thought if only his father had been here then none of this would've happened. How wrong! How wrong. A lifetime of conviction, two years of belief, shattered over a day or two when reality has dawned.

Barney raises his arms to the side. He could run, but now that the end is near he feels he must accept his fate. Where would he run to this time? He's been running, and it isn't for him. Neither is prison. He must accept what must come.

'There's something ye want tae tell me,' he says to Blizzard. Almost has to shout, as a great howl of wind pummels them, and they both lean into it.

Blizzard stands with rain pouring down his face, greatcoat blowing in the storm.

'What dae ye mean, son?' he says.

Barney swallows. Can feel the beginning of a tear coming to his eye. His father. About to engage that special bond which he has never truly known.

'Ye know what Ah mean,' he says. 'Dad.'

The rain cascades off Blizzard's face, turning it into a cruel parody of the Niagara falls. Streams of black have begun to run down his forehead, from where the hair dye has finally given up the good fight. His mouth opens, his nostrils flare.

'What?' he says.

'Dad,' says Barney. 'Ah know it's you. Ah forgive ye!'

Blizzard spreads his arms, much in the manner that Barney is employing. 'Ye forgive me for what? What the fuck are ye talking about, son,' he says. 'Dad? Ah'm no yer dad. Where'd you get that fi'?'

Barney swallows again. The tears suddenly dry up. He takes a step back. Self-assurance vanishes into the rain. He suddenly finds himself looking at an old man with no hold on him, with no part to play in his future. Except that of being his death. Just another mad old bastard, with no connection.

'Why are ye gonnae kill me, then? Why did ye lead me up here?' he says.

Blizzard shakes his head and raises an eyebrow.

'Kill ye? Is that what ye think o' me, Barney? After ye saved my shop? Ah'm no gonnae kill ye, Barney, for God's sake. Why'd ye think that, son? That's pants, that is. Pants! Ah thought it would be the polis bloke following me. Didnae realise the nampy-pampy eejit would stay behind tae look after his bird.'

'Oh,' says Barney. 'Oh.' Not good in an unexpected situation.

'Why did ye think Ah was yer father?'

Barney's brow furrows as he attempts to think. It had all seemed so obvious a few seconds ago. The dream, the madness, the omens; they had all been coming together.

'Ah don't know,' is all he says. Has not stopped to think that this life of his may be incredible, but it is not supernatural.

'Ya bloody eejit,' says Blizzard, smiling. Face black with running dye, old white teeth showing, mad eyes glinting. 'What happened tae yer father, then?'

Barney shrugs. Buffeted by the wind.

'He died when Ah was six,' he says.

'Six! Who the fuck did ye think Ah was, then?'

Barney stands looking at the old man. Wet and cold, clothes sticking to him. This feels as if he is back where it all began. The last few days he has faced the inevitability of his death, and now that it will be denied to him, does he know what he will do with himself?

'Ah thought Ah'd come up here tae die,' says Barney, ignoring the question. 'Ah don't think Ah know anything any more.'

'Die?' says Blizzard. 'That's just a load o' mince, son. Ye've got years in front o' ye. Mind you, Ah don't think we can go back tae the shop, 'cause yon polis'll know where tae find us. Unless ye killed the bastard before ye left.'

'Naw.'

'Oh, ach well. You and me, son. We can move on. Start another shop some place else. Just the two o' us. Blizzard and Thomson, barbery wi' a smile and a knife.'

Barney is struggling. Brain in overload. Immediately begins entertaining the prospect; at the same time knows that this man is a murdering psychopath. Cannot yet escape the thought that he is his father, so sure was he. Cannot escape the dread of the dream and the belief in his forthcoming death.

'Come on, Barney. Ah know what ye must think o' me. But you and me, we're the same. This kind o' thing follows us around. But if we go somewhere there's no Santa Clauses, we'd be set up. Ah'd be fine, son, Ah promise. We could go tae Africa, or somewhere like yon. Asia, or something. Somewhere miles away fi' this bollock-freezing place. How about it?'

The rain seems to increase in intensity, the wind blows strong. Old Leyman seems to grow taller and more imposing in the black of this long midnight. Barney Thomson stares through the night and sees his future stretch out long and strange before him. Perhaps it is not his fate to die after all. Perhaps there are adventures still to be had. It is an enormous world out there, and so far he has tasted the highs and lows of Scotland. There must be more than this; that's what he has often said to himself. This could be his chance to find out. The possibilities are infinite.

Blizzard takes a step towards him.

'Come on, son, I know where Ah'm going. Ah'm making a break over these hills, Ah've got some money in my pocket, and Ah'm never looking back. This is it, son. Out future awaits.'

Barney looks into the passionate eyes. A world of

opportunity awaits him. And then suddenly he thinks of
the eyes of Arnie Medlock and Billy Hamilton. The eyes
of Katie Dillinger, which will never see again. How can
he possibly spend a life with this man? He himself has
been responsible for the deaths of others, of that there is
no doubt; but he is not a murderer. And this man who
stands before him, he is. Most definitely. A loose
cannon, a maverick, an unfettered beast. How could he
ever trust him? How could he help to protect such a man
from the authorities? It is madness to even consider
travelling on with him.

He shakes his head. His is a solo path, and that is what
he must follow. The adventure can continue, but it must
be on his own terms and in his own company. He takes a
step back; Blizzard's eyes go wild, his mouth opens, his
hand is outstretched.

'Ah have tae go it alone,' says Barney.

And the sentence is barely free of his lips when it is
followed by a loud cry as his foot slips from the edge of
the rock. Blizzard reaches towards him, Barney frantically grabs at his extended hand. Their fingers touch,
hands clasp; and then slip in the rain, and come free.

Barney makes one more attempt to regain his balance;
a frantic swirl of arms and legs and lunging body; and
then he is falling off the side, heels making one last
contact with the rock edge as he plummets to the grave.

A short drop, no more than fifteen feet. In daylight,
feet first, anyone could manage it. But in this storm,
Barney is out of control. His head cracks into a rock with
a sound that Blizzard can hear; his neck snaps; his body
crumples into a fuddled heap, head twisted back at a
hideous angle. And the rain falls and the wind blows.

Old Blizzard looks over the side, and so dark is this
night that he can barely see the body below. He stares

391

long enough and at last the pale stretch of Barney's neck looks up at him through the storm. Snapped like a Twiglet. He can see it. And the old man knows.

He backs slowly away from the edge of the rock in this bloody rain and howling gale. The brief few days when he imagined he might have found a soul mate of sorts are over. His is to remain a lone furrow after all. He takes one last look over the edge and swallows. Another simple future has been blown to the wind.

For Barney Thomson is dead.

'Bugger that, well,' says Blizzard, as he turns and begins the long walk to nowhere, dog collar soaked to his neck; a piece of clothing to which he may well remain attached. Barber? Minister? What the hell, it's all about making people feel good about themselves. Or otherwise. 'Wonder what I can have for ma supper,' he mumbles into the night.

21
i'll be your jade weapon

The police arrive just a little too late. Forty-three minutes too late. The doorbell rings and, with Hertha Berlin gone, no one answers.

Inside the house all is peaceful and quiet. Not a mouse stirs. On the third floor Annie Webster rocks slowly back and forth on her crossed legs, over the strangled body of Ellie Winters. To and fro, slowly rocking, eyes wide and staring at the pale skin of Winters; a dead duck. Behind the closed door of the lounge, Morty Goldman indulges in another Christmas feast.

Sergeant Marcus Grooby stands outside. Not dressed for the rain, having dashed the ten yards from his car. Under the awning outside the front door, his hair soaked; he looks cold. Rings the bell again, eventually tires of waiting. Wonders if this silence points to the reason for the call.

Marcus Grooby, thirty-one years old, as good-looking as you're going to get in Scotland, dragged away from an evening at the station with Constable Caitlin Moore, and the usual Sunday night romantic dance. No crime, just idle chatter and harmless flirting. A decent bloke, unused to the careless world of the serial killer. About to be given a rude awakening.

He tries the door and it swings open before him. Warmth and the serenity of thick carpets ooze out at him, and he takes the giant step across the door into the house.

Rugby on a Saturday, church on Sunday, occasional golf on Sunday afternoon, runs the Scouts on a Friday, every day at work a little bit different from every other. Uses words like *ma'am* and *homicide* because he watches too many American TV shows.

Grooby steps gratefully in out of the cold, walking into the center of the great hall. Thick carpet, pictures on the wall, and he takes it all in. Knows not yet what unfolds no more than ten yards away, behind the unlocked door.

So, a few short steps, first door he comes to, hand to the knob, and in he walks.

Morty Goldman looks up as the door opens. About to be rumbled, but he does not care. He has already done enough to satisfy his primal urge. And if he should end up in prison for the next few years, then so be it. The things that matter to him; well, they exist in plenty, whether in prison or not. Means nothing to a man such as Morty Goldman.

Sammy Gilchrist lies dead; bloody, hacked apart, but untouched thereafter. Morty preferred the medium dry with a hint of petrol fume claims of Fergus Flaherty's body. Shirt ripped open, knife into the chest, and the heart cut out. The black gap in the ribcage, where the ribs have been torn apart and splintered, the blood on the turquoise shirt, are the first things that Grooby sees. Then the virtual stump, where Goldman has torn off Flaherty's arm, using nothing but brute force. So an unclean, messy split.

Then Grooby sees Goldman himself, the scene whipping through his brain and his sensibilities in a nanosecond. Covered in blood, cross-legged and relaxed, in much the same position as Annie Webster. Except while Webster stares solemnly at her victim, Goldman eats his. Heart already gone; Grooby interrupts him with the arm up to his face. Blood everywhere, food on his teeth, quiet slurping and munching sounds fighting for space with the murmur of the fire and a subdued 'O Come All Ye Faithful'.

'Jesus Christ,' gasps Grooby.

He immediately feels the surge from his stomach, and he turns away and vomits violently into the corner.

Goldman sits and rocks and stares and is not concerned with his audience. He is sated, but is content to munch away until he is officially interrupted. Presumes that Grooby will not take that upon himself. Throwing up indeed! When that knob Lecter does it, it's chic! It's nineties-retro, it's fava-tastic, it's now; it's almost comedic in a BBC sitcom kind of a way. Bastard. Sings along in his head to the song; his own words.

> O Come let us adore him
> O Come let us adore him
> O Come let us adore him
> Morty is cool.

✂

The police arrive in force some twenty minutes later as a result of a desperate call from Grooby. He sits in the hall, propped against a wall, bum going numb. Can see the edge of Goldman's arm through the crack in the open door. Making sure he doesn't go anywhere, but without confronting him. Unaware of the death of Ellie Winters upstairs, while Webster rocks back and forth, humming a low tune 'Rocking around the Christmas Tree . . .' And within minutes the house is opened up, Webster is discovered and not a room is left clear of investigation.

And not a trace do they find of the handyman or of young Hertha Berlin. For at least these two people have escaped this night with their worlds intact.

But they still have Hertha Berlin's words on the peculiarity of the group who went calling at the church, and so of the twenty-three police officers who turn up in the first wave, four are dispatched to the kirk of the late Reverend Rolanoytez ...

... where shepherds watch their flocks.

Katie Dillinger lies dead, an arrow in the back. Plundered her lung, and she was gone, gone, gone. And she has already joined her husbands in eternal misery, in a very special place.

Mulholland sits cross-legged, quite still. Holding Proudfoot's head in his lap. Constantly talking, encouraging responses from her. Attempting to keep her going until the ambulance arrives. Never talked so much in all his life, and she smiles occasionally and can barely understand what he's saying.

He holds her head, hopes not to cry. Ignores Socrates sitting close by, recently returned from attempting to find a phone. Had discovered all the lines in the area had been cut; the work, he assumes, of Leyman Blizzard; although, as it happens, it had been the afternoon's work of Sammy Gilchrist, who had been intending a little mayhem of his own, before being overtaken by events. Socrates had searched the manse of the Reverend Rolanoytez for more modern telecommunications equipment, but had found only a 1930s gramophone. That, as well as a large collection of animal traps, several hundred Commercial Off The Shelf (COTS) porn mags, and two bodies. Had decided not to make the trip back up the road to the old house as he suspected things might have become a little intense by now. And so now he sits, close by, trying not to listen to Mulholland's endless embarrassing chatter. Many words of love, and he cringes at most of them. Men can be such saps for a bird with an arrow in the chest.

Mulholland talks of times past; the first occasion they met; her uninterested face; losing his temper, giving into romance, the great breadth of emotion in the thrall of which he has been held. A life in seconds, and then minutes, and on and on. Over an hour they wait before they hear the siren of the police car approaching. Over an hour with the occasional word from Proudfoot, and the faint heartbeat, and gentle gasps of air. And he has hope.

Finally, after all this time, they are approached by Sergeant Barnes, late of Grampian CID. Socrates sees him first. Not traumatised by the uniform like some of the others, and pleased in his way. Was beginning to think that he really ought to make more of an effort to get to a phone than just walking the fifty yards to the manse.

Mulholland looks up, can say nothing.

'Better get an ambulance, Big Man' says Socrates. 'The lassie's got an arrow in the chest, of a' things. Gonnae ruin her tits if it's no taken out soon. Whacked her napper 'n' a'. And she's one o' your mob, so you better get a shifty.'

And Sergeant Barnes quickly bends over Proudfoot to check for himself, then radios for the ambulance.

And soon the other policemen enter the church. Gallacher, Watson and Torrance, three of the Borders' finest. And they spread out and start to thump their way around the church.

'You do this?' says Sergeant Barnes to Socrates.

And Socrates shrugs and remains cool.

'Naw, it was some auld guy. Buggered off out the back

about an hour ago. Long gone by now, I imagine. Long gone.'

Mulholland looks up at the sergeant. Head muddled, no more substance there than the endless stream of consciousness he has been babbling.

'He's right. It was a hour ago or more. He killed the lassie up the top there first, then shot the sergeant.'

Barnes leans over and takes a closer look. One of their own, indeed.

'Nice-looking bird,' he says. 'She still breathing?'

Mulholland glances up. Proudfoot's eyelids flicker open.

'Aye,' they say in unison, her voice barely audible.

'Right enough,' says Barnes.

Then he stands up and looks around at this bleak place, now illuminated by the dull and mundane electric lights. Looks properly for the first time at the two bodies dangling from the rafters, notices that the eyes are gone. Turns away.

'What the fuck were you doing here anyway?' he asks.

Mulholland looks up again. That should be what the fuck were you doing here anyway, sir? he thinks.

'Getting married,' he says. 'That was the plan.'

And he shakes his head and looks away from the pale face, drained of blood. But everywhere he looks he sees death, and he can take no comfort from it. Turns back to her, runs his fingers along her brow.

'The ambulance is coming, Erin. You've got to hang in there. Won't be long.'

There is a slight movement in his arms, she lifts her eyes, her lips part.

'See me,' she says. 'Jade Weapon. Tough as old shite. I'm not dying yet.'

'You better not. If you're Jade Weapon, we've got some amount of shagging still to do.'

The smile stays on her lips as she lets her eyelids close.

'You're on. I'll be Jade Weapon, you can be Buzz Lightyear.'

Mind not quite in gear.

And as best he can, he holds her tightly. And in the dim, dreary distance, the ambulance is diverted from the house to the church, and Sergeant Barnes directs one of his men to cover up the faces of the two hanging bodies.

Socrates watches Mulholland and Proudfoot from a few yards away, eyes narrowed and shaking his head.

'Buzz Lightyear?' he says quietly to himself. 'What the fuck is that all about?'

epilogue

a warm evening in august

A warm evening in August, the handyman does his final rounds. Checking doors are locked, computer terminals switched off, bins free of anything the cleaners ought not to be getting their hands on. It's been two years since Professor McLaurity left a severed foot in the bucket, but it was first thing the handyman was warned of when he arrived.

Not long in the job, but he already feels at home. Check the place out at the end of the day and at weekends; a few odd jobs around the building; share a few cups of tea and the odd burger with the scientists; a few hours a day, and that's all it needs. Ten to twelve in the morning; a couple of hours of his choosing in the afternoon; nip over from the house at close of play – sometimes after eleven – to check everything's been locked up. Easy. Hertha keeps house for Professor Snake, who is about as nice an old man as you could wish for, and the two of them couldn't be happier.

The handyman wipes some dust off a laboratory table

and makes a mental note to check it again tomorrow after the cleaners have been in. Keep them on their toes. Wouldn't find dust like that in here if Hertha was cleaning, he thinks. And he laughs to himself.

'She sure is a feisty lady,' he says quietly, with a smile.

Hertha has blossomed. In a whole range of ways.

Still shaking his head and laughing, and already thinking of the night to come, he opens up the door at the end of the laboratory and sticks his head round. Looks at the long line of large jars filled with pink fluid.

Did a bit of travelling, the handyman and Hertha Berlin. Went to all the handyman's old haunts. Memphis, Hawaii, Vegas, a few long, lonely highways. There were some who recognised him, but no one liked to say. After a few months they had returned to Scotland, for few can tear themselves away from this Land of Kings for too long. Answered an ad in a local newspaper, and have now settled down in the employ of the University of St Andrews.

The handyman looks along the line of jars and shakes his head.

'There sure is some amount of weird shit going on,' he says. 'Weird goddam shit.'

The innocently titled Department of Human Biology contains many jars, with many body parts kept therein. In formaldehyde, or whatever fluid they could lay their hands on at the time. Limbs, organs, entrails, appendages, brains. They are all here.

The handyman looks into the brain room. Jar after jar of human brains. And in particular, since this is in support of Dr Gabriel's fifteen-year study on the physiology of the psychotic mind, the brains of ex-criminals; each jar neatly labelled. Malky Eight Feet. Brendan

Buller, the Brechin Bastard. Wee Janice Twinklefingers. Dr Crevice. Captain Nutcruncher. Big Billy One Hand. And so on the jars go. And right at the end, at eight months the most recent addition to the troupe, in a jar much like any other, the brain of the greatest serial killer that Scotland has ever known.

The brain of Barney Thomson.

The handyman shakes his head again, and flicks the light switch. Pulls the door closed and turns the key. Moves up to the secondary lock, then throws the dead bolt – as if any of the brains are getting out. Turns the tertiary lock, then locks the four padlocks. Finally zips round the combination.

The Brain Room is the prized asset of the Department of Human Biology.

The handyman shakes his head again and smiles.

'Weird goddam shit,' he says, twiddling the last knob. 'Still,' he adds, beginning to walk off, already thinking of the quadruple pork burger with extra fries and mayonnaise which awaits him at home, 'there ain't no way there's any brains gonna get stolen outta that room. No way. There's none a these brains getting stolen and put into some weird goddam Frankenstein monster type a shit. No brains getting taken outta there, no siree. No siree.'

The Long Midnight of Barney Thomson

Douglas Lindsay

Barney has never had the knack of talking drivel to complete strangers, and it irks him. Certainly, he can talk about the weather with the best of them, but when it comes to uncompromising, asinine bollocks, he just doesn't have it...

Barney Thomson's success as a barber is limited. It's not just that he's crap at cutting hair (and he is); it's because he has no blather. He hates football for one thing. He hates most people. He hates his colleagues most of all, and the glib confidence with which they can discuss Florence Nightingale's sexuality or the ongoing plight of Partick Thistle.

But a serial killer is spreading terror throughout the city. The police are baffled. And for one sad little Glasgow barber, life is about to get seriously strange...

'an impressive debut novel'   *Sunday Mirror*

'Lindsay has succeeded magnificently in putting the lowly barber centre-stage'   *Time Out*

'pitch-black comedy spun from the finest writing. Fantastic plot, unforgettable scenes and plenty of twisted belly laughs'
New Woman

'Gleefully macabre...hugely enjoyable black burlesque'
The Scotsman

'Hair-raising'   *Daily Mail*

The Cutting Edge of Barney Thomson

Douglas Lindsay

With the press accusing him of every crime since Jack the Ripper (including Don Masson's missed penalty against Peru in 1978), Scotland's most notorious – and misunderstood – serial killer Barney Thomson is on the run. The Holy Order of the Monks of St John seems the ideal hide-out for a sad little Glasgow barber with a fear of small talk. As 'Brother Jacob' he's even managing to keep his hand in with some part-time barbery – even if his legendary creative genius is limited to just three styles (Mike McShane in *Robin Hood*, Sean Connery in *The Name of the Rose* and *Cadfael*.) Only, with the police hot on his trail, Brother Jacob has just discovered that he's chosen the only monastery in Britain that already has its full complement of serial killers!

Praise for *The Cutting Edge of Barney Thomson*:

'a mad, macabre romp with surreal characters and cutting black humour...clearly a talent to watch'

Sunday Mirror

'Comedy so dark it needs a candle to find its navel...with more talent than Irvine Welsh could dream of, Lindsay has crafted a macabre little masterpiece'

What's On

'highly entertaining'

The Scotsman

Cruising for Murder

Susan Sussman

with Sarajane Avidon

When a friend begs her to help out on a cruise ship, actress Morgan Taylor can't resist. She tells herself she's escaping from a brutal Chicago winter. She is definitely *not* running away from her relationship with homicide Detective John Roblings. *Honest.*

But her friend has neglected to mention two things. One: Morgan has to share a cabin with the room mate from hell. And two: the girl she is replacing in the cabaret hasn't just moved on...she is dead. Killed in an accident that doesn't look particularly accidental to Morgan.

She had hoped to soak up some sun and enjoy a three-week paid vacation with a little light singing thrown in. But, given Morgan's knack for finding trouble, it's clear that this trip isn't going to be plain sailing...